ONE ROUGH NIGHT AT THE CIRCUS BAR

ONE ROUGH NIGHT AT THE CIRCUS BAR

DAVID R. ODELL

LitPrime Solutions
21250 Hawthorne Blvd
Suite 500, Torrance, CA 90503
www.litprime.com
Phone: 1-800-981-9893

Published by LitPrime Solutions   11/29/2022

ISBN: 979-8-88703-036-4(sc)
ISBN: 979-8-88703-037-1(e)

Library of Congress Control Number: 2022913531

Contents

PART THREE

One Rough Night at the Circus Bar

David R. Odell

One rough night at the Circus Bar didn't start that way. A quiet drink with a friend was all he planned to do. All the good intentions are not always enough, things don't always go your way. You plan on going right but end up going left and things are different over there.

One rough night at the Circus Bar, nothing planned. A night with friends or family after a long week at work. It all comes down to how you feel as the night gets underway. Still, as you look around the room you can see things are just not what you thought they would be.

One rough night at the Circus Bar, a smile or two and it is all good. However, the frowns are something else. The look is wrong the fight is on in the blink of an eye. Good intentions don't help now the fight is on. There is trouble at the bar the good times are over.

One rough night at the Circus Bar, It didn't take much at all. With a sour look and an evil smile, the fight is on at last. No need to worry about what went wrong there will be time for that later. The rough night has now begun, hold on tight the shotgun is coming out.

One rough night at the Circus Bar, It all started with one word. The words have been said the darkness is there it can't be unsaid. Everything just needs a spark, it really won't take much at all. The line is drawn with a word and the fight is on though it won't last long Laurie has the shotgun.

One rough night at the Circus Bar. The word has been said, no one can take it back. One rough night starts with a word then the rough night starts with a smile as well. It is the first it will not be the last trouble always comes in threes they say.

One rough night at the Circus Bar. It did not start that way, it was going to be a good time they thought. Not everything goes their way, and not every smile is a kind one. Not every word is a good one some words should never have to be heard.

One rough night at the Circus Bar. The word has been said no one can make this right. The fight is on now there is no turning back. The looks have changed but the hearts remain the same. What it seemed would last forever has changed, it has a time limit now. One rough night leads to all the rest, the fight goes on.

Thoughts

Late one night Luke Richardson sat at the picnic table in the yard looking at the night sky. Time had passed a lot had changed or so most people thought. As he remembered things people were always talking about his father and Mrs. Linda Fields. It was all just talk but even talk can hurt.

His mother never said a word about any of the talk around town. She was friends with Linda Fields as far as Luke could tell. His Mom seemed to be friends with everyone in town. She always seemed to be happy no matter what was going on around her. She was the family anchor.

Luke like his father was a truck driver. They said his father drove because he liked it, as well as out of guilt, over his wild youth and other things. Luke drove to escape his home life which was not what he thought it would be. There was a bit of truth there though not the way people told it. Luke had never planned to be a truck driver he had never planned to leave town.

It all started back when Luke's father started driving a truck for a young couple who took a big chance. They started their own business which meant they needed a truck driver which Roger was happy to do, the job seemed to fit him. He liked the job because it made him feel like the boss with none of the worries. All he had to do was drive from here to there and then back again.

Roger had a wife as well as a child on the way which meant he needed a steady job. As far as he could see he had done just what he needed to do. He had the job at the time they could buy a house. He was on the right road in more ways than one. Nothing could stop him from getting what he wanted from life.

Luke's mother was a quiet woman who ran her house, cared for her children, and managed over the years to get food on the table no matter how little money they had to work with. She had worked in the Rice family factory for a time until Luke was born. After that, she worked at home doing different jobs. She had watched other people's children, been a hairdresser, cared for a couple of older people in the neighborhood then become a bookkeeper.

As a married couple, they had suffered through some bad times and celebrated through the good times. They had helped their children as they grew to adulthood the best they could, even when that meant letting them do things that would hurt them in the long run. It had not always been easy though most of the time it had been the right thing to do.

Linda and George's Fields were good friends of the family some people said while other people said other things. George had been a truck driver before he bought a bar. When he became a bar owner his wife Linda became the bartender. This was a job she seemed to do well when she wasn't having children. She was friendly as well as a very good bartender as long as no one caused trouble in the bar.

She may have tended the bar as well as waited tables in her bar but she didn't dress the part. There were no low-cut blouses or short skirts, no heavy make-up no high-heeled shoes. She seemed to be a good woman who ran a bar. In time Luke learned that everything is not always as it seems. He also was learning that the same thing is true of all people.

Back when he was young there were pictures on the wall at the Circus Bar most were pictures of people standing at the bar glasses raised. There were three pictures above the rest one was George next was Linda the third one was his father. They said it was because he was the first truck driver to walk into the bar when they opened it. They said his father had talked the place up which made it a truckers' hangout.

Other people in town disagreed and his Mom never said anything about it. As far as he knew his Mom was never in the bar. This was something that was not surprising if you knew anything at all about how his Mom had been raised. Luke's grandparents had come over on a ship from Europe at the turn of the century. They had met and been married on the ship which had not gone over well with her family. Still, they did help the young couple get started.

They bought them a large house that was close to the church the family attended. After that, they found his grandfather a good job which he was going to need. They had twelve children eight girls and four boys. The entire family went to church every Sunday and all the girls sang in the church choir. They all learned to say grace before each meal as well as to pray every morning and every evening.

Luke's Mom took this all in and did what she was told she even planned to marry the man her family had found for her. He wasn't rich though he did have a very good-paying job. He came from a good family which was very important at the time. It was all arranged his Mom was going to have a very good life.

When Mom met Dad the guy with the good job and good family was left behind. Mom and Dad were married less than a year later. This did not make her family happy but in time Dad won them all over even though he was only a truck driver. Mom took to the family life though they had their rough times here and there over the years. Dad made sure they always had a roof over their heads as well as food on the table. If they were poor they couldn't see it because they seemed to have everything they needed.

They learned that marriage like life wasn't always perfect but it lasted until death and maybe even after hearing his Mom talk. Mom wasn't perfect and neither was Dad but most of the time they never seemed to notice. That was what marriage was you didn't expect perfect nor did you want the other person to change you just accepted them for who they were. At least that was what they believed when they were young.

Luke had married at a young age, to a girl he didn't know. Once they were married he bought a farm as well as some animals. He bought a flatbed truck and then worked for people around town as a local delivery man. He would deliver anything and everything for a fair price. It seemed he had it all just like his parents.

When Luke's wife left him he bought a sleeper cab. He gave his brother his flatbed truck then he became a long-haul trucker. His brother took over the farm during the week then they would work together on the weekends. It was the perfect arrangement for the time, everyone seemed to have what they wanted.

At least that was how Luke saw things back then. He had failed to keep his marriage together he was ashamed as well as feeling sorry for himself. The truck was the best thing for him as he was better off alone. He was a failure at the one thing that he was not supposed to fail at.

Luke had learned the hard way that not everything is as it seems or as you would like it to be. Luke had learned a great deal about his life and the lives of the people around him. All it took was one rough night at the Circus Bar to get everything started.

Even now as he sat there looking back at everything that had happened It seemed hard to believe that he had not seen where he should have been all along. It was hard to believe that things had gone the way that they had. Just when he had been so sure that life had changed and would never be good again he had learned differently. Life seemed to have more twists and turns than anyone could handle.

One Rough Night at the Circus Bar

PART ONE

Chapter 1

Sunday afternoon on the farm after the haying as well as the chores were done seemed like any other Sunday. There were a few more people there than usual which no one seemed to mind. Luke had been gone longer than usual. He had not called home as he usually did. His Mom had been worried as had other people. Everyone wanted to know just what had happened to him.

Roger Richardson looked around the table. His wife Rachael was sitting at the other end of the table. To his left sat his oldest son Luke the long-haul truck driver. Beside him sat Emily Rice a young lady from a good family in town. Beside her sat his son Dan a young man who ran his local delivery service around town.

On the other side of the table across from Dan sat Rhea Conner the Pastor's daughter. She is an unlikely match for Dan if you believed everything you heard around a small town. Roger didn't listen to anyone he trusted his judgment which told him they could be a good match given a little time.

Sitting to her left was a young man by the name of Steve Benson a young man who was doing his best to keep up with the changing times. He was working for a new company learning how to manage their computer systems. He had to travel from time to time helping others learn the computer game.

Roger's daughter Emma was sitting beside Steve they had been quietly dating for over a year and they had known one another even longer than that. Emma said they were friends but Roger knew better. Still, it was best not to argue with her about that. It was best to let her think that she was in control of that part of her life.

Roger looked at his eldest son. "Luke, your mother has been worried about you all week. You know she worries about you so would you please tell us why you never called?"

"It was a rough week with a lot more going on than usual."

"We are not going anywhere so why don't you tell us just what kept you so busy."

Dan laughed. "Yeah, why is Emily here?"

Roger looked at Dan. "Why is Rhea here?"

"Yeah, Dan, what is the story?", Luke asked.

Roger looked at his sons. "Boys I want to know what is going on."

Emma laughed. "Yeah, boys, just what have you been doing?"

Roger sat back in his chair looking at his daughter thoughtfully. "You know this is the first time Steve has come out to the farm to help with the haying."

Emma took a quick look around the table. She had stuck her foot in her mouth she was going to have to think fast. "Dad, Steve has always wanted to come out here to see how things run and to work out a little."

Steve looked at her. "Are you saying I am getting fat?"

Emma laughed. "If the shoe fits it must be your shoe."

"Okay, Cinderella."

Roger smiled. "Luke, I didn't forget you I still want to know why you were gone for a second week."

Luke sipped his coffee. This wasn't going to be easy nor was it going to be believed by everyone. There were times as he thought about what had happened when he wasn't sure it could have happened. That Friday afternoon seemed more than a week back.

Luke could have said a lot about what had happened but there was no need. There were just some things they didn't need to talk about. He would keep the story short which would be best for everyone concerned. When you were telling a story about your time away from home you better tell the truth because Dad already knew most if not all of the story. There was nothing to do but keep the story as short as you could.

The Short Version

"Alright, I will tell you just how it was. I got home Friday afternoon which as you might remember was a little warmer than usual. I cashed my check paid the bills then ran into Emily. We went over to your house so I could mow the lawn while Emily was talking to Mom. After that, I took Emily with me when I went to mow the lawn at my place.

Emily made us something to eat and it was really good. I had told her I would take her out so we went to the Circus Bar where we had a couple of beers while we were waiting to use the pool table. We talked to you then after you went home we played some pool until the fight broke out. Once that happened we thought we would call it a night.

I took Emily home and we talked for a bit then she asked me if she could go with me to make a delivery the next time I went out. Well, I had a load on the truck so I figured it would be okay. You have to understand it wasn't a long run so I thought it would be a down and back. When we got there the place was closed and to be honest I needed some sleep.

I was really tired while Emily was wide awake so I found a place where there was a mall and lots of stores to keep her busy while I was sleeping. When I woke up we tried to deliver the load. I should have stopped by the house or called but the place was closed. We talked about going back but decided we would spend the weekend or what was left of it. The plan was to deliver the load early Monday morning then I could drop her off in town on my way back through.

The more we talked the more she told me what she wanted. What she wanted was a vacation so I thought it would be okay if we delivered a few loads instead of just one load. I should have stopped by the house or called I know but I was having fun talking to someone besides Jack for a change.

As it turned out the week was a longer one than usual or at least that was how it felt. The truck acted up which it never does and the weather was bad more so than usual it seemed. I did the best I could to get us back by Friday. We didn't make the last delivery until late

Saturday which is something that rarely happens. I had to get some sleep so I couldn't get back until today."

Roger looked at his son thoughtfully. "Why didn't you take Emily home?"

"I did but she asked if she could come help with the haying so I brought her with me."

"That is all you have to say after being gone for a week?"

"Dad, that is all there is I don't know what you are looking for."

Roger looked around the room. "Dan, what do you have to say?"

Dan did his best to look confused even though he knew what his father wanted to hear. "Dad, I was not the one gone for two weeks. I was right here in town doing my job the way I always do. When I wasn't working I was here taking care of his animals and stuff. If it wasn't for me he wouldn't have a place to come back to when he got the urge."

Roger smiled. "You know I have eyes which means I can see Rhea sitting here at the table with us. She is a lovely young lady with good parents. Which has me asking questions. Why is she here spending time with you? I haven't seen the two of you together for years until this past week."

"Dad, are you telling me she is not allowed here?"

"No, I was just wondering what a nice girl like her sees in you that no one else does."

The good thing was Dan knew what his father thought of him otherwise he might have gotten mad. "Last week Friday I had a date with Rhea so after work I came here. I did the chores and then drove over to your house. Mom had washed my clothes for me. I got ready for my date then drove over and picked up Rhea at her house. I was running a little late but she didn't seem to mind. We went out to eat at the country club where the food is very good by the way.

"We were going to go to a movie but we went by your house then we went to the Circus Bar though we didn't stay long. There had been some trouble there and I cut my hand on some broken glass. Rhea drove me to the truck stop where she cared for my hand then drove me home. I let her take my car home which is why I saw her on Saturday.

"I cared for the farm over the weekend with everyone's help then went to work on Monday. Like always I worked all week not missing a day even when we had that heavy rain. I did what I usually do I worked then I worked some more. There was nothing special about it except that Rhea stopped by a couple of times. Mom and Rhea both bought food for the house which is the only reason we are eating so well today.

"The only other thing I did this week that I have not done before bought myself a tractor. That is all I can tell you because that is all there was."

"You boys sure can spin a yarn better than most but you seem to come up just a bit short each time. I may not be the one in the room with all the education but I know a good line of bull when I hear it. I am a trucker from the old school I can spin a line with the best of them which is miles ahead of both of you."

Rachael looked at her husband with a smile on her face. "Roger, don't you think you are being a little hard on the boys."

Roger smiled a smile that none of them wanted to see. "You could be right they always seem to leave things out when they are telling a whopper. I think it might be best to talk to someone who can tell the truth."

Dan shook his head. "Emma, you are next."

Roger looked at his daughter. "Emma, would you like to tell us all just why you brought Steve with you today."

Emma nodded her head. "First of all I didn't bring him here he brought me. We have been friends a long time so I don't know what the big deal is. If you want to know if we are dating I can tell you that we are talking about it. You want to know what I did this week I had a very rough week at work last week. It was so bad that I went to talk with Laurie a couple of times I even took Friday night off. I worked a double shift during that big storm we had because some of the girls couldn't get to work. Other than that it was a week like any other except that I have been working out here two weekends in a row."

Roger shook his head as he looked at his children and their friends if they wanted to call them that he would let it go for now. "We have to finish bringing in the hay tomorrow afternoon. I hope the three of you can find your way to the truth by then.

"Rachael, we should get going they have a lot of thinking to do."

Once his parents were gone Luke went into the kitchen and then came back with six bottles of beer. "I can't speak for the rest of you but I need at least one of these after all of that."

Dan looked at his brother. "If it wasn't for you we wouldn't have had to go through that."

"You can say that if you want but we all know better."

Emma looked at Dan. "He is right Dan, we said a lot but nothing that mattered."

Luke looked around the table. "We all have something to say so it might be best if we talk about it while we are all here to help one another get it right."

Chapter 2

The Long Version

The Richardson Family Stories

Roger Richardson was in bed looking up at the ceiling thinking about all the plans he had made for his wife Rachael and himself. He wanted to travel the country and see all the sights they had only read about. He was a truck and driving was his life he could drive around the country in one of those campers with his wife beside him it would be fun. The kids were grown and on their own for the most part they might even do better if they were on their own for a little bit.

Rachael brought him his first cup of coffee. "Here you go this should help get you moving."

"It always does. Did I ever tell you that you make the best coffee in the world?"

"You may have mentioned it once or twice over the last thirty years."

"Well, the truth is the truth it never hurts to say it from time to time."

Rachael smiled. "Where are you going today?"

"Out near Boston, I should be home early if everything goes okay."

"Would you like some breakfast this morning?"

"Yes, I think that would be a good idea, I might even have another cup of coffee with my breakfast."

"Then you better get moving or it will be cold before you get to the table."

Rachael took his empty cup and then left the room going down to the kitchen. Roger took a quick shower and then got dressed. He looked at himself in the mirror. He was a handsome devil even if he had to say so himself. Rachael was a lucky woman to have him all to herself. Life was good for the most part he had more than most, a good wife as well as three good kids. He was lucky to have kids who were smarter than most. His job was just right for him and the people he worked for were his friends. A man could not ask for more nor want more if he were smart.

Going down to the kitchen he took his seat at the table where the second cup of hot coffee was waiting for him. He lit a cigarette and then took a long drag from the first smoke of the day. The first one was always the best though for him they were all good. He should quit but then he would have nothing to do while he was driving for hours at a time. He had cut back at the house doing his best not to smoke in the house. The first smoke of the day you had to have with your morning coffee.

"Rachael we need to take a vacation this summer."

"Okay, where do you think we should go?"

Roger looked at her thoughtfully she was just as beautiful as the first time he saw her. "Let's go to the ocean."

"My sister has a place in Connecticut by the ocean. She might let us stay there."

"It would be nice if they were there with us we haven't seen them in a long time."

Rachael looked out the kitchen window. There were tears in her eyes she knew they would never take the trip to the ocean. "I can call her and see if we can work something out."

Roger finished his breakfast then got up from the table and kissed her. "I will see you tonight for supper. Have a good day and tell Dan we need more eggs."

Rachael watched her husband go out the door then she cleaned up the breakfast dishes. He was no different now than he had been the first time she saw him. They had been through so much and they should have a long time ahead of them but she had a feeling that things were about to change. There was no reason for her fear that she knew of but she was afraid just the same.

How can a person let go of something they can't explain? How do you explain a fear you do not understand? It comes out of nowhere and then holds you so tight you have to fight for every breath you take. Rachael sat down at the kitchen table shaking so badly she thought she would fall out of the chair. This was real life the part we never talk about.

Thirty years of marriage good times as well as bad then you get what? That was the question just what was next? How do you prepare for the unknown? The best thing to do was clean the house so that she could think about something else for a time. It couldn't help but it wouldn't hurt her.

Luke and Jack got out of the truck and then went into the diner hoping to get some breakfast before they started their day. It had been an average week so far nothing to brag about or complain about. If you knew your business you never had any real problems. That was how they did their job they did it the way it was supposed to be done.

The waitress smiled a warm friendly smile. "What can I get the two of you to drink this morning?"

Luke smiled his best smile. "Carol, I would like a hot cup of black coffee and Jack would like some water."

"I will bring that right over."

Luke looked at Jack. "You just take your eyes off of her butt. You know she is a happily married woman."

Jack wagged his tail as he looked at Luke. Jack was a black and white border collie sheepdog with no sheep to care for. He did his best to care for Luke though it was a hard job to be sure. He thought it might be best to give up on him after all he was only a human.

"Don't look at me like that you are not as smart as you think you are."

Carol came back to the table with the coffee and the water. "The two of you arguing again."

"We never argue there is no point he never says a word he just looks at me."

Carol smiled. "I am not sure what to say about that."

"I know what to say. I will have steak and eggs this morning. Scramble the eggs, make the steak well done and give Jack the bone."

Carol wrote it down and then smiled. "Will there be anything else?"

"Just keep the coffee coming until I float out the door."

"I think I can do that for you."

Luke sipped his coffee thinking about how things had been going over the last couple of years. He was driving a lot though he didn't drive on the weekends when there was work to do on the farm. He should just sign the place over to his brother. Dan didn't like the place much but it would grow on him if he gave it a chance.

. The other problem was that he wanted the farm because he never intended to drive long haul for the rest of his days. He had bought the farm because he planned to be a farmer. One day he would sit on his front porch looking out at his land and his cows and horses grazing in the field. While they grazed the chickens would walk around the yard clucking as they pecked at the ground.

That was his dream while Jack and the truck were his reality. A man did the best he could today while he dreamed of what he would do when he could be in charge of his life. Right now the bank was in control which was the way it would stay until the farm was paid for. It seemed no matter what you did with your life someone was always telling you where to go as well as how to get there.

Carol brought the food as well as more coffee. Jack chewed on his bone while Luke ate his breakfast. When they were done Luke took Jack for a walk to get his business done. When Jack had found the perfect spot he made his deposit. Once he had done that Luke put him in the truck. Luke went back into the truck stop to take care of his own business a little disappointed that Jack always had to go first.

Once they had both done what they had to do Luke drove out onto the highway. They had a load to deliver which meant no more time to sit still. It was a three-hour drive to drop the load than two more hours to get the next one. He had no idea where he would be going next which was nothing new, He shifted gears as he hit the highway. Jack looked at him then sneezed.

"Oh keep your opinion to yourself."

Dan got up before the alarm went off. He got dressed and then went down to the kitchen. He stirred up the hot embers in the wood stove then added some small stuff to get the stove going. He set the old coffee pot on the stove to heat the coffee.

When that was done he started a pot of coffee going in the new coffee pot his mother had bought them. Putting more wood on the stove he poured himself a cup of coffee before going into the bathroom to take his shower.

When he was done with his shower he got dressed and then poured himself a fresh cup of coffee from the new electric pot. Dan poured the coffee the pot into the old pot on the stove. When he was ready he went to the barn. He grained the horses and cows then milked the two cows. After taking care of the chickens he turned the horses and cows out to pasture.

With the milk, eggs, and his empty coffee cup he went back to the house. Another cup of coffee then put wood in the stove then strain and bottle the milk. He cleaned the eggs before putting them into a carton. With the chores done he took some milk and eggs to his truck placing them on the seat. Going back into the kitchen he filled a travel mug with coffee. He placed the other cup in the sink then mug in hand he went out to his truck.

Driving into town he goes to his parent's house where he leaves the milk and eggs. Driving over to the feed store he backs his truck up to the platform. The Carr Family Feed and Grain store was run by a young couple Lucy and Kieth Carr. They were young but they were good at what they did. Lucy ran the register while Kieth loaded the bags of feed into cars as well as trucks. They had two children one boy and one girl with a third child on the way.

Dan walked into the store with his travel mug in hand. He poured some coffee into the cup from the pot on the desk behind the main counter. "Good morning Lucy, how are you feeling this morning?"

"Like shit. Kenny didn't sleep much last night, I think he has another tooth coming in. Kieth never stopped snoring all night long so I want to kill him too."

"You want me to kill him for you?"

"No, but I might let you break a small bone or two."

"Which one would you like me to break?"

"Never mind it would just mean more work for me."

Dan smiled as he put the lid on his mug. "If you are sure that is the way you want it I won't touch him."

Lucy shook her head. "Why are all you men so full of shit."

Kieth walked into the store and answered the question before Dan could. "We only have what you women give us."

Lucy had a slight smile as she looked at him. "In that case don't plan on getting anything from me tonight."

Kieth smiled. "Okay then. Dan, you want to give me a hand? We have a couple of big orders for you this morning."

"No problem, I think I have worn out my welcome here this morning."

The two men went off to work while Lucy sat by the cash register drinking her second cup of coffee. She loved them both though Dan she was never going to tell anyone about. He had taken her out once and then told her about his friend Kieth. She loved him for that. In one movie a pizza then he found her a husband. He was a good man as well as a very good friend.

On Wednesday night after work, Emma Richardson went from work at the hospital to the truck stop where Steve Benson was sitting at a table waiting for her. He had cold drinks on the table and had ordered food for them. Steve smiled at his waitress Rhea Conner. "Rhea, you are looking good as always."

Rhea smiled. "I thank you. I must say you are looking good tonight too."

"Emma is meeting me here and I wanted to look my best."

"I must say you seem to have done a fine job."

"You don't think I overdid it?"

"A three-piece suit in here would be overdoing it you look just fine."

Emma walked in and took a seat beside Steve. "What are you two talking about?"

"Steve was talking about you as he always does."

Emma smiled. "Do you think I should keep him?"

Rhea smiled. "He will be a hand full but you should keep him if you want him."

Rhea went off to get their food as Emma smiled at Steve. "I am late I know but we had a longer meeting than usual."

"It isn't a problem I don't need a lot of time I wanted to ask you if you would move in with me when I get back?"

Emma looked at him as if she were surprised. "I don't know I mean this is all so sudden."

Now it was Steve's turn to look surprised. "We have talked about it before."

"Yes, we have but never seriously."

"I was always serious about it."

"I didn't know that, I just assumed you were joking."

"Why would I joke about something like that?"

Emma looked at him thoughtfully. "I have wondered that very same thing myself. Living together is a very serious step and I don't think it is something we should be joking about."

"I am not joking, I am going to be leaving tonight and I won't be back until Monday evening."

Rhea brought them their food and then went off to another table as Steve sat wondering what he should do next. He had thought Emma would say yes or no and not be surprised that he had asked her. It was not the first time he had asked her to move in with him. He sat eating his food not looking at Emma he was wishing he could get up and walk out of the truck stop. He might have if he had not been the one sitting against the wall.

Emma looked at Steve with a smile on her face. "I should let Mom and Dad know that I am moving. They will want to know if we are going to get married. What should I tell them when they ask?"

Steve almost choked on his food; he had all he could do to get it down. "I wasn't going to bring that up just yet I thought we might want to see how things go before we talk about marriage."

"I am so glad to hear that I was afraid you were going to get ahead of yourself."

"You are trying to drive me out of my mind aren't you?"

Emma smiled. "I am not trying to make you crazy I was just trying to get all the facts right."

"You still haven't answered the question."

"I told you I would let Mom and Dad know I was moving."

"I thought that was if I asked you to marry me?"

"Are you?"

"Not yet."

"Do you plan to?"

Steve smiled. "I am thinking about it."

"Do you want me to wait until you do before I move in?"

Steve was feeling confused he had been in control of things before he started talking to Emma. Now he was not even sure what they were talking about. "I would like you to move in with me. If we live together for a bit and no one gets killed we can talk about getting married."

Emma smiled. "I will pack this weekend."

Steve smiled. "You are going to be waiting for me when I get back from my trip?"

"As I always do."

"You are going to be at my place?"

Emma smiled at him. "No, I will be at our place."

"I have to get going I have places to be in the morning."

Emma was still smiling. "I will walk you out."

"Thank you."

Chapter 3

Roger Richardson was up early as usual. Rachael fed him breakfast as always then he kissed her good-by before going out the door. He drove over to the yard where his rig was parked and cleaned it out as he did at the end of every week. When that was done he drove over to the Circus Bar and went in the back door taking a seat at the bar. Linda Fields placed a cup of coffee on the bar in front of him.

Roger smiled. "Thank you, how are things going this morning?"

Linda looked down the bar at the small group sitting there. "My day is off to a good start. I have customers here, the crowd is the same as always. It looks like the start of another great day."

"I took the day off and I might just take tomorrow off too."

"You seem to be in an awfully good mood this morning. I think you should take time off more often if it makes you this happy."

"I work all the time and I can't remember the last time I had a couple of extra days off."

"I can my daughter and your son didn't come home after going to the movies with friends."

Roger laughed. "I forgot all about that."

Linda looked at him. "I doubt that."

"Yes, I might remember something about that."

"They scared the crap out of all of us."

"Things might have been different if we had known where to look for them."

"We didn't know they had the jeep and we surely didn't know they had driven it through the woods."

Roger shook his head. "I never knew all those old logging roads came together. Though I have to be honest I don't think I would have looked for them on that road even if I had known about it."

Linda refilled his coffee cup. "I thought for sure those two had run off and gotten married. I was so afraid that I couldn't think about anything else."

Roger laughed. "I was thinking about the beating Luke was going to get when I finally found him. Rachael talked me out of it once we finally had them home."

"I thought they would have to be dating before they ran off to get married but I was told that was not always true."

"Once they were home safe I sat down and thought about it and I have to admit it scared me to think that they might have gotten married."

Linda smiled. "The fact that they got to the fire tower before they ran out of gas was hard to believe. Then Laurie tells me that the gas can on the back of the jeep was empty. She says they talked it over and decided it was late so they went to sleep. They knew they were going to have to walk down the mountain to get gas. Once they had the gas they might have to walk back up with the gas. Laurie said it never crossed their minds to call for help. She said they knew what they had to do and you told them if they got themselves into trouble they would have to get themselves out of it."

"I guess it was a good thing we found them filling the gas can then."

Linda shrugged her shoulders. "I guess it was a good thing for them that we found them when we did."

Roger laughed. "If you had a better bladder we never would have found them at the gas station."

"Well, I can't hold it for eight hundred miles like you wild truckers do."

"We are very good at what we do."

"You are all full of shit and that is the only thing you are good at, holding it."

Roger laughed. "On that note, I have to leave Rachael is home waiting for me."

"Tell her I said you are a shithead."

"I will not, I don't want her to come over here and hurt you."

"Get out of here I have work to do."

Roger left the bar and sat in his car. They had all shared some good times over the years. That was the good thing about spending your life in the same town. You knew everyone and everyone knew you which was the bad thing about spending your entire life in the same town. Roger needed to get home he had to get ready for his afternoon appointment.

Roger started for home with a smile on his face. Life had been good to him for the most part. He had married a good woman and they had three wonderful children. Nothing was perfect they had not shared just good times there had been bad times as well. Together they had gotten through everything and he knew they always would. Rachael was a good woman and she liked him most of the time.

Rachael was sitting on the porch waiting for him when he pulled into the driveway. She got into the car and looked at him. "You are late."

Roger shook his head. "No, I have never been late for anything. I have been early, I have been on time or I have never arrived but I have never been late."

"If you don't show up you are late."

"If I was never there I was never late."

Rachael shook her head. "You are so full of shit."

Roger smiled. "I am a truck driver I hold everything in."

"I happen to know you can't hold it forever I have waited for you to come out of the bathroom."

"You leave all the good reading material in the bathroom."

"If you are tired you should sleep in our bed, not in the bathroom."

"I never sleep in the bathroom our daughter is always banging on the door when I am in there."

Rachael laughed. "She is banging on the door when anyone is in there."

At this point, they had reached their destination. Roger parked the car and the two of them went into the three-story brick building. They went into an office on the third floor. They were in there just under an hour. When they came out they were not talking.

Roger drove Rachael back to the house after they finished the appointment. He needed to walk for a while to think about everything. Over the years he had not thought about the future he took each day as it came. Now things had changed he was thinking about all that he had done over the years. He stopped by the diner and got coffee to go.

Roger sat on a bench in front of the library watching people as they passed him by. How many times in his life had he been in such a hurry to get somewhere that he had not seen the wonderful things around him? He was thinking about his younger days and all the plans he had made. He had been a factory worker but a friend needed truck drivers so he started driving a truck. It was going to be for a short time but he was good at it.

Roger had gone to school with Jason Conner, Walter Rice, George Fields, Big Jim Campbell, and Patrick Benson as well as all the girls that they had married. Walter started a business where all the women worked. He had teamed with George, Jason, and Patrick who were the truck drivers for the company. Their wives worked in the factory Big Jim took care of all the machinery as well as the trucks.

Roger remembered how they had started with box trucks and then worked their way up to tractor-trailers as Walter's business grew. On Friday nights they all went out to the bar where they had a great time then went home to their families. Those early years were great years that they were sure would never end.

They had been wrong about that Roger remembered the accident as if it had happened yesterday George was crippled but he survived. Big Jim died that day and the whole world changed. Jason and his family left town. Linda and George had the bar, Walter and his family had the factory, Patrick became a long-haul trucker and Roger worked for Walter.

Roger finished his coffee. Everything was so different now. All the children were grown Jason was the pastor at the church. Patrick was long since gone. He had gone off in his truck one day and never come back. Nothing was what it had once been.

He had planned on buying an RV when he retired so that he could take his wife out to see the country. He had always wanted to see more of the country just as soon as he had the time. That had been his plan.

Roger got up he wanted a drink but this was not the time it would be best if he went home he needed to talk to Rachael about everything. They had been together a long time and they talked about everything before they did anything. Once they had talked he would feel better. She always made him feel better. She was his wife after all and she liked him. At least he was pretty sure she liked him. Yes, he was sure he would feel better about his plan once they had talked.

As he started toward home he thought about big Jim he missed him they had been good friends. He thought about Linda and George they were going to want to hear from him. Rachael had been with him earlier so she would understand. It might be a good idea to go talk with them before he went home. Yes, he was sure that was a good thing to do before he went home. George was going to understand him after all they were good friends. Besides once he went home he would not go back out.

Rachael Richardson sat in the kitchen with a small cup of coffee that was getting cold. She was thinking about the first time she had seen Roger. He had been with friends laughing as they were having a good time. When he saw her looking at him his smile got even wider. He walked away from his friends and up to her table. Without a word, he stole her heart. The following night they went out on their first date.

Roger was not a perfect man or a perfect husband however he was a good man as well as a good husband and father. He would do anything for the family as well as friends expecting nothing in return. He would help strangers as quickly as he helped his family. He was a good man even if everyone didn't think so. Even those that talked about him behind his back would ask him for help when they found themselves in trouble.

Rachael set her cup of cold coffee in the sink and then went into the bathroom. This was the only room in the house where she could be sure no one would walk in on her. Roger would be home soon she needed to get her emotions under control before he got home. He would need her to appear a lot stronger than she felt. Life was never easy always full of changes which they had managed to deal with so far. This was different this was the part they had never seen coming.

Rachael was a smart woman she knew how the world worked. The thing was she had blocked out the things that she thought would hurt her. Now the time was forcing her to think about all the things she had hidden away for so many years. It was all unfair yet it was a life that meant there was nothing she could do about it. There was nothing she could do so she decided to do the laundry. She could dust the house again even though she had done it the day before. There was always dust somewhere.

Emma Richardson went to work at the hospital a little early she had heard Joseph Taylor was back in the hospital. She worked on the second floor which was where the surgical patients were. Before the start of her shift, she went up to the fourth floor to see how her friend was. Joseph was in and out of the hospital due to his fight with cancer. Joseph was one of the tough ones he was a fighter he had overcome a lot to get to where he was.

Emma went into his room with a smile on her face. "Joe, you are looking good as always."

"Emma, you are lovely as always. You are early today."

"I heard you were here so I wanted to come up and see you."

"Are you going to run off with me today?"

"I was thinking we could run off at the end of my shift tonight."

"That sounds like a good idea I will be ready to leave by then."

"How is the family doing?"

"They are doing okay but this is getting hard on them."

Emma nodded. "They love you so they want the best for you."

Joe gave her a sad smile. "No, they want me to live and I am not sure that is what I want anymore."

Emma knew what he had been through and she understood that the treatments were not easy for him. "You are a tough man I am not sure I would be able to go through all that you have been through."

"No one is as tough as they think they are when it comes to something like this."

"Is there anything I can do for you?"

Joe smiled. "Live a good life."

Emma left the room with tears in her eyes. Joe was not going to recover it was something that everyone knew. They had all expected him to die at least six months back when he had been in very bad shape. He had fought his way back and now he was back for some minor work before he started another round of treatment. He would be back in the hospital again she was sure of that.

The night was quiet on her floor everything going the way it should. She was tired as she did the end-of-shift report. She needed to go home and get some sleep if she could stay awake long enough to drive that far. Even though she didn't live that far from the hospital she was very tired for some reason.

Marion Cross was a nurse from the fourth floor she was a friend of Emma's. They had gone to school together Emma had been part of the wedding party when Marion got married. When Emma saw her by the elevator she didn't want to talk to her.

"Marion, what is it?"

"I am sorry but Joe died about a half hour ago."

"What happened?"

"He went to sleep and his heart stopped. He was scheduled to be released in the morning. We were all surprised at how well he was doing we couldn't believe he was gone. I don't think there was any member of the staff that didn't cry."

The two of them got on the elevator. As they started for the first floor Emma could finally speak. "He was a good man. You know there are days when I hate this job."

"It isn't the easiest way to make a living."

As they walked out of the building they stopped looking at the parking lot. Emma shook her head. "It isn't fair the good ones die while the ugly ones live because they have money to pay for better care."

"Emma, we do the best we can."

"I know that but we can't always give them the best because we don't have it."

"The system may not be perfect but at least we care about them."

"Yes, I just wish we could do more."

"Emma, go home and get some sleep."

"I am tired. I will see you tomorrow."

Emma went to her car but didn't leave she just sat there looking at the hospital. As much as she loved what she did, there were times when she wished she was a truck driver like her Dad and her brothers. Being a nurse was not always that great, like tonight. It was time to go home but it might be best if she spent some time talking to Laurie.

Instead of going home, she went to the Circus Bar where her friend worked as a bartender. Laurie had been her best friend since she was in the same class as her brother Luke. It took a long time for Emma to realize that Laurie was more interested in her older brother Luke than she was in her.

Even after Laurie lost her interest in Luke she still stayed friends with her. Emma looked at her as the big sister that she never had. They had learned to tell each other everything they couldn't tell anyone else. Tonight Emma wasn't sure what she needed but she was sure Laurie would know. Laurie always knew just the right thing to say.

Laurie had two beers in hand as she led Emma to an empty table. "Okay Girl, what is it this time?"

"Joe Taylor died tonight."

"Emma, I am sorry I know you liked him and his family."

"It isn't just that, he had been doing good the doctor was going to release him in the morning."

"M, you can't fight fate you know that."

"So what am I doing then?"

"You are helping people. None of us are going to live forever but you help them recover from everything that happens to them on their journey through life."

"Losing sucks."

"You didn't lose you did everything there was to do so he could die in his time with dignity."

"You make me sound like a saint or something."

Laurie smiled. "You're a nurse and sometimes people may see you as more but you are a nurse and a very good one."

Now Emma smiled. "No need to butter me up anymore I will pay for the beer."

"M, you don't have to pay for the beer I put them on Luke's tab."

"I thought you were done with him years ago."

"I was but I still remember he dumped me."

"I thought you dumped him?"

"To be honest I don't remember who dumped who I just blame him so I can make him pay for our drinks."

"Okay, that is fine as long as we don't have to spend any money."

"I knew you would understand."

"Do you think he would mind buying one more round?"

"Not at all, he used to like me."

As they talked they drank though not at the same speed. Emma had several drinks while Laurie had just one. It was a little trick her mother had taught her. When you owned the bad the last thing you wanted to be was drunk on the job.

Emma looked at her friend. "I think my brother has bought enough beer tonight."

"He can buy us another if you like. We are friends and like I said he used to like me,"

Emma smiled. "We were kids back then."

Laurie laughed. "Yeah, back when he was good looking you mean."

"Yeah, way back then."

"You do know that I can still send you to a bad place if you are not careful."

Emma looked at her. "We are not going to talk about that either."

Laurie looked at her a slight sign of a smile in her eyes. "Okay, we are not going to talk about my first boyfriend or yours again."

"Why what is wrong with my brother?"

"He has you for a sister."

"Luke is a good guy who can't find the right girl."

"You better go home before a fight breaks out here."

"I thought you had a gun?"

"I do and I am thinking about using it on you."

"I need to go home before I have to hurt you."

"Keep dreaming shorty."

Emma smiled. "I may need a ride home."

Laurie shook her head. "You think? I will have my brother drive you home."

"No meed I can walk."

Laurie smiled. "Girl, you can barely stand."

"You might be right. Do you think your brother would drive me home?"

"He might."

"Laurie, you are a good friend. I am going to move in with Steve this weekend."

"Emma, you are lucky to have someone like Steve."

"Laurie, I am afraid that if I move in with him something will go wrong."

Laurie understood the feeling. "Emma, you don't have anything to worry about you know that he loves you."

"I do, and I think I should go home."

"That sounds like a good idea."

Chapter 4

Dan Richardson got in his car and drove to the Clover Corner Restaurant where Lucy and Keith Carr were waiting for him. They had made plans to have a night out which they did from time to time. The three of them had become good friends since Dan had introduced them to one another. When they started running the feed and grain he started delivering things around town for them. Usually, they would get together at least once a week. From time to time Dan would bring a date though it was not something he liked to do. When he took a girl out with Lucy and Kieth she always thought it meant more than it did.

Dan was well known around town as a ladies' man. It was said that he had dated every date-able girl in town at least once. Dan never said one way or the other if the story was true.

On this afternoon he was alone planning only on spending some time with some friends. He was the last one to arrive at the restaurant he was taken to a table by the window. His friends were there waiting for him. Being late was not a new thing for him he was always on the go with too much to do and too little time to get it all done.

Dan sat looking at his coffee cup wondering what he was going to do. There was a lot of talk around town about him and the rest of his family. There had to be some truth to the stories or they would not be talking about them.

He was well known but then so was his whole family. They talked about his father as well as his older brother. They talked about his younger sister because she was a good nurse as well as the fact that she had been leading that Benson boy around by the nose for a long time. Everyone in town felt sorry for that poor boy he seemed to like too nice a boy to be mixed up with the Richardson family.

Everyone in town felt sorry for poor Rachael. Between her husband and her children, it was a wonder the poor woman was as nice as she was. Her husband miss treated her. Her sons were no better than their father they had no respect for people at all. The town thought that as nice as Rachael was she must be soft in the head to put up with all that she did. There was no way in the world that she could not know what was going on right under her nose.

Everyone in town knew all about Dan's family and though they felt sorry for his mother they believed she should have left his father years ago. There was no way the whole town could be wrong about him. Dan knew all the stories as well as all the people involved. He had to admit he had questions about what had happened back when his parents were young.

When Lucy and Keith saw Dan had arrived they ordered his coffee. Lucy could tell his mind was elsewhere so she ordered for the three of them. It was not the first time she had done it. Lucy looked at Dan with a smile as he sat looking out the window. "I thought you would have someone with you."

"I had to pay my bills today so I have no money except for my meal."

"I heard that you were doing a really good business these days."

"I am doing alright but I still owe money on the trucks."

Lucy smiled. "Is this your way of saying you need more work?"

Dan shook his head. "No, it is my way of saying I have bills to pay just like everyone else."

Keith sipped his coffee and then smiled at Dan. "I thought you were independently wealthy. I have heard wealthy people tend to ignore people they feel are beneath them."

"You two are very funny tonight. Have you been smoking something without me?"

Keith shook his head. "We have children we don't do things like that anymore."

Dan nodded. "They say guilty people say things like that all the time. I would think you two respectable people would stay away from someone like me."

Lucy laughed. "We like to get back to our roots from time to time. Some of you lower class people are quite interesting in an odd way."

Dan looked at her. "That depends on who you talk to as I understand it."

Lucy laughed. "I have heard that too. I will never tell you not to eat or even what to eat. I may find it necessary to tell you how to eat."

Dan shook his head. "You are so helpful I am amazed I got this far without you."

Keith smiled. "Speaking of Rhea how is she doing these days?"

"No one was speaking of her. We had one date, we may never have another in this town."

Kieth set his cup down. "I heard it was two."

"Not yet that will be tomorrow night."

Lucy sipped her drink. "I like her she seems very nice."

Dan nodded. "She is nice maybe too nice for me."

Keith laughed. "I think the two of you make a nice couple. You have only had one date don't worry just yet."

"I wasn't you two were the ones with questions. When do I start to worry?"

Keith laughed. "When you are sitting in the kitchen thinking about what your life would be like without her."

When they finished eating Lucy and Keith went home to their children while Dan went off to have a drink or two. He had to be up early in the morning so he could not stay out long. He didn't have much money so he was not going to drink that much.

It was getting late, Dan was sitting at a table at the Circus Bar when his sister walked in and sat down at a table with Laurie. He was not used to seeing his sister at the bar on a weeknight. Emma was the kind of girl who only went to the bar on the weekend and was never alone. She had her boyfriend Steve the one no one was supposed to know was more than just a friend. Everyone who cared about Emma knew about Steve.

The fact that her brothers knew about him was not important because they didn't care. Dan thought she was okay but she was his sister which made her unimportant most of the time. He smiled when he thought about it. She was unimportant and their brother was never home so he didn't matter either which meant that he was the only one that mattered.

He sat watching them glad that they had not noticed him. As the thought came to him he knew it was not completely true after all Laurie knew he was there. Whatever had brought his sister to the bar must be important or Laurie would have told her he was there.

He watched them until his sister left. He should have talked to her. There was no need to talk to her Laurie wasn't going anywhere. She would tell him what was going on. He had never dated her and then dumped her.

As Laurie started past him he smiled at her. "Laurie, what was my sister doing here?"

"She was having a drink with me which you are paying for by the way?"

"Why me?"

"Because you are here."

"Oh, okay I guess."

"You should go home."

"Give me one good reason why I should."

"We are closing."

"Right, I knew that. I think that is a good reason so I think I will go home now."

"You just sit right there I will have my brother drive you home."

"That is nice of you but there is no need for me to have my car."

Laurie shook her head. "I am sure you do but you are in no shape to drive it."

Dan pointed a finger at her. "You are right, I think I like you."

"Don't, I am not doing it for you I am doing it for your sister."

"Okay, that works for me right now."

Laurie walked off as Dan sat at the table alone; his friends had left as soon as they heard the place was closing. It didn't matter that they had stayed longer than they had intended to. They had left him alone in the bar. What had they been thinking?

He hadn't planned on getting as drunk as he was. Things just happened as they were sitting there having fun. He usually didn't go out on a Thursday night but it was the only night his friends could get a babysitter.

Dan looked at what was left of the glass of beer in front of him. What was he doing? This was not him he didn't get drunk during the week or most weekends for that matter. He had to be up early in the morning he had work to do. It was not like he could call off work. He was a hard worker, he was the only employee as well as the boss. Things were supposed to be different when you were the boss.

That was a joke, he wasn't the boss after all he wouldn't have anything if his brother hadn't given it to him. Big brother Luke had it all so when he was tired of something Dan got it. Everything he had was hand-me-downs from his brother. Luke his big brother gave him everything toys, clothes, a bike, a car, a home even his job.

Yeah, having a big brother meant you didn't need a lot of money if you didn't mind second-hand shit. Dan hated second-hand shit. He hated his brother for giving him everything that he no longer wanted. He was surprised he didn't try to give him his wife when he was done with her. There was nothing funny about having nothing that was yours.

Roger Fields walked up to the table. "Dan, give me your keys and we can get you out of here."

Dan handed Roger the keys as he stood up. "Roger, I like you because you are a nice guy. Not everyone would give me a ride home this late at night."

"My big sister told me to do this or she would slap the crap out of me."

"'" You believe her?"

"Yeah, after all, it wouldn't be the first time."

"Oh, I didn't know that."

"Older brother or older sister it is, all the same, they think they are royalty or something."

Dan shook his head. "It isn't right."

Once they were in the car and on their way Roger spoke up. "You are right but that is the way that things are."

Dan nodded. "You think we should stage a revolt and kill them?"

"Not tonight it is much too late."

"I think you are right we can kill them in the morning."

"That sounds like the best plan."

"Did you know that my friends left me there alone? They got me drunk in your bar with no way home."

"Dan, you were alone at the bar."

Dan smiled. "Oh yeah, I think I forgot that."

Roger smiled. "It happens from time to time."

Dan looked at Roger. "You are a good friend."

Roger smiled. "You know we should kill everyone younger than us too. I am sure they will try and kill us when we are the oldest."

"That is an awful lot of killing isn't it?"

Roger shrugged his shoulders. "Two or ten we have to do what we have to do."

"Okay, but it can wait until morning right?"

"Sure we will kill them right after we have coffee."

Once Dan had gone into the house Roger walked to the end of the driveway where his sister was waiting in her car to give him a ride home. "Okay we can go home and I can go back to bed."

Laurie started driving back home. "Roger, you are alright even if you are a guy."

"If you don't like guys why did you wake me up to help Dan get home?"

"He is my friend's brother."

"Speaking of Emma what was she doing at the bar tonight?"

"A patient that she liked died tonight."

"People die at the hospital all the time don't they?"

"Joe was a nice guy with a nice family and she felt bad for them."

"It sounds to me like she should be in another line of work."

"I think she would have agreed with you tonight."

"Laurie, I thought you had a date tonight?"

"I did but he canceled on me."

"He canceled or you did?"

"Does it matter?"

"I am not sure yet."

"Mind your own business."

"I would but you have a more interesting life than I do."

"Only in your eyes pal, I promise you. It is only in your eyes.", Laurie told her brother as she drove back toward town.

Dan got as far as the kitchen where he sat in a chair by the table. His parents and sister were already sleeping so he sat in the dark. No matter what he did he was always one step behind his brother. He had a business his brother had given him and people said he did the job almost as good as Luke had. No matter how hard he worked he always seemed to be one step behind his big brother.

Dan stumbled up the stairs and fell on the bed. There was something he was supposed to do but he couldn't remember what it was. That was the trouble with his life so much to do he just couldn't remember it all. He would talk it all over with his mother in the morning.

Luke Richardson was sitting at a truck stop at a table with Jack and a cup of coffee. As they sat there Luke had his eyes on a waitress who was not working their table. He had been on the road four days and he was hours away from home. Luke might have made the run home if they hadn't seen the waitress. Luke had been living alone more or less for a couple of years. It was true that he went out on a date now and then, but he had no steady girl.

Luke could have done a lot of things but he liked driving trucks most of the time. The thing was he had never wanted to be a truck driver he wanted to be a farmer but he needed money so he started a delivery business. Everything would have worked out fine if Linda had been the woman he thought she was.

Now Linda was gone and he had lost his interest in the farm but he owned it along with the bank so he had to make enough money to pay for it. Even if he wasn't going to be a real farmer he planned to keep the few animals that he had. One day he might find that he wanted to be a farmer again or maybe the place would just be a good investment.

Jack had been with Luke for eight years which was six years longer than his wife Linda had lasted with him. He had seen him with several other girls but none that lasted more than a weekend or two. Luke was a nice guy but he had no luck with women at all. Jack knew he was the only real friend Luke was ever going to have.

"Jack, don't look at me like that. You may not think that she will like me but I know I am going to get a date with her."

Jack shook his head and then rested his head on the table.

Luke put up his hands and then placed them on the table. "You are a dog what do you know about women?"

A waitress was refilling Luke's coffee cup. "The dog is right Debbie just got married she isn't interested in you."

Before Luke could say a word Allen Fields sat down at the table next to Jack. "Evening Luke, how are you doing?"

"Al, what are you doing out here so late?"

"They sent me after machinery."

Luke was surprised. "I thought my Dad always did those runs?"

Al nodded. "Usually but he turned it down this time and said it was time one of the kids learned to be responsible."

"He must have had other plans."

"Yeah, that is what he says every time he doesn't want to do something."

"Yeah I know, you would think home would be a little different than work."

Allen looked around the room. "How are you doing with the waitress?"

Luke shrugged his shoulders. "I am not interested so I am not getting anywhere."

"Why?"

"I don't know I just don't feel like being turned down again I guess."

"You don't want them just in case they are like Linda."

Luke smiled. "You would think I would be over that by now."

Allen nodded. "You would think. Maybe you just need to find the right girl."

"Did you have someone in mind?"

"If I did I would be dating her myself."

"Right, well it never hurts to ask."

Allen laughed. "You are a trucker just like your Dad. If you want to be a family man you have to love a woman more than Jack or your truck."

Luke shook his head. "I can give up the truck for a woman but never Jack."

"I can understand that. Jack, you can count on but a woman is always a question."

"Right, I knew you would understand."

"What I understand is that you are out of your mind."

"Yeah, I think you might be right about that."

"I am, you should start dating my sister again so she will move out of the house."

"You sound like you are trying to get rid of her."

"I am, she is my sister. Why in the world wouldn't I want to get rid of her?"

"You want her room."

"I do, it is bigger than mine. Luke, I have to get going it is getting late."

"If you don't want her around why would I?"

"Damned if I know. I have to get going I will see you when you get home."

Luke smiled. " Maybe if she was a dog instead of a girl. A dog can be trusted."

Allen laughed. "You might have a point. I need to get going."

"I have a load to drop in the morning and another to pick up before I can head home."

"I am going to head home I plan to take the day off tomorrow. I was thinking I might go fishing."

"That sounds like fun I might do that myself."

Allen smiled. "If you don't want to do the work why not just get rid of the animals or the whole place for that matter."

Luke nodded. "I have thought about it but I like the horses and the cows. Chickens are okay as long as they are providing eggs for my breakfast."

"I need to get going I will see you this weekend."

Luke finished his coffee after Allen left then went out and walked Jack around before they went to the truck. Luke needed to get some sleep but it was the last thing that he wanted. He was looking for a quiet night without much time to think which meant he needed to get some sleep.

Sleep didn't come so Luke drove to his next delivery site. As soon as the place opened the truck was unloaded. Driving across town he picked up a load from another place then he headed home. He was going to be home early which would be good. He was going to have time to get his bills paid and have a little fun before he went to the farm. This was going to be a good weather weekend so they were going to be working the hay field through the weekend.

Chapter 5

Emma Richardson was up early Friday morning she had been hoping to have breakfast with her father but it was too late he had left for work. She was up so she might as well go down to the kitchen for coffee and some breakfast. She got dressed and then went down to the kitchen for the coffee which she needed desperately.

When she reached the kitchen she found her father sitting at the kitchen table drinking a cup of coffee. "Dad, don't take this wrong but I didn't expect to find you here this morning."

"I took the day off."

"Good, we can have breakfast together. What would you like?"

"Eggs and sausage I think."

"I think I remember how to do that."

"I didn't know nurses knew how to cook."

Emma poor herself a coffee and then refilled her Dad's cup. "We have to know a little bit about everything just in case we find someone in need."

"Did you find someone in need of a cook?"

"Dad, all men need a cook."

"I don't know I can cook pretty good."

"You should tell that to someone who hasn't had to eat your cooking."

"You never complained before."

"That is because Mom does most of the cooking."

"You know why that is don't you?"

"Yes, her food tastes good."

"Better than mine that is true."

This was her chance to tell him about Steve. "Dad, I do know a man who needs a good cook."

As Emma was speaking Roger spoke. "Emma, I have cancer."

Emma put the eggs in the pan and then began to beat them. If they had been alive she would have beat them to death. "We are having scrambled eggs this morning."

"That is fine with me. Did you say something about a man?"

"No, I said it is good you like scrambled eggs. We are out of eggs and I beat the shit out of these."

"Did it help?"

"Yes, in a very small way."

"Wish you had some more I would try it too."

Emma looked at her father. "Dad, people do survive sometimes."

"I know Emma, I haven't given up though I am mad and scared. I always figured I would die in a truck wreck never home in bed."

"I don't want to talk about that right now it is time to eat."

Emma put the food on the table and then sat down next to her father. "Boston has a good-looking team this year."

"I don't know I haven't seen them all yet."

"Are you going to date one?"

"That depends on just how much money he is worth."

"I always thought you would marry for love."

"I will the second time I have to be sure I have a nest egg first."

"That seems wrong to me. I must say it is good to hear that you are planning though."

"You always said it was best to have an outline."

Roger smiled. "I didn't mean it that way I meant a good man to take care of you."

Emma looked at her father. "I have you so it is all good."

The two of them sat there eating their breakfast talking about nothing that mattered. When they finished eating Emma refilled their coffee cups and then cleaned off the table. Leaving the dishes in the sink she hugged her Dad and then went up the stairs with her coffee in hand.

Emma sat in her room with tears in her eyes but she didn't make a sound. She had sat in the kitchen with her Dad talking over eggs and coffee. Somewhere over the second cup of coffee or maybe the first he had told her as if he were telling her he wanted more coffee. He had not sugar-coated anything he just came right out and said it. He looked at her holding his cup in both hands as he tried to smile.

Emma had just stood there beating the crap out of the eggs. This couldn't be happening it wasn't fair he was young yet not even fifty-five. She was a nurse she knew the odds it was certain he would never reach sixty. She had told him the treatments could help him even though they both knew it was a lie. Then they just sat there talking as if cancer was something you could fix with a band-aide.

She was supposed to be sharing the good news with him about Steve asking her to move in with him. She was sure once they were living together it would not be long before he asked her to marry him. Steve was one of the good guys he believed in marriage he would want to get married. She had planned on saying yes. Now everything had changed there was no way she could leave her parents now.

Her bedroom was big but as she sat there she felt the walls closing in on her. She had gotten through breakfast without crying though she had started before she reached her room. How was she going to hold it all together long enough to go to work? She needed to talk to someone she had to get it all out before she went to work.

Stephen was the one she wanted to talk to but he was out of town. That meant she was going to go over and talk with Laurie. They had been friends all through school and if she couldn't talk to Stephen she would talk to Laurie it might be better this way.

Now that she knew what she was going to do all she had to do was get out of the house without crying. That was easier said than done. She was having trouble sitting in her room alone without crying. Her Dad would not want to see her crying he felt bad enough she was sure.

She got ready for work and then went down the stairs to the kitchen. Her mother was in the kitchen cleaning up the dishes. "Mom, I have some things I need to do before I go to work. I will come right home from work."

"Emma, are you okay?"

"Mom, are you?"

Her mother smiled. "Drive carefully."

Rachael stood in the kitchen at the sink doing the breakfast dishes. She had cried and she would cry again many times she was sure. She had hoped Emma would talk with her but she was her father's daughter she would talk to Steve and Laurie first. This was not going to be easy on any of them as they did their best to deal with the news. Rachael knew that she would talk with her daughter when Emma was ready.

Emma waved and then ran out the door to her car. Sitting in the car she did her best to stop crying. She knew she couldn't drive like that but she had to leave her Dad would be watching. Pulling herself together again she headed for Laurie's place. It only took a couple of minutes to get there it was in the center of town. She didn't want to bring this to Laurie but she had to talk to someone. She would understand she was more than just a friend she was more of a sister.

Parking in the parking lot out back she ran up the old wooden stairs to the second floor. Knocking on the door she was having second thoughts about being there. What was she going to say? Did she want to say anything at all? Should she say anything after all her Dad might not want anyone to know.

Laurie opened the door. "Emma, come on in the coffee is on."

Emma walked inside taking a seat at the kitchen table. "Let's skip the coffee I need a beer."

Laurie set two beers on the table and then sat down. "I am guessing something is wrong."

"Dad has cancer he told me over coffee this morning. We sat there eating breakfast and drinking coffee while we talked about it. It was as if it were nothing at all."

"I knew something was up my Mom was crying last night. I am sorry Emma."

"It isn't fair he had all these plans for Mom and him when he retired."

"I understand, I was young when Dad was hurt but I thought he was going to die. I still remember how that felt I couldn't seem to even breathe right."

"It isn't fair and there is nothing I can do to change the way things are. I have talked to God but nothing changed. I know the odds I know just how it will go. Nothing helps because there is nothing that I can do to help him."

Laurie sipped her beer. "I have had to live with a lot and it is never easy or fair it is life and it sucks."

"No shit, all the training I had and I don't know a damn thing I can do to help him."

"All you can do is be there for him and you're Mom. Don't try to do anything but be his daughter. That is all he wants right now."

"It doesn't feel like it is enough."

"I know, I feel the same way every time I look at my Dad. There is only so much any of us can do about anything."

Emma shook her head. "I don't know if I can manage to go back home without crying."

Laurie understood how she felt. "Some days you will while other days you won't be able to. It can be hard to stop crying at times. Birthday parties will make you cry at times even on holidays or there may be a day that was special for some reason. You may just cry for no real reason at all, that is just the way it is."

"It sucks."

"Now you have got it, "life sucks," and then you ignore it and move on for I bit."

"Steve left town right after he asked me to move in with him. Joe died of cancer last night. Dad tells me he has cancer this morning. Just what am I supposed to do now?"

Laurie was smiling. "Girl, did you just say that Steve asked you to move in with him?"

"Yes, he did right before he left town on a business trip."

"You said yes didn't you?"

Emma nodded. "I did but that was before I knew about Dad.

There is no way I am moving out of the house now. Mom and Dad will need me."

"Girl, you told Steve you were going to move in with him you can't change your mind."

Emma shook her head. "I didn't change my mind the situation has changed. I can't leave my parents now they need me."

Laurie's voice was calm. "Steve needs you too."

"He will understand how I feel."

"Maybe."

"Laurie, if he doesn't, do I want him?"

"Girl, you are growing up."

"My big sister is to blame for that."

"Yes, I am."

Emma smiled. "I have to go to work. Thanks for everything I think I can handle things for at least eight or nine hours."

"Call me if you have trouble and I will try to help you."

Emma nodded then walked out the door and down the stairs to the parking lot. She was feeling better as long as she didn't think too much. Her mind was full of thoughts none of which made her happy. There was no way to stop thinking about it. Her Dad was dying, she was a nurse, she knew the odds, and she knew the outcome. She knew too much.

Jim Campbell was standing by Emma's car a smile on his face. "Hi good looking, you got some free time I think I can make you happy."

Without a word, Emma kicked him where it counted. The look on his face made her feel a little better. She would have done it again but he was on his knees already. Then there was the fact that she needed to get to work. She was smiling when she drove out of the parking lot.

Emma drove to the hospital but didn't stop, she just drove on by. She knew she should go to work. The truth was she just couldn't bring herself to do it. What she needed was some alone time. To be honest she felt that just maybe she needed something more.

Emma wanted to get drunk but she couldn't bring herself to do it alone. If she couldn't drink she would just keep driving. That was when she stopped the car. With nothing else to do she just sat there crying. She was crying for her parents as well as her brothers and herself.

When she stopped crying she sat in the car wishing there was something more she could do. Life wasn't fair. This was supposed to be a time for her to be happy. What had she done to deserve something like this? Yes, she was being selfish because she was scared as well as hurt. There was not a damn thing she could do about it.

She was back in the parking lot of the Circus Bar. Laurie was sitting on the back porch. Emma got out of the car and then walked slowly up onto the porch. "I couldn't go to work."

Laurie nodded her head. "I know I have been sitting here waiting for you. You left Jim on his knees as white as a sheet."

"I am in a bad mood and he is a pig."

"Chuck says the same thing about him."

"You think I should have kicked him again?"

"At least one or two more times it might have helped you."

"I will remember that for next time. The thing is I don't think it will help. To be honest I don't think there is anything that can help."

Laurie nodded her head in agreement. "Why don't we go inside and get something to drink."

"No beer."

"I think I might be able to find you something a little better than that."

"Laurie, getting drunk isn't going to help anything."

"No, but it isn't going to hurt anything either. There is a time when it is just something you have to do. The good news is that my parents own the bar and today your drinks are free."

"Laurie thanks but you really can't do that."

"Emma, do you think my Mom is going to let you pay?"

"No, I don't think she will."

"What do you want to do?"

"Drink."

"After that?"

"I want to run away from home but I can't. I want to forget what Dad told me but I can't do that either."

"You could always learn to drive a truck."

"I have driven the trucks but it is not for me."

They walked into the bar where Laurie's mother poured them each a drink and then gave Laurie the bottle. The two of them found an empty table where they sat drinking and talking. They were good friends which is something that the people in town seemed to think was odd. Their parents had a history that the whole town thought they knew.

Laurie poured a drop in her glass and then filled Emma's "You want to learn how to tend bar?"

Emma smiled. "Right now I would drink more than I sold."

"Mom wouldn't like that."

"I should go home while I can still walk."

"I can get you a ride home if you want."

"You mean I can drink more."

"I think that would be one thing you could do."

"I will drink to that."

Together Laurie and Emma sat there Emma drinking mixed drinks Laurie drinking coke. Just as the sun was setting Stephen Benson walked into the bar and got a beer. He took his beer and then went to the table where Emma and Laurie were sitting. "Ladies, can I join you?"

Emma looked up at him. "What the hell are you doing here? Dad has cancer I am going to lose him. Sit down my neck hurts looking up at you."

"I think I should take you home."

"It is too early for that and we still haven't finished the bottle."

"We finished one."

"Laurie, we should be careful we could get drunk."

"No, Mom shut us off."

"I am not ready to stop."

Stephen smiled. "I will take you home."

"I don't want to go home. Let's go drink at your house."

"Let's go girl."

Emma stood up. "Can we go to your places?"

Stephen smiled at her as he put his arm around her. "We can go wherever you want to."

Emma put her arm around Stephen. "I will go anywhere you want as long as you take me. You will take me home when we are done having fun won't you?"

"I think I can do that for you if you want me to."

Emma smiled as she looked at Laurie. "I like him."

Laurie watched them go then took the bottle and glasses back to the bar. "That didn't take as long as I thought it would."

Linda looked at the empty bottle. "How much did you drink?"

"I had one I didn't want it she did. Thanks for calling Stephen."

"He got here faster than I thought he would."

"He would do anything for her."

"Are you going to work tonight?"

"Sure I am in the mood to be around happy people."

"With thoughts like that, you still want to tend bar?"

"Mom, the sound of the cash register always makes me smile."

"Will you watch things I want to go sit with your Dad for a few minutes?"

"Not a problem."

Chapter 6

Luke was back early which always seemed to be a good thing on a Friday. He had parked his rig in the yard and with his check in his pocket, he got in his pickup with Jack. Their first stop was the bank they cashed his check then he made his payment on the farm. Coffee was on his mind but the warm weather had him thinking of soda. By the time he parked the pickup in the parking lot of the grocery store, he was thinking beer.

He could have bought a cold drink at the grocery store if he had wanted to. There was no shade near the grocery store so he started walking along the street. It wasn't a long walk down the street to the small store where he could get a cold drink. He went out of the store to sit on a bench in the shade. In the afternoon heat, it seemed as though it had been a long walk even to Jack.

When he had been in the store he had wished they sold beer. He joked with the clerk about the heat and the lack of beer for sale before going out to the bench. The bench was in the shade which made it seem cooler than it was. He liked sitting in the shade just sipping his drink while he watched the people walk by. He spent most of his time with Jack so he didn't want to talk to them. It was enough to just watch them go about their business.

When he had gotten to the small store to get his drink he had changed his mind again. When he walked out of the store he had a bottle of water which was not what he had planned. He sat there on the bench in the shade while Jack lay down beside the bench. They watched as people walked back and forth along the street. He smiled at them all, some of them he knew others he didn't. He was happy, it felt good just to sit quietly for a little bit watching people as they walked by him.

He was sitting outside in the shade thinking of all the things he could be doing if he had a little more money. The payment on the farm had taken most of his money. He didn't mind that after all, he didn't need much money. It had been a long week but the week was over. It was Friday afternoon everyone he knew was getting ready for the weekend. He had no weekend plans other than mowing his parent's lawn as well as his own.

The weatherman was saying the weekend was going to be sunny and warm. Tomorrow he was going to have to cut some hay then Sunday he would bale it up. With help from his brother, he would put it in the barn. Other than working around the farm he hadn't had any weekend plans. It had been that way for twenty months, fourteen days, and eighteen hours give or take a couple of minutes.

When he was nineteen he met Linda and they had gotten married six weeks later. It had seemed like a really good match they liked the same things they even liked one another. They had a lot of the same friends they had everything they thought they would need as long as they were together.

What they didn't have was a place to live so they bought one in cooperation with the bank. The bank loaned them the money to get the place and in return, they agreed to pay the bank a whole lot more than they had borrowed. It didn't matter they planned to live there together for the rest of their lives. What they didn't tell people was without his parents co-signing the loan they wouldn't have gotten anything.

They bought a small farm with a couple of horses, two dozen chickens even a couple of cows. Linda loved to work in the garden so they had a big one. He had bought a flatbed truck and then talked a few places into using him and his truck to make their deliveries. He only took jobs delivering locally so he was home every night as well as on the weekends.

For two years everything was perfect then one Friday night he got home late and she was gone. There was no note, nothing was missing but her belongs she sent him divorce papers a month after she left. He simply signed them and then sent them to her mother. That was the last he heard from her he never went looking for her he never asked anyone about her it was over.

There was nothing to worry about now he had everything he needed two horses, two dairy cows, and two dozen chickens. He milked the cows twice a day right before he collected the eggs. His brother helped him take care of things when he needed help. It wasn't a perfect world he was living in but it was his. It was not bad after all it was what he had wanted.

Maybe it wasn't that good after all, marriage was supposed to last forever. Why had his only lasted two years? He had failed even though Linda had left him he must have done something wrong. If he hadn't she would never have left him. You didn't have to have a college education to figure that much out.

It was a small town and everyone in it knew he was a failure. There was nothing he could do to change it so he sold the flatbed truck to his brother. He made sure everyone would work with Dan then he bought a sleeper cab and a box trailer. He was now a long-haul trucker gone all week home most weekends during the summer.

Sitting on the bench he was thinking about what he wanted to drink soda, coffee, water, or a beer. It was too hot for coffee and too early for beer so it looked like soda or water. He had already had water so it seemed soda had won by default. Or maybe not because he was going to have to get off the bench to get the soda which was something he didn't want to do right then. He would have been on his way to his parent's house if he wanted to get up off the bench.

There are times when just sitting quietly was the best way to finish out a day. This was that kind of day everything just seemed to tell him to sit and enjoy the beautiful afternoon. That was it then his mind was made up he was going to sit right where he was until the sun went down. It had been a long week in some ways a short one in others but it was over now.

The sun was warm the sky was clear and she had some great-looking legs! He had no idea who she was but she had some shorts that moved well on her as she walked. She had on a yellow shirt that fit her quite well. To make things perfect she had long red hair. She was going into the drug store on the other side of the street. It was about half a block away not far at all. Now might be a good time to go get that coke he had been thinking about.

Getting up he walked along the street to the store and then went inside. The redhead .was by the cooler that had the soda in it. This would be way too easy. He was going to get a date with her. There was nothing that would stop him now that they were this close

"Excuse me young man can you let me by."

He smiled at the elderly lady as he stepped aside. She reminded him of his grandmother. "Yes Mam, it sure is a nice day isn't it?"

"Yes, it is."

Looking back toward the coolers he saw that the redhead was gone. He hadn't looked away for more than a minute or two but that was all it took for her to disappear. Well, that was that it was just not meant to be. He got a coke and then got in line behind the elderly lady.

The woman looked at him. "You were looking for the redhead."

"Yes."

"Today must be your lucky day. You should buy a lottery ticket."

"I don't feel very lucky she disappeared and I don't even know her name."

"Luke, as I said it is your lucky day she lives near me. Her name is Cassie and she is fifteen years old."

"She is fifteen years old?"

"Yes, she is in my history class just as you were when you were her age."

"Mrs. Hoffman?"

"Yes."

"It is good to see you it has been a long time."

"Not that long though it might seem like it to you. You were good at history you learned a lot in my class. Cassie isn't a very good student she doesn't understand that history is a life lesson the way that you did."

"Maybe I will buy a lottery ticket."

"I think that would be s a good idea for you right now."

Mrs. Hoffman left and he bought a lottery ticket and a coke. The coke was cold the ticket was worth a hundred dollars. One hundred dollars richer he left the store. As he walked back to his pickup he was still thinking about the redhead. A girl that looked that good shouldn't still be fifteen years old. He knew girls a lot older that never looked that good.

"Jack, I think we got lucky thereby not getting lucky."

"Luke, what are you doing sitting here? I thought you didn't talk to the dog anymore."

Emily Rice was standing on the driver's side of the truck looking at him her hands on her hips. He hadn't seen or heard her walk up to the truck his mind had been on the redhead. "Emily, what are you up to?"

"I am not chasing jail bait or talking to my dog, I can tell you that."

"What are you talking about?"

"You walked right past me chasing that fifteen-year-old redhead. Even Jack stopped and wagged his tail when he saw me."

"How is it everybody seems to know she is fifteen but me?"

"I know her older sister we used to hang out together when we were kids."

"Where are you going?"

"Nowhere really I was just walking along the street hoping to run into someone I knew. All I found was you and Jack."

"Sorry, I guess everyone else had somewhere else to be this afternoon."

"It is okay I can hang with you and Jack if you don't mind."

"I was on my way to mow my parent's lawn. If you want to come along we can go out later and maybe have a couple of beers."

Emily looked at him thoughtfully. "If you had caught up with the redhead and if she wasn't jail bait would you have asked her to go with you to your parent's house?"

"I most defiantly would not have taken her to see my mother."

"That is what I thought. I think I should be insulted on some level."

Luke smiled as Emily got in the truck. He hadn't seen her in a while and she looked even better than he remembered. "I don't think so you are two different people that is all there is to that."

"You take her home to your bed you take me to your Mom and Dad's to help you mow the lawn."

"I know you can handle a lawnmower."

"I don't know about you."

This time Luke laughed as he drove toward his parent's home. "I would have taken her to a motel she never would have seen my place. As for you, I trust you which is something I don't say about most of the girls I know."

"You trust me because I don't look as good as the redhead?"

"I never said that, in some ways, you look better than her. I trust you because I know you and I know you are a good person."

"I am a good person because I am a good person or because I am engaged to another man?"

"I have known you a few years you have always been honest with me."

"You mean honesty is that important to you?"

"Yes, people tell others what they think they want to hear so you never know the real person the way you think you do."

"Then I guess you should know Jim dumped me for some girl he met at the diner a couple of weeks ago."

"Sorry, I thought you two would be the ones to make it you seemed like the perfect couple." It was a lie but there was no need to tell her he thought she was stupid for staying with him as long as she had.

Emily smiled a sad kind of smile; she had a far-off look in her eyes. "I thought we would live happily ever after too at one time. I guess we were lying to one another as well as to ourselves."

Luke nodded his head thinking of his past and his own mistakes. "It happens to the best of us. I was there and I did that and then I got married. I knew it was a mistake."

"Then why did you do it?"

Luke smiled. "Seemed like a good idea at the time."

"That is stupid."

Luke nodded his head. "It sounds stupid now I guess it sounded stupid then too."

"You know this is not the first time he has done this we got engaged after the last girl dumped him."

"Why in the world would you do that?"

"I don't know, I guess it seemed like a good idea at the time."

Luke shook his head. "I always liked Jim but then I guess I never really knew him. I never thought he was like that I thought he was honest."

"No, that was his Dad. I think he is everything but honest."

"People are hard to understand at times."

Emily laughed. "Now there is an understatement if I ever heard one."

Luke parked the truck in the driveway. "Mom is in the house I don't think Dad is home yet. Why don't you go talk to her while I mow the lawn."

Emily looked at him thoughtfully. "You don't want me to help you mow the lawn?"

"No, I think I can handle it. I think it would be nice if Mom had some company."

Emily smiled a warm smile. "Come along Jack I have a feeling he wants to work alone."

Emily went into the house with Jack while Luke went to the garage and got out the old push mower. He put in oil and then gas before he stood there thinking about Emily. Why had he brought her with him to the house? He smiled as he started up the mower. The only reason he could think of was that it seemed like a good idea at the time. He hoped things were not going to go the way they had the last time he said that.

The lawn was not that big but it was going to take him about an hour to mow the yard. That would be just enough time for his Mom to enjoy the company which was not bad. He was thinking that Emily was someone his Mom would be happy to see again.

Rachael Richardson smiled at Emily. "Would you like some ice tea?"

"Yes thank you."

"Emily, how is Jim doing?"

"We broke up he is a bum."

"I heard you two were planning to get married."

"As it turned out I was the only one that was planning to get married I guess."

"That happens sometimes, you should just take your time the right man will come along."

"I am not sure I want to find a man I think it would be best if I spend some time alone."

"Sounds like you have things well in hand. Luke has been on his own for two years. He seems to be doing just fine on his own. I have hopes that he will find a nice girl soon I would like to have some grandchildren. Still, I think he has to do things in his own time. It is hard to say what is best. You never know just how long you have on this earth."

"Have you told Luke that?"

"No, I think it is best to wait until he has found a nice girl before I say anything about grandchildren. As for the other thing, he will find out about that soon enough."

"I think you are right I bet something like that would scare him half to death."

"I never said anything to Linda about grandchildren she didn't seem like she would be a good mother."

Emily smiled. "It would seem you were right about that."

Luke's Mom smiled. "Would you like to see some pictures of the kids when they were young? I think there may even be a couple of you in there."

"I think that would be fun."

Luke forgot about everything as he was mowing the lawn. It was something he liked to do as long as it wasn't too hot. He had mowed his first lawn when he was seven years old. Over the years as the mowers got better the lawns seemed to get bigger even though they only moved twice and never left town. The first lawn had been the biggest and he had mowed that one with a reel push mower.

By the time he was done it was after five he needed to get home and mow his lawn as well as help Dan with the chores. He hadn't realized just how late it was. He put the mower in the shed and then stood looking at the lawn making sure he hadn't missed anything. When he was satisfied that he was done he went into the house.

Jack barked at Luke as he walked into the house. "Jack, why do you always bark at me but not at anyone else?"

Emily had a hand on Jack. "He is glad to see you that is the reason he barks at you."

"An afternoon with Jack and you know how he feels."

"He is a smart dog you should be more like him."

"Right, what have you two been doing while I was mowing?"

"We had some ice tea and looked at some pictures. I never realized I was over here that much when I was a kid. There are pictures of us playing together as well as some nice pictures of you naked in the tub."

"Mom, you have to be careful who you show those pictures too."

"Luke, I always am after all I never showed them to Linda."

"I have to go over to my place so I can mow my lawn. Would you like me to give you a ride home?"

"I thought we were going to go out for drinks?"

"Right, well in that case we do have to get going I want to get something to eat before we go out."

"Would you like me to fix the two of you something before you leave?"

"No thanks Mom, I need to get moving before I run out of daylight."

"Are you sure I can't fix you something?"

"Mom, Dan is going to be wondering where I am as it is."

Rachael watched her oldest son and Emily Rice leave the house with Jack. She wanted to tell him about his father. Roger had told her he would tell the children and he had told Emma. The boys still needed to know but Roger had gone for a walk after Emma left for work and still had not returned. It was so hard for her to watch Luke leave the house thinking everything was as it always was.

There was nothing for her to do so she went into the kitchen to make a salad. She got out a few onions to peel and then sliced it up. As she worked she cried. Roger would tell the children but she hoped Dan would talk to his father before she saw him. Rachael was not sure she could keep quiet if Dan got to the house and Roger wasn't there.

Chapter 7

Dan Richardson was up early he started the coffee and then washed up. He had plans for Friday night but first, he had to get through the day. He poured himself a cup of fresh coffee and then went out to the barn. He fed the horses and then grained the cows. He cleaned the barn and then milked the cows.

Before going back to the house he fed the chickens and then collected the eggs. Putting everything but his empty coffee cup in the wagon they had made to hold everything for the trip to the house he left the barn.

Once everything was in the house Dan got another cup of coffee and then took care of the milk and eggs. Once that was done he fixed himself something to eat. He looked over his delivery schedule while he ate then washed the dishes before taking his shower and getting dressed for work. With the last of the coffee in his cup, he went out to his truck and then headed for town.

As he drove toward town he remembered how the night before he thought Roger Fields had dropped him off at his parent's house. He had not realized until he woke just where he was. He usually didn't drink that much and he couldn't say why he had done it.

The grain and feed store was his first stop Lucy Carr was in the office waiting for him. "Good morning Dan."

"Lucy, how are you doing this morning?"

"I could be better the baby had me up half the night."

"Sorry, is he okay?"

"He is with his grandmother sleeping he is fine. I am the one that is going to suffer all day."

"Sorry for you but glad he is okay."

"We got two more orders late yesterday."

"Of course, you did it is Friday."

Lucy smiled at him. "Weekend plans?"

Dan nodded. "I have plans for tonight not sure about the rest of the weekend yet."

"Do I know her?"

Dan just smiled and then went out to the loading dock. They had talked about Rhea the night before. Lucy was always doing her best to get him going. It was a game with her she enjoyed watching him turn red.

Keith Carr was already loading the truck. Dan gave him a hand with the bags of grain and other supplies. Within a half hour, the truck was loaded and ready to go. The two of them went inside where Lucy had the paperwork as well as two cups of coffee ready for them.

Keith sipped his coffee and then looked at Dan. "How are things out at the farm?"

Dan waved his hands. "Wide open and filled with fresh country air."

"Horseshit."

"Yeah, we got that too."

"Dan, you should find yourself a wife to help you with all the farm work."

"I think I will pass on that one. I am not ready for that just yet."

Keith laughed. "You think we were? You don't pick the time a time picks you that is how marriage works."

Dan laughed. "You make me sound like fruit on a tree."

"You just might be."

Dan finished his coffee. "I have to get on the road."

The good thing about deliveries is you have a lot of stops and people to talk to at each stop. This all helps the day to move along as well as gives you different things to think about as the day goes on. Dan liked that about the job not that he had any worries his life was looking good. He had a job he liked as well as some friends he hung out with from time to time.

In the afternoon he delivered furniture with the help of Allen Logan. Allen was married and worked the third shift in the factory five or six nights a week. He had a young son who was about a year old. His wife Joanne worked days at the truck stop while her Mom watched the baby. They were saving up to buy a house not far from her Mom's house.

Dan liked to go over to visit them from time to time they always seemed so happy with what they had even though they didn't have much. They always made him feel that he was missing something by not being married. Then he would think of his brother and his two-year marriage to Linda. Marriage was gambling with your life, feelings, and everything that you owned. He was sure he wasn't ready for that.

By the time Dan got home he was running a little late too late to mow the lawn. He did the chores then took a shower then got ready for his date. As he finished his second cup of coffee he was thinking he didn't mind helping out on his brother's farm. He did get a place to live and he was alone most of the week which didn't hurt his social life at all. Most of the girls he knew liked the farm, especially the horses.

Getting into his car he drove home to mow his parent's lawn. When he got home he found the lawn had already been mowed. He got the milk and eggs which he had brought with him out of the car.

As he walked into the kitchen he asked. "Mom, I was going to mow, who mowed your lawn today?"

"Your brother did he was here earlier with Emily Rice."

"I was at his place caring for his animals and he was here mowing the lawn?"

"Yes, did you bring the milk and eggs with you?"

"I did I put it all in the fridge in the kitchen."

"Good we are getting low on both your father was afraid he wouldn't have milk for his morning coffee."

"Where is my brother?"

"He said he was going to go home and mow his lawn."

"He should have done that before he came over here then he could have cared for his animals."

"Dan, why are you so mad at your brother?"

Dan thought about it for a bit. "I guess I am just mad because he is gone all the time."

His mother looked at him. "You told your brother you were glad to help him."

"I was and I am I just am not sure why I feel this way."

Rachael knew she had felt the same way before Roger had told her about feeling sick. "Are you going out tonight?"

"I do have a date with Rhea which I will be late for if I stall around much longer. I have to go to the car wash I need to clean the car inside and out."

"Rhea Conner is a nice girl I know her parents they are very nice people."

"Mom, the whole town knows her parents. This is only the second time we are going out together. Please don't start planning the wedding just yet."

"Do you want something to eat before you leave?"

"No, I promised her we would eat out."

"Take her someplace nice no fast food."

"Mom, I am not my brother I don't take my dates to burger joints."

"Your Dad needs to talk to you but he went out I guess it will wait until tomorrow."

Dan smiled at his mother. "Mom, Rhea, and I will stop back here after we go out to eat."

"You should call first just to be sure your Dad is back before you come over."

"Mom, don't worry we will swing by the house and you can say hi to her while I talk to Dad. I have to get going."

Dan was in a hurry he was going to be late but he liked talking with his Mom she was always doing her best to help him impress the girls. It was true her advice was always the same but it was good advice.

Rachael Richardson watched her youngest son drive out of the driveway. She hoped he didn't come back to the house with his date he should be alone with his father when they talked. She didn't dare say anything Dan would know something was wrong. It would not be easy for him to hear maybe Rhea would help him deal with the news.

Dan moved as fast as he could to get the car clean. He worked fast doing his best to be ready on time. When he was finally ready he was late. He called Rhea and told her he was on the way just before he left the car wash.

When Dan got to the house Rhea walked off the porch and down the walk toward the car. She was dressed in a white blouse and black skirt. Her shoes were black with what Dan called a half-heal. She had a small black handbag in her hand. Dan could tell just by the look of her that there was only one place she was dressed for. They were going to be eating at the country club. It was the best place in town with good food as well as high prices.

Dan got out of the car and opened the passenger side door for Rhea. She smiled at him as she was starting to get into the car. "Thank you."

Dan watched her as she got in the car afraid he was in over his head. Rhea was not the kind of girl that he was used to dating. This was going to be a very different kind of night. Dan closed the door then went around the car and got behind the wheel. Looking at Rhea now he was amazed she had agreed to a second date with him.

Chapter 8

The farm was bigger than Emily thought it would be, after all, he only had two horses, two cows, and a couple of dozen chickens. She wasn't sure how much land he had but it was clear he had a lot more than he needed for the animals he had. At least that was the way it seemed to her. Emily was not a farmer or even a farmer's daughter so she knew she was not the best judge of these things.

When they got out of the pickup Jack ran down to the fence to check on the animals. It was clear he was as much a farm dog as Luke was a farmer. Emily was thinking they were the perfect pair. She wished she was as free as the two of them seemed to be. She was a prisoner of a life that she never chose for herself.

"Emily, you can have a look around or go into the house. There is soda, ice tea, milk, and beer in the refrigerator you can have what you want. It is going to take about a half hour to mow the lawn so think about where you want to go out to eat."

"We are going out to eat too?"

"We might as well I am not as good a cook as you might think. Besides I told Mom I would take you out to eat so I will take you out to eat."

"To be honest I didn't know you could cook."

Luke smiled. "That is what I call it other people may call it something else."

"I bet they do."

Emily watched Luke as he went off to get his mower out of the shed. She was surprised that he seemed to trust her alone in his house. Even though they had not seen one another in a long time he trusted her enough to leave her alone while he worked on the lawn. To be honest they, like so many people had lost touch once they were out of school. They saw each other on the street from time to time or at the Circus Bar but that was all.

They hadn't talked to one another in years though there had been one night. They had been at the bar; they had talked about their school days. It had been a good time once they had forgotten everyone around them as they talked. There had been a point when she thought it was going to turn into something more but the moment had passed. Jim had come into the bar and joined them. Luke left the bar with some friends while she left with Jim.

Luke was sitting on the mower in the shed wondering what he was thinking asking Emily to come out to the farm. Word would get around people would start to talk his Mom would look at him with that silly grin on her face. He should have left her in town but there was just something that came over him. He didn't want to be alone when he went out he was sick of being alone.

Luke started the mower and then drove out of the shed. He started mowing the lawn thinking about everything that had happened since he had graduated. He had gotten off to such a good start he thought, then Linda left him. This left him wanting to get out of town. He hadn't wanted to run away just spend some time alone. The farm would have been good for that if he didn't have to have a job to make the payments on the place. He had wanted to keep it because he liked it. He liked it even more than he told himself he had liked Linda. That was what he told himself even though at first he wasn't sure it was true.

Dan needed a job so they made a deal he gave Dan the flatbed then he bought a used sleeper rig as well as a used box trailer. By the time he was done he was in more debt than he liked but it was what he needed to do. The first year he drove all the hours that he could so he could pay off as much as possible as fast as possible.

Now the tractor and trailer were his and he had paid off half the debt on the farm. He could have kept on pulling the extra loads but he needed to be home on the weekends. He missed working around the farm more than he let anyone know. His brother Dan did a good job but it was not just Dan's farm he needed to be there too. He would have gone back to the job he had before Linda left him but he liked driving his rig. It was best to do it now one day he might have to be home more for one reason or another.

After finishing the lawn he put the lawn tractor back in the shed and then went into the house. He left his boots by the door and then started for his room. As he walked past the kitchen he caught the smell of something good.

"Emily, you are cooking."

"Yes, I thought that since you were being so nice to me today the least I could do was cook you a meal."

"Do I have time for a shower?"

"Just as long as you don't stay in there too long you should have time."

"I won't be that long I promise you."

Emily laughed as she heard him trip on his way up the stairs to his room. He ran back down the stairs with his clean clothes slamming the bathroom door. She laughed again knowing he had not intended to slam the door. Searching the kitchen she found the plates as well as silverware and glasses. Everything was surprisingly well organized when you took into account that no woman lived in the house. Emily wasn't sure but it seemed most likely that his Mom cleaned the house for him. The place was just too clean to be the work of a man.

When Luke came out of the bathroom all cleaned up he was dressed in his good clothes. Good clothes for a man usually meant jeans and a shirt with a collar. He was just in time the food was just going on the table. He got a soda and then took his seat at the table. The food looked as good as it smelled all that he had to worry about was the taste.

Emily took her seat at the table. "You look worried."

"No, I was just thinking that everything seems so good I hope the food tastes as good as it looks."

"You don't think I can cook?"

Luke smiled. "Just thinking that it all looks so good, I want it to taste as good as it looks."

"Well, you are never going to know if you don't try it. I am sure you will be disappointed if you let it get cold."

Luke nodded his head and then tried the food, it was very good. "You are a very good cook."

"Thank you, my Dad taught me. My Mom can't boil water she just never liked spending that much time in the kitchen."

"In our house it was different neither one of my parents could cook though Mom tries real hard. Dad has trouble making toast."

"What about you?"

"I don't cook I open up cans. If I can heat it I can eat it."

"You eat in restaurants or fast food places most of the time."

"That is me not the best way to live but at least I eat."

"Do you smoke?"

"No, I never really liked the look of people who smoked so I never had the urge to try it."

"I don't smoke but I know a lot of people that do. I did try it but I didn't like it not even a little bit. They used to tell me all the cool people smoked I guess I just never cared that much about being cool."

Luke smiled surprised at her willingness to talk about herself. "I was thinking we could go to the Circus Bar if you want or we can go someplace else. I think you should know that I have a lot of work to do here this weekend so I will not be drinking much."

Emily lied. "I have to be home by one in the morning or I will never get up in the morning."

"Then we agree we don't drink much and we leave before the bar closes."

Emily laughed. "We sound like we are planning a battle not a night out."

"Not a battle just talking about what we each want so we know what we are going to do and just how long we have to do it."

"It still sounds like a battle plan to me."

"Then we should let the war begin I guess."

Emily shook her head. "You want to leave right now?"

"Not just yet this is too good to feed to Jack."

Emily laughed. "I am really glad you like it."

Luke smiled realizing that for the first time in a long time he was having fun. He had gone on dates with girls he didn't know which had been okay but nothing had been fun. It seemed that most of the time it was simply something to do on a Friday night. He was with someone he didn't know or care about. Just as he started to get to know a little about the person he was with the date was over. The truth was he had given up on finding a woman he could trust.

Once they were done eating they climbed in the pickup with Jack and then headed for town. They didn't talk much they seemed content to sit thinking about what they were about to do. Luke was not worried about what Emily had on her mind he was thinking about the hay he was going to have to mow after he took care of the animals in the morning.

Emily had plans to meet her Mom in the morning for breakfast. They needed to talk about everything that had gone on that week. She was wondering what she would be telling her Mom about this night. She thought she might be able to say it was a nice quiet evening with a friend. Her Mom would smile and nod her head but she wouldn't say a word. Her Dad would want to know everything about her friend.

When they got to the bar all three of them went in Jack went to a spot in the far corner that he liked. Emily was with him she sat at the corner table waiting for Luke to get the beer and bring it to the table. She sat there watching Luke. She was still trying to figure out just what the two of them were doing together. He was never going to be around much because of his job. She was not going to run off with the first man who was nice to her.

Jim had found himself someone new, another tramp he could play with. As always it wouldn't last it never did. He would come crawling back begging her for one more chance. Not this time this time she would not take him back.

"Emily, what are you doing here with my son?"

Emily looked up at Roger Richardson he looked younger than his years and he had a warm friendly smile that she liked. "I am waiting for him to bring me a beer."

Roger sat down at the table with her. "You know he got married when he was nineteen. I am afraid it didn't go the way he had hoped it would. I have to tell you that I never really liked her much she never seemed real to me."

Luke walked back to the table with two beers. "Dad, how are you doing?"

"I have been better. How are things with you?"

"I am paying the bills."

"Did you go by the house to see your mother?"

"Yeah, I even mowed your lawn."

"Thank you."

"You are welcome. Would you like another beer?"

Roger looked at his oldest son. "No thank you. I have cancer."

"Does that mean you are going to stop drinking?"

"No, I am just going to stop for tonight I think."

"Are you going to cut hay tomorrow?"

"That is the plan."

Roger nodded his head. "Your mom and I might swing by for lunch."

"That would be nice though I am not sure what we will have."

"I am sure your mom will bring something."

"That might be a good idea."

"I always have good ideas."

Luke looked at his Dad but couldn't say a word. He looked at Emily. "Emily, Linda says those two boys at the pool table should finish up in about an hour. If you want to try a game or two I will claim the table."

Emily just sat there she couldn't say a word she just nodded her head. He couldn't have heard what his father had said. Luke didn't react he just seem to go on as though his father had just told him about the weather. How could anyone do that? Why would anyone tell their son something like that in a bar full of strangers?

Roger looked at his son. "Luke, what was your Mom doing when you were at the house?"

"She was having fun showing Emily some of those old pictures of us all."

Luke sat at the table not looking at his father. Roger got a big smile on his face. "Did I tell you two that I used to work with George before he bought this place?"

Luke still didn't look at his father. "Dad, I have heard this story before."

"Emily hasn't heard it I bet."

"I haven't heard it from you. I would love to hear it if you don't mind."

Roger smiled at Emily. "I would love to tell you all about it but I have to get home my wife already thinks I got lost."

"Dad, Mom knows right where you are."

"She calls here every time I walk in the door she knows where I am at all times."

Luke shook his head. "Dad, you call her when you get back to town then you come here. You have a couple of beers and she calls you when the food is just about ready to go on the table. It is all so you have a good excuse to leave here."

"You know about that."

"Dad, I lived in the house for eighteen years it wasn't hard to figure out."

"Speaking of your Mom I think I should get home before she sends your sister after me. It was nice talking with you Emily, don't keep my boy out too late he gets cranky if he doesn't get to bed on time."

Roger left the bar waving to everyone as he went out the door. Emily looked at Luke. "Why don't we get out of here?"

Luke shook his head. "No, let's just sit here and have a beer or two."

"Luke, wouldn't you rather be with your Mom and Dad?"

"No, I would rather be sitting here talking to you."

Emily was starting to catch on. "Are you going to tell me the story?"

Linda Fields set two beers down on the table. "What story are you telling?"

"Dad was going to tell her about how he and George used to work together. He would then have to tell her how you bought this place. You know he didn't have the time he had to go home Mom is waiting for him."

Linda smiled a smile that had a touch of sadness to it. She had tears in her eyes. "Your parents are very good people, the best I have ever known. These two beers are on the house."

Emily watched the woman walk back to the bar. A lot was going on here Luke was upset as he should be but he wasn't talking. Linda was very upset as well. It was clear that she knew about Luke's father too. Emily did the only thing she could do she played dumb. "What was that all about?"

Luke went right along with her. "Right after they bought the bar George fell asleep behind the wheel of his truck and then went off the road. People said he should have died but my Dad wasn't far behind him he radioed for help and then got George away from the truck before it exploded. Between the fire and the explosion, there wasn't enough left of that rig so you could say for sure that it had been a rig."

"I thought he was always unable to walk."

"George can walk from that chair to his bed but they say the pain would be too much for most other men to deal with."

"I was told he never left the chair except when his wife put him to bed at night."

"There are a lot of stories about them but they are the only ones who know what the real truth is. I do know that my Dad was here every night after the truck wreck and my Mom was here during the day while we were in school. Between them, they had this place up and running before George got out of the hospital. They had an elevator put in while they turned the upper floor into a home for the family."

Emily looked at Luke she could tell there was a lot more to the story than he was going to tell her. It was clear he had something else on his mind. "I take it that is all the story that you are going to tell me tonight. I am not going to get the whole story tonight?"

There was an angry edge to Luke's voice now. "We are here to have fun not tell stories everyone in town seems to know more about than the people who lived through it all. You can't tell the whole story if the story isn't over quite yet."

"Not all of us listen to the bull that gets tossed around this town all the time. My parents don't talk about any of it at all. They act as if it had nothing to do with them."

Luke nodded his head but there was anger in his eyes which said more than the half-smile on his face. "Not as many as you might think. I am not surprised to hear your parents don't talk about it."

"I know a lot of the story I know George was working for my Dad when the accident happened. I know a lot of lives were changed that night. I know it is the reason my Dad is the way he is today."

"We should play some pool before we leave."

Emily was okay with not talking after all she had secrets of her own. That was one of the things about a small town everyone knew everything that happened over the years they just didn't remember it the same way. Each story had several different endings it all depended on who you were talking to.

When the pool table opened up they took it over not that either one of them would ever make a living at it. They might not have been the best but they were having a good time as they talked, joked, and teased one another. They didn't notice the passage of time or the people who came and went from the bar. It was the most fun either of them could remember having in a long time.

All good things have to come to an end eventually. Emily stood up after missing a shot she was smiling until she saw Jim and the redhead sitting at a table not far away. She wanted to ignore him she was having fun but he looked at her and smiled as he put his arm around the tramp he was sitting with.

Emily could let a lot of things go but that stupid look on his face as he start to make his move was one she had seen too many times before. How could she have been so stupid as to trust a pig like that? Her temper may be on the rise but she could control it she was better than some people who had no self-control!

Jim stood up he looked over at Emily then his smile got bigger. As he bent over to kiss the redhead something snapped inside Emily. She was calm on the outside a smile on her face as she walked toward Jim. Emily tapped Jim on the shoulder, as he turned to look at her she broke the pool stick over his head. The redhead screamed as Jim yelled then raised his fist to hit Emily.

There were a lot of things Luke tried to stay out of but tonight he had himself in a mood. He might have let Jim slap Emily after all she hit him first with a cue stick. Tonight he had a lot on his mind and he wanted to hit somebody, he needed to hit somebody. He couldn't hit Emily so Jim was his target.

Emily didn't move she didn't care if he hit her all she cared about was the fact that he now knew she wasn't going to take his crap anymore. Someone grabbed her arm and sent her toward to pool table on the run as she tried to stay on her feet. There was a loud crash then Emily was against the pool table looking toward the bar where Linda Fields stood shotgun in hand.

Jack brushed against Emily's leg his hair on end a low growl sounding as he looked across the room. Emily looked in the same direction Jack was, Luke was standing between her and Jim. Luke never said a word he just started hitting Jim as hard and as fast as he could. There was a loud crash as Jim hit the floor.

There was anger as well as surprise in Jim's eyes as he lay there on the floor looking up at Luke. Everyone in town knew Dan Richardson would rather fight than talk. Luke wasn't a fighter he was the one that would talk to you before he hit you. Jim was not ready to accept the fact that he was on the floor at his feet.

Emily was surprised when she saw Jim his face was starting to swell below his right eye and there was blood on his face as well. As he started to get up off the floor he looked up with anger in his eyes. Emily could see that the fight was not over yet.

Jim was up then he was down again. Luke stood over him with a look in his eyes that no one had seen in a long time. Jim might have gotten up again if he had not been looking toward the bar. He had a feeling he was better off on the floor for several reasons.

Emily heard Linda's calm voice from behind the bar. "If you boys are smart you will leave your trouble right where it is because you make another move and I will not take sides I'll shoot you both."

Luke lowered his hands and then backed away from Jim. "No more trouble Linda, Emily and I are done playing pool so we are going to leave now. Jack is tired anyway."

"Emily, those sticks cost money and I promise you are going to get a bill for the one you broke."

"I will pay it."

Linda never looked at her but her voice was cold when she spoke to her. "Your damn right you will."

Luke took Emily's hand and then took her out the back door Jack with them watching their backs. The three of them got in his truck and headed anywhere but where they were. Luke didn't say a word but he still wanted to hit something harder than he managed to hit Jim.

Linda Fields lowered the shotgun and then set it back under the bar. "You still want to fight?"

Jim shook his head. "No, I think I have had enough."

"Follow me to the kitchen and I will get you some ice for that eye. Send your date home first she isn't old enough to be here."

Chapter 9

Dan took Rhea to the best restaurant in town which was at the golf course. Though he didn't play golf he had done some work for them which got him the right to eat there as a member. The place was a large room with paintings on the walls. Most of the paintings were outdoor scenes painted by the best local artists. The tables were covered with white tablecloths and had candles in the center.

They got a table for two in a corner of the room by the window looking out on the golf course. They ordered a drink and then sat looking at the menu. Dan was wishing he had picked a less expensive place to go. As he sat looking at Rhea he was sure they were in the right place.

Rhea smiled at Dan she had enjoyed their first date. They had gotten something to eat at the truck stop and then go to the movies. She had enjoyed it and been home early which had made her father happy. They had talked and laughed but he never talked about anything. It had all been small talk as if he didn't know what to say.

"Dan, do you bring all your dates here?"

"No, and after I wash dishes here to pay for our meal I will not be coming back here again."

"I will help you wash dishes."

Dan smiled. "I was kidding about that."

"So was I."

"I do have more than enough money to pay for the food. I knew what I was getting into when I brought you here."

Rhea put her menu down. "Why did you bring me here?"

Dan put his menu down. "I looked at you and couldn't think of any other place you would fit into."

"Because of the way I am dressed?"

"Because of the way you look in those clothes."

"Thank you."

"I think I should be thanking you. All the guys in here wish they were me right now."

Rhea sipped her drink. "I like the way you think though I think you are going a little far. I don't think every man here is looking at me."

"You are right of course the gay ones are looking at each other."

"They might be looking at you."

Dan shook his head. "I think I need another drink."

"I have only been here once before tonight. A friend of mine had her wedding here."

Dan nodded. "I have never eaten here before though I have been told the food is worth the money."

"When I was here for the wedding the food was very good."

"I am surprised you haven't been here more often."

Rhea smiled. "I do not go out much."

Dan sat back in his seat as the waitress took their food order. "I would think you would get asked out a lot."

"I have been but most of my dates expect me to be someone different."

"I was not sure what to expect. You are the pastor's daughter, a Sabbath school teacher as well as a waitress at the truck stop."

"Yes, I am my parent's daughter. My mother was a waitress and she worked in a factory for a time. My father in his younger years was a truck driver."

"Sounds like my parent's right up to the pastor part."

Rhea smiled. "We have more in common than you thought."

Dan nodded his head. "I guess I could have found a cheaper place for us to eat then."

"No, this is the perfect place for our first date."

"This is our second date."

"No, the other time we were together was our predate meeting to see if we should have a date."

"That was the first time I ever auditioned for a date."

"I see it as more of an interview."

Shaking his head Dan smiled. "Whatever it was it was a first for me."

Rhea smiled but didn't say a word. She had him right where she wanted him. He was going to put his best foot forward or he would take her home if he was less of a man than she thought he was.

Dan smiled. "The food is very good here."

"Yes, they have a very good chef here."

The rest of their time at the country club went better than Dan had expected it to be. He was happy as he thought of asking Rhea for another date. She had him interested, he wanted to know more about who she was. She had him thinking about just who he was with, she was more than the Pastor's daughter. There was a light in her eyes a joy that he wanted to know more about. He had to know just who she was.

When they left the club Dan was happier than he could remember being for a very long time. He couldn't wait to tell his mother all about Rhea. There was just something about her that brought a smile to his face. It was crazy even though it felt so good. Nothing the world could do to him could take away how he felt now.

As they drove over to his parent's house to talk to his Dad Dan wasn't worried about a thing. The night was going so much better than he had ever expected it to be. Rhea was just not who he had thought she should be. For a pastor's daughter, she seemed almost a little too calm.

When they got to the house they just walked in as he always did. His parents were sitting in the kitchen having coffee. His mother gave them each a cup of coffee then they all sat around the table looking at one another.

Roger sipped his coffee and then looked at his son. "I have cancer."

Dan didn't know what to say he just sat there trying to think of something to say. "I guess I should say something but I can't think of anything to say."

"There is nothing to say it is what it is, now we just go on and do the best we can."

"Dad, I wish I could think of a way to do that."

Roger smiled. "Just do whatever it was you were going to do. I think I will watch the news then I will go to bed."

Dan looked at his mother; she had a smile on her face and tears in her eyes. "Mom, what are you going to do?"

"Whatever your Dad wants me to."

Dan stood up. "I think I should get Rhea home it is getting late."

His mother looked at him. "It will be alright."

Dan smiled as he lied to his mother. "I know."

Without another word, Dan took Rhea by the hand and then walked out of the house. They got in the car and then drove off toward no place in particular. The only thing he could think to do was keep on driving.

Rachael stood watching her son and his date as they left. She had expected him to react differently. He had acted more like his older brother than himself. She thought he would ask more questions. Now as she stood there she was worried about what he would do next.

Dan drove past Rhea's house twice then out of town for ten miles before he turned around and headed back toward town. Dan was not sure what he should do or if he should do anything at all. How did anyone deal with news like that? Was there anything that you could do or say?

Rhea never said a word she just sat quietly looking at Dan. It was hard to say what she would do if her father had told her he had cancer. They were close so she was sure she would not be as confused and hurt as Dan seemed to be. The problem was she just couldn't be sure of that. How could anyone deal with the news?

Things were awful quiet for a Friday night when Rhea Conner and Dan Richardson walked into the Circus Bar just after midnight. Dan still had that stop at his parent's house on his mind. After he had taken Rhea out to eat he should have taken her to a movie or home. She should not have been there with him. They had planned on going to the late show at the movies before they stopped at his parent's house.

After talking with his Dad Dan only had one place he wanted to go. He needed a drink or maybe more than one.

Dan knew getting drunk was not going to help. He knew that it would be best if he took Rhea home. If she was going to get to know him she might as well see all sides of him. What was she going to do to walk away from him? This would be the best time for her to do it. This was a family problem there was no reason she should go through it with them.

Jim Campbell was at the bar with two of his friends. George was sitting in his wheelchair at his table watching the bar. It was clear something was different. Laurie Fields was working the bar while her mother Linda was standing beside her husband. It had been a hard night for them and it wasn't going to be getting any better.

Rhea sat down at a table near the pool table while Dan went up to the bar to get a couple of beers. Rhea had only been in the bar a couple of times. She usually didn't go to a place that didn't have a dance floor. It wasn't that she wanted to go out dancing that much. It was just that most of the boys that took her out thought she wanted to go dancing. They never took her to any place they would take most of their other dates to.

Dan sat down at the table after he gave Rhea her glass of beer. "Have you been in here before?"

"I have been here once or twice."

Dan looked at her trying to figure her out. "I guess this is not a place you would like to come to if you had a choice."

"I don't drink much so I don't spend much time in bars."

"Laurie told me my brother was in here earlier with Emily Rice."

"I didn't know they were going out I thought she was going to marry Jim Campbell."

"From what Laurie says the wedding is off."

"I am glad she finally dumped that jerk."

"Would you like another beer?"

"I haven't had any of this one yet."

"I need another one I'll get two just in case you change your mind."

Dan went off to get a couple more beers leaving half a glass of beer on the table. He was upset which meant he was not thinking clearly. His mind was still trying to deal with what his father had told him.

Rhea looked around the room at the other people in the bar. She felt as though she was peeking behind a curtain. She knew most of the people she saw from one place or another. There were a few that she had seen at church more than once. There were a lot of truck drivers there that she knew from the truck stop where she worked as well.

As she looked at them it was clear most seemed to be drinking more than they should be. There were married men with women that were not their wives as well as married women who were not with their husbands. There were married couples there as well as single people just having a night out.

Sitting there she couldn't help but think about what Dan's father had told him. She was wondering how Dan could just seem to go on after what his father had told him. She knew he was upset though he didn't seem to show it as much as she had thought he would.

Rhea knew if her father had told her something like that she would never have left the house. Men were different they did their best to hide their true feelings most of the time. At least some of them did while others were very emotional. Dan was one of the quiet ones.

"You are Rhea Conner aren't you?" Jim asked leaning over her.

Rhea didn't like this boy he smelled bad and looked even worse. "I am but I can't say that I know you."

"Sure you do, my name is Jim I saw the boy you came in with he is okay for a boy but I am better. What you need is a man like me."

"I wouldn't say anymore if I were you I already have a date and I am not looking for another."

Jim reached out and took Rhea's hand as she stood up which was when he heard a calm voice. "Let her go and we can have a drink."

Jim wasn't in the mood he let go of Rhea then turned and swung at Dan. Dan moved a little to the side causing Jim to miss which made him almost fall on the floor. Dan waited for Jim to get his balance then he hit him in the jaw just as hard as he could. Dan was still holding two glasses of beer one of which he hit Jim with. Jim fell backward and tripped over his own feet going down on the floor. His face was bleeding again and there was blood, glass, and beer on him as well as on the floor around him.

It took a minute for Jim to get started back to his feet as he did he grabbed Rhea's leg. They were beside the pool table and there was a stick on the table. Jim looked up just in time to catch the back end of the stick in the face. Jim was back on the floor Rhea raised the stick again. She wasn't going to hit him again unless he moved.

Dan set the glass of beer down on the table where they had been sitting. He had drunk half of it as he waited for Jim to get up off the floor. Once Jim was back on his feet Dan hit him several times in the stomach as well as in the face. This time when Jim went down he didn't move he just lay there on the floor looking up at Rhea and Dan.

Laurie Fields was still behind the bar she had the shotgun aimed at Jim. "You two best get out of here the cops are already on the way over to get the trash on the floor. Leave the cue stick on the pool table we already lost one tonight."

Rhea and Dan went out the back door to the car. Rhea looked at Dan. "Let's go over to the truck stop so I can take care of your hand. Give me the keys I think I better drive."

Dan looked at his hand then gave Rhea the keys. "That doesn't look that bad but it hurts."

"You are crazy."

Dan shrugged his shoulders. "People keep saying that."

"Then there must be some truth to it. You might want to get some help."

"I thought you were helping me?"

"Oh shut up."

Dan stood by the car looking across the parking lot. "My sister's car is here. I should go in there and look for her."

Rhea shook her head. "She isn't in there I heard someone say she got drunk and left with a friend."

"I guess Dad talked to her too."

"Did you think he wouldn't she still lives with your parents?"

"I never really thought about it. I can't think clearly when I am in pain."

Rhea looked at him she didn't know if she should hug him or hit him. Whatever she did he would probably tell her it hurt him. She didn't want to hug him she was thinking hitting him would be best though she wasn't sure. In the end, she just shook her head. "Nothing ever really changes."

Dan looked at her he had no idea what she was talking about. "What is that supposed to mean?"

"Never mind you are in no condition to understand"

"Okay."

Without another word, they got in the car and Rhea drove off toward the truck stop. She had never expected anything like what had happened when she agreed to a second date with Dan. There was a reason for everything that happened she had been told. Right now Dan needed her help.

Back in the bar, Jim was starting to move until he heard Laurie's voice. "Campbell, if you move I promise you they will be able to pick up your head with a mop and sponge."

Jim seemed to turn whiter than he was though Laurie was sure that wasn't possible. She was smiling on the inside because she knew the shotgun wasn't loaded. Jim was afraid of an empty gun which he should be because she would have fun beating him with it.

Chapter 10

Emily and Luke didn't talk to one another when they got in the pickup with Jack on the seat between them. Even Jack seemed concerned as he looked from one to the other of them. Emily had not expected Luke to become involved in her battle with Jim whom she had never intended to hit. It had never occurred to her that Luke would jump in and punch Jim the way that he had. As she looked out the side window she realized Luke was still in the mood to hit someone. After his talk with his father, Jim should be thankful Luke had not killed him.

Luke had not said a word since he had led her out of the bar to the pickup. He had never expected her to hit Jim with a stick breaking it over his head. She had never seemed like the type of girl who would do something like that. She was a giving person as well as a very understanding person. He couldn't believe she had let someone like Jim Campbell make her that mad. It was clear to Luke that Jim wasn't worth it. Why she had never noticed who Jim was before the redhead came along.

He had stepped in but it wasn't to defend her. To be honest he was just in the mood to hit someone, anyone. He knew it couldn't change anything it hadn't even made him feel better. He was angry because what had happened to his father wasn't fair.

Luke glanced at Emily and then back at the road. "Do you want to go home?"

Emily thought about it for a minute. "No, I think I need to calm down a little more before I go home."

"We can go out to the truck stop for coffee I know that usually calms me down when I am upset."

"Is it true that truckers drink coffee by the gallon?"

"The old-time trucker maybe but now we drink it by the cup full most of the time. I drink a cup or two mostly in the morning."

"So what do you drink when you are on the road?"

"Soda, ice tea, and bottled water with coffee in the morning if I am in a truck stop."

Emily smiled as they pulled into the truck stop. "That doesn't sound like any trucker I know."

"I am not trying to be like everyone else."

"I have noticed that you mow your parent's lawn even though you have a place of your own. People don't usually do that these days."

"It is not that big a thing we are a family we look out for one another."

"So I have noticed. Does that mean that we are family now that you looked after me while trying to knock Jim's head off?"

"I don't like him."

"I noticed that."

They all got out of the truck and went inside where they sat in a booth. Emily was on one side of the table Jack and Luke were on the other. Luke ordered two sodas and a bowl of water. "Emily, you want to tell me what in the world you ever saw in that jerk?"

"The same thing you saw in Linda I guess."

"You got anything else you want to talk about?"

"We can talk about truck drivers if you want."

Luke nodded. "Emily, you must know that all truckers are not the same. We do what we do for our reasons we are no different than anyone else."

"I think you are different but not always in a bad way. I worry about the drivers who are in it for the money I think they would drive too fast and take too many chances."

Luke smiled at the waitress who brought their order. "You are right there are some who are just in it for the money but everyone is working to make money no matter what job they have. Some drivers like the job while others hate it, that is just the way it is."

"Why do you drive?"

"I like it because for me there is a sense of freedom about it even though you work for someone you spend most of your time alone. The boss tells you where to take the load as well as when it has to be there but once you leave the yard you are on your own."

"Are you?"

Luke laughed as he thought about it. "Maybe not the way my Dad and my Grandfather were. I have a CB and a radio in my truck. I can shut all of that down at times if I am in a quiet mood. I have been known to shut everything down for an entire week which can be nice. Of course, Jack makes a lot of noise which can be hard to ignore at times."

"I sit in an office five days a week where everyone seems to know my job better than I do. That is what you would think if you heard them day after day telling me where I went wrong or just how they want it done. It is enough to drive me crazy."

"Sounds to me like you need to find a different job."

Emily looked at him thinking about what he had said it wasn't like she hadn't thought about it. "I have thought about it but my parents own the company, as you know. It wouldn't be right to just walk out on them they count on me."

"Yes, I suppose they do but maybe it is time to take a vacation so that when you get back you can keep doing your job."

"You know Jim works there too I would rather not see him for a while."

"Go home pack a bag then just take off and don't tell anyone where you are going. Take a week or more and have some fun in the sun by the ocean or by a pool. It doesn't matter as long as you take the time and just enjoy yourself."

"That sounds like a great idea I think I will do it but I will have to go home first and get some clothes."

"You don't have to leave tonight you can leave in the morning after a good night's sleep."

Emily shook her head. "No, I have to leave tonight if I am going to go at all. I know if I wait until the morning my parents will talk me out of it just like the last time."

Luke sat back in his seat looking across the table at her. She wasn't talking about a vacation anymore she was talking about Jim Campbell. Things were a little clearer now though only a little. Thinking about it he still couldn't see her with Jim. After what he had done to her she shouldn't be afraid they would still be getting married. He couldn't see them getting back together after what she had done to him. If they did get back together there was something else going on.

"Okay, I will help you get out of town."

"Thanks, I know I am asking a lot but I have to go tonight."

Luke paid for the sodas on the way out to the pickup then Jack and he drove Emily to her house. She went into her bedroom where she packed a bag then went back out to the truck. She put her bag in the back of the truck before she got back in closing the door quietly.

"Where do you want to go to the bus station? Or would you rather go to the train station?"

"I would rather go with you if you don't mind."

"I am going back to the farm and get a good night's sleep I have a lot to do this weekend."

Emily looked straight ahead she didn't cry she just looked out the windshield at the road ahead. "You might as well just leave me here then."

"Emily, I don't understand?"

"I know but the truth is that I don't get to take a week off unless I go someplace with Jim. If I am going to go I want to be someplace where they will not think to look for me. I don't want to have to worry about waking up and finding Jim there. I don't know why they like him so much I just know that they do.

"They will make me feel guilty about leaving even though I know I am right. My parents only want the best for me and they think that is Jim. I don't care what they think they see in him. The truth is they don't know him."

Luke shook his head. "I get the feeling I am going to have to do something I had never planned on doing."

"You are going to take me with you?"

"Yes, but that isn't what I was talking about. If you are going with me we are going to need a thermos to hold our morning coffee in."

Luke drove home where he packed some clean clothes into his travel bag. He checked on the animals then they all got back in the pickup and drove to the yard. Parking the pickup Luke put the bag in his rig and then walked around the truck giving everything a quick look.

Climbing up into the cab he did his usual check and then started the old girl up. Turning on the lights he climbed back out then walked around the truck again checking all the lights the tires and everything else even if he knew it was okay he checked it anyway.

Once he was satisfied that everything was as it should be he told Emily and Jack to climb up into the cab it was time to go. He locked up his pickup and then climbed up in the cab with them. "We will stop at the truck stop for a few things then we will be on our way."

Emily had set her bag behind her seat. "Luke, are you sure you want to do this?"

Luke smiled. "Hell no, but this might be for the best for both of us."

They were in and out of the truck stop in no time at all Luke knew just what he wanted as well as right where everything could be found. The thermos needed coffee he let Emily take care of that while he got everything else.

They both finished at the same time and then went back out to the rig where they stored everything before heading out. He couldn't stay home he needed time to think time to try to get used to the idea. That was what he told himself even though he knew it was not true. He was never going to get used to the fact that his Dad was dying.

Chapter 11

Dan looked over at Rhea she was not the girl he had thought she was when he first caught sight of her. There was a lot more to her than most people would think. When they saw her walking down the street her clothes determined who they saw. All dressed up she looked good there was no doubt about that. She looked like she was used to all the best things life had to offer. Working the truck stop she looked good but approachable.

It was true that even dressed in her waitress outfit you knew she was meant for other things. You could tell she was not a soft helpless kind of girl though she might appear to be. There was more to her than just a princess. It was clear she could be the princess as long as you didn't make her mad. She would stand up for herself when the situation called for it.

Rhea knew the stories about Dan he was not the kind of guy to stay with any one girl for more than a date or two. They said to give him what all guys want and you will never see him again. He didn't have the time or the need for someone who wanted anything more from him. He wanted nothing more than a little fun for a night or two. He had very few friends; he was busy with his job and his brother's farm. If a girl was looking for more than a night or two on the town; it would be best if she looked at someone else.

Rhea had not expected him to be anything more than his reputation. As much as people liked to talk they usually lost the truth of the story as they passed it around. At first, she thought they might have got it right this time but then things changed. He was not the man they said he was there was more to him than that. He was not his father or his brother he was his person. Rhea was curious about this man no one else seemed to know.

Her father said she should never judge a book by its cover. He also said that people were not books. He could be a real pain in the neck at times while he was driving her crazy with his father's talk. It was a mix of father wisdom, pastor wisdom, and worried father talk. It all made her angry, happy as well as a bit confused. He wanted the best for her, he wanted her happy and he wanted to keep her safe. They both knew life didn't always let you have all of that.

Dan looked at her. "You should get home I know you have to work tomorrow."

"I don't have to work tomorrow. I don't have to work today I have the weekends off. It is almost one in the morning I was going to be home before this.

"Let's go over to the truck stop we can get your hand taken care of there. After that we can get a cup of coffee then I will get you home. Once you are home I will drive home and get some sleep. I need to go to church with my parents I have a class to teach."

Dan laughed as he thought about what she had told him. "You do remember that this is my car don't you?"

"I remember but you are in no shape to drive it."

"Oh, I guess you might be right about that. You are not the person that I first thought you were."

"I can say the same about you."

They were sitting outside the truck stop as a rig was pulling out of the parking lot headed south. "I am going to run inside and get what I need to fix up your hand though I think it would be best if we went to the hospital and let someone there look at it."

"I will have my sister look at it in the morning she is a nurse."

Rhea didn't argue though she doubted he would let Emma see his hand. She didn't say anything she just went inside and got what she needed. It didn't take long she knew right where everything was. When she went back to the car she set everything on the seat and then gently began to care for Dan's hand.

Dan didn't argue he just went along with what Rhea said. He didn't want to think about anything though that was proving impossible. It had been a rough night even though he was with Rhea he couldn't forget what his father had told them. He couldn't forget what he had done to Jim because of it. He didn't want coffee but the beer wasn't going to change anything so coffee with Rhea was good.

He watched her face as she was working on bandaging his hand. She looked like an angel. Her blue eyes were so beautiful, her hands so soft as she worked with his hand. If he was not careful he would fall in love with her. He had to be careful because that was the last thing he needed right now. He couldn't let that happen his mother was going to need him.

Rhea worked carefully doing her best not to hurt Dan. As she worked she thought about what his father had said. She felt so sorry for Dan and his family. Looking at his father it was hard to believe it could happen to him. Even though she knew it could happen to anyone it was still hard to believe.

Roger Richardson was as strong as a rock with a heart that seemed to be able to care for an entire town. Her father told her he was a man at war with himself as he did his best to do what was right. Roger was a man who feared letting anyone see his true self. He was afraid he would appear weak. Better to appear cold and unfeeling than to let someone see him shed a tear.

Rhea never stayed out this late her parents were going to want to know what she had been doing all night. What were they going to think of her when she told them? What would they say about everything that had happened at the bar? What would they think of Dan because he had taken her there? She couldn't be sure but she had done what she had to and she hoped they would understand that.

Dan watched Rhea's face as she was caring for his hand. He wondered what she was thinking. The night had not turned out the way he had planned it. He felt bad because he felt she deserved better than what she had been put through. He thought he would be lucky if she spoke to him again. He had put her in a bad position when he took her to the bar. He had not been thinking. She was lucky she had not been hurt. He should have taken her home after talking with his Dad.

He had been selfish he had not wanted to be alone. Dan knew what he should have done but he had been hurt and angry. His father had ruined his night out with Rhea. Why didn't he wait until they were alone to tell him? There had been no need to rush he could have waited to tell him that he was dying.

Rhea worked on Dan's hand. It didn't take long though she had seemed to have too much time to think. The night was never supposed to turn out this way. It was the first time in a very long time that she had felt this good about someone she dated.

When she was done she smiled at him. "Let's go in and get a cup of coffee before those truckers drink it all."

Dan smiled. "How many cups of coffee is this fancy nursing job going to cost me?"

"We can settle that over the first cup."

"I am sorry for the way the night turned out."

"Don't be it was a night I will never forget."

"I am sure of that."

"I am glad I was with you tonight."

They went to the truck stop and sat at a table for about an hour drinking coffee. They talked about a lot of things except what had happened that night. Rhea asked a lot of questions about the farm which Dan thought a bit odd. He didn't mind talking about the farm after all it was better than talking about his Dad or the fight at the bar.

When it was time Rhea drove Dan home and then went home to try and get some sleep. She wasn't sure about much by the time she was trying to sleep. She was tired and she didn't think she would last through church without the sleep she was not getting.

Rhea sat up on the edge of her bed thoughts of Dan and his family filled her mind. She prayed for them all then lay back down thinking about Dan. This was not the time to start dating him too much could go wrong. It would be best to slow things down. What would Dan think of her if she walked away from him? Would he understand? Would she be able to do it?

When her alarm went off she got ready for church and then went down to the kitchen where her mother was fixing breakfast. "Good morning Mom."

Her mother handed her a cup of coffee. "You got in late last night. I noticed the car in the yard do you know who it belongs to?"

"It belongs to Dan Richardson he let me drive it home last night."

"Why did he do that?"

"He hurt his hand and couldn't drive."

"It was a good thing you were with him."

Rhea felt uncomfortable. "I guess it was."

"Did you have a good time?"

"I did though I didn't think I would at first."

"Are you going to see him again?"

"I am sure I will I have to bring his car back to him."

Her mom smiled at her. "I think that would be a good idea I am sure he will need it."

"Mom, his dad has cancer."

"I thought something was going on I saw Roger talking to your Dad yesterday."

Chapter 12

Emma woke up to a pounding headache that would not let her open her eyes. She wanted aspirin and coffee just as soon as she could force her eyes open. One of the other things that worried her was moving. Would she be able to move once her eyes were open? If she opened her eyes and if she could move would she find herself in a place she knew?

Emma remembered a lot of things about the night before but the end of the night was more than fuzzy, it was so dark she couldn't see it. She remembered going to talk to Laurie but after that, all she remembered was that the drinks were really good. She was hoping she hadn't done anything really stupid.

It was the first time that she had drank that much in a long time. It was the first time she could not remember how she got home. It was the first time she didn't know if she was home. It was the first time she found out her father was dying.

Carefully she opened her eyes to find that she was right, the light hurt her eyes. It took time but she realized that she was in her room. Though she was relieved there was still the question of how she had gotten there. The good news was she knew where the aspirin was. She was going to have to get to the bathroom.

Very carefully she sat up on the edge of her bed. This was one of the hardest things she had ever done. That was only until she walked to the bathroom. Looking into the mirror she didn't like what she saw mostly because she wasn't sure who was looking back at her. A couple of aspirin, as well as a shower, would be a start.

When that was done she stood back at the mirror. She needed more so she got dressed and then left her room for the kitchen. Emma walked slowly hoping she would not fall down the stairs. When she was down the stairs she was glad she hadn't fallen.

There was a pot of coffee sitting on the counter she got a cup, filled it with the hot black liquid then took a sip. When she opened her eyes she saw her Dad sitting at the table. She hadn't even seen him when she sat down at the table.

He looked at her over the rim of his glasses. "A rough night I take it?"

"Not that I remember."

"You didn't go to work last night."

"I was with a friend and lost track of time."

"I have done that a couple of times over the years myself."

"I am not the boy's Dad, I live here."

"Yes, you are also a nurse so you know what is involved here."

"Dad, what do you want me to do?"

"I want you to be there for your Mom and I want you to stop counting my days and live them with me. I am not ready to die just yet."

"Dad, I am having a little trouble with that one I know what will happen."

"Emma, we all die that is the way things go there is no way we can live forever. It is all a matter of when and where."

"Dad, you are only fifty- three it isn't fair."

"If you think I am going to argue with you I am not. All I can do is fight this the best that I can. I want to do the most I can with the time I have left."

"Dad, I don't want to let you down but I can't promise I won't just start crying."

Rodger smiled at his daughter. "That makes two of us."

"Don't make me laugh my head hurts."

"You didn't go to work you went to the bar last night."

"I went to talk to Laurie and while we were talking we started drinking."

"Laurie worked the bar last night."

"She is a better girl than me it seems."

Roger smiled. "She didn't drink as much as you did is more likely."

"That makes sense she is always in control."

"I saw Luke at the bar last night I didn't see you or Dan there."

"I don't remember much of anything about last night. I started in the afternoon. I can't tell you how I got home."

"Steve brought you home. Your Mom put you to bed."

"Steve was here? I thought he was out of town until tomorrow?"

"He was he came back to get you home then he left again."

"I don't remember calling him."

"He said Laurie called him. He said you would never call him you are too proud. He said you should call him to let him know you are okay."

"I can't call him after what I did, mostly because I can't remember any of what I did or didn't do."

"Don't worry he knows you are not going to call him."

"Dad, he is my friend I didn't want him to see me like that."

"I am sure he has seen you drunk before."

"Not like I was this time."

"You think he might not be your friend anymore?"

"The thought crossed what little is left of my mind."

Rodger had poured himself another coffee. He sat back down at the table looking thoughtfully at his daughter. "I don't think you need to worry he is not that kind of guy."

Emma got another cup of coffee. She wanted to sit down but she was afraid she would not want to get back up again. "I suppose you are right."

"You still won't call him will you?"

"No."

"What are you going to do?"

"I have the day off I think I will go back to bed."

"Try a shower then you should have another cup of coffee while you are talking to Steve."

Emma smiled the best she could. "You are telling me I have to call him? What is this I already took a shower."

"Are you going to argue with your poor sick Dad?"

"No, I will call him but I am not going to take another shower."

"I wonder what else I can get you to do."

Emma didn't say a word she just took her coffee up to her room. There were tears in her eyes but she didn't make a sound until she was safely in her room. The shower was a good place to cry so she took a long shower before she went back down to the kitchen. Her parents were gone so she sat down at the table with a fresh cup of coffee.

The phone rang she didn't want to talk to anyone but it might be something important for her Dad. When she answered the phone she was glad to hear Steve's voice. "What do you want?"

"I wanted to find out how you were doing. Your Mom called me and said it would be best if I called you instead of waiting for you to call me."

"You call me once or twice a week."

"Yeah, your Mom said I was thinking about giving you time when you needed to talk."

"Were you?"

"No, I was going to call you."

"That is what I thought."

"You were a little drunk last night."

"I was a lot drunk last night and I am a lot hung over this morning. If I were you I would listen to me. It is best if you don't mess with me."

"You think I would give you a hard time after what we did last night?"

"We didn't do anything last night."

"Okay, I can go with that if you want."

Emma smiled. "You can be a real ass at times."

Stephen didn't know what she remembered but he was having fun. "That was one part of my body you were interested in last night."

"What does that mean?"

"Nothing but I had a hard time getting you to keep your clothes on last night."

"You are full of shit."

"Are you sure?"

Emma laughed. "I am now pal, I am now."

"Was it something I said?"

"No, I just remembered I have better taste in men."

"Ouch!"

They talked for over an hour about everything but her Dad. Steve knew she would talk when she was ready. He had known her long enough to know that about her. They had met at a meeting one day and just hit it off right away. They didn't date they just spent time together it was best that way. People were stupid they let themselves get involved with people they didn't know. The next thing you know they are married, they have kids and they don't even like each other. Emma called it the five-year marriage plan.

Emma went back up to her room her head still felt like someone was hitting her with a hammer. Thinking about her Dad wasn't helping her she needed to lay down in a dark room. The whole thing was more than she wanted to deal with. The quiet of her room was all that she wanted for the moment.

Chapter 13

The sky was going from black to light blue as Luke drove south thinking about everything that had happened. The fact that it was Saturday morning and he was headed south instead of being home caring for his animals was bad enough. There was also the fact that he had been in a fight the night before.

He had left in the truck with Jack the two of them going south out of town Emily with them. It had been after midnight he hadn't told anyone where he was going and he didn't want them to know. The whole thing was so unlike him. He had learned not to do this sort of thing after Linda had left him in the same way.

Emily and Jack were sleeping which was something he wanted to do. He had been up to long he was two days ahead of schedule which meant he couldn't deliver his load until Monday morning. He was going to have to find a truck stop. No, it would have to be a motel that they could stay in until Monday morning. A truck stop was fine for him and Jack but Emily needed a place to stay that didn't smell like diesel fuel.

It wasn't that he thought the rooms at the truck stop smelled like diesel fuel but he lived in his truck so he just might not notice the smell. Emily was not a truck driver she would notice the smell if it was there. He smiled as he thought about it after all he was worried about someone who started fights in bars.

Once the fight was over she ran away from home in a truck with a guy and his dog. When you thought about the whole thing like that it seemed kind of silly. She was running away from home so she wouldn't make her parents unhappy. She couldn't tell them she wouldn't marry a man who cheated on her. She could run away from home though. The more he thought about it the worse it sounded to him. He needed to get some sleep.

He managed to find a motel across from a truck stop with a couple of fast food places as well as a large number of stores all on the same side of the street. He had never had a woman in the truck before. His sister as well as his Mom loved to wander in the stores so this seemed like a good place to stop. He parked in the truck stop parking lot and then just sat there thinking about going into the truck stop for breakfast.

Luke looked back at Emily who was sound asleep on the bunk with Jack. It was something he thought he would never see. Jack never slept on the bunk with him. Old Jack must be getting lonely after all his time on the road.

Jack got down off the bunk as Emily sat up and smiled at Luke. "This bunk is a lot more comfortable than I expected it would be."

"Glad you like it."

Emily sat in the passenger's seat looking out at the parking lot. "What do we do now?"

"We go inside and get something to eat then you and Jack can spend some time together while I get some sleep."

"What would you do if I wasn't here?"

"I would get something to eat then Jack and I would get some sleep in the truck."

"Then I guess it is a good thing for Jack that I am here at least he will have someone to keep him company."

"We best get in there or I will just go to sleep without breakfast."

They got out of the truck locked it behind them then went inside. There was a good-sized crowd already there having their morning meal. Luke found them a booth at the back of the room it was the only one open.

The waitress walked over with a smile on her face. "Good morning Luke, we rarely see you and Jack in here on a Saturday. It is nice to see that the two of you aren't alone today."

"Dory, as always it is nice to see you too. I need a coffee and Jack needs a small bowl of water."

"What about you?" Dory asked looking at Emily.

"Coffee as well please."

"I like her she is nice. How did she ever end up with the two of you?"

"I like Jack."

Dory nodded. "He is the better of the two of them."

Dory left to get the coffee and Luke looked around. "Emily, you sure you wouldn't rather be on vacation at a nice fancy hotel with an ocean view?"

"Are you and Jack tired of me already?"

"No, it is just that this isn't my idea of a vacation this is my job."

"I needed to get away and I didn't want to go alone. Besides I like spending time with Jack."

"Yeah, he seems to have that effect on the ladies."

"You must know a lot of young ladies because of him."

"You are asking about others but you want to know about Dory. Her husband and her son like her a lot. As for me, I can tell you when she brings me my food it is hot."

Emily laughed. "I was going to tell you I should go back home today but I think I will stay with you a little longer."

"Good because I can't get rid of this load until Monday morning."

"You are kidding! What am I going to do all weekend?"

"There are quite a few stores here as well as a few places to eat. We will get you a room in the motel so that we will both have a bed at night."

"You think we are going to share a motel room?"

"No, I was thinking we might share the bed for a little bit before I went back to my bed in the truck."

"I don't think so."

"Which is why you get a motel room and I get the truck."

"You have a collar and a leash for Jack?"

"Yes, I have them in the truck. There are a few places we go where Jack has to get dressed up to get in."

"You are not right in the head."

Luke shrugged his shoulders. "Are any of us?"

"Not that I have noticed I guess."

"Then it oddly is all good."

Emily smiled. "Damn that almost makes sense."

"Scary ain't it."

They placed their order when the waitress brought them more coffee. Sitting there with their coffee things got quiet all at once. They seemed to realize what they had done as well as where they were. In effect, they had both run away from home after a fight in a bar. That didn't sound good nor did it feel good all of a sudden. What had they been thinking? Had they been thinking at all?

"Luke, I am sorry I talked you into leaving home I should have just taken the bus as you said."

"Emily, I could have said no and left you standing there at your house. I didn't have to sit and wait for you to come back with your clothes. Once you were out of the truck I could have run off and left you."

"Why didn't you?"

"I didn't think of it at the time."

"What about now?"

"We have come this far we can hang out together a little longer I guess."

"I am not going to be hanging out with you I am going to be with Jack. Do you think he will help me meet a nice guy?"

"He likes you he might help you if he doesn't think he already got you together with the best."

"Meaning you are the best there is?"

"It seems Jack thinks so."

"Of course, he does you feed him."

"Yeah, but I gave you his seat in the truck he might want to get rid of you so that he can get it back."

Emily laughed. "I never thought of that."

After they ate they went back to the truck where Emily put Jack's collar on him and then hooked him on the leash. Luke watched the two of them walk off then climbed into his bunk and went to sleep.

He might have been worried about bad dreams but the fact was he slept like a baby.

By noon time Emily and Jack were sick of the stores and all the walking. They needed time to relax and maybe try something different. After standing looking at their choices they went to the truck stop for lunch. Emily was getting tired even though she had slept well in the truck. For some reason, she felt she could use more sleep.

Everything she had done since Thursday afternoon was now going through her mind. Jim had left her for another girl again which should have been the last time. For some reason, her parents were on his side, not hers. Though it made no sense at all her parents liked him for some reason. They never seemed to notice that he was not the honest hard working young man that they wanted him to be.

Everyone in town seemed to know he was a creep, that was strike one. There had been several girls before they were engaged. He simply said that it was her fault because she failed to commit to their relationship. That had been another strike. She had made up her mind. She knew what she wanted, she wanted someone better. She hated him for that but they were engaged though she wasn't sure just how that had happened. That was strike one for her.

Once they were engaged she told herself he wouldn't cheat on her anymore. That was strike two for her. She had been wrong about that and she knew it when she said it. Once he had cheated on her she had known in her heart that he would do it again.

Once again her indecision he said had caused him to doubt her commitment to their plans. This time they would set the wedding date. He now had three strikes against him and it was her turn at bat. She had hit him with the cue stick just as hard as she could. It might not have solved anything but it was a home run in her book.

This last time he simply told her that he had never really cared about her at all. She had liked the idea of being married, she just didn't like him. The truth was she didn't like the idea at all, she was sure it was the wrong thing to do.

The truth was out there for everyone to see, he was a creep. No that wasn't right he was something that would creep along the ground.

She never wanted to see him again she surely didn't want to marry something as slimy as he was.

Running away had seemed to be her only option. Had she been wrong about that? She had run from him because she had no choice or did she? She was going to have to go back home she knew that much. All she knew for sure was that she didn't have to go now.

When she did go home her parents would be there with Jim waiting for her to return. They would tell her how worried they had all been so that she would feel guilty. Jim would hold her and she would hold him then before she realized what she was doing, she would take him back. When the day was over she would be left feeling guilty that she had caused everyone so much pain.

Why did she have to go back? After all what was back there for her? There was nothing but more mistreatment, more guilt, and the fact that she had lost control of her life.

Back home she was little more than a puppet living the life that others wanted her to live. She didn't want to go back to that but she did want to go back home. No matter what she did nothing was going to change. After all, she was still the same person she had always been. Nothing could change if she didn't change.

Emily looked at Jack thinking how lucky he was after all he had people who cared about him. He had everything because someone cared about him Emily was given what she needed so that her parents could get Jim to marry her. They didn't want her they wanted Jim she was nothing more than bait.

Luke walked into the truck stop and took a seat in the booth across from Emily and Jack. "You two look all worn out."

Emily nodded. "I am worn out and sure I feel as though I have lost control of my life."

"No, you are just tired."

"I am tired of being used by everyone around me."

"Jack and I will go easy on you."

"I think I will go over to the motel and relax."

"You go ahead Jack and I will meet you here in the morning."

"Aren't you going to walk me over to the motel?"

"No, that would be controlling or at least saying we do not trust you to do it on your own."

"Now you are just being a smart ass."

Luke smiled. "Maybe, you get used to a thing even if you don't like it."

"Meaning I am used to being controlled so I want everyone to tell me what to do?"

"No, I am just giving you a hard time because it is fun and I am in a good mood."

"I don't think you are funny at all."

"Then stop smiling it makes people think you are having a good time."

Emily stood up. "I need to get my things out of the truck."

Luke handed her the keys. "Make sure you lock it up when you are done."

"Do you want me to bring them back to you?"

"No, I will come up to your room and get them from you."

"I will bring them back as soon as I get my bag out of the truck."

"If you want you can do it that way."

"You just want to get me alone in a motel room."

"I live in a motel on wheels and I had you in there what is the big deal about your motel room."

Emily smiled. "A bigger bed."

Luke laughed. "Okay, you have a point."

"I will be right back."

Luke watched her as she walked away. "Jack, if you are not careful you might start to like her."

Emily sat in the truck thinking about everything and wondering just what she was doing. She didn't want to start anything with Luke it was too soon. She wasn't ready for that and neither was he. He didn't want to be alone after learning about his Dad. If they were not careful they could end up doing something stupid.

PART TWO

Chapter 14

Saturday morning the sun was up before Dan which was unusual though not unheard of. He lay on the bed looking at the ceiling thinking about the night he had spent with Rhea. It had started with him being late to pick her up which had not been good. Then there was the way she had looked as she walked toward the car. He knew she was good looking he just hadn't realized she looked that good.

The meal had been perfect and the talk had been less than memorable. They had talked about nothing much at all. In truth, she had seemed more interested in Luke's farm than in him. They had talked but he still didn't know much about her. She had a way of talking around herself but not about herself. Dan was going to need more time with her if he wanted to know who she was.

Dan never wanted more than two dates because he knew what would happen after the third date. After the second date all the girls he knew started making wedding plans. After the third date, they treated him like they were married. He wasn't sure if she was like that though he doubted that she was. There was something different about her. He wasn't sure if it was good or bad it was too soon to tell. A smart man would stay away from her but he couldn't do that.

Dan looked around the room a few minutes before he realized he was in the guest room on the farm. This wasn't his room he was supposed to be in his room. He didn't remember going into the guest room or did he? What in the world had he been thinking?

Rhea had wanted to see the house when she brought him home. He had given her a tour of the place. When they reached the guest room he was feeling tired so he sat down on the bed. They had been talking while he was sitting and that was the last thing he could remember. He must have fallen asleep while she was talking to him.

Dan needed coffee which meant he was going to have to get moving. He got up and went to his room to get some clothes. While getting his clothes he remembered his hand was hurt. The pain traveled up his arm until he stopped using his hand.

He got dressed carefully and then went down to the kitchen. He got a pot of coffee started and then went to take a shower. He took the wrapping off his hand carefully. He noted that it didn't look as good as he hoped it would.

He took his shower hoping it would help. When that was done the coffee was done. He poured himself a cup and then went out to help his brother care for the animals. It was going to be rough working with a bad hand he might have to let his sister have a look at it.

As he reached the barn he realized that his brother wasn't there he hadn't come home. Once again his brother was off having a good time while he was there working the farm. It wasn't fair after all he spent more time caring for the place than his brother did. The only time he had was on the weekends and even then he helped his brother with the haying. The truth was he had no time for a life of his own. He was always too busy taking care of his brother's dream.

Dan shook his head and then started doing the chores. He fed all the animals and then cleaned the barn before milking the cows. Once that job was done he opened the stable door to let the cows and horses out for the day. He was still mad when he collected the eggs before heading back to the house.

Once he was back in the house Dan set the pales of milk on the table and then poured himself a cup of coffee. He needed the coffee he had stayed out too late now he was tired. They were supposed to mow hay today so they could bail it on Sunday. He wasn't sure what he should do about that. He wanted to skip it but the animals hadn't done anything to him. For two cents he would move out of the house so his brother would have to stay home to care for his animals.

As he strained and then bottled the milk he thought about the hay. This was Luke's farm not his but he seemed to be doing most of the work most of the time. He had morning deliveries to make the mowing would have to wait. There was nothing he could do about his brother so he was just going to do what had to be done. He should be in a hurry but he was going to make time for another cup of coffee before he left the house.

There were grain deliveries in the morning and then building supplies in the afternoon. It was the way it went every Saturday the loads were a little different each week but that was all. He didn't stop for lunch on Saturday he wanted to get done early. Today he was already running late. That was the start of his day the problem was that it was also the easiest part of his day.

Luke never came home Dan did the mowing that his brother should have been doing. It wasn't that he didn't like the job it was a simple fact that it wasn't his. Luke should have been there instead of being shacked up with whoever it was that he was with. His brother was allowed to find himself a woman as long as he did it during the week. After all, there was a time for everything and the weekend was the time for haying.

When the mowing was done Dan did the evening chores. When they were done he got cleaned up before he fixed himself something to eat. As he sat there drinking a cup of coffee he thought about his father. He always thought that his Dad would be there to hold and play with his grandchildren. Now Dan knew that would not be happening.

Dan was finishing his coffee when he heard a knock on the door. Very few people ever came to visit the farm. The few that did come were family mostly which meant they didn't ever knock. That was when he remembered Rhea still had his car.

Dan opened the door with a smile on his face. "Hi, how are you?"
Rhea smiled. "I am fine. How is your hand?"
"Okay, thanks to you. Come on in. Would you like a cup of coffee?"
"Yes, I would love one."

They walked into the kitchen where Dan poured two cups of coffee and then set them on the table. "I had a busy day Luke never came home last night."

"You forgot I had your car didn't you?"

"Never even thought about the car until you knocked on the door."

Rhea laughed. "I thought you might have when I didn't hear from you today."

"I am afraid I got busy and I had a lot on my mind as well. I am mad at my brother and my father as well as being mad at myself."

"That is a lot of mad for one person to be walking around with."

Dan nodded in agreement. "I know and I know it is crazy but that doesn't change anything."

"You should talk to my Dad he is good with this sort of thing."

"I would hope so he is a pastor."

"Owning a farm doesn't make you a good farmer."

"True."

"I am telling you he is good at this sort of thing, you should talk with him. You could take me to church on Saturday morning if you think that will help."

Dan laughed. "I thought you might bring that up."

"Well after that fight we had in the bar last night I think we both need to go to church."

"You might have a point there."

"I went to church today."

Dan smiled. "That is right this is Saturday."

Rhea pointed at his hand. "Let me see how your hand is doing."

"It is fine I cleaned it then wrapped it again."

Rhea took the wrapping off Dan's hand. She carefully cleaned it up and then wrapped it again. "That should keep it from getting infected."

I thought it looked good."

"It is not bad but you should have Emma look at it."

"I will."

"I would love to sit here and talk some more but I need to get home."

"I would think you would. We should get going."

"Are you going to take me to church next Saturday?"

Dan smiled. "We will talk about it."

Dan drove Rhea home then drove back to the farm and poured the last of the coffee into his cup. He liked Rhea a lot but he had the feeling he was in over his head. He was going to have to worry about that another time tonight he had other things on his mind.

Dan finished his coffee and then went up to his room. As he got ready for bed he was still thinking of his Dad. No matter what he knew he could not imagine life without him. What would happen to his Mom how would she go on without his Dad? What would she want to do? Where would she want to live?

As he went to sleep in his room he was wishing he was anywhere but on the farm. He had nothing against his brother owning the place. He didn't even mind having to do the chores during the week. The weekend was supposed to be his, but Luke wasn't home. He wanted to have the weekend to do what he wanted to do. Even as he drifted off to sleep he knew he was not upset about working the farm he was upset because his brother was not at home to face his father with him.

Chapter 15

Sunday morning Emma was up early she was tired but she didn't want to try to sleep. Her night had been long with little sleep but a lot of bad dreams. All she had seen was her life without her Dad. Her brothers had seemed to go on as if nothing had happened. She couldn't understand how they could do that. She would be at home every day all she had to do was smile and make believe nothing was wrong.

Emma lay on her bed she couldn't cry anymore and yet tears filled her eyes though she made no sound. She didn't want to have them hear her crying it was all too hard on them already. She was glad they had each other but she was still alone.

She needed her morning coffee or something stronger but it was a bit early for that. She just lay there thinking about her parents she could not imagine how hard everything was on them. She got up got dressed then went out to her car. She wanted coffee and maybe something to eat she wanted to be alone. The truck stop would be her best bet she rarely went there.

The drive was a short one and she was glad because she wanted to be around people she didn't know. When she first walked in she knew she had made a mistake Laurie was there. At least it was Laurie and not one of her brothers' friends. Laurie understood her almost as well as Stephen did and of course, they had other things they could talk about.

"Laurie, what are you doing here?"

"I had a breakfast date but it seems he stood me up. What are you doing here?"

Emma sat down across the table from her friend. "I came here to spend some time alone."

"In that case, we both lost out this morning."

The waitress Sheri Carson brought them coffee. "Good morning. Are you ready to be older?"

Emma looked at her. "I will have the pancakes."

Laurie looked up at Sheri. "I think I will have the same."

Sheri smiled at them. "Alright I will bring your order out to you shortly."

Emma looked at Sheri. "I thought you worked nights?"

"I do but one of the girls called off this morning so I am filling in for her."

Laurie smiled. "You want to fill in for me tonight?"

Sheri didn't say anything about that. "I will get your order in."

Emma sipped her coffee. "Laurie, I am afraid I am not handling all of this very well."

"I am amazed you can handle it at all, it can't be easy."

"It is the end of everything even if he lives which is very unlikely at this point it simply won't be the same."

"That I do understand I remember how I felt when they told us my Dad would survive but he would never walk again. He was still Dad but he wasn't. I had to get to know him all over again. He has changed and so has I it isn't easy anymore."

"I know the whole world looks different, I feel like a lost little kid. You think you are on your own but you still depend on your parents more than you think you do."

Laurie nodded. "We simply don't want to see things as they are because then we have to face the fact that one day they will be gone and we will be alone."

Emma put her cup down on the table. "Where do you go to feel safe when they are gone?"

"I think about that all the time and I still don't have an answer."

"Good morning ladies, I hope you are talking about me.", Stephen said as he sat down beside Emma.

"Steve, what are you doing here?"

"Laurie, I am here to get some food and some coffee. I didn't expect to find either of you here this morning."

"We were talking about our parents."

"I am an only child and my parents left me when I was a kid so I can't say much about that life."

Emma shook her head. "You had a family."

"I did I had my grandmother but it is not the same."

Laurie looked at Stephen. "You have your parents and your sister."

Stephen shook his head. "I do have parents but they left me with my Grandmother when they left town. As for my sister I have never met her." "They don't live that far away."

"I guess it is quite a long way away or they would have come to town when Gram died."

The food came and the talk went from family to other things. Steve had been out of town so he had some wild stories to tell about the people he had seen. No one was sure if the stories were true but they were fun to listen to. He had crazy driver stories, a story about a girl with long blue hair, a guy who couldn't keep his pants on right, there was a woman with four screaming children, and an older guy who was sleeping in the park. He always had stories as well as a look in his eyes that made you wonder if the stories were true.

Laurie was wishing she had stayed home while Emma just laughed. "You are so full of it."

"You say that like you don't believe me."

Laurie ignored Steve she was looking at Rhea. "She was at the bar with Dan Friday night."

"Mom said they had a date."

Steve looked at Rhea. "Isn't she the pastor's daughter?"

Laurie looked at her empty cup. "Yes, she is."

"Did you know Luke was with Emily Rice on Friday night? They were at the bar too."

Emma was surprised. "They were both there?"

"Yeah, though they were there at different times. Emily and Luke came in first then after they left Rhea and Dan came in. Emily hit Jim Campbell with a pool stick breaking it over his head. Jim started after her but Luke got in between them. I have never seen him like that he beat the crap out of Jim.

"A little while after they left Jim was telling everyone what he was going to do to Luke when he saw him again. Just as he finished up Rhea and Dan walked in. Jim was trying to take Rhea out to his car I think. Dan was talking then they were fighting then I had the shotgun.

"I had Jim covered while Rhea and your brother went out the door. The redhead Jim was with was under age so the cops took them both to the station."

Emma smiled. "We all beat up on Jim."

"Yeah, he looked really bad the last time I saw him."

"It is getting late I have to get home."

Steve looked at Laurie. "Jim got bailed out of jail by Emily's parents I saw him in the coffee shop this morning.

Emma looked at her friends. "I think we should all get out of here before the lunch crowd starts coming in."

Chapter 16

Sunday morning Emily was up early she showered then went over to the truck stop for breakfast where Luke and Jack were already seated at a booth waiting for her. Jack was happy to see her but Luke just sat there looking toward the door.

She sat down and the waitress brought her a cup of coffee."Luke, you don't look very happy to see me."

"It isn't you, I was watching for someone else."

"You have a girlfriend here?"

"No, I saw a truck in the parking lot that belongs to someone I know and don't want to see this morning."

"What is wrong with him?"

"He is a she, her name is Georgia and everything is wrong with her."

"What is wrong does she have the hots for you?"

"No, she has a girlfriend."

"Oh, I see."

"No, you don't. I don't care what she does at home. Georgia is nice enough but she is going to come in here and there is going to be trouble."

"Why?"

"Because she is who she is and she just can't help herself."

Georgia Stewart walked into the room and then just stood there looking around until she saw Jack. The good thing about Jack was that he brought Luke with him everywhere he went. It was a good thing too because Jack didn't talk much. If she was completely honest he wasn't much of a driver either.

Georgia didn't know who was sitting with them but that didn't matter. The way she saw it people were people half were nice half were not. You had to sift through them to find the best ones. She walked over to the booth and sat beside the girl.

"Luke, I thought you and Jack didn't work on the weekends?"

"Gee, you here because you are on the way someplace, or are you just here to bust my butt."

"I just thought we could talk while we eat."

"You are not going to give me a hard time?"

"You have your dog with you as always, now you also have a girl with you. The cab of your truck must be crowded when you all try to get in that small bunk of yours. Why would I give you a hard time about any of that?"

"It isn't that small."

Gee looked at Emily. "My name is Georgia but everyone calls me Gee."

"Hi, my name is Emily."

"Emily, I hope you two haven't been dating long because he has never mentioned you before."

"We aren't dating we are just traveling together."

"Can you drive?"

"Not the truck."

"Too bad I was looking for someone to be my co-driver."

Luke shook his head. "Gee, you can't stand to have anyone else in your truck."

"I know but I might be willing to try to change if I found the right person."

"Jack might have puppies too."

"Emily, I have no idea how you can spend any real time in a truck with these two."

"I don't know I like Jack."

They all laughed then Georgia pointed at Emily. "You best be good to her I like her."

"Gee, you like everybody as long as they let you pick on them endlessly."

"Luke, I don't pick on everyone after all there are some of these old farts that I would love to run over."

"Not everyone is as nice as me."

"I have news for you I like Jack more than I like you."

Emily looked at Jack. "Doesn't everybody?"

"That is true I hear Luke is hard to live with."

"Jack likes me."

Gee nodded her head. "That is the only reason you have any friends at all. To be honest he is all you have going for you. Everybody likes him from what I hear."

"Gee, why is it every time I see you all you do is bust my chops?"

"Because Jack can't talk so I have to speak for him."

Emily laughed. "When she is right she is right."

The four of them sat there for almost an hour then Georgia left. Luke looked at Emily thinking about how she had seemed to fit right into everything. The last time this happened to him he ran away with her. He let it talk himself into a marriage that lasted two years. She could be a great person but he wasn't going to make that mistake again.

"She seemed nice."

"She is though I have to admit I didn't think I was going to like her when I first met her. She was defensive back then. A lot of the old truckers used to give her a hard time because she is short. I thought she was just another crazy girl trying to prove she could do anything a guy could do. The truth is she just likes to drive."

"You don't care that she is gay?"

"I don't think it is any of my business what she does in her own home."

"So you don't care what she does as long as she keeps it at home."

Luke smiled; he had been down this road with a few people before. "I have not changed my view on people in a long time. Live and let live, I don't judge a person that is not my place. If you want to know the way I see the people in this room I can tell you. I don't know them well enough to tell you if they are good or bad."

"I have seen you make quick judgments about people before and most times you are right. So what happened with Linda and Jim?"

Luke looked into his coffee cup wishing he was not having this conversation. "Linda was never going to stay with me and I knew that right off but she needed me right then and we lied to each other as well as to ourselves because we were afraid for different reasons but we were both afraid.

"When she left me it hurt because I hate to lose even when I know from the start that I am going to lose. You tell yourself that it won't hurt but it does because you care. Even though you knew from the start it was wrong. Even though you knew it would never last. People say it is because I hate to lose that I hold on too long or I don't want to see the truth when I make a mistake... The truth is I cared even though I knew she was going to leave me and I didn't want to let her go because I was afraid of what my parents would think of me."

Emily looked at him she had never realized he had known all about Linda. Even though he knew the way she had been. He had said nothing so they had been married. "What about Jim and me?"

"Another lost cause right from the start, Jim lies to himself so he lies to you. He lets most people see him as a nice guy who is misunderstood by you. Yes, he has cheated on you but it is your fault not his after all you say one thing when you mean something else. You say you love him but you are afraid to commit to him.

"People can see the fear in you so they believe it is because he is right. The truth is you know who he is and you are afraid of what life will be like if you marry him. You stand beside him because you believe if you do he will change even though you know better than that. You think you have to defend him because you are a couple. We all do the same thing, right up until we have had enough then we get angry then we start looking at the truth. It is never easy but with a little bit of help and time we usually find our way."

"I didn't face anything I ran away."

"You hit him over the head with a pool stick I think he got your message."

"I guess you are right but I still ran away."

"So did I and I am still running."

"When do we stop?"

"You have got me."

"What do we do now?"

"Damned if I know, I have been looking for the answer to that question for two years."

Emily laughed. "I meant what are we going to do now that we have finished breakfast?"

"Oh, we should go have a look around and see what they have."

"Jack and I have already done that."

"Yes, you did but you haven't checked this place out with me."

"What does that mean?"

"That means you have missed something special."

"Okay, what did we miss?"

"You missed seeing everything from my point of view."

"Oh shit. It seems one of us is full of it."

"The restroom is over in the corner to drop your load. Jack and I will wait right here for you."

"I am not the one that is full of shit."

"Jack and I went when we got up this morning."

"Why do I talk to you."

Luke smiled at her. "I am with Jack."

Emily shook her head. "That must be it."

Chapter 17

Dan was up early Sunday morning he started the coffee and then went out to the barn. He fed the horses as well as the cows and then milked the cows. Once that was done he fed the chickens and then collected the eggs. He took the eggs and milk to the house and set them on the table everything could wait until after he had his coffee.

By the time he had finished bottling the milk and cleaning the eggs, he was ready to head for his parent's house. The whole farming thing wasn't bad but it wasn't his farm it was Luke's though he seemed to be doing all the work these days.

Dan was upset because he wanted his brother home so that they could talk. Their world had changed they needed to talk about what was going to happen as well as what they would do after it did. What about their Mom? What would they do about her once their father was gone? It might seem a bit early to be thinking about it but he could not help it.

What would he do go home or bring Mom to the farm? What about Emma would she want to stay in the house or move out to the farm as well? There were a lot of questions that needed to be answered. They needed to talk it all out but they could not do that without Luke.

When he was ready and the coffee was gone he put some milk and eggs in his car and then started for town. He was thinking about asking a couple of his friends to help him with the haying. Any other time he would have asked his father for help, things were different now his father was sick.

Dan drove over to his parent's house where his Mother was the only one up. "Good morning Mom."

"Dan, where is your brother this morning?"

"I have no idea. He didn't come home again last night. I was hoping maybe you would know where he is."

"Your Dad said he was at the bar Friday night when he left. Maybe you should stop by there and ask if anyone knows where he is."

"You think he might be spending time with Laurie again?"

"No, he was with Emily Rice Friday when he was here."

"Then where could he be? I know she still lives with her parents."

"Laurie or her parents might know something that will help you."

"I will try to remember to stop there."

His Mom looked at him. "Where are you going now?"

Dan put the milk and eggs in the fridge. "I have to get help with the haying today."

"I will send your Dad and your sister Emma over to help you so don't worry about that. I will help too it will be a nice family day."

"Mom, it might be best if I get a couple of the guys to help me."

"Dan, you should let your Dad do this just like he has before."

"Mom, are you sure?"

"I am sure it will hurt him a lot more if you don't let him do it."

Dan understood though he still wasn't sure if it would be the best thing. "Right a family day on my brother's farm with everyone except my brother should be fun. This should be the time when he walks through the door."

His Mom smiled. "It would have been nice if it worked out that way."

Dan shook his head. "I will swing by the bar on my way back to the farm."

His Mom smiled at him. "Dan, this is the right thing to do."

"I will see you at the farm."

It was just after ten on a beautiful Sunday morning When Mrs. Linda Fields opened up the Circus Bar for business. They served breakfast and nothing stronger than coffee until noon. People said she would bend the rules for her regular customers though no one had ever proved that she did. People loved to talk and they loved to tell stories about people they knew. People had to talk even if they didn't know if the story was true.

Linda Fields was the subject of a lot of the talk around town. They told stories about how she was a very good mother to her six children. It was also said that she treated her husband better than she should in almost every way. They said her husband was no longer able to care for himself, because of a complete mental breakdown. It was said she did everything for him before she could leave the house each morning. A nurse sat with him during the hours when his wife was tending the bar or so the story went.

Dan knew almost all the stories about her it was hard not to after all it was a small town and he was a Richardson. They said she had taken almost every man in town to her bed at least once. They also said she never let her husband know but people believed that he knew.

They said that must have been what drove him out of his mind. It was also said that all six of her children were not his. Two were said to have the same father though no one knew which two. It was said that few people agreed on who it was who had fathered any of her children.

Dan let people talk it seemed to be the only thing most of them could do. The fact that most of the time they had no idea what they were talking about never seemed to bother them. He had learned at a young age that most stories people told had a single truth. The rest of the story was just filler to make the truth a little more interesting. If you took that little truth mixed it with most people and their love of a good story. Then added some alcohol well that was how stories were made.

Dan walked into the bar and then just stood by the door looking around the room. All the Sunday morning regulars were there even Mr. Fields sitting at his table in his wheelchair. That was something people never talked about after all the truth never made a good story. No, when it came to the truth it was all just too normal.

Mr. Fields had been injured in a truck accident about ten years earlier. He lived over the bar with his wife and children not in a house across town as some of the stories said. He had never had a nurse and he could be found right there at his table most days as well as nights. As long as the bar was open he was at his table with a deck of cards or watching the TV.

"Mr. Fields, I am looking for my brother I hear he was in here late Friday night."

"He was in here with Emily Rice until about eleven I saw them. I don't remember seeing them after things settled back down. Linda got the shotgun out than folks just calmed right down."

"What started the fight?"

"Not what who, Emily hit Jim Campbell with a stick from the pool table. She hit him right in the head just as hard as she could. Jim went after her but found your brother instead. When Jim got up off the floor he went after Emily but ran into your brother again. Your brother was not in a good mood I would guess because he put Jim back on the floor. He might have gotten up again but Jack was there as well as Linda with her shotgun. Emily, your brother, and Jack disappeared while everyone was watching Linda and her shotgun."

"Well, that explains why Jim was acting the way he was when Rhea and I got here."

"Jim isn't the smartest kid I have ever met though he probably is the most bruised this morning."

"I guess he should be after Luke and I got done with him."

"Your sister kicked him where it counts Friday afternoon."

"I didn't know that."

"You should talk to your sister more."

"I guess. I should start looking for Luke in other places around town."

"Speaking as someone who once drove a truck for a living you might want to check for his truck."

"Thanks I think I should have gone there first."

"Dan, if you don't find him or his truck go over to the truck stop they might be able to help you."

"Thanks, George, I am afraid my mind is not working right these days."

"I understand, your father is my best friend."

"Take care of yourself."

George nodded "I will do my best."

Dan left the bar it was getting late he had work to do there was hay to get in and the family would be waiting for him. He started for his car thinking about his brother right up until he saw Rhea Conner walking toward him. He forgot all about his brother as well as whatever else might have had on his mind.

"Dan, it is a bit early in the morning isn't it?"

"Rhea, I wasn't in there for that I was looking for my brother."

Rhea smiled at him. "It is Sunday morning they serve coffee with breakfast I am told. What else are you doing today besides looking for your brother in bars I mean?"

"We are going to the farm to bring in the hay."

"Sounds like fun can I help you?"

"You want to go work in the hay field on my brother's farm even though my brother isn't there?"

"It sounds like you can use the help."

"I can always use more help."

They got in the car then he drove to the farm forgetting to look for his brother's truck when they went by the lot where he parked it. The afternoon went by quickly they got the hay in then milked the cows, fed the horses, and the chickens and then collected the eggs. When everything was done they ate before his parents and sister went home. Rhea sat on the porch with Dan drinking ice tea as the sun was setting.

Rhea was thinking about a lot of things that she had done on her days off this day was right at the top of her list, she had enjoyed it. "Dan, thank you for letting me help you and your family. I don't think I have had that much fun in a long time."

"I am glad though I can't believe you liked working in the hay field."

"When I was a kid my uncle had a farm I used to help him all the time."

"I never pictured you as a farm kid."

"Can you tell me why not?"

"I don't know I guess it is because you look like a city girl."

"Because you judge me by the clothes I wear and the way I look?"

"Yeah, I guess that is why."

Rhea smiled. "I am not sure how I should feel about that."

Dan all at once felt very uncomfortable. He had the feeling that all of a sudden he was way over his head. He had planned to ask her out again now he wasn't sure he should they seemed to be moving a lot faster than he had planned. "I should go look for my brother."

"Would you like some company?"

"I would."

"It has been a good day."

"It was a good day as long as you like working all day in the hay field."

"It was the most fun I have had in a long time."

"I better get you home."

It didn't take long for Rhea and Dan to find out that the rig was gone, Luke had stopped at the truck stop on his way out of town. They also found out that Emily had been with him at the diner. There was other news as well Emily was wanted for questioning in the assault of her ex-boyfriend. Luke was also wanted for questioning though it didn't seem like that big a deal to the police who had Emily's ex-boyfriend locked up again.

The police also wanted to talk to Rhea and him about the trouble at the Circus Bar on Friday night. Rhea agreed they should talk to the police right away just to get it out of the way. They went to the police station where they sat waiting for someone to talk to them for almost a half hour.

When they were finally seen the officer wanted to talk about the fight in the bar. He listened to their story then thanked them and told them they could go home. In a way, they both were feeling a little disappointed it had not been anything at all.

It had been a long day they were both tired as well as a bit disappointed by what had happened at the police station. They needed to get home but they needed a cup of coffee more. The truck stop was the best place to go for coffee so they went back there just to relax and try to end the day on a good note.

Everyone already knew about Emily, Jack, and Luke being wanted by the police they also knew what Rhea had done with her day off. They had a couple of questions about their time at the police station and once they knew it all they just walked away smiling. It was a small town but word still seemed to get around faster than it should.

Everyone seemed to be worried about where Emily and Luke had gone off to with Jack. Dan wasn't worried he was mad. His brother was gone and he had to run the farm. He looked at Rhea, he was way over his head with her. He needed to spend some time on his own or he was going to start something that he wouldn't be able to stop.

There are times when a person just knows how things will turn out. They know that they should run but for one reason or another, they just can't do it. Right at that moment that was how Dan felt when he looked at Rhea. He knew he should run but his legs just wouldn't move. He had a feeling that this could be something special. There was something about her, he felt as if he had known her all his life.

Dan knew this was not the time to get involved with Rhea or anyone else. He should be spending all his time with his parents as well as his sister. He should be putting himself last while he helped the family. What if he was just using Rhea to avoid dealing with his Dad's illness? Was he being fair to her or himself? It was all just more than he wanted to think about. Why did everything have to happen at the same time? He had to go to sleep before his headed exploded.

His last thought as he drifted off to sleep was that it was all just so unfair to him. There was the thoughts of the family, there were the thoughts of Rhea in his head going round and round. How could he sleep with all of that going on in his head?

Chapter 18

Monday morning Emma was up early dressed then ran down to the kitchen pouring a cup of coffee then grabbed her car keys. She wanted to catch her brother Dan before he left the farm. She had made up her mind that they needed to talk. With Dan, it was always best to catch him in the morning before he left the farm. Most days Emma could get through to him any time but this was different. This was not a phone call thing this was a face-to-face. They needed to talk about their Dad.

When Emma got to the farm she parked beside Dan's car. She should have called before she drove over. He was family there was no need to worry. Dan was not one to bring his one night's stand girls home to the farm. Walking up to the door she knocked as she walked into the house.

Dan woke up Monday morning in his bed on the farm wishing he was not there he looked out the window. He might want to have a farm someday but that day was not today. A farm would be a great place for him now that he knew Rhea liked it too. Maybe he could get Luke to sell him the farm after all he was almost never here. Two dates and a day working the hay field together was all it had taken. He couldn't stop thinking about her.

Dan took a cold shower then he took another he was losing control. He got dressed and then started a pot of coffee before he went out to do the morning chores. By the time the chores were done so was the coffee. On his way back to the house he was thinking about the day ahead of him there were a lot of things he had to do right after he took milk and eggs to his parents.

The coffee was good as it always was when he made it. He should fix himself something to eat but he really didn't want anything. He took care of the milk and then put the eggs in a carton. He wished someone else could be there to help him. He should be loading up his truck to make his first delivery by this time. It was hard doing things this way which was no doubt why his brother wasn't doing it anymore.

"Good morning Dan, how are you doing?"

Dan spun around almost spilling his coffee. "Emma, you could have knocked. What are you doing here so early in the morning?"

"I came for a cup of coffee and to talk about Dad."

Dan got out a cup and then filled it with coffee. "What about Dad?"

"Dan, he is dying."

"We all are it is just a matter of when."

"Don't give me that hard-nosed crap. This is our father, not some person we don't know."

Dan sipped his coffee looking out the kitchen window. "Emma, you are a nurse what is there to talk about at this point? Dad has a year or two maybe even less than that. What can we do for him besides being there for him?"

Emma had tears in her eyes but she didn't make a sound. When she spoke her voice was strong even as her tears fell. "Dad will need us to be there for Mom and Mom will want us to be strong for Dad."

"So we all agree to lie to one another and everything should be just fine."

"Don't get mad at me!"

"Emma, I am not mad at you I am just mad. This isn't right; there are a lot of evil people in the world why can't they die instead of Dad."

Emma looked at her brother. She had been wondering the very same thing the last couple of days. "I don't know."

"Emma, I wish I didn't know about this."

"If he had died on the road we would be wishing we had more time with him. Well, we have the time and it still isn't enough."

"You will let me know what is going on with him right? You know Mom and Dad are not going to tell me anything."

"I was planning on it. You are going to let me come over here and cry when I need to?"

Dan smiled. "Sure as long as you let me cry with you when I feel the need."

"Okay, coffee in the morning."

"Okay, we can do that and beer after work."

Emma smiled. "We have a deal."

It was late by the time Dan started his deliveries and he was going to be late getting done. He was going to be in a bad mood all day which was not going to help him at all. He couldn't think of any good reason why he should be mad at his brother now. Things were different now after all this was Monday and he was almost always gone on Monday. Luke had a job he liked, he may be gone a lot but he had told Dan many times to make the farm his home. Maybe if he did he wouldn't be as angry as he was.

What if he stopped fighting the farm and learned to enjoy it? There had to be a way to do that, after all, it wasn't like he hated the place. There had to be something he could do that would make him feel like he was a part of the farm. He should do something so he would feel like he was doing more than just caring for it while his brother was out of town.

By noon his anger had turned to a search for a way to belong on the farm. The problem was that no matter what he came up with it always involved more animals which meant more work. He was sure he was missing something but he could not imagine what it could be. After all, a farm was animals and more animals meant more work.

Dan parked his truck at the truck stop then just sat there looking at the building. What was he doing there? He should be at the store getting something cold to drink or at the diner in town getting a sandwich to go. He didn't have time to go in there and get a meal.

That was when he saw Rhea walking out of the building headed right for his truck. She shouldn't be there her shift had ended two hours earlier. Dan watched her as she got in the truck and sat on the seat beside him a smile on her face.

"Good afternoon, where are we going?"

Dan was shocked he hadn't expected to find her there. Why was he there if he didn't expect to find her waiting for him? "I'm working."

"I know, that is why I asked you where we were going."

"Don't take this wrong but what are you still doing here?"

"I was waiting for you. I am not sure why I just had this feeling that you would be here so I waited. Why are you here?"

Dan shook his head and laughed. "Damned if I know. I never come here when I am working. To be honest I seldom come here at all."

"I know so why are you here now?"

"I was thinking about the farm and I have been mad all morning I wasn't really thinking about coming here."

Rhea smiled a knowing kind of smile. "Why don't you give me a ride home and we can talk a bit? You never know I might be able to help you with your problem."

Dan didn't know why but her smile made him nervous. "I can give you a ride home but I don't think you can help me with my problems."

"Maybe not but if you don't mind I would like to try."

"I don't mind at this point all I have managed to do is make myself mad."

"Okay, tell me what you want to do and I will see if I can come up with something that will help you."

"The problem is that I am mad at Luke for doing what he said he was going to do. I told him that I would care for the farm while he was on the road. Now I am getting mad at him because it is his farm and they are his animals. I take care of them more than he does. I am doing most of the work and I have nothing there that is mine."

"So buy a horse, cow, or some chickens."

"No, the last thing I need is more animals I have enough work to do."

Rhea smiled at him again with that same smile that made him nervous. "I am not sure I understand what you are looking for. Tell me a little more about how you agreed to take care of things for Luke in the first place."

"After Linda left him he wanted to get away to have time to work things out for himself. He sold me this truck and got all his customers to sign a contract with me then he bought a sleeper and box trailer. He found a company to work for and hit the road. He told me to treat the place like my own he even had me put on the deed so that I wouldn't have any trouble while he was gone.

"I was happy that he did that but I knew it was his farm and one day he would stop driving and start running the farm again. He really likes farming he just needs time to work things out."

"Dan, maybe you are looking at the wrong things. You want to feel like you belong there without it causing you more time and money."

"Right I don't want more animals I work hard enough with the ones that are there already."

"Can I ask you where you sleep when you are at the farm?"

Dan was really worried now. "I sleep in the spare room."

"It isn't the spare room it is your room so start thinking of it that way. It isn't Luke's farm the place belongs to both of you so try to remember that."

"Luke and Emma tell me the same thing but everything belongs to Luke it is his farm."

"Then go out and get your own things. There are a lot of things on a farm besides the animals."

"I don't know what to get Luke has everything he needs."

"Maybe he does but what would you like to have?"

Dan smiled as he thought about what he would like to have. "I think I would like to have my own tractor."

"Would you like anything else?"

"I think that is enough to start with don't you?"

"I am not the one who lives there. I think it is all up to you."

"In that case, I think a tractor is a place to start. I will have to see what that is going to cost before I do anything else."

Rhea looked at him still smiling. "Now that we have solved that problem I have a question to ask you. Why did you just drive by my house?"

Now it was Dan's turn to smile. "I guess I was enjoying talking to you and I was in no hurry for it to end."

"I can spend some more time but I at least need a change of clothes before we go riding around town."

Dan turned the truck around then went back to her house. He parked the truck in the driveway and then looked over at her. "Take your time there is no rush I only have a few deliveries this afternoon."

Rhea was only in the house long enough to change her clothes and then leave a note for her parent's so they would know where she was. She was having fun with Dan he was nothing like what other girls had told her he was like. She wanted to help him find himself or at least help him realize there was more to him than just being Luke's brother.

By the end of the day they had made plans to look at tractors and then go to the farm to care for the animals. After that the plan was to go out to eat then Dan would take Rhea home. That was the plan before they got to the farm.

When the sun went down that evening they were still at the farm. They were talking about farming mostly; they were surprised by how much they both seemed to like the same things. They seemed to have enjoyed it from childhood though they had found other interests as well. Rhea had gone to college only to end up a waitress at the truck stop. Dan had gone to college and was now a delivery boy.

Rhea made them something to eat though there wasn't much food left in the house. Dan was good at his job as well as around the farm but he wasn't much of a shopper. That was the way most guys were it seemed. They didn't need much; if they got hungry there was always fast food. If they got sick of that there was canned food or they could cook a burger or some mac and cheese.

After they ate they sat on the front porch drinking ice tea looking at the stars and talking about nothing special. There didn't seem to be any need to say a lot they were happy just sitting there. Dan hadn't thought about his Dad for over an hour. Sitting there looking at Rhea Dan had forgotten to be worried about his Dad. He had also forgotten about what he might be getting himself into with Rhea.

Chapter 19

Monday morning about an hour before sunrise Emily walked into the truck stop dining room where Luke and Jack were already waiting for her. Coffee and breakfast with very little conversation then Luke had the waitress fill the thermos as they were about to leave. They didn't have to go far they were only about an hour or so from where they had to deliver the load.

Emily couldn't understand why Luke was so quiet after all they had seemed to have had fun Sunday. They left Jack at the motel then they had gone to a movie. After that they had gone to the mall where they bought odds and ends then they had lunch. After dropping everything at the truck they went for a couple of drinks while they played a little pool. It had been fun so she couldn't understand why Luke was so quiet.

Before they left the truck stop Luke got on the phone and asked the company where he had to go next. There was only the owner in the office she told him where to go. He had nothing much to say his mind was on where he was going. He looked over at the passenger seat surprised to see Emily sitting there he had forgotten she was in the truck. He was so used to being alone he had simply forgotten about her.

"Sorry, I forgot you were here I am so used to having no one to talk to but Jack."

Emily smiled at him; she had been worried about what he thought about her. In a crazy way, it was a relief to know that he wasn't thinking about her at all. "I understand you have been on your own for a while."

"Yes, but we have been together since Friday afternoon you would think I would at least remember you were in the truck."

Emily laughed. "I guess we haven't done anything memorable yet."

"It should all be memorable after all it isn't something I do all the time."

"This will be a memorable trip I am sure."

"Are you planning something?"

Emily smiled. "Not yet."

"You will warn me if you start making plans for something memorable won't you?"

"That depends on the situation."

Luke glanced at her then back at the highway. "Right, all you have to do is keep answering my questions that way and I will remember this trip."

"Don't get nerves just yet we have time to get crazy no need to rush into anything."

"That doesn't do much to ease my mind."

"Was that what you thought I was trying to do?"

"I thought you might want to after all that you have done so far."

"Exactly what do you mean by that?"

Luke never looked at her but he did grin. "I was not the one that broke a cue stick over someone's head."

"No, you are the one that beat the crap out of him when he came after me."

"He was going to hit you I can't stand someone who mistreats women."

Emily shook her head. "You pushed me halfway across the room."

"I had to get you out of the way so Jack could keep you safe while I dealt with Jim."

"You almost took his head off."

"Yeah, he should have gone someplace else with that redhead I guess."

"Yeah, well I think you got that message across to him."

Luke glanced at her again. "I wouldn't count on it."

Emily nodded her head. "No, I guess he isn't smart enough to change."

When they got to where they were going Luke backed the truck up to the loading dock and then looked at Emily. "Wait here I have to go see the man about getting this old girl unloaded. One more thing keep the doors locked I don't want Jack getting out."

"You are worried about Jack? What if we have to go to the bathroom?"

"I'll take Jack when I come back and you can use the bucket in the back if you really have to go."

"I think I am going to kill you."

Luke laughed then went into the building carrying his load book with the information about the load in it. There was rarely any real paperwork for him to do anymore. Helen made sure all the information was right When she made out the paperwork. He didn't like the way things were done now. He went to the shipping and receiving office where Mrs. Sharon Griffin was waiting for him.

"Luke, you are early even for you today."

"I had to get out on the road the house was closing in on me."

"I have had that happen to me from time to time but I have a husband and three kids. You didn't get married did you?"

"Not me, if I had I would be late, not early. If I had gotten married I would still be in the honeymoon stage of our marriage. I might still be on the honeymoon."

"Luke, I think that only lasts a short time then life hits you right between the eyes."

"I was here last week how short is the honeymoon stage these days?"

Sharon handed him back his book. "Have Jeff sign that when he finishes unloading your trailer. The answer to your question is just as soon as the money runs out and money doesn't buy what it used to anymore."

"You aren't telling me anything I don't know. I was married once right up until she found someone else with more money."

"I settled for a man that looked good I figure we can always win the lottery."

"Good luck with that."

Sharon looked at the monitor that had the outdoor cameras hooked to it. "Luke, I think someone is trying to steal Jack. Some girl is walking him across the back lot by the loading dock."

"She is not stealing him she is taking him for a walk. I told her to stay in the truck until I got back but Emily has a mind of her own as does Jack."

"Emily? I don't think I have ever heard you mention her before."

Luke shook his head. "I never did as far as I can remember."

"She doesn't look like my idea of a lot lizard."

"She is a nice girl I went to school with her she wanted to take a trip so I brought her along. To be honest I think she might be wishing she stayed home the trucking business isn't very exciting."

"Maybe not but she seems to be getting a lot of attention right now."

Luke was already on his way out he had told her to stay in the truck. He should have known she wouldn't listen to him she had a mind of her own. The more they talked the more he thought they had nothing in common. He stopped at the truck long enough to leave the book in it.

Luke was thinking about everything he should have done as he started around the building. If he had been thinking he would have put her on a bus before going home to bed. Yes if he was smart he would have put her on a bus and send her home on Saturday when he had finally gotten some sleep. He could have done either one if he had been thinking about anything but his dad when things got quiet.

Jack may have been told to wait in the truck but he hadn't looked like he could wait. Emily wasn't used to just sitting around waiting for someone to tell her what to do next so she had decided Jack needed to get out of the truck. Everything had been just fine until the four guys came out of the building to smoke. Cigarettes were not enough for them they were going to have to give her a hard time.

"Hi, good looking were you looking for me?"

"I wasn't looking for anyone but now that you are here you can clean up after Jack he dropped a load right about where you are standing."

"She is right Bill, you are standing in it."

"Shut up Don, or I will make you lick it off my shoes."

"While you boys are having breakfast Jack and I will be going back to the truck."

Bill looked at her there was something in his eyes that told her she had gone a little too far with him. "I think you and I should get to know one another. I have a car in the other parking lot."

"Good morning Bill, I see you and your friends have met Emily. I am so glad you all are out here to make sure that Jack gets to walk around the yard."

"I have no interest in the dog."

"I know but Emily has no interest in you so I thought maybe you were smart enough to figure that out. I am sorry I misjudged you."

Bill went after Luke while his friends stood by and watched. Bill took a swing which missed but Luke didn't miss he broke Bill's nose. The whole thing was over in seconds there wasn't even time for a deep breath. Bill's friends took him inside while Luke took Emily and Jack back to the truck.

"Sorry I should have stayed in the truck."

"Emily, I had a reason for telling you to stay in the truck as you now know. Things might have gone a little differently if I had told you why I wanted you to stay in the truck."

"I didn't think anyone would bother me while I was walking Jack."

"You had Jim these folks have Bill. They don't all look alike and they do not wear a sign but they seem to be everywhere. Can you hand me the book I have to have Jeff sign it when he finishes unloading the trailer?"

Emily handed it to him. "I really didn't mean to start any trouble."

"Don't worry about it he would have gotten hit by somebody the way he is around people."

Luke walked into the building just as Jeff took the last skid off the trailer. "I saw what happened and I want to thank you I have wanted to hit him for months now."

Luke handed Jeff the book with his copy of the paperwork in it. then took it back after it was signed. "No problem he seems like one of the fools we have back home."

"Yeah, I guess we all have to have at least one around."

"Catch you next time."

"You bet."

That was the first stop in what could be a long day if it went on as it had started. Luke climbed back in the truck put the book in its case then checked the computer to see where he was going next. His next stop was just a couple of miles away. There was a load of paper headed west waiting for him nothing he hadn't done before an easy drive no big deal. As he pulled out onto the road a car going out the other driveway was taking Bill to the doctor.

It didn't take but a few minutes and he was backed into another loading dock ready to pick up a load of paper. Emily looked over at him as he was getting ready to get out of the truck. "Can I use the lady's room here?"

"Come on we will get you in there. We will have to go to the front office which means we will have to walk around to the front of the building."

Leaving Jack in the truck they went around to the front of the building. Kellie Pike looked up from the papers on her desk when they walked in. "Luke, it has been a while since I have seen you in the office."

"You got married no need for me to come up and see you anymore."

"You can still stop in my husband doesn't work here. Lucky you got here when you did I have to leave. Some trucker punched Bill in the nose and broke it."

Emily blushed. "Sorry about that."

"Bill is okay but when he is with the guys at work he can get stupid."

Luke looked at Emily and then back at Kellie. "She needs to use the restroom."

"It is right there go ahead."

Once Emily was gone Luke did what he had to do. "Kellie, I am the one who punched Bill in the nose. He was showing off and things got out of hand. I don't think he likes me very much."

"He hates you because of that one night before we got married he still thinks you and I went off together that night. I told him you were gone and I was with my sister and my mother but he thinks we were together."

"He is lucky to have you."

"You got that right. I have to leave tell your friend not to worry this isn't the first time he has had his nose broken."

Kellie left then Emily came out of the restroom. "I didn't know you knew that guy you hit."

"I have only talked to him a few times but that is the second time I have broken his nose. I don't like him and he doesn't like me he is always trying to pick a fight with me."

"That is why you told me to stay in the truck so there wouldn't be any trouble."

While they were talking they were walking back to the truck. "I thought if he didn't see you I might get out of there without any trouble but there was no guaranty on that."

"I thought you didn't want people to know I was with you because they would talk. I should have known better that is not the kind of person that you are."

Luke looked at her a smile on his face. "If I had a girlfriend I might want to hide you in the truck but the truth is you are the only female I have spent this much time with in over two years."

As they reached the truck she looked at him thoughtfully. "I am not sure that you could handle someone like me."

"I have to go talk to a man about a truckload of paper."

Emily climbed up into the cab of the truck she sat in the seat petting Jack thinking about what she had gotten herself into. She wasn't having a bad time but she wasn't having a good time either. In a way, it was like a bus ride with a stranger and his dog. Luke seemed to be different when he was in the truck he didn't talk much nor did he seem as friendly when they did talk. It was like he was two different people the one in the truck and the one that lived on the farm.

Emily looked out at the empty lot watching as someone mowed the lawn. Things here seemed to be the same. People didn't seem any different they mowed their lawns, went to the store for food, they went to work though most of them would rather be somewhere else. They took their children to the babysitter or school depending on the time of year. They lived and died just like everyone else but all the lives they wanted to be different to be more or just have more.

Emily had never thought much about anything but her work, her family, and Jim it seemed. The more was away it seemed the more she thought about it. There was always so much to do she didn't have time to think about things that didn't seem to matter. She wondered how Luke did it day after day you would think it would all start to drive a person mad.

She had been so lost in her thoughts she didn't realize Luke was back in the cab beside her. When he spoke to her she screamed. "You scared me!"

Luke smiled. "Where were you?"

"I was thinking about a lot of things which is something I usually don't have time for."

"That is one thing you have a lot of time for in a truck, thinking."

"I don't know how you can be alone day after day with no one to talk to it would drive me crazy."

"I have Jack to talk to and there are people that I talk to every time I stop to get a load or drop one off. There are different places I stop and talk to people."

"You spend most of your time alone with only Jack to talk to. That has to affect you no matter what you think."

Luke drove the truck out of the parking lot heading west doing his best to stay away from the conversation that Emily seemed determined to have. "When we get to a truck stop we will stop for lunch."

"We have enough coffee in the thermos for each of us to have one last cup."

"That sounds good."

"You don't think that part of the reason you never remarried is that you spend all your time on the road?"

"You have never been married are you going to blame that on my truck too?"

That was the end of that conversation though they did talk about other things none of which had anything to do with either one of them getting married. Luke had brought up a good point that Emily didn't want to think about. She had run off because she didn't want to be forced to marry Jim though that wouldn't happen if she could bring herself to tell her parents that she wasn't going to marry him even if they did like him.

"You know I like spending time with you and Jack."

"We are a fun couple of guys."

When they got to the truck stop they went in and got something to eat then had the thermos filled with water for Jack. This was a stop where Jack was not welcomed as he was at other places. Emily and Luke talked about where they were going next as well as the weather and road construction.

Emily brought the water out to Jack while Luke paid for their meal. He was finding that he liked Emily more than he was ever going to tell her. There was something about her that told him he would be better off if he kept his distance. The truck was getting smaller with every mile they traveled together.

Jack was enjoying his water while Emily was ready to get back on the road she was beginning to enjoy the trip. Luke got in the truck he seemed a little upset. "Is something wrong?"

"We have a flat tire on the trailer the garage can fix it in a few minutes but it is going to take some time before they get to it there are other trucks ahead of us."

"What are we going to do while the tire is being changed?"

"We are going to sit and wait there is nothing else we can do."

By the time everything was done they had been there a total of three hours. Luke wasn't talking which left Emily with too much time to think. She was wondering how things were going back home without her at her job. What were her parents doing? What did they think about what she had done? She hadn't called them on the phone.

Once the tire was fixed they got back on the road. Luke still was not talking so Emily started thinking about her friend Christen. She was thinking she could call her and find out how things were going back home. Christen wouldn't be able to tell anyone what she was doing if she didn't tell her. That was the good thing about a phone it didn't tell people where she was.

Thinking about using a phone she looked at it. The thing was everywhere they went there was a phone. "The next time we stop I need to make a phone call."

"If that is what you want."

Emily looked at him surprised that he had agreed with her so quickly. "Just like that no argument about it."

"Yeah, just like that. We agree it is a sign! We have to get married now."

"Let's drop the trailer and head for Las Vegas."

"Let's sell the load on the black market then head west with our money."

"Are we getting married or gambling?"

"If we get married we are already gambling."

They were laughing when Jack barked and the air pressure gauge dropped down. Luke started to gear down as he eased the rig to the side of the road. When he brought the rig to a stop he shut everything down. He was sitting there thinking he had not had any trouble with the truck on any of his other trips. This was looking like he had found all the bad luck that he thought he had left behind him two years before.

"What happened?"

Luke shook his head. "My worm of life has turned I think."

"What does that mean?"

"Something else is broken on the truck."

"What do we do now?"

"I don't know about you but I am not buying any lottery tickets today."

"I don't think I should either. "

"Well, I best see if I can fix whatever is broken or patch it to get us to where we can get it fixed."

"You carry spare parts with you?"

"Yeah, that is why I tow a trailer everywhere I go."

"You think you are a funny man but if I were you I wouldn't quit my day job to tell jokes for a living. I am sure you would starve to death if you did."

"I have a couple of spare lines as well as a very large roll of duct tape. I am sure we can at least get to a truck stop where we can get what we need."

"You think I am bad luck don't you?"

"Well if I believed in that sort of thing I might but the truth is tires go flat and air lines fail."

"Do you need some help?"

"No, but Jack could always use a walk while I am checking things out."

It took about a half hour to get the truck back on the road which wasn't bad all things considered. Once they were back on the road they didn't talk much as they went along the highway. Luke was used to not having anyone to talk to and Emily thought it best not to remind him she was there.

Emily looked out the window as they went along the road. She had a smile as she sat there feeling like she thought Jack must feel when he was sitting on the seat looking out the window. That was something she never thought she would do, sit looking out a window and comparing herself to a dog.

Chapter 20

Luke had the truck on the road early Tuesday morning. He was running a little behind but it wasn't anything he couldn't make up with a little luck. The way things had started he was going to need a lot more than a little luck. He didn't want to say that Emily was bad luck but right now she was no four-leaf clover.

Monday had not gone well they had been delayed twice and Bill had a broken nose. In truth, he couldn't really blame Emily for any of that. He knew things go wrong from time to time still this was a bit more than that. Trucks break down and Bill was Bill which was something only he was to blame for. He knew Bill would have found another reason to start trouble if Emily had not been there.

"What are you thinking about?"

"I was thinking that we need a good day if we are going to make up the time we lost yesterday."

"I was thinking about Jim."

"Are you sorry you hit him now?"

"No, I wish I had hit him harder he is a no-good pile of crap."

"Don't hold back tell me how you really feel."

"He wasn't like that when we first started dating he was good to me then something changed."

"That is what I used to say about Linda until I realized that she had always been the same I just didn't want to see it."

"So what made us blind or stupid or a little of both?"

"I don't know I guess we want to see the good in people even if it isn't there."

"Is there ever any good in them? Mom has told me there is good in everyone if we look for it."

Luke thought about it doing his best to remember what it had been like with Linda when they first got together. "I think at first we want to believe so we tell ourselves that together we will be okay. The trouble is you can't change people they have to do that for themselves. If they think they are okay the way they are then there is no reason for them to change."

Emily seemed to understand though her view was a little different. "What happens if we see the problem but we feel we have to keep on trying until we are sure there is no hope?"

"Everyone has to do what they think is best even if no one else agrees with our view on things."

"I never really loved Jim you know. I liked him he was a lot of fun but there was something about him that just wasn't right."

Luke smiled. "Linda was hot enough to set a house on fire though looks aren't everything. She was far away no matter how close we thought we were she was never really with me. I knew it and I didn't care because I was no better than she was. We were both looking for something but we settled for each other for a couple of years."

Emily looked out of the window concerned that she was looking at her life passing by as she ran through it alone. "You know you are starting to depress me."

"Yeah, I was thinking we should talk about something else."

The conversation didn't change they just stopped talking. They dropped off a load of paper and then picked up a load headed for a warehouse in Pennsylvania. It was a short haul which was okay because they needed to make up some time.

By the end of the day, they were sitting in a truck stop in Ohio with a load of custom-made chairs headed for a warehouse in Illinois. They ate in silence still wondering about where they were in their lives. Emily was thinking she should have taken the bus though she was glad she had not.

Luke was wondering why he had let her in the truck. It had seemed like a kind thing to do. He thought he would be getting her to a bus station so that she could go where she wanted to. Luke never expected her to want to stay in the truck and call it a vacation. Was that true or had he wanted her to stay with him? That was a question he didn't want to answer or even think about.

"Luke, if you don't want me to stay with you in the truck I can take a bus home."

`"Emily, I am not going to tell you I don't want the company I just don't understand why you want to ride in the truck when you could be on a beach someplace."

"I like Jack and I think I can put up with you until we get back home."

Emily, you have to know you are a little on the strange side."

"You think I am strange? You are the only man I know who would throw a good-looking woman out of his truck."

"I would never do that and I will prove it to you just as soon as we find one."

"Watch it you can be replaced."

"Emily, you can't replace something you don't have."

"We could get engaged or married then I could replace you."

"I have done all of that once already I do not think I will do it again anytime soon."

"Then we will just have to be friends. Do you mind traveling around the country with a friend?"

"No, it might even be fun."

"We should get back to the truck it is getting late."

"You sure you don't want to get a room here after all we only have one bunk in the truck?"

"I thought about that but I don't think it would be a good idea I would be safer in the truck."

Luke sat there looking at her thinking about just how he was going to get out of this one. "Well if that is what you want to do I think I know how we can do it and both be happy. Let me go get it all set up then I will come back and get you."

"Are you sure you don't want me to help you?"

"No, you just wait right here I will be back in a little bit."

Luke left Emily sitting alone with her thoughts which was not a good thing right about then. She was thinking she might have gotten herself in over her head after all she had just gotten rid of Jim she didn't need another man right now. She liked his sort of but this was not the time. She should stay at the truck stop or he should. As soon as he came back she would tell him.

When Luke came back for her he had a big smile on his face. "Tonight we sleep together in the truck."

Emily smiled but she was very nervous even a little scared. "Are you sure about this?"

Luke nodded. "I am as sure as I can be. I mean you never know how things will work out until you try."

"What if it doesn't work out?"

"We can try some other way of doing it."

"You want to do this?"

"Yeah, don't you?"

"Yeah, I really do."

Chapter 21

Dan was sitting at the table Tuesday morning eating the breakfast Rhea had fixed him before she left for work in his car. He couldn't believe what had happened the night before. He had told himself time and time again that he wasn't going to let anyone stay overnight in his brother's house.

That may have been what he had done before Rhea. She was different he had let her stay. He had promised himself a lot of things that he seemed to forget when Rhea was around him. After all, she was driving his car to work and no one was ever going to drive his car. This was the second time she had driven his car. Dan knew he was way over his head so why did he smile when he thought of her?

He washed the dishes when he finished eating and then went out to his truck. He sat in the truck looking at the list of deliveries he had for the day. It was an easy day for a change as long as nothing else came up. He thought of what Rhea had told him before she left in his car. She wanted him to pick her up at the farm after he made his last delivery. He had said "Okay" before he realized what he was saying.

Driving toward town he thought about his Dad wondering how anyone could get news as he had and get up the next morning to work or just face the day. What can you do when you know that your days are numbered? What do you do when your life has an end date stamped on it? What did it feel like to look at someone you have shared your life with knowing she will have to go on without you?

Dan pulled into the parking lot and then backed up to the loading dock. Shutting down the truck he got out and then went inside the feed store. Lucy looked at the clock and then at Dan. "You are late. Did you have a rough night?"

"Lucy, I had a good night's sleep."

"You must have gone to bed early to get a good night's sleep; I saw your car at the truck stop this morning."

"I wasn't there this morning."

"I know I saw your car this morning."

"The car was there I wasn't."

"I thought you didn't let anyone else drive your car?"

"I didn't but it was a special circumstance."

"What is her name?"

"I am sure you know her, Rhea Conner."

"I know her and her parents. Her Dad is the pastor."

"Yes, I know he is I go to the church."

"I never thought she would go out with you."

Dan sipped his coffee before he said anything. "I thought we were friends?"

"We are I just never thought she would go out with someone who didn't go to church."

"I go to church."

"Dan, you are not what I would call a churchgoer. I think you would need to go more than three times a year."

"Lucy, I think you are saying I am not good enough for Rhea."

"I am sure that is not what I am trying to say."

"What are you saying?"

Lucy laughed. "I am not sure anymore."

Dan refilled his travel mug. "I have to get going."

Keith walked back inside. "What the heck is with Dan this morning?"

"Rhea Conner is driving his car today and if I had to guess I would say it is not the first time."

"Rhea Conner and Dan Richardson that is a match I never thought I would see."

Lucy smiled. "You know I think she will be good for him."

Keith shook his head. "I don't know I have heard that preacher's kids can get pretty wild."

"Not Rhea she is one of the good ones."

"She might have been before she met Dan."

Lucy poured a little coffee into her cup to warm up what was in there. "You should go find something to do."

"I was doing something I was talking to you."

"Keith, go to work."

"I thought you loved me?"

"I do but we have a customer so we will have to get to work."

"People keep dropping in here."

"Yes, which is good we need them to pay our bills."

Keith smiled. "We will go out for lunch today."

Dan drove down the road doing his best to think of anything but his talk with Lucy. If she knew Rhea was driving his car other people in town must know as well. They were going to be the talk of the town which was nothing new to his family. It seemed people were always talking about his family for one reason or another.

There were extra deliveries that day but nothing that took him out of his way. He had his route all figured out before he had left the yard. It was going to be a short day there was nothing to deliver after lunch. He had made plans for his free time which he was having second thoughts about now.

When Dan finished he called Rhea to let her know he was on his way to pick her up. He still had trouble believing that she wanted anything to do with him. He wasn't anyone just a delivery truck driver nothing more. She could do better than him he was sure of that.

It was not that there was anything wrong with him or his job after all he did okay. Still, there were guys in town who had more money for their own homes or apartments. Dan lived on his brother's farm, he was well known for all the wrong reasons. The entire town knew about his family they were all the same, trouble.

They were not bad people but in a small town that didn't always matter. People had to talk about something his family seemed to be the most interesting. To a lot of the people in town, Linda Fields was the most interesting. The problem there was talk about her always getting around to his father as well as his brother. Everything they did seemed wrong no matter what it was.

When Dan got to the farm Rhea was standing on the front porch looking at him. Dan stopped the truck by the garage and then walked back to the house. He went in and cleaned up then changed his clothes. Going back out to the porch he and Rhea got in the car. He had watched her walk from the porch to the car. No one else could walk like that.

Dan got in the car with a smile on his face. "Where do you want to go?"

"I thought we could go buy you your tractor."

"I have a couple of places that we can go to look at them."

"Did you have a type of tractor in mind?"

"I was thinking about something the size of an old Ford 8N they seem to work best around here."

Rhea nodded her head. "Doesn't Luke already have one of those?"

"He has three tractors I will just have one."

Rhea smiled at him. "You don't mind having the same kind of tractor that your brother has?"

"No, I want what I know to work, not something different."

"You know what you want all you have to do is find it."

"I could buy something Luke doesn't have but what would be the point if it didn't do the job? Besides I like the old 8N's they are dependable."

It took time to find just what he was looking for. They made a deal and then set things up to close the deal and pick up the tractor the next afternoon. Rhea seemed quite happy with the tractor though she was looking at other things. Dan wasn't sure what she was looking for and he was afraid to ask.

After they picked out the tractor they went out to eat then Dan took Rhea home. When they got to her house Rhea went inside leaving Dan on the front porch with her father. "Afternoon Pastor Conner, it turned out to be a very nice day."

"Is that because of the weather or because my daughter called you?"

"To be honest I would have to say it is a little of both."

"Rhea will be back out in a minute it takes her a bit to get the ice tea while talking with her mother."

"I enjoyed your sermon last Saturday."

"Last Saturday you were not in church."

"No Pastor, Rhea had a tape of it which she played for me Sunday afternoon."

"She is a very good girl."

"Yes Sir."

"Dad, go easy on him I like him."

Pastor Conner looked at his daughter and smiled. "He was just telling me he likes you too."

"That doesn't worry you does it?"

Pastor Conner smiled. "I never worry I let your mother take care of things like that."

"That is good to know."

"I will leave you two out here to talk. I am sure that your mother needs me for something."

Dan was smiling but he was nervous for several reasons. "I can't stay long I have to get back to the farm and care for the animals."

"Did my Dad scare you?"

"Not enough to make me want to leave. I just need to get back to the farm to care for the animals."

"Alright we will finish our tea and I promise I will let you leave."

"That sounds like you want me to leave in a hurry."

Rhea smiled. "Not really but we will see how things go."

Dan shook his head. "I think I had less to worry about when I was talking to your Dad."

"We will see how things go."

Dan left right after they finished the pitcher of tea. He was late getting back to do the chores which the animals let him know. There was no doubt that he was in over his head with Rhea. A smart man would try to slow things down. The way things were looking he wasn't a very smart man.

That night when Dan went to bed he had a hard time falling asleep.

He was thinking about Rhea and his family. People in town had been talking about his family for years. It was never good but that was because of his Dad he wondered what they would say after he died. There were times when he hated living in a small town.

That night his dreams were not dreams they were nightmares. There was nothing good about them. The people had no faces just shadows warning him that things were not what they seemed. Everything was going to come to a sudden end and he would find himself alone.

Dan was up early Wednesday morning he did the chores and then went over to his parent's house. They were not there but his sister was in the kitchen with a cup of coffee. Dan put the milk and eggs in the fridge and then got a cup of coffee.

Dan was still upset trying to get the dreams out of his mind. Why was he so worried? Nothing had changed yet. Yes, they all knew it was going to but it hadn't. He was sure it was too early for nightmares.

Sitting down at the table he smiled at his sister. "Emma, where are Mom and Dad?"

"Dad had a doctor's appointment so they left early."

"How are you doing?"

"I am getting used to the idea I guess. I am not crying as much as I was over the weekend."

"It isn't easy for me either I keep thinking it is all going to turn out to be a mistake even though I know it isn't."

Emma looked at her brother. "What are we going to do?"

Dan smiled. "You are asking me? You are the nurse you should know more about that than I do."

"I was thinking about what we should do after he is gone."

"We do what he would want us to do we look after Mom and just keep on going."

"It isn't going to be that easy."

Dan finished his coffee. "No, it is not going to be easy but we did it when our grandma and grandpa died it wasn't easy either. The scary part about it is that it isn't as hard as you think it should be. You get up you go to work you talk to people. After a time there are days when you forget that they are gone. The problem is they were not Dad and it will be harder when he is gone. I have to go to work."

"You say that then you just walk out the door?"

Dan smiled. "That was the idea, something tells me I should have moved a little faster."

"Dan, what are we going to do?"

"We take the days one at a time and we hope for the best while we prepare for the worst."

"You should go to work I need to get this place cleaned up."

"Emma, we will do what we need to do and we will do it together."

"I will remember you said that."

"You better."

Dan had wanted to be on the road early Wednesday morning. He had to get his work done as soon as he could so they could pick up the tractor that he wanted. If he had wanted to get an early start he shouldn't have stopped by his parent's house. Talking with his sister had taken too much time as well as keeping his nightmares in his head. Talking with her had not helped. His mind was still holding tight to his bad mood.

At lunchtime, he would swing by the bank to get the money that he needed. He was going to need to be in a good mood for that. When all his deliveries had been made he would pick up Rhea and together they would go get his tractor. At least that had been the plan before his mood had turned to crap. This was not the mood he wanted to be in.

It was as if he was finally a part of the farm even though Luke had always told him it was a family farm he had always thought of it as Luke's farm. He knew it was ridiculous but it was the way that he felt after all if everything belonged to Luke it was Luke's farm he had no stake in it. Once he bought a tractor of his own he had an investment in the farm. He was thinking of other things he could do that would make it easier on them as they tried to get things done around the farm.

At noon he got the money from the bank and then went back to work. He had fewer deliveries in the afternoon so he had everything done by four. He went over to Rhea's house where he found her father sitting on the porch waiting for him. Dan took his time getting out of the truck and then walked slowly up to the porch.

"Good afternoon Pastor, I am here to get Rhea she said she wanted to go with me when I get my new tractor."

"So she told me. She seems to think that you are doing good things at the farm."

"I am helping my brother it is his farm."

"Rhea tells me that you and your brother share the farm."

"Everything belongs to my brother I own nothing but that is about to change I will soon have my own tractor."

"It seems to me that your brother sees things a little differently than you do."

"I know he does but I want to earn my way not have him just give it to me."

"I see."

Rhea walked out of the house. "Dad, what are you doing to him?"

"Nothing we were just talking that is all."

"Dad, with you there is always more going on."

Pastor Conner smiled at his daughter. "Not every conversation is a sermon."

"Dad, this is not going to end up as a sermon or you and I are going to have a few words about fathers and daughters."

"Dan, if I were you I would be careful my daughter is set on her path we are only along for the ride."

"Yes Sir."

Rhea and Dan climbed into the truck then Dan drove it out of the driveway. "My Dad likes to talk don't let him bother you he is a father he can't help it."

"I know my Dad thinks he knows me and most of the time he does but not all the time."

"Parents can't help being parents."

"When do we get to be adults too?"

"Where are parents are concerned we may never be though I think that may not be as bad as it sounds. It all depends on how we see ourselves."

"Rhea, your father is not the only pastor in your family."

"You tend to carry certain traits of your parents with you as you grow up I guess."

"So it would seem though that is not always a good thing."

Dan looked at the road he was thinking of his father who had been a truck driver most of his life now Luke was driving long hauls something their father had not done that much of. Dan was driving a delivery truck which though it was short and not in their eighteen-wheel class was still a truck and he could drive a tractor-trailer if he had to. That was the part that worried him he didn't want to go out on the road for a week or more at a time but it was in his blood.

"Dan, I thought you were going to get your tractor from the ford place?"

"I am we should be there in a minute or two."

"I think it will be a little longer than that we just passed it."

Dan laughed. "I guess it is a good thing my brother is the long-haul driver in the family I can't seem to find my way around town."

"What are your nerves about the tractor you are going to buy or the fact that I am with you?"

"I want the tractor and I like the fact that you are with me."

"Is it my father?"

"No, it is my Pastor."

Dan turned the truck around and then drove to the place that sold the tractors and farm equipment. It didn't take long to pay for the tractor and then load it on the truck however it took just long enough so that the rain was already coming down by the time they had the tractor secured. As they drove toward the farm the rain came down harder and faster filling the streets.

The rain was falling faster than the drains could handle. Traffic slowed to a crawl while some people just found a parking spot to wait until the rain at least slowed down a bit. Dan drove slowly he was in no hurry he was only going to the farm. As he drove into the driveway at the farm the rain eased up a little but it didn't last.

Dan backed the truck up to the back door of the barn which served as a loading dock because it was a good four feet off the ground. Because of this Dan was able to back the tractor off the truck right onto the main floor of the barn. Once that was done Rhea drove the tractor out of the barn and then to the garage. Dan drove the truck to the front yard and then went into the garage.

Once they were both in the garage the rain started to come down harder. They stood there for a while watching the rain fall. "Rhea, you know if we run to the house now the rain will slow down or stop altogether once we are inside."

"If we stand here waiting for it to slow down or stop it will rain like this all night."

"That is one of Murphy's laws."

Rhea laughed. "Is that really one of Murphy's laws?"

Dan nodded his head. "I learned them all or at least how to tell when I heard one of them."

"Do I have to learn all about his laws as well?"

Dan looked at her a little surprised. "I didn't think you would believe in those laws."

"I don't but I think I will enjoy them just the same."

"So we make a run for the house?"

"They say that you get wetter if you run."

Dan laughed. "Do you really want to walk to the house when it is raining this hard?"

"No!" Rhea yelled as she ran toward the house.

Once they were both in the house they were soaked. They both needed a change of clothes. Dan had clothes he could change into but Rhea had nothing else to wear. Luke's ex-wife Linda had left some things behind so Dan got the box of clothes out of the attic so Rhea could find something to wear. There wasn't that much to choose from Linda hadn't left that much behind still there was enough for the most part.

Dan had put the box in the bathroom and then gone up to his room to change his clothes. When he got back to the kitchen Rhea was sitting at the table drinking a cup of coffee. Dan got a cup of coffee for himself and then sat down at the table too. "I see you found everything you needed."

"Not everything I needed but I can make do with what I did find."

"You look like you found everything you needed."

"I am glad to hear you say that I think."

Dan poured a cup of coffee and then handed it to Rhea. "What was missing?"

Rhea took the cup as she sat down at the table. "I think it is best if some things are not known by everyone in the room."

"I am sure you are right after all what good is life without a good mystery now and then."

Rhea looked at the clothes she was wearing. "I wonder what mystery you are referring to?"

Dan had several thoughts on that subject which he thought might be best kept to himself. He had never thought of himself as the guy who would be dating the Pastor's daughter. Rhea was not the kind of girl he thought of when he thought of the Pastor's daughter. The girl he pictured was a little more on the wild side. He thought of the movie and TV version of what she should be like.

"Would you like me to make you something to eat or would you like to eat out? We could stop someplace when I drive you home."

Rhea smiled at him. "Why don't you go take care of the animals and I will stay here and make us something to eat."

"The part where you do the cooking sounds good. I don't like the part where I go back out in the rain. Still, as long as you are doing the cooking I think I can live with your idea."

Dan grabbed his raincoat and then went out to the barn to care for the animals. Rhea checked the cupboards there wasn't a lot in them she was going to have to do something about that if she was going to be spending more time around the farm. She had promised herself that she would not let herself get too involved with Dan after all he wasn't the kind of guy she had seen herself with.

Rhea liked Dan but he didn't make it to church every week or at times not even every other week. He would get drunk from time to time as well as go out with more than one girl at a time. He didn't seem to have enough faith in his ability or his worth as a human being. He didn't seem to notice that he was smart enough to run the business that he was running.

Rhea was talking herself into something or was she talking herself out of something? She told herself she wasn't sure what she was trying to do. She was sure she was going to do something which usually meant her mother already knew what she was going to do. She was in trouble.

Dan finished milking the cows and then put it in the large milk can which they would keep cold then when it was full they would bring it to a friend who would make cheese with it. They worked hard trying to make sure that nothing went to waste. Most of the ideas were Luke's all Dan did was the manual labor around the farm.

Right at the moment, his main worry was Rhea. She was a good person maybe just a little too good for him though he was nothing like what people said he was. He had a bad reputation but that was because he didn't want just any girl he wanted the right girl. It only took a couple of dates to figure out if a girl was the right girl or not. So far all the girls had been the wrong girls.

Rhea might be different though it was hard to say because she was a different kind of girl. She wasn't trying to change him she seemed to be trying to help him to find himself. That was causing him great concern. He didn't know if she liked him for him or just if something broke that she needed to fix. He wondered if in time she would consider him fixed and then simply move on. She might just drive him crazy.

Dan went back into the house just as Rhea was getting the plates on the table. As he watched her he realized that there was so much more to her than just her good looks and warm smile. He thought she could be the one if she thought of him in that way which was the one thing he just didn't know.

Rhea finished putting everything on the table then she looked at Dan with a warm smile on her face. "Well, what do you think?"

"It all looks perfect to me."

Rhea's smile seemed to get a bit bigger. "I put my clothes in your dryer, I thought it would be best if I went back home with the same clothes I was wearing when I left."

"I think that would be best for both of us."

As they sat down to eat Rhea was thinking of all the times she had sat at the table. No one would believe the story if she told them everything that had happened at that table not even Dan. She wondered just how long it would be before she could talk about all of it to someone who knew what she was talking about.

Once they finished eating Rhea got her clothes out of the dryer and then went into the bathroom. Once she had changed back into her own clothes she went back into the kitchen. Rhea helped Dan put the dishes away then they went out to the car.

Dan drove Rhea home dropping her off but not staying. They had not talked much there seemed to be nothing to say. Yet that might not be true it just might be that there was too much emotion between them for either of them to say anything. Whatever was going on between them it would work itself out in time. That was what was bother both of them they were not sure what was going to happen next. Life was never easy they just didn't have time to deal with whatever this was Dan's Dad was what was important now. Everything else was going to have to wait, wasn't it?

Chapter 22

Wednesday morning it was raining very hard Luke ran into the truck stop wishing he could park the truck for the day. The rain didn't bother him but most people didn't do well in the rain which meant they all wanted to be in front of him. Speed was a bad thing any time but on wet roads, it would get you killed a lot quicker than it would on a dry road.

Luke had the thermos filled and then got their breakfast orders to go he wanted to get moving before something happened. It was a very good idea because it would be slow going they were going to need the extra time. When he got back to the truck he found that Emily had everything in the truck in its place ready to go.

He handed her everything then fired up the truck and headed west. It was raining hard but it had rained hard before there was no need to worry as long as he was careful. No matter what the weather a driver had to be careful. Everything seemed to be going well enough, Luke even managed to eat his breakfast before it got cold.

Emily was in a good mood talking about old friends from school as well as things they had all done before they became responsible adults. "Do you remember Ted Stanton?"

"Ted the brain."

"Yeah, that is him. Everyone said he was so smart."

"They were right until it came to zipping up his fly."

Emily laughed. "What about Mary Johnson."

Luke was laughing. "Steady Mary, she went out steadily with every guy in the school."

"Does that include you too?"

"She thought so we walked to class together a couple of times."

Emily shook her head. "There were a lot of people in our school who were normal so why are we talking about these two?"

"They were fun and they were nice but like the rest of us, they were not perfect. They were the ones that everyone talked about."

Emily thought about it for a moment. "What about Tina Wilson?"

Luke shook his head. "Tina the office rat, she was someone we all disliked."

"She died last year in a car crash."

"I heard about it she was working at the school in the office wasn't she?"

"Yes, she was liked by everyone at the school. It is funny how she didn't do well in High School until after she graduated."

"I think she always was a little ahead of herself."

"She was more responsible than we were I guess."

"So it would seem."

Emily looked out the window. "Do you remember Toby?"

Luke smile. "You were all over him I thought the two of you were glued together back then."

"Yes, we got older and more responsible."

"I guess we did."

Luke knew that was a stretch after all if they were that responsible he would never have married Linda. It was nice to have something to talk about as well as someone to talk to. By noon they were close enough to where they were going so they could stop for lunch. This was something he would not have done if Emily was not with him.

Once they were at the truck stop they sat enjoying their meal talking about the things they had planned before everything got messed up. They were laughing about how everything had turned out for them as well as what they had done to Jim at the bar before they left town. In a very short time, it seemed they had to get back on the road.

Gordon Dean was standing by their table looking at the two of them. He was surprised to see Luke with a young woman. Luke never seemed the kind of guy to pick up women at a truck stop. "Luke, where are you headed for?"

"Gordy, I am going west."

"You better call ahead they are closing a lot of roads out that way due to flooding. Interstates are open but a lot of the local roads are closing."

Luke went to the phone to call his boss. Helen answered the phone and told him the company he was to deliver to was closed. The road to the business was closed and water was running through their building. It was clear they would be closed for a day or two. He thanked her and then hung up. "The place I am going to has six inches of water running through it like a river. They told Helen they would call her when the rain stops. I have to call her tomorrow to see if I can make the delivery."

Emily looked at him worried about what they were going to do. "What are we going to do while we wait?"

"Stay here I guess they have a motel across the street with a large parking lot we can park the truck in. We can get a room and a good night's sleep at least."

"Why don't we just stay in the truck?"

"I want Jack out of the truck for a while he needs to be able to walk around for more than ten minutes at a time."

"Separate rooms?"

"Separate beds at least Jack doesn't like to sleep in a crowded bed."

Gordon Dean was still standing by the table though Emily and Luke seemed to have forgotten all about him. "If I wanted a room I would get over there right away before there are no rooms left."

"Thanks, Gordy, we will go over there right away."

Luke paid for their meal and then went after Jack. While he was doing that Emily ran over to the motel to get them a room. By the time Luke got to the motel with Jack and their bags, the young woman at the desk smiled at him. "You must be Luke Richardson. Your friend said you would be along with Jack. She described Jack quite well I would have known who you were even if I had never seen you before."

"Hi Mary, how are things going?"

"Not as well as they seem to be going for you I am still married to the same man. I am happy about that but we have been married six years and we have three kids. Our idea of a really good night is when we get to sleep the night away."

"What room are we in?"

"Three eighteen, it was our last room so I hope you are happy with it."

"Do you have room for my truck in the parking lot?"

"Sorry, you will have to leave it across the street."

Luke took the key then he went out of the lobby taking the elevator to the third floor. The room was halfway down the hall on the right which meant the window in the room would look toward the truck stop. He opened the door and stood there looking at the room it was just like every motel room. He closed the door set the bags down under the clothes rack then looked at the bed.

There was one bed a big bed but just one bed. Jack whined and Luke smiled at him. "Yeah Jack, I see it there is only one bed someone is going to have to sleep on the floor."

The bathroom door opened a bit and Emily stuck an arm out. "I need my bag."

"So come and get it."

"I just got out of the shower I am naked."

Luke set the bag by the door. "I have seen naked women before you know."

"Not me you haven't. We only have one bed in this room. I asked them about a roll-away bed but they seem to all be in use at the moment."

"I don't have a problem with one bed you can always sleep in the truck on your air mattress."

"You go sleep in your truck on your bed."

"I would but I already paid for the room."

"I will give you the money you spent on this room."

"No thanks, I think I will just stay here with you. I am sure we can work out the sleeping arrangements later."

"I will give you twice what you paid for the room."

Luke was looking at the bed thinking it would be nice to sleep on a big soft bed. "Thanks but I think I would rather sleep in this bed it is very comfortable."

Emily walked out of the bathroom and placed her bag beside Luke's. "We can share the bed."

"I guess we can but I sleep in the nude."

"Good I could use a good laugh before I go to sleep. By the way, I also sleep in the nude."

"Then why didn't you come out of the bathroom and get your bag?"   "I didn't want you to stand there speechless when you saw me."

"I don't think I would have been speechless I am sure I would have had something to say."

"I bet you would. What were you planning to do in this room while we are waiting for the weather to clear up?"

"The two of us in this room with one bed you mean?"

"Yes, that is what I mean."

"I thought we could watch TV or play a game of cards. Oh, we could play strip poker if you are not a sore loser."

"You are starting to get on my nerves."

"Let me know when you are down to your last one."

Emily gave him the evil eye. "I am pretty sure I am already there."

Luke smiled a kind of twisted little smile. "I hear they have a lounge where we could go down there and have a couple of beers."

"Why, so you can take advantage of me later?"

"No, I thought we could have a look around there might be a guy in there you want to hit with a stick."

"You mean besides you?"

"That is what I was hoping."

"What about Jack?"

"He quit drinking years ago."

Emily looked at him with a gleam in her eyes. "Okay you buy the first round then we will see how it goes from there."

"I am not carrying you back to the room. I will push you on a luggage cart if the need arises."

They left the room taking the elevator down to the first floor. Emily didn't say a word though she did stare at him with a smile in her eyes.

He did his best to appear not to notice. He was having fun as was she which was something neither of them had done much of as of late.

The lounge was not a lounge it was a bar, some stools, four tables, and twelve chairs. There was a TV with a ball game on as well as a few well-stocked shelves behind the bar. The beer was on tap and it was cold. They got two beers and then sat at one of the tables.

Emily looked around a little disappointed at what she saw. "It isn't much."

"No, but the beer is cold."

"There isn't any music."

"I can sing for you if you want music."

"I think it would be better if we watched the ball game."

"I thought you didn't like watching the ball game?"

Emily smiled at him. "I hate watching the ball game."

"I think you are going to need more than one beer if we stay down here."

"I may need to drink a case or more."

Luke ordered two more glasses of beer. "This should be fun."

"It could be if I can find a good-looking guy."

"I thought we talked about this already? I think it would be best if you just have a few drinks and let me find a good-looking gal to spend the night with."

Emily smiled at him. "Why were you looking to get married again?"

"Not any time soon."

"Your problem is you have no idea what you want so you take the first thing that you find."

Luke ordered two more beers and then looked at Emily. "I didn't take the redhead."

"You would have if you hadn't found out how old she was."

"I didn't take you."

"Not yet."

"Is that an offer?"

Emily laughed. "Fella, I will have you know I have standards."

"Okay, you were dating Jim and I am a whole lot better than him."

"Not tonight you're not."

"You want something to eat?"

Emily shook her head. "I can't eat while I am drinking."

"Fine, I can wait."

They sat there for over three hours before they walked slowly to the elevator. Emily pushed the up button then looked at Luke and smiled. "You want to come up to my room fella?"

"I would love to."

"Well, you can't I already have Jack up there waiting for me."

"Jack and I are friends we share almost everything."

"You don't share me, Bub."

Luke smiled but didn't say a word he was thinking that she was not the girl that he remembered from school. She wasn't wild as some people might think, she was angry. She was angry at Jim as well as her parents. They had convinced her that she was the one at fault even though she knew better. Luke knew she was as mad at herself even more than she was at anyone else. He was worried about what she would do once they were in the room.

When they were back in their room Emily smiled at Luke then her eyes got big and she ran for the bathroom. She didn't close the door she just got down on her knees in front of the toilet bowl. What came next was what you would expect. Luke stayed with her until she was asleep then he left Jack to watch over her.

Luke was not sure how he felt about how the evening had gone. He liked Emily she was a good person which is why she was having so much trouble leaving Jim. It wasn't just Jim it was her family too. She was being told she had to stay with him he was a good man. Why they didn't see the truth he couldn't say.

Luke went to the truck and lay down in his bunk thinking about the week they had gone through so far. It was nothing like he had ever expected it would be. He never had any real trouble on a run that was for sure. He liked Emily even though she was nothing like she had been when they were younger. That wasn't true because she was that person she had been but right now she wanted to be someone else.

He couldn't help but wonder just what it was that had made her want to get out of town with him and Jack in the truck. She was mad at everyone as well as herself he knew but there was more to it than that. She was searching for something but he wasn't sure what it was. It might be just her way of sorting things out so she could decide what to do with her life now that she had broken away from Jim for good.

Lightning flashed as thunder rolled across the night sky. Luke didn't want to think about what could happen between them he wasn't ready for a full-time commitment. Emily seemed to be running away from hers which meant the best thing he could do for both of them was drive off and leave her behind. He couldn't bring himself to do something like that to her. It would be impossible after all she had Jack.

She had gotten drunk because she wanted to forget even for a short time. Luke just wanted to get some sleep there was nothing else he could do. He was going to talk to Emily in the morning over coffee. That was his plan as he drifted off to sleep.

Chapter 23

Thursday morning like Wednesday morning it was raining the only difference was it seemed to be raining a little slower but it was still raining. The place Luke was supposed to deliver to was still closed, water was still running through the building. The loading dock parking lot was under close to a foot of water and still rising. There was nothing to do but spend the day at the motel and truck stop.

Luke climbed out of the truck and then went to the motel where he got two cups of coffee before going up to the room. He knocked on the door but no one answered so using his key he unlocked the door. When he went inside he was thinking about what he might find. As he closed the door with his foot he saw Jack sleeping on the bed alone.

Luke set the coffees on the desk and then went to the open bathroom door. Emily was lying naked on the floor between the toilet bowl and the bathtub her head under the sink. Taking hold of the door handle Luke paused to think about what he would do next.

He could just stand there holding the doorknob and wake her up. This could be very amusing when she woke up and then realized she was naked. She would turn red from head to foot and he could see it all. He would laugh she would never speak to him again and she would never get back in his truck again. The chances were very good she would never speak to him or anyone else again. Chances were good she might even move to a foreign country just to be sure no one would ever mention this to her.

He could put a towel on her before he woke her up which might make her feel a little bit better but not enough to matter. The chances were still very good that she would leave him and Jack to drive home in the truck without her. Though she might one day speak to him again the chances were good it would not be for some time.

His third option was to simply close the door then knock on it and tell her he had coffee. She would think she had closed the door so she would believe that she was the only one that knew she was naked on the bathroom floor. This idea could be more fun than the other two over some time. Leaving her in there naked was going to leave her with one big problem. How was she going to get her clothes without letting him know she was naked?

Option number three seemed to be the best way to go after all he would know more about her than she thought he did. Besides he was getting so he liked having her in the truck with him and Jack. He quietly closed the door and then knocked on it.

"We have coffee out here. Are you coming out of there before it gets cold?"

Emily woke up with a start, she started to get up hitting her head hard on the bottom of the sink. This almost knocked her out. She got out from under the sink and then just sat on the cold tile floor holding her head and crying softly. Her head hurt so bad she didn't feel the cold tile against her skin. Even though this was bad it didn't beat the shock she got when she looked up into the mirror. That was when she saw that she was naked. She looked into the large mirror hanging on the door. This was when she wished she was dead.

Emily moaned as she looked at herself trying to remember just what had happened the night before. They had gone down to the lounge to have a few drinks she remembered that much at least. There wasn't much after that she could remember clearly. They had both been drinking, there was one bed in the room and she ended up naked on the bathroom floor. No matter what had happened in between she couldn't remember any of it.

"Emily, the coffee is going to get cold."

"I'll be out in a bit. Jack needs to go out."

"Are you going to take him?"

"Luke, take your dog out I will be ready by the time you two get back."

"Come on out we will have some coffee first Jack is in no hurry."

"If I could come out and get it I would but I am not finished in here yet."

"Alright, I will even bring you back another cup of hot coffee."

Coffee was what she needed hot coffee or warm coffee she would even drink it cold. She heard Luke close the door as he left the room still she opened the door a crack just to make sure he was gone. She had wrapped herself in a towel before she opened the door.

Running out of the bathroom she looked for the coffee but there wasn't any in the room. Grabbing clean clothes she went back into the bathroom locking the door behind her. She took a fast shower which was when she discovered she had a cut on the top of her head. When the shampoo got into the cut it burned as if her head had been set on fire. Even after she rinsed the shampoo out of her hair the cut still hurt.

She yelled then cried then felt helpless and foolish. What was she going to do now? Telling the truth was out of the question Luke would never let her live that one down. It didn't matter what she told him he was going to pick on her anyway. Knowing that she decided the best thing she could do was to lie to him.

By the time Luke got back, she was dressed and just about done in the bathroom. She was going to have to have him look at her head just in case it needed stitches. It wasn't bleeding much but that didn't mean anything she knew that. What was she going to tell him? She didn't want to tell him the truth but she was going to have to tell him something.

Luke was sitting at the desk with two hot cups of coffee on the desk in front of him. "Emily, I thought you were going to be out of there by the time we got back?"

Emily walked out of the bathroom with a damp washcloth on the top of her head. "I would have been but I slipped in the bathroom and slammed the top of my head on the side of the tub. It is bleeding a little but I couldn't see how bad it is. You are going to have to look at it."

Luke got up looking at her surprised. This was something he hadn't thought he would be doing. He was not the medical person in the family. He was worried because if she needed help there was nothing he could do.

Emily took the cloth away and then tilted her head a little so he could see the spot where she had hit her head. "How does it look?"

"You split your head open alright? It isn't bleeding much but you are going to have to have someone look at it. You might need a stitch or two I really can't tell."

"You have got to be kidding!"

"No, I think you have to go to the hospital emergency room so that you can be sure you are okay."

"That is not going to happen."

"Then I suggest you start walking home because you are not going to die in my truck."

Emily looked at Luke. He wasn't kidding and she could also see that he was worried about her. "I don't think they are going to put stitches in my head."

"Maybe not but we are going to let a doctor tell us that."

"What about breakfast?"

"We will grab something on our way out of here they have some food downstairs with the coffee."

"They better have something more than a doughnut."

When they got down to the lobby there were no donuts left just blueberry muffins. The muffins were small which didn't do anything for Emily's frame of mind. Luke helped Emily into the cab of the truck and then dropped the dolly legs on the trailer before unhooking the lines from the trailer and securing them to their spot on the back of the cab. He pulled the pin on the fifth wheel then climbed up into the cab and eased the cab out from under the trailer.

As he drove toward the hospital he thought about what he had just done. He had never left a loaded trailer sitting alone at a truck stop before. He had never let a woman ride in the truck with him before not even his Mom or his sister. He had never found a naked woman on the bathroom floor in a motel room before. The whole trip was filled with firsts for him some good some not as good.

It was the first time Luke had ever been to the hospital it was a small place and very busy. They checked in and a nurse looked at Emily's head then she told them to have a seat. Time passed slowly as they sat waiting for someone to look at Emily's head. Even when they were the only ones left in the waiting room no one called them.

Emily was losing her temper as Luke did his best to keep her calm. It was almost five hours before Emily was called in to see the doctor they wouldn't let Luke go in the exam room with her so he sat in the waiting room watching the rain fall. They finally released Emily with two small stitches on the top of her head it was after three in the afternoon.

Luke stood up as Emily walked back into the waiting room. "Are you okay?"

"No, I have stitches in my head, a pounding headache and I am starving to death."

"You forgot that you are also cranky but it is okay I noticed that one right off. The rain has stopped."

"I'm not in the mood. I don't need a reason to slap the stupid out of you. With your mouth running like it is I have several good reasons to hit you already."

"You want to hit me because I know you get the rooms in a motel mixed up. You are supposed to jump on the bed, not in the bathtub. The bedroom has the bed the bathroom has a tub and other hard things."

Emily shot him a look that might have killed a weaker man if looks could kill. "What is that supposed to mean?"

"It means if you are going to fool around fool around in the bedroom there is less chance of ending up with stitches in your head."

"I still think I should hit you."

"I am hungry."

Emily was sure she should hit him but he had reminded her she hadn't eaten all day. "Fine let's go get something to eat before it starts raining again."

Together they went out to the truck. Luke helped Emily into the truck and then climbed up in the truck with Jack and Emily. He had spent most of his time going back and forth between the waiting room and the truck. He didn't like leaving Jack in the truck for a long time even if the ac was on.

Jack was a good dog he needed someone with him all the time. It might be time to start leaving him with his Mom when he was out on the road. Luke would miss him but it would be better for Jack. It might even be good for his Dad. He had heard that some people with cancer did better if they had animals living with them.

Emily didn't look at Luke she just sat quietly looking out the window as the rain started to fall again. She was thinking about finding herself naked on the bathroom floor. She now remembered going back to the room with Luke the night before. She had almost thrown up in the elevator twice once when it started moving and again when it stopped.

She had thrown up right before she changed into her pajamas. She had almost fallen in the bathtub while she was getting into her pajamas. She remembered falling into the bed the room still spinning as she fell asleep or passed out. She really couldn't remember what she had done. That was the last thing that she remembered before she woke up naked on the bathroom floor.

She thought it was odd that she would remember to close the bathroom door when she went in there. If the room had been spinning and she was feeling sick when did she have time to close the door? If she was throwing up why would she even care about the door? She could have kicked it shut while she was sleeping on the floor there really was no way to be sure about that.

There was one other question. Where were her pajamas? She had been wearing them when she went to sleep. When she woke up on the bathroom floor they were not with her. If she had taken them off they would have been with her. She had to stop thinking about it because it made her head hurt even more.

Emily had to stop thinking about the whole thing. Even thinking about breakfast was making her head hurt. Her head was hurting more even though they had given her something for the pain. She wondered what they had done the night before though she didn't think they could really have done anything. If she had been sick enough to sleep on the bathroom floor, what could have happened?

Luke had held the room for another night calling the desk from the hospital and explaining that they were at the hospital and would be around for at least one more night. He didn't tell the desk clerk Emily had been hurt in the motel he didn't see the need. Luke went to the drug store where Emily got her pain prescription filled. Once that was done he drove back to the truck stop. When he got there he hooked back up to the trailer before going inside to get something to eat.

While they were eating Emily looked at Luke with a very serious look on her face. "Where did you sleep last night?"

"I slept in the truck."

"Why did you do that?"

"You were looking a little green around the gills and I thought I would be better off in the truck."

"If you were in the truck why did I close the bathroom door?"

"Maybe you didn't want Jack to see you or maybe you thought I was still in the room. If I had to guess I would say it was just that you did it out of habit."

"I guess that makes sense."

Luke didn't say a word he just filled his mouth with food and then looked out the window. He had a feeling that one day the truth about what happened would be known. He was pretty sure he would at least tell her. Then again maybe he would just think back on it and smile.

With a slight smile on his face, he thought that if his brother and sister found out what had happened that would be too bad. They were going to find out one night that was for sure. Jack always talked too much after a couple of beers.

Chapter 24

Dan sat in the kitchen drinking his morning coffee looking out the window at the falling rain. The day before he had taken Rhea with him and they had picked up his tractor and brought it to the farm. There had been a small problem when they got to the farm it was the rain. By the time they got in the house, they were soaking wet. She had found clothes to wear in the things Linda had left behind. Linda's clothes were a little tight on her but they were good enough while her clothes were drying in the dryer.

Her clothes had dried so that she could wear them when she went back home. Dan had taken her home in his car. She had still gotten wet going from the house to the car but nowhere near as wet as she had been going from the garage to the house. The rain had slowed down a little by the time he took her home though it was raining hard again when she ran from the car to the front door of her house.

It was still raining Thursday morning with no sign that it was going to stop any time soon. The deliveries would have to be made with the box truck today. That was something Dan had done to improve the business since he had taken it over he had three trucks now. There was the flatbed his brother had started with, the box truck that he had bought and he had the car hauler that he had just bought off a friend who had closed the garage he had been running.

Dan had also been thinking about buying his friend's garage. It had three repair bays as well as an office. There was a room in the back with a bed in it. Dan thought that might be useful, in case he needed a place to spend the night away from everyone. He thought about it every time he drove by the place. Right then that was something he just didn't have the money for. It was a nice dream but for now, that was all it was. Dan finished his coffee and then placed his cup in the sink as he was on his way out to the truck.

As Dan reached the door his sister walked into the house. "Dan, we need to talk."

"Good morning Emma, won't you come in and join me for a cup of coffee?"

Emma walked into the kitchen where she poured herself a cup of coffee. Coffee in hand she sat down at the kitchen table. "I am afraid Mom and Dad have lost their minds."

Dan poured himself a cup of coffee and then sat down at the table with his sister. "What is going on?"

"You know that garage you have been talking about, Dad bought it."

"What the hell does he want with it?"

"He wants you to have it."

"He can't afford that."

"Mom told him that. He just smiled at her and then told her he would get a job when he gets to his new home."

Dan couldn't help but smile. "That sounds like Dad."

"He sold his truck and his pickup."

"What did he do that for?"

"He said it was so we wouldn't have to worry."

Dan was confused. "Worry about what?"

Emma shook her head. "He didn't say."

"Must be he paid for his arrangements once he is gone."

"I never thought of that."

"I wouldn't have if you didn't tell me all this."

Emma was still confused. "Where did he get the money for the garage then?"

"Knowing Dad he took out a loan."

"With his medical condition, that is crazy!"

"No, that is Dad. I am sure he has an angle he always does."

Emma got up and poured the last of the coffee into her cup. "I think you might be right about that."

Dan looked at his empty cup. "I need to go to work."

"What do we do about this?"

"I think that was nice of him but he needs the money. I will go over to the house and talk to him."

"You can't you are not supposed to know about it."

"I can't say anything because I am not supposed to know what he did. So why is it you know all about it?"

"You got it, just keep quiet."

"So why are you here?"

"I thought you should know. You just can't let them know you know."

"Then why did Dad tell you about it?"

"He didn't I heard him and Mom talking."

Dan sat back in his seat. "What the hell am I supposed to do?"

"Say thank you when he tells you."

"Emma, you are not helping."

"No shit, they are going to sign the house over to me."

"We can't let them do this."

"Dan, you think we can stop them?"

"No. I guess we can't but we should."

"I know but they want to do this for us and it would hurt them if we refused it."

"What are we going to do?"

Emma finished her coffee and then smiled at her brother. "I am going back home. I think you should go to work."

"I was going to do that before you showed up."

"What are you saying it is my fault you are going to be late?"

"Okay, that works for me."

"Later bonehead, you need to get to work while you can still get out of here. The water in the brook is looking more like a river. I think it will flood the road before the day is over."

Dan watched his sister go out the door thinking about what his Dad had done. So many times he had thought about that place wishing he could buy it. There was a parking lot behind and on both sides of the garage. He had always liked that about the place.

Dan was thinking that there were times when he seemed to want to do everything without thinking about where the money would come from. It was a good thing his Mom had taught him how to control the urges. The urge to jump into the dark he had gotten from his Dad. Still, he liked the idea of the garage but it was something he couldn't do on his own. He wished his parents had not bought it but at the same time, he was glad that they had.

He wanted to call Rhea and tell her but he couldn't because he wasn't supposed to know. He got in the truck and drove toward town still thinking of Rhea. He liked her more than he should after all he didn't know her that well. There were times when he knew he would be better off leaving town. Then he thought of his family and now Rhea, he knew he wasn't going anywhere.

Rhea finished her shift at the truck stop and then went home. She had no plans for the day other than going shopping with her Mom. They usually went every Thursday as part of her Mom's plan to avoid the weekend rush at the stores. It really didn't seem to help much as the stores were always crowded when they went no matter what day it was.

Rhea never got a cart of her own they just shared the one cart because she never bought much she just liked going with her Mom. They usually went as soon as she got home from work but everything was running late today which her Mom blamed on the rain. Rhea couldn't understand what the rain had to do with the fact that her Mom couldn't seem to find her car keys.

They were late getting started which was why the store was crowded or at least that was what her Mom was saying. Rhea had gotten her own cart and then walked along behind her Mom. As they walked they talked and filled both carts something Rhea didn't realize she was doing until she was standing in line at the checkout. She had known she was putting food in the cart she just didn't think about it until she was standing there at the checkout taking everything out of the cart.

Rhea realized she had set her mind to do this the night before when she saw how little food there was at the farm. She hadn't told anyone what she was going to do. She had done so good a job ignoring what she was doing while she was doing it that she even surprised herself. Her Mom never said a word about what she had done until they got to the car.

"I don't seem to have as much as you do so I will put my groceries in the trunk you can put yours in the back seat."

"Alright, can I borrow the car when we get the groceries put away?"

"You can take the car after you help me get my bags into the house. I can put everything away myself. You might want to get the things you bought out to the farm so you can get them to put away before Dan gets home from work."

Rhea smiled and blushed. "Mom, it is not what you think."

"You may be right about that or I might be right. I guess we will just have to wait and see how things turn out."

As they drove back to the house Rhea did her best to explain what she was doing as well as what she was feeling. "Dan is very nice and I do like him very much but he isn't the right one."

"I think you are right, he just is not right for you. Even though he seems to be a very nice young man you can never be sure about these things."

"Mom, he is nice but a lot of boys are nice. Right now he needs some help as he tries to work a few things out."

"Does he know you are just trying to help him find himself?"

"I am not helping him find himself he has to do that on his own I just don't want him to starve to death while he is working things out."

"I am sure you will have things all worked out by the end of the summer."

"Mom, you have that look."

"Which look is that?"

"The one that says you know something I don't know."

"Rhea, I am your mother I know a lot of things you don't know."

"Okay, but you don't know Dan better than I do."

"No, I don't know him as well as you do that is true."

"I always hate it when you agree with me it makes me feel like I missed something."

"I wouldn't say that you missed anything you simply don't have the same view of things that I have."

"Mom, now you are telling me I have a blind spot."

"Rhea, don't worry, you are doing just fine everything will turn out just the way it should."

"Now I know for sure you know something that I don't know."

"What I know is that we are home and we need to get these bags inside."

They were at the house and Rhea helped her Mom bring her groceries into the house then she ran back out to the car. The drive to the farm in the rain was slow which gave Rhea too much time to think about what her Mom had said to her. She hated it when she was left feeling ten years old again. Mom was always right even if she was wrong she was right in part and that was what scared her.

By the time she got to the farm, it was after four which was much later than she had planned on being there. She was going to have to hurry if she was going to get out of there before he got home. It wasn't that she didn't want to see him she just wanted him to get used to the fact that she had bought the groceries for him before she saw him. By the time she had everything where it went and was putting the bags under the kitchen sink, she heard the truck pull into the yard.

'She checked the coffee pot it was empty so she put it on the stove to make a fresh pot. Going to the cupboard she got out two cups and then got out two plates as well as silverware. Putting everything on the table she started to fix them something to eat. If she did this right he wouldn't notice the food she had bought until after she was on her way home. As she started cooking she forgot about her need to get out of the house.

Dan walked into the house hung up his raincoat then went into the kitchen. Rhea handed him a cup of hot coffee, he sat down at the table watching as she was cooking. "What are you making?"

"It is something for us to eat."

"I was hoping it wasn't for the cats."

"You know I was wondering why you had five cats and a dog."

"Jack isn't a dog he is part of the family. As for the cats, they sort of came with the farm. One was living here when Luke bought the place and the rest just moved in over time. Luke said they could stay as long as they worked and we haven't seen many mice around here. As for me, I like cats more than dogs they can take care of themselves and they don't bark."

"You don't like dogs?"

"I like dogs I just don't like the barking that comes with them. Had one back me into a corner when I was a little kid. It didn't bite me just stood there barking at me. I was scared to death while my brother thought the whole thing was very funny."

"Whose dog was it?"

"It was our dog."

"What did you have that the dog wanted?"

"Her bone Luke gave it to me then called the dog."

"That was a mean thing to do."

"Yeah, Luke liked to tease me when we were young it seemed to make him happy. Dad said we were just being boys but Mom thought it was mean and she got after him about it."

"So he stopped doing it?"

"No, he just did it when Mom wasn't around. He stopped as we got older I guess he got smarter or it wasn't as much fun as when we were younger."

'"Did he pick on your sister too?"

"Not nearly as much, though he used to get her to help him pick on me until she got wise to him. We teamed up on him for a bit but we were getting older and it was easier to just ignore him so we did that. There was a time when we didn't talk to him much at all but that ended once we got out of school."

"The food is ready."

"Good I am starving. What did you make?"

"Don't worry you are going to love it."

After they ate Rhea helped Dan with the chores then after she took care of the milk she went home. Dan stood by the window watching the lightning as it flashed across the night sky. There were a lot of things going through his mind as he stood there. He never thought that he would like veggie burgers and now he knew he was right. He liked vegetables but in place of meat, they just didn't work.

Dan also liked having Rhea around but he had a feeling they were just too different to be anything more than friends. After all, she seemed to want to be more of a mother to him than anything else and he already had a mother. He liked her and didn't want to lose her as a friend but he was sure that a friend was that she was ever going to be to him.

He put his cup in the sink and then started for his room. Tomorrow would come quickly so he had best get some sleep. As he started for the stairs he saw the car come into the driveway so he went back into the kitchen. Rhea walked in and stood looking at him.

"Did you forget something?"

"The road is flooded I can't get past that small hill about a mile from here."

"If that is flooded then the other road out of here will be too. You should call your parents and let them know. You can spend the night here in the spare room next to my room."

"I will call my parents then I am going to need a cup of coffee."

"That makes two of us that need coffee. I will make fresh pot while you are talking to your parents."

Chapter 25

Emma got back to the house early Friday morning after working back-to-back shifts at the hospital. Because of the heavy rain and flooding, a lot of people could not get to work. Other people had not been able to get home. Emma had stayed to help even though it had turned out to be a slow night.

Now that she was home all she wanted was a small cup of coffee before she went to bed. Her mother was sitting at the table having a small cup of coffee. "You had a long night?"

"Yes, a lot of people couldn't make it in because of the flooding."

"Your father is still out there helping people."

"You let him go out there by himself?"

"There was no way I could have stopped him even if I had wanted to."

"Mom, he has cancer! You can't just let him wander around town as if he were healthy."

"Emma, he is your father and he will do what he wants to do just as long as he can. If we stop him he will die before his time."

I know but I still worry."

"Don't worry he won't give his cancer to anyone."

"Mom, you are making fun of me."

"No, I am doing my best to laugh whenever I can because that is what your father needs us to do. I am also making fun of you a little."

"It is hard, I worry I can't help it."

"So do I but I don't let him know."

"I need to get some sleep."

"Emma, your Dad and I have signed the house over to you. It isn't final yet there is still some paperwork that we need to take care of but you are going to get this house."

"Mom, I don't know what to say. I love the house but it is your house."

"Yes, and soon it will be your house."

"I am not sure I should be the one to get the house."

"Your brothers do not need the house but you do."

Emma smiled. "Thank you."

"You are welcome. Can your father and I live here with you?"

"I don't know. Can you afford to pay the rent?"

"I can send you to your room little miss smart ass."

Emma smiled. "I will cover the rent."

Emma went upstairs and then went to the bathroom for a shower. While she was in the shower she cried. It was too much she wasn't going to be able to handle this on her own. What was she going to do as it all moved along through the course of cancer? Another bout of tears caused her to stay in the shower a little longer. She got out at last and smiled, at this rate she was going to wrinkle up like a prune.

She wanted to call Steve but he would be at work so the call would have to wait. She thought she could call Laurie but she really needed to get some sleep. Everything was going to have to wait she had to be up in a few hours to go back to work. Sleep was the important thing so she put her head down on the pillow.

Right after she put her head down the alarm went off. As she shut it off she looked at the time. It told her hours had passed but that couldn't be right she had just put her head down on the pillow. She sat on the edge of her bed wishing she could just go back to sleep for a few minutes. She knew if she didn't get up now she wouldn't make it to work on time.

Emma got up and then got ready for work even though it was hard. Once she was ready she went down to the kitchen for a large cup of coffee. There was no one in the kitchen so she stood by the counter drinking her coffee afraid to sit down at the table. Even though the coffee would help one cup wasn't going to do it.

Rachael walked into the kitchen; she looked at her daughter with a smile on her face. "Emma, you look like hell this afternoon. Are you going to be able to make it to work?"

"Mom, I was hoping for a little support."

"Are you having trouble standing up?"

"I am leaning on the counter, what does that tell you?"

Rachael smiled at her daughter. "Would you like me to make you something to eat?"

Emma shook her head. "No thanks Mom, I am too tired to chew right now."

"Would you like me to drive you to work?"

Emma thought about it for a few minutes then she shook her head.   "No thanks Mom, I will take some coffee with me. I think I will be fine once I get started. I am almost sure I will be okay."

"How is Steve doing?"

"He is fine why?"

"I was just wondering you haven't said much about him."

"He has been working as have I so we haven't talked this week."

"I see, well you are both hard workers."

"Yes, we are but we will see each other this weekend."

"I am sure you will talk with him this weekend."

Emma start feeling uncomfortable. "Mom, I am going to work."

Rachael smiled. "That is good."

Emma shook her head. "Mom, we are good friends and we have been for a few years now."

"It is always nice to have a good friend."

Emma filled her travel mug. "Mom, I need to get going."

"Linda called me yesterday. She was asking me when you were going to move in with Steve. I told her I wasn't sure the two of you were still talking. I really didn't want to tell her she knew more than I did about your plans."

Emma knew her face was red and she wanted to run out the door. She hated small towns and people who couldn't keep their mouths shut.

"I told him I couldn't move in with him now you and dad needed me here."

"I think your Dad and I can manage just fine if you want to live with Steve."

"Mom, why would I move out of a house you just gave me?"

"Are you going to ask Steve to move in here?"

"MOM!"

Rachael hugged her daughter and then watched her go out the door. When she was gone and the house was empty Rachael poured herself a cup of coffee. Sitting at the table she didn't make a sound but there were tears in her eyes. She found it hard to keep a smile on her face when she was alone with her thoughts.

As she sat there she was thinking about all the things Roger was going to miss. She was also thinking about the things they had planned to do that they were never going to be able to do. She was going to grow old alone and that thought made her mad. It wasn't fair! She had been a good wife and mother. She had gone to church, she had taken her children to church and now she was going to be left alone. It simply wasn't fair at all.

No, it wasn't fair to her family but that was nothing new in her family. Her mother had died before Luke was born and she lost her father a year later. Her sister had died young and her cousin had died a month after her sister. Life was not fair it was just life. She sipped her coffee and then got up to clean the house even if it didn't need it.

Roger was sitting in the office at the garage he had bought for Dan. It was quiet here no one knew he had bought it except Rachael and George. Rachael wouldn't come to the garage looking for him and George rarely left the bar. The truth was that the last thing he should be doing was spending time away from his family. Still, he needed time alone to think to plan to get his life in order.

How did one go about getting his life in order? How did one prepare to suffer and die? No matter how he tried he couldn't come up with a plan that made him feel any better. Life was not something you were supposed to plan for the last day.

Before he knew he had cancer his plan had been to work until he was old enough to retire. When he retired he would buy a small camper then with Rachael they would drive around the country. There were things he wanted to see and share with Rachael. Well, that had been the plan before the doctor had told him he would not be alive that long.

He thought about not fighting the cancer but that didn't seem right somehow. The plan was to cut him open and remove what they could. The doctor was hopeful but Roger was a realist. No matter what they found Roger knew he would be lucky if he lived more than three years. In reality, he probably would not live three years but he had to have a little hope.

He smiled a sad smile; he was hoping to live three short years. It wasn't long at all and yet he would be happy to have that long. Roger sipped his coffee. Had he expected to live forever? What had he thought about how long he would live? In truth, he hadn't thought about it at all. There was no need to think about it after all he had a plan nothing could happen to him until his plan was complete.

Well so much for that line of thought. Now he had to make a new plan a short-term plan that only lasted two years. Anything he got after that he would live day to day. Day by day until the days were all used up.

Roger looked into his empty cup. His time was running out and there was nothing he could do about that. He could not change the past or the future. Still, he could walk up the street to the doughnut shop for another cup of coffee. Roger smiled as he thought about another cup of coffee. All the things in the world at this point in his life and all he wanted was another cup of coffee. As he walked along the street he laughed until tears came to his eyes. Who was ever going to notice his tears in the rain? He was Roger Richardson he didn't cry.

By the time Emma went to work her father was on his way to the Circus Bar to talk with his friend George. It had been a good day for Roger he had learned to laugh again. He knew it would not last but he had it back for now. George would help him hold onto it for a while. They had come a long way together.

The rain had stopped the wind had picked up the clouds were moving out. Roger walked into the bar and right to the table where his friend was sitting. "George, you look like hell."

"So do you."

Roger smiled. "We need a beer."

"Damn right we do."

"Just one?"

"We have to start somewhere."

"So we do."

"How was your day?"

Roger smiled. "I started rough but I found a smile or two as the day went on."

"You found a mirror. Your face always makes me laugh too."

"Have you looked at yourself lately?"

"Nope, they put the mirrors up to high for me to use."

"Just as well Linda would not want to spend her day picking up broken glass."

"You want another beer?"

"That depends, are you buying?"

"Hell no, I bought the place so I could drink for free."

"Free beer tastes best."

George smiled. "You are right about that."

Roger laughed. "After all these years you would think we would have learned to handle life's little disappointments better than we do."

"Oh hell we are broken old men and we still handle things better than most people."

"I know but I would like to see someone younger than us with at least half the brains we have."

"Our kids are about half as smart as we are."

"In that case, we have done well we should have a drink to celebrate."

"I have to say that you come up with ideas that sound good to me."

"It is a gift."

"It is bull shit."

"It is still a gift."

Chapter 26

Dan was up early Friday morning he got the chores done and then went back to the house for his morning coffee. Rhea was already up she had showered, dressed, and had breakfast on the table. He got cleaned up and then sat down to eat. The food was good the coffee was hot it was the perfect start to the day. The only downside to the day was the fact that it was still raining.

Rhea had already taken care of the milk while Dan was getting cleaned up. The eggs would wait until after they ate. They didn't talk at first as Rhea was waiting for Dan to say something about the food or the coffee. When he didn't say anything she thought it was time to get him talking.

"Now that we have spent the night together a second time my Dad will expect us to get married."

Dan sipped his coffee doing his best not to look scared to death. "I was thinking we would be getting married now. After all, with your Dad being the Pastor it would look bad if we didn't. So would a week from now be good for you or would you like a little more time?"

"I think a week from now is a bit of a rush, don't you? I mean people would start thinking we had to get married."

"They are going to do that anyway after all you are the Pastor's daughter and I am my father's son they can't get much farther apart than that."

"I like your Dad."

"Most people do but he is never going to be a deacon in the church."

"I don't think that matters to us."

"No, I guess not, after all, we are going to be busy getting to know one another once we are married."

Rhea laughed. "Dad isn't that bad though he will have a few questions when I get home this afternoon."

"Your Mom might want her car back before then."

"No, she told me to take it to work she had no plans until this evening."

"If you need me for anything just give me a call."

Rhea looked at Dan she was smiling even though she didn't feel like it. "Are you telling me that one night together and we are finished?"

"I was thinking that you will most likely be under house arrest after spending the night with me again."

"I see what you mean, if I come up with an escape plan I will call you."

Dan looked at her thinking about the time they had been spending together. It seemed as though they had been together longer than a week. Still to be honest they were not together they were just getting to know one another. They had done a lot of things together but they had only gone out on two dates.

Dan went to work while Rhea was cleaning up the kitchen. He had told her not to worry about it but she needed to do it. She had a lot on her mind and it helped her to think if she kept busy. The biggest problem she had right now was that she was thinking too much.

Rhea was a helper she couldn't seem to keep from helping people she liked. Dan was someone she had always liked even though he seemed to be a little on the wild side. If you believed all the stories about him, that is. Rhea was learning that he was not as wild as people seemed to think he was. The truth was he was really quite nice.

Her plan to help him was not going the way she had thought it would. She liked him more than she thought she would though she had no plan to marry him. She might one day though she did want to get to know him a little better before she thought about that. He made her happy because he didn't seem to want anything from her. He seemed to like her as much whether she was wearing jeans or a dress.

He didn't seem to mind who her father was even though they joked about it from time to time.

Dan liked her cooking but he also seemed to like to take her out to eat. He listened to her no matter what they were talking about he even laughed at most of her jokes. He laughed because he thought they were funny not because of how she looked. His only plan seemed to be friends which were starting to worry her. She had found a friend which was not what she had been looking for. She had expected one thing and found something else she wasn't sure what she should do next.

Dan spent the morning making his deliveries doing his best to think about anything but Rhea. They had joked around about getting married and he was having a very hard time thinking about anything else. He didn't want to get married but he liked having her around. He could take her to a fancy restaurant or the Circus Bar and she would fit right in.

She helped around the farm as if she had lived there all her life and she liked it. No matter how he felt about the whole thing it just seemed too good to be true. She was as close to perfect as she could get so there just had to be something wrong with her. No matter how hard he tried he just couldn't think of one good reason to get rid of her. That in itself might be a good reason. He had thought enough about it no one was that good. No one could be that good, no one but Rhea.

By noon he was sure he was going to go crazy he hadn't been able to think about anything but Rhea all morning. The funny thing was he was to the point where he thought that was okay. He had had enough for one day so he made his last delivery and then went home.

The rain had stopped around nine in the morning, and the weather forecast called for four days of sunshine. Dan could see no reason to just sit in the house so he got Luke's tractor out and started mowing. If everything worked out he could cut even more tomorrow afternoon. It would be easy for he could do it while his sister and his Dad were raking and bailing the stuff he was going to cut now. It was simple enough all he had to do was quit when it was time to do the chores.

The plan was simple all he had to do was keep busy as long as he could. By the time he stopped, it would be dark. It would be too late to call Rhea at home he would have to wait until tomorrow. That was a good plan just stay too busy to see her.

All at once, Dan realized he had been so busy thinking about Rhea he had forgotten about his father's cancer. He was planning on working with his father to avoid Rhea. What kind of son was he that cared more about some girl than he did about his poor sick father?

The afternoon went by quickly and Dan was late getting to the barn to take care of the afternoon chores. As he got off the tractor Rhea walked out of the barn a smile on her face and a milk bucket in one hand. She waved to him and then went on with the chores. Dan stood there for a minute not sure what he should do. There was no need for him to stop mowing Rhea was doing the chores so he got back on the tractor.

He went back to mowing around and around the field until it started to get dark. Parking the tractor near the barn Dan stood there wishing he had a reason to stay out of the house until she left. He shook his head as he started toward the house he knew she wasn't going to leave until she saw him.

"Dan, I was beginning to think you were going to be out there all night."

"No, I was out there a little longer than I should have been but everything was going so well."

"Wash up so we can eat I have to get home before it gets much later."

Dan got cleaned up thinking about how natural it seemed for Rhea to be there. He was thinking about a lot of things mostly he thought about Rhea. He needed to slow things down even though he didn't want to.

Dan sat down at the table. "I didn't expect to see you today. I am grateful for the help."

Rhea set the food down on the table and then took her seat. "I wasn't going to come out here this afternoon but then I was here so I put myself to work."

"I am a bit confused."

"I was going for a ride after work then I was going to go home but instead I came here."

"Sounds a lot like my day I did the whole thing in a fog."

"We should talk about this."

"We should but where do we start?"

Rhea smiled at him they seemed to be having the same thought. "We need to talk but not tonight, not about this we just don't have that kind of time tonight."

"I think we need to talk soon before we do something without thinking."

"Dan, you think we are going to do something that crazy?"

Dan reached across the table and took her hand. "I think it could happen right here right now if we are not careful."

Rhea drew her hand back slowly. "I think I best get these dishes washed so I can get home I am already late."

"Don't worry about the dishes I will take care of them."

"I think you are right. Will I see you at church in the morning?"

"I will see you early say about eight? We can talk some before church."

"That sounds good I will see you then."

Rhea ran out the door then Dan cleaned off the table putting everything in the sink. He poured himself another cup of coffee and wished he was a smoker he sure could use a smoke. His whole life was going to change direction in the morning and he had no idea what was going to happen.

How could any of this be happening now? His Dad had cancer and he couldn't stop thinking about Rhea. What kind of a son was he? How could he be so heartless as to just forget about his father?

He was angry with himself as he did the dishes. How could he be thinking about anyone other than his father? What would he do when his father was gone? How could he think of himself and his future when his father was dying?

By the time he went up to bed he was so angry with himself that he didn't know if he could sleep at all. He knew his parents would want him to get on with his life. They would be happy for him but was it right? Was this the right time for him to be thinking about his own life? His father would smile and his mother would tell him she was happy for him.

How could he be happy at a time like this?

Chapter 27

Friday morning Emily and Luke had breakfast at the truck stop before the sun had even started to rise then they headed off along the road. The rain had stopped during the night so they had been cleared to deliver the load at noon. At noon they arrived to find the loading dock parking lot still had half a foot of water in it but that didn't stop Luke.

There was no visiting at this stop everyone was very busy cleaning up after the flooding of the building. They unloaded the trailer quickly so they could get him out of their way as they were still getting some water out of the building. It would take them at least a week to get everything back to normal if there was no more rain.

Luke grabbed a load going east then drove through the afternoon and into the night to get it where it had to go. They delivered that load just after nine that night. They couldn't pick up another load until morning but the place they had to go to get it was not far from where they were. Luke stopped at an all-night diner to get them something to eat. It was a small place which was fine he didn't want to live there he just needed something to eat.

Emily went inside and got them a table while Luke took Jack for a tour of the area. Jack wasn't impressed but then he had seen it all before. Usually, by this point in the week, they were home or a lot closer to home. Jack had his own worries after all Emily had been in his seat all week.

Emily was sitting in the diner looking at the menu when she saw

Luke walk through the door. She also noticed that the waitress who seemed to be about their age was looking at him too. She seemed to have been working too much she was looking at Luke as if he were on the menu. It was none of her business after all she had no claim on him they were just friends.

Still if "Bedroom Eyes" didn't get her eyes off Luke there would be trouble. The woman could keep her mind in the gutter as long as she kept her hands off Luke. Emily thought she was going to slap the woman up just for the hell of it.

Luke ordered a soda and then joined Emily at the table. The waitress walked to a table as she was going to get his drink. Her eyes were on him not watching where she was going. With a waitress like that there was going to be trouble one way or another unless she got her act together.

"It serves her right."

"Emily, what are you mumbling about?"

"The waitress just walked into a table because her mind isn't on her job."

"Nora is okay she has been working here about three or four years I don't remember which it is. She told me once but it wasn't that important so I seem to have forgotten what she said."

"She likes you a lot."

"She does? I wish I had known that before I might be married again."

"You like her?"

"I like to look at her and I have talked with her a little not sure if I like her enough to marry her. You never know about a person until you really get to know them. You know how it is. You have to spend some time with a person before you know who they really are."

"You mean you have never asked her out?"

"No, though I have thought about it. The trouble is she is here and I don't live around here. I see no point in starting something that is going to be a long-distance thing. You know what they say about long-distance romances they never work out."

Emily started laughing, she was tired and she was laughing way too hard. "You are a long-haul truck driver on the road for at least a week at a time. Any relationship you have is a long-distance relationship."

"I guess you are right but I have a home I would want my wife there not a couple of hundred miles away."

"You mean you don't think she would move from here? Do you want me to ask her for you?"

"No, I don't want you to talk to her unless you are ordering something to eat."

"So you have thought about her in a caveman kind of way."

"Emily, I am twenty-four years old and single I think of most pretty girls in a caveman kind of way but that doesn't mean I would really drag them off to my cave."

"I noticed that, what does it take to get you moving? Do you have to see a woman naked before you make a move?"

Now it was Luke's turn to laugh right after he spits soda across the room as well as choked. He laughed until tears came to his eyes and his side started to hurt. When he finally calmed down he looked at her still smiling. "There are times when I wouldn't even do it then I would have to say."

"I don't understand you. I was afraid you were going to turn out like Jim but I don't think you even like me."

There was a time when I could have but that was before Linda taught me a few things."

"She taught you woman can't be trusted?"

"No, she taught me to take my time and get to know a person before I make what is supposed to be a lifetime commitment. Last Friday if anyone would have asked me if I knew you I would have said I did because I thought I did. This week I have seen a side of you that I never could have imagined existed.

"You beat Jim with a cue stick; you drink like a sailor that hasn't had a drink in months. You are running away from everything and everyone important to you. It seems you have no idea where you are going. We are headed home and you are not sure you really want to go back there. I thought I was the real lost kid in the woods until you came along."

Emily didn't cry she just sat there looking at him as if she were seeing him for the first time. "I never realized you still blame yourself for Linda leaving you, even though you know it isn't true."

"Marriage is supposed to last a lifetime, mine didn't. I would have to say I did something wrong."

"Like what?"

"I should have gotten to know her better; I jumped in before I realized just what it was I was jumping into. I didn't think it would end because I thought it couldn't. I know that doesn't make sense now but it made sense when I was nineteen. You think you know everything when you are a teenager. Even if you are sure a thing won't last you really can't see beyond the day."

"I understand that I felt the same way when I first started going out with Jim. We learned the hard way that life sucks and then you die. It may be a bad way to look at things but it is the way it seems to be."

"Mom says that life is what you make it which still leaves me in a bad spot."

Emily looked out at the darkness. She had a lot on her mind none of which seemed to go along with what they were talking about at the moment. "It is getting late we should eat then get some sleep."

"You can sleep on the bunk tonight I will sleep on your air mattress."

"No, that is okay I will sleep on the air mattress, I like it."

"I had planned to ask you to share the bunk with me at one point on this trip."

"Why didn't you ask me?"

"I realized I just didn't know you well enough."

"Since when do most people our age care about a little thing like that?"

"Since my marriage fell apart I have learned that you have to take your time and make sure you are with someone you care about. You want to be sure that person cares about you as well."

"I guess you are right after all I would be doing is going from Jim to you with no real time to think about anything."

"Now you have it."

They ate in silence doing their very best to ignore one another as they ate. They both knew where they were and they were both worried after all this could be their only chance to get it right. No matter what they did next it was a roll of the dice it was always a roll of the dice. Six days or six years it was always the same you just never really knew for sure what was going to happen in the long run. You had to just take the whole thing on faith and hope you got it right.

Emily looked at Luke he had a small piece of something on his chin. "You know if you go too slow trying to make sure you get the right person that person might just pass you by."

Luke looked at her wondering just what it was she was trying to say. Was she talking about Nora or was she talking about herself? The whole thing was starting to give him a headache. "I guess that is true though I never thought of it before."

Emily finished her meal first then she went out to the truck and took Jack for a long walk. She had come with Luke because she told herself it felt like the right thing to do but the truth was she had not wanted to be alone. Now she thought she might have been better off alone. Even if that were true it was a little late for that now. She didn't want to go back to the truck but she had no place else to go. She needed to get away she needed time to think.

Luke sat in the diner looking at the waitress. She was very good-looking too good-looking to still be single or unattached unless she liked being free. Some people liked the single life. They could do whatever they wanted with whoever they wanted. The last thing he needed was another one of those types. One had been enough for him he needed someone who believed in the whole forever thing. It didn't have to be perfect it just had to be two people working together and doing their best to get along.

Trust was the hardest part for a lot of people for one reason or another but other things got in the way. Money was one of the big things that people fought over. It didn't matter if they had a lot or a little they seemed to have to fight about what they should do with it. There was always something to fight over unless two people learned to work together. That could be hard if you didn't know how to talk to one another. You had to know one another as well as trust one another to pull that one off.

Luke was in the diner Emily was standing by the truck. The only one that was happy was Jack he had his seat back. It was getting late and the only thing that Emily and Luke could agree on was the fact that they didn't seem to agree on anything. It was going to be a long night if they just didn't move.

At last, Luke walked out of the diner as Emily stood by the truck watching him. "Emily, how is your head?"

"It is fine even though I still have a slight headache which has nothing to do with the stitches in my head."

"We should get some sleep."

"I don't want to be alone anymore."

"Neither do I."

"So what do we do about it?"

"I guess we should just keep each other company until we can figure out what to do."

"You don't mind hanging out with me?"

"No, I am getting used to you."

Emily smiled a shy type of smile. "Is that good?"

"Well, it isn't bad."

It was early Saturday morning Luke stood outside the truck looking up at the dark sky. There was a faint light in the eastern sky as the very first light of day began to push the night sky back to make way for the sun. Luke had seen this many times before still it never seemed quite the same as it had before. Like a snowflake the start to each day seemed different and unique he thought.

The night had been long only because he hadn't slept much but then why should the end of his trip be any different than the start of it had been? He had a lot of regrets in his life he thought but none that would matter when he was in his forties. Only one was memorable and even that one would fade with time though not completely. Linda was not something he would ever forget even though he might wish he could forget her. He really wanted a coffee but he had promised Emily he would wait for her and she had walked off with Jack.

Emily was walking along the sidewalk with Jack not noticing anything around her she was lost in thought. She had a lot to think about, Jim had dumped her on Thursday night right after a lovely meal at the best restaurant in town. He finished his meal had two more drinks then told her he had found someone new and he wasn't waiting for her anymore. With that, he wished her well then got up and walked out leaving her to pay the check.

Friday she had put in for a week of vacation which was okayed as she knew it would be. It seemed best to get an early start on her vacation. She finished up her work early then she took the afternoon off as well. She left her car at the house and walked down to Main Street.

Emily had no idea what she was going to do with a week off from work. The good news was that she had the rest of the afternoon to figure it out. How hard could it be to figure out how to spend a week out of work? It turned out to be a little harder than she had thought it would be.

By the time she got Jack back to the truck, the eastern sky was a beautiful light blue. The diner waitress was standing out front having a smoke and Luke was pacing by the truck. She put Jack back in the truck and then looked at Luke with a smile on her face. "Were you worried about us?"

"No, I need to go to the bathroom and you were taking too long getting back. Let's not stand here we need to get in there."

"I thought you boys just found a tree?"

"Not where people can see us. You can get arrested for that these days."

"I never thought you guys worried about a thing like that."

"We do we just don't talk about it."

"There is a bucket in the truck right?"

"Order me a coffee to go with my steak and eggs please."

Emily sat down at a table near the window where they could keep an eye on the truck. It seemed odd to her that he had let her walk around with Jack but he had to keep an eye on the truck at all times. She might understand the value of the truck and the load but she thought she should be worth more after all you could buy another truck.

The waitress brought the coffee and took the breakfast order all before Luke made it to the table. "I am sorry I didn't realize you had to drop a load I thought you just had to pee."

"That is what drives me crazy when it comes to you gals. The sun isn't even up yet and you are already talking shit."

"We wouldn't but you guys seem to like to get the crap out first thing in the morning."

"It is always good to be regular they say."

"You are so full of it!"

"Not anymore I am a morning person."

"You are going to be a dead person if you keep this shit up."

"You are the one holding onto it I delivered my load already."

"You are a pain in my ass."

"No, that it is not me that is you. It will go away once you make your daily deposit."

"I give up."

That is the reason why you still have pain. You have to learn to let go of your inner discomfort so that you can enjoy the day."

Emily was laughing as she shook her head. "I don't care about that I am still going to kill you."

"That is going to cause a lot more shit for you."

"Will you knock it off!"

Luke smiled at her. "I could but then what would we talk about?"

"We could talk about last night."

Luke sipped his coffee and then looked out the window at the truck. "We were tired and we should have gotten more sleep than we did."

"Meaning you would rather have been sleeping last night?"

"No, I just mean we should have gotten more sleep."

"It was a long day."

"We should get home around noon today if everything goes right."

"Luke, I don't think I am ready to go home just yet."

"Emily, I am not staying out here another week Jack needs to spend some time out of the truck."

"Right I forgot about Jack for a minute."

"How could you forget Jack he gave up his seat for you?"

"I guess it is because I haven't finished my morning coffee."

"Do you remember who I am?"

"Yes, though I have been doing my best to forget this whole conversation we have been having."

"I can understand that I mean it really stinks doesn't it?"

"I swear I am going to kill you before the day even gets started."

Luke smiled at the waitress and thanked her as she refilled his coffee cup. "We should be on the move if we expect to get home today."

Emily sat back in her seat looking at him thinking about what she was about to say. "I am not ready to go back home today."

"I believe you already said that but we are going to go home just the same."

"Can't we deliver just one more load before we go back?"

"We could but I have to get home to the farm."

"I know but Dan is there and he can hold things together for one more day I am sure."

Luke shook his head. "It is a good thing you don't travel with me every week I would never get home again."

"I could you know."

"You could what?"

"Travel with you every week."

"You could but you have a job with your family and I really don't think you want to give that up."

"Luke, Jim is there and I do not want to see him again."

"He isn't going to quit because you are there so why let him push you out?"

"You are going to try and shame me into keeping my job?"

"No, I was just asking you a question the question everyone else is going to ask if you quit your job."

"Can we talk shit again?"

"I thought we still were."

"Now I know why you drive a truck you couldn't make it as a comedian."

"That is right but it wasn't because my jokes were not funny it was because my dummy ran off on me."

"I know what that is like I lost mine last week."

"I heard something about that."

Emily had a smile on her face even though she was scared to death. She could honestly say she was doing something she had never done before. She felt like she was back in school with a boy she liked even if they had never really talked to one another. It was crazy but it felt good at the same time.

Luke put his coffee cup down on the table and then looked at what food was left on his plate. He remembered the first time he saw Linda and all the time from then to the day that she left. There was nothing there that was like this morning. What they had shared was a living space with a little something extra that they thought was marriage. Last night and this morning had been like nothing he had ever expected. It was something he would remember all his life in those times when the world was crashing around him he would remember this time.

Luke was still thinking about it as he pulled back out onto the road after he had picked up his load. The load was to go to a warehouse in southern Connecticut. He headed that way still thinking that he had to get home even as he headed southeast.

They drove all day to get where they had to go late in the afternoon. As it turned out there was a crew working overtime so one of them unloaded the truck and did the paperwork. Luke thanked him and then headed for the closest truck stop. They both needed to sleep they also needed to eat they hadn't had anything since their early morning breakfast. He was going to have to figure out what he was going to put in the log as well.

When they got to the truck stop Emily took Jack for a walk while Luke worked on his log book. Emily was glad to be out of the truck they had barely talked at all. They had talked a little about water, and weather and they had stopped a couple of times for Jack. They drank soda and water while they ate some crackers.

She had been left to think about the night and the morning that they had shared. It had been a special time even though most people would say it was really nothing special at all. No matter what anyone else might think she was sure they had shared something special. Still, they had never said anything about what they were going to do next if they were going to do anything at all. That was the thought that was driving her crazy as it had been all day.

Emily put Jack back in the truck then climbed in and took her seat. "Did you get it all figured out?"

"It took a little doing but I got it all figured out."

"You lied to it a little."

"Baby, I lied like a rug!"

"I thought you said you couldn't do that?"

"You aren't supposed to but a friend of mine taught me a couple of tricks that work as long as you don't try to push it too much."

"What do we do now?"

"We eat then we call it a day and get some sleep. I don't know about you but I have had enough for one day."

"You mean to say it has only been one day?"

"I am afraid so. If you don't believe me just check the log."

"You just said you lied to the log which means the log would lie to me."

"You talk a lot."

"We really need some sleep."

Luke smiled. "Now you are talking."

Chapter 28

Dan was up early he took a shower then went out and took care of the animals. When he got back in the house he heated a cup of day-old coffee and then started a fresh pot going. He got out some good clothes and then took another shower. By the time he was dressed for the second time the coffee was ready so he poured himself a cup and then sat down at the table.

He was as nervous as a kid going to a new school for the first time. What was going to happen? Was she going to like him or was she going to kick him to the curb? He knew he liked her but that didn't mean anything if she didn't like him in the same way. There were so many things that could go wrong he wasn't sure why anyone would put themselves through this ordeal more than once.

Sitting there thinking about it he realized this was not the first time he had ever felt like this. There had been that girl he liked in the second grade. Though he never talked to her he had loved her just the same. She sat in front of him all year she even sat in front of him on the bus. During the summer she had moved away which had broken his heart. He could still remember her long blonde hair but not her name.

Dan got another cup of coffee and then looked at his watch if he left now he would be an hour early. It would be better to be on time rather than early there was no point in rushing to meet her just so she could tell him to get lost. He had to do something just sitting there was starting to make him crazy.

Dan finished his coffee and then left the house even though he would be an hour early he had to do something. He could always stop by the coffee shop to kill a little time. Dan couldn't believe he was going so crazy after all she wasn't the first girl he had ever dated. If she dumped him this morning that would not be a first either so why was he making this such a big deal? Whatever was going to happen was going to happen no matter whether he worried about it or not. That was when he realized they had never said where they were going to meet.

Rhea was up early her morning shower was a little longer than usual though not that much longer. She picked out three different things to wear tried them all on in front of the mirror then went back to the closet for three more outfits none of which seemed right. In the end, she settled on her newest dress. She had bought it to wear to church. It was a plain light blue dress there was nothing special about it.

Rhea fussed with her hair trying to find a way to make it look just right. In the end, she settled for simply brushing it out as she did every day. Going down to the kitchen she poured herself a cup of coffee and then looked at the clock. If she left right now she would be an hour early. She was going to have to wait a little longer so there was time for a second cup of coffee.

Her Mom walked into the kitchen got a cup then made herself a cup of tea. "Rhea, you look nice."

"Thank you."

"You are up early this morning do you have plans?"

That was when Rhea realized that she did have plans to meet Dan but they had not said where they were going to meet. "I do I am just not sure where I need to go."

Her Mom smiled at her and then sipped her tea. As she looked at her daughter she set her cup on the table. "I would think the two of you would have talked about that if you were making plans to meet this morning."

"I was in a hurry to get home."

"So it would seem. You need me to give you a ride but you have no idea where I have to take you."

"I guess I should have taken the time to find out where I need to be this morning."

That was when her Dad walked into the kitchen. "Rhea, is there something we need to talk about?"

"Dad, I already have one problem this morning, and Mom and I are talking it out."

"I have a problem this morning too. I want to know why Dan Richardson is sitting on the front porch."

Rhea and her Mom smiled. "Dear, I will explain it all to you while you are having your morning coffee."

"Dad, you are the greatest."

Rhea hugged her Dad and then went out the front door. He stood there looking after her. "What in the world is going on? Do I really want to know?"

His wife smiled at him as she handed him his coffee. "I think you should know that Rhea will be going to church with Dan this morning."

"Is that all I missed?"

"I think it is so far."

"I guess we should go to church."

His wife smiled. "A little prayer right now would be a good thing."

Rhea found Dan sitting on the front porch. "Good morning."

"Good morning. We didn't say where we were going to meet so I came here."

"This will work out just fine unless you would rather go somewhere else?"

Dan thought about it for a moment, the truth was he would rather be someplace else but this would do as long as they could be left alone. "I think this will work as well as anywhere else."

"Good, would you like some coffee?"

"Maybe later I think we should talk first."

"I know but I was doing my best to put it off a little longer."

"I know what you mean I was up early then stalled around until I realized that we hadn't said where we were going to meet so I came here."

"I was up early too I wanted everything to be just right I had plenty of time until I realized I had no idea where to meet you."

Dan was more than a little uncomfortable. He had no idea what the right way was to say what he wanted to so he just kept on talking. All he could do was hope he got it right. "You were supposed to be a one-time date because I thought we were just so different you would never say yes to a second date."

Rhea smiled he was saying everything she was thinking. "I had no intention of going out with you a second time but you surprised me you were not the person that people said you were."

Dan looked off toward the road. "You are doing your best to change me and I might not like that. If I didn't know that you are not trying to change me as much as you are trying to show me what I can do. I might not be talking to you now."

Rhea smiled at Dan. "I liked you because you were not the guy people said you were. You treated me like a person you didn't treat me like a nighttime sporting event."

"You like the farm, you are not afraid to break a nail."

"So where does that leave us?"

"Rhea, I think that leaves us getting to know one another."

"We are dating even as we are working on the farm?"

"I promise to take you out to the movies or anything else that we agree is something we both want to try."

"You want that coffee now? We are dating you can come in the house."

"Great I really could use a cup of coffee."

"Mom and Dad are gone they will be glad to hear we had this talk."

Dan followed Rhea into the house. "I am willing to bet my Mom and Dad already know we are dating now. I wish I knew how they do that. Rhea, now that we are dating does that get me a bigger cup of coffee?"

"I can give you the whole pot if you ask me that again."

"I think I will just have a small cup."

"You are smarter than some people say you are."

"You have to stop talking to my brother about me."

"I would never talk to your brother about you. I have been talking to Emma."

"That is fine I am sure she likes me most of the time."

"That was what she said."

Dan looked out the kitchen window. He was standing in the Pastor's house talking to his daughter and there was no one else home. All at once, he felt very uncomfortable as if everyone in town was watching him. Maybe it wasn't the town he was worried about at this point. Dan felt as though he should be looking for lightning bolts being aimed at him. Rhea was a pastor's daughter.

Dan put down his cup. "We should go."

Rhea put both cups in the sink. "If that is what you want."

Emma was up early she had decided it might be a good idea to go to church. When she got to the kitchen she found her parents at the table waiting for her. They were dressed in good clothes and drinking coffee. Emma poured herself a cup of coffee. "Okay, where are you two going?"

Her Mom smiled. "We thought we would go to church with you this morning if you want to go."

"That was my plan."

"Good, we can all go in your car."

"Dad, do you want to drive?"

"No, I am going to sit in the back with your mother."

"Are you sure?"

Roger smiled at his daughter. "Yes, I haven't had your mother in the backseat of a car in a very long time."

"Dad, I think that is more information than I need."

"Emma, you know the last time your mother and I were in the backseat of a car together we were on our way to a wedding I think."

Rachael smiled at her husband. "No, we were on our way to the bar, and as I recall we didn't come home that night."

Roger sipped his coffee. "You know I think you are right. As I recall you slept on the floor that night. You had a tablecloth for a blanket."

"We shared that table cloth as I recall."

"That was some night."

Rachael put her cup down on the table. "It was the last time we were all together."

"Yeah, everything changed after that night."

"Not everything, we still had good friends we just were not together anymore."

Roger put his cup in the sink. "It was a long time ago."

Rachael stood up beside her husband. "It wasn't that long ago but it does feel like it was."

Emma looked at her parents she had no idea what they were talking about. What was scary was she was afraid to ask them what they were talking about. There were some things she didn't want to know. Right now this felt like one of them. "I think we should get going or we will be late."

When Rhea and Dan walked into the church they were surprised to see his parents and sister already there. They took a seat beside Rhea's mother keeping a close eye on Dan's father. Things were going okay as the service got underway. Most people in the church seemed to be watching Dan's father after all he was rarely in church. The town would have plenty to talk about once this service was over.

Roger Richardson was a very good truck driver, father, husband, and friend but as a singer, the best you could say about him was that he was loud. Being loud was not a bad thing if you could carry a tune. Roger was loud, he couldn't carry a tune in a fifty-three-foot trail but he could be heard.

After the service, the pastor complimented Roger on his strong voice which he said was a pleasure to hear. Dan asked his parents and sister for help on the farm. They all seemed a little too happy when they said they would be glad to help him. The entire morning seemed more like a dream than anything else. It was almost enough to make some people forget Roger was sick.

Rhea and Dan left the church to go back to her house so that she could change her clothes. She needed a change of clothes before they could go out to the farm. By the time they got there his parents and his sister were already there. Emma was already raking the field using his tractor. His Dad was greasing up the baler getting it ready to go to work. The baler was hooked to the Case tractor as it always was. Luke's Ford 8N had the mower on it.

Dan got on the 8N and went off to do more mowing. Rhea stood there watching him go wondering what she was going to do. She had been so glad to be with Dan on the farm now she stood alone feeling out of place.

"Rhea, you have stacked bales on a truck before we know that so you can do that again."

She looked at Dan's mother. "Yes, I have it is not that hard I kind of like it."

"Fine, you will be the one to stack the bales, I will be the driver and Dan can pick up the bales. Things will change as we go but that is how we will start. Would you like some iced tea?"

"I would love some."

"Well let's go in the house they aren't going to need us for a couple of hours."

Dan's Mom got the iced tea while Rhea was getting out two glasses. The two of them sat down at the table Dan's Mom was smiling while Rhea was nervous. "Rhea, you have been spending a lot of time with Dan lately."

"He lets me help around the farm which is something I have not been able to do since my uncle sold his farm."

"I went to school with your uncle. Stanley asked me out a few times before he met your Aunt Jane. She loved him and she loved the farm. He couldn't stay here after she died which is why he sold the place to Luke."

"I didn't think anyone remembered him but me."

"I even remember you coming over to the house when you were here visiting your Aunt and Uncle. The boys don't remember but you were all young back then."

"I was glad when I heard that Luke had bought the place I thought he would take good care of it."

"It takes the whole family what with the two boys always working I am surprised they still have the animals. You know I don't think anyone has ridden those horses in over a year."

"Dan told me that no one has ridden them since Linda left. He did say that he has thought about it but has never done it."

"Rhea, Dan doesn't ride he never has and I am not sure why."

"Maybe he just doesn't think he has the time."

"With Dan that is possible, he is always in a hurry even when he has nothing to do."

"I have noticed that."

Two hours later they were all working in the field. Dan had stopped mowing to put bales on the truck as his Mom said he would. Emma finished the raking and then took over driving the truck while her Mom went to do the chores. By the time they were finished getting the hay in Dan's Mom had the food on the table. They talked about the plan for the next day as they were eating. Rhea was included in the planning for the next day. Emma would be late she had plans for noon so Rhea was going to have to learn how to run the rake and do the raking in the morning.

Everyone left after they ate except for Rhea who was doing the dishes while Dan was getting the laundry going. Saturday night was laundry night which was not a big deal after all there were only two of them living in the house and Luke hadn't been home all week. What really took the time was putting the clothes away once they were clean. Even that didn't take that long after all there just wasn't much there.

The clothes were in the dryer right after Rhea finished up in the kitchen. They walked out of the house and looked at the night sky. Rhea looked at Dan. "I am running the rake in the morning does that mean I am accepted as part of the family?"

"No, if you were family he would have had you walk around the field with the hand rake and pull the hay away from the woods."

"I have done that here before."

Dan looked at her surprised. "You have?"

"I did it when I was a kid and my aunt and uncle owned this farm."

Dan started to laugh. "That was a long time ago we were what ten years old? I remember you were always in the barn in the hay you loved to jump in the hay."

"We were eight, Luke used to tease you all the time and slap you on the back."

"As I remember you thought that was funny."

"That is why you don't ride the horse we locked you in the stall with the old horse my uncle had."

"That horse never did a thing to me but look at me. I was so upset about not being able to get out."

"You didn't remember me did you?"

Dan smiled. "I remember that little girl but I didn't know you were that girl."

"I thought it might be that you just didn't remember me at all."

"Rhea, you don't look anything like that little girl anymore. I liked her but she liked Luke. All the girls liked him when we were young."

"Dan, I liked you both but Luke made me laugh."

"That is something I have heard before."

"I would never go out with your brother now he is not as nice as you are."

Dan smiled. "Yes he is, he just hides it more now so people will leave him alone. Linda is to blame for that. He trusted her and she let him down so he keeps to himself most of the time now."

"I can see where that could happen but he has to learn to get over it."

"He has been with Emily Rice for over a week now that is a good sign."

"If he didn't drop her off somewhere then go on his way."

Dan smiled. "Take it from me she is still with him or he would have been home by now."

"I should get going."

"I know it is getting late and I only have enough coffee in the pot for two cups."

Rhea smiled at him. "Maybe we should finish that off so we can have fresh coffee in the morning."

"You think that would be best?"

"You can't go wrong with fresh coffee in the morning."

"Then I will heat it."

"I'll get the cups."

When Dan went to bed that night he was glad to be living on the farm. Rhea loved the farm he was going to end up on the farm with Rhea if he could talk his brother into moving off the place. Luke was rarely there so why would he want to hold onto it? Linda was not coming back; even if she did Luke wouldn't want her. As he drifted off he was thinking of Rhea with him on the farm.

The night wind blew gently across the land as the moon looked down on the farm the light and shadows changing the look of things. Everything was changing, some for the good as well as some for the bad. Everything was always changing we were not always smart enough to notice. The wind moved the trees as well as the grass while time moved everything else. Mysteries lay ahead while history lay behind.

Chapter 29

Emma got dressed and then went down to the kitchen for her morning coffee. It was after nine her parents had already gone to the farm to help Dan. Sunday was breakfast with Laurie at the diner in the center of town. This was something they did at least twice a month just to spend some time maybe go shopping after they had something to eat. Usually, she would walk over but today she had to go to the farm after they ate.

Laurie Fields was sitting in a corner booth when Emma walked in. She waved at her and then waited as she sat down across from her. "You are looking a little rough this morning."

"Thanks, I never say things like that about you."

"I know but I was told to always tell the truth."

"Laurie, can you tell me why I am still talking to you?"

"I would say because you don't have a sister?"

"Okay, Dan is dating Rhea she is even helping on the farm."

"I guess that means I will have to find another guy to drink with."

"Luke doesn't have a girl."

"He might do if you don't mind?"

Emma laughed. "I would love to see that one work for more than two dates."

"I don't want to date him but I might take him out for a night or two."

"You are a very bad girl."

Laurie smiled. "I can't help it I like to have a good time now and then."

"We better order I have to get out to the farm."

"I am going home to get some sleep."

Emma shook her head. "I think I hate you."

Laurie laughed. "I know."

"What about Luke would you go out with him?"

"You know I hung out with him before Linda came along."

"Where are you dating him back then?"

"We were talking about a lot of things back then."

"So how did he end up with Linda then?"

Laurie sipped her coffee. That was a good question and one she had no real answer for. "Luke and I were talking like I said and Linda wasn't talking she was giving it away."

"So the two of you never..."

"We never talk about it."

Emma smiled. "Our food is here."

"Thank God."

"Just because we are eating we don't have to stop talking."

"I was afraid you were going to bring that up."

"Laurie, I want to know why you let Luke end up with Linda?"

"Emma, you know your brother does what he wants not what we want him to do."

"You wanted him to stay with you?"

"To be honest I am not sure what I wanted back then. I was hurt when he went off with her though he never stopped talking to me. We are still friends."

Emma smiled. "What would you do if he started talking about marrying Emily?"

Laurie sipped her coffee before she said anything. "Like I said whatever your brother does or doesn't do we will still be friends."

"Is that enough for you?"

Laurie smiled at her friend. "That is something you and I are never going to talk about."

"You don't want to talk about your friend?"

"No, I am not going to talk about my friend so you will have nothing to tease me about later."

Emma laughed. "What makes you think I would do a thing like that to you?"

"You are his sister and you both pick on me if I give you a chance."

"Well, I need to get going. You are no fun right now so I have to go."

"Bite me."

Emma smiled. "I will leave that kind of thing to my brother.".,

Steve was standing by her car when Emma walked outside. "Where are we going?"

"I am going to the farm where are you going?"

Steve smiled. "With you."

"Oh shit."

Luke was up early he took Jack for a walk then got him some food and fresh water. Emily was up standing outside the truck waiting for him so they could get something to eat before they headed home. They hadn't talked much the night before sleep seemed much more important at the time. Now breakfast was at the top of the list before they started home. At least that was what they thought when they took their seats.

"We need to get home I have to talk with my parents."

Luke smiled at her. "Emily, your parents think you are on vacation mine don't know where I am."

"You could have called or sent a message from your boss."

"Helen told my Dad what was going on she always does. He always knows where I am though he never says anything about it to me."

"Might be they thought you would call them if something was wrong. Why didn't you call them?"

"I don't know I guess they would have asked me things I didn't want to talk about."

"Like the fact that I was with you?"

"You didn't want anyone to know."

"No I didn't but I don't think they would have told my parents."

"Yes they would, I am sure of that."

"Luke, what are we going to tell everyone about this week when they ask us?"

"We can always tell them the truth though I would leave out the part where you fell asleep on the bathroom floor if I were you."

"What makes you think I was sleeping on the bathroom floor?"

"Jack doesn't climb up on the bed unless it is empty and he doesn't stretch out unless he has been there for at least a couple of hours."

"You are trying to tell me that the dog told you that I slept in the bathroom?"

"That and the fact that your bag was where you left it and I saw the outfit you wore that day hanging on a hanger."

"Which lead you to think I was sleeping in the bathroom?"

"You were not taking a shower and if you were taking a dump you had been at it for a long time so I think you were sleeping on the bathroom floor or in the bathtub."

"You got all that from the fact that Jack was sleeping in the bed?"

"No, I also happen to know that you had quite a lot to drink and chances were good that you tossed your cookies again after I left the room."

"I did."

"Dad always said you learn more by looking and listening than you do talking.'

"Something tells me that there is more to this story than you are telling me."

"There is, you forgot to lock the bathroom door. I had a real hard time talking myself out of opening it."

"What did you expect to see if you say you knew I wasn't in the shower?"

"You want some more coffee while the waitress is standing here listening to our conversation?"

"Oh shit! Could we please get a little more coffee?"

"Don't worry Honey, I have heard a lot worse working here."

Emily looked at the waitress a nasty look in her eyes. "Not from me you haven't."

Luke smiled. "I guess it was a good thing you remembered to close the bathroom door or this conversation could have gotten someone punched in the nose."

"We should talk about something else."

"I suppose we should though I thought this conversation was just starting to get good."

"We could talk about that little redhead you were chasing last time you were home."

"We could but I hear she has a new boy in her life I think his name is Jim."

"I should be so lucky."

"We should get going if I am going to get back to the farm in time to help with the haying. I bet Dan is about ready to kill me for being gone so long."

"Why didn't you just sell him the farm you are never there."

"I like the farm but it cost a lot and I need this job to meet the payments every month."

"You need to get more cows and sell the milk to the dairy."

"Sure Dan would love that, more work on him while I drive around the country."

Emily shook her head. "You have to spend money to make money."

"True but you need to be able to pay the bills and right now that is all that I can afford to do."

"You could make a deal with Dan."

"I could but not if he doesn't like the place which he doesn't."

"I could help you."

"What are you going to do move in with Dan and me?"

"I might think about moving in so I can help you but I am not going to live with you and your brother."

"Dan is a nice guy."

"Who said I was talking about getting rid of Dan? I always liked your brother."

"I see how it is now spend a little time with me so you can get a chance to get to know my brother."

"Yes, but as it turns out I think Dan is dating Rhea Conner isn't he?"

"They have only gone out once or twice they will never make it as a couple they have nothing in common."

"I like Rhea."

"So do I but that doesn't mean she is going to like my brother."

"You don't think your brother could make her happy?"

"I think he could I am just not sure she would want him to try."

"What makes you so sure?"

"I guess it would be the fact that they seem to travel in different circles these days. It is not like when we were kids on the farm."

"What are you talking about?"

"When we were kids Rhea's uncle owned the farm. He sold it to me when he moved to Florida."

"I didn't know that."

"She used to be around during the summer but Dan was into sports and didn't see her after that one summer."

"But you did."

"Yes, from time to time over the years."

"Did the two of you ever date?"

"No, we were just friends."

"Then you don't think she is too good for your brother?"

"No, Dan is a really good guy after all he helps me with the farm, watches out for Mom while Dad and I are away from home and he has his own business to run."

"We should get going I need to get home."

"Do you want me to stay with you or just drop you off?"

"Just drop me off I will be fine."

Luke paid for breakfast then they went out to the truck. Luke had to admit he was going to miss having her in the truck. He was just getting used to having someone to talk to that could talk back. It wasn't that Jack didn't communicate he just didn't talk. "Emily, are you ready to go home?"

She smiled. "No, but I do think it is time."

The truck rolled out of the truck stop heading for home. Jack was on the bunk still wondering when Emily was going to get out of his seat. They didn't say anything to each other until they were in the pickup. They agreed they had to swing by the police station which they did. Once that was done they drove over to Emily's and then parked in the driveway.

Luke looked at her. "Call me and let me know how things go."

"Luke, I don't think I have ever had a better vacation."

"It was a fun week for me too."

Emily got out grabbed her bag out of the back then went up on the porch. She waved to Luke as he drove away and then went into the house. She had enjoyed herself which was something she hadn't done in a very long time.

Luke felt like he should wait to see how things went but she was a big girl she could handle whatever she had to. He was going to miss her though he was sure that she would forget all about him once she went back to work. Her vacation was over now it was time to get back to the real world.

Chapter 30

Emily put her bag down by the door happy to be home. She had been scared when she first left the house after Jim had dumped her again. She had been hoping that she would be able to finally get away from Jim. She was glad to be home, she was looking forward to starting over without Jim.

"Mom, Dad, I am home you are never going to believe the great vacation that I had."

Jim was sitting in the living room with her father. Jim looked more at home than she was feeling right then. "Emily, you are looking good. I am glad you are back I have missed you."

"Dad, why is he here?"

"He is here because he is going to be part of our family soon."

"Why? Are you going to adopt him?"

Jim gave her a cross look. "Don't talk to your Dad like that."

Emily smiled at him. "Jim, would you do something for me?"

"I would be glad to, what do you need?"

"Go to hell, you cheating bastard!"

"Emily! I want you to stop that right now."

She looked at her father with fire in her eyes she had put up with these two long enough. "I see you have made your choice. You took the cheating child molesting rapist over your own daughter. This time you have gone too far because I am not going to bow down to you anymore. I hope you two are very happy together. You can give him my room I won't be using it anymore."

Emily turned and walked back to where she had set down her bag. Picking it up she turned back to face her father. "I am sure you know what you can do with my job. If you have any trouble getting it in there just have Jim help you out. Giving people the shaft is something he is a pro at."

With the bag in hand, Emily turned and walked out the door. It felt good to be rid of it all at last. She was free she could do anything she wanted to now. She could get another job working for anyone that wasn't family. She was halfway to Main Street before it came to her that she had no idea where she was going. She sat down on a park bench and started to cry.

Luke stopped by the store and bought a case of soda and a case of beer then went to his parent's house. There was no one home which meant they were all at the farm with Dan. He was going to be in a big trouble by the time he got there. His father was going to want to know everything that had happened.

It was not the first time he had ever been gone this long but it was the first time he hadn't called home. It was true that they could have called him but that wouldn't matter after all he hadn't let his mother know what was going on and that was what would get him into trouble. He knew he should have called but he had never been sure of what to say with Emily right there in the truck beside him.

That was when his house phone rang. It was Emily and she needed him to pick her up she wanted to go to the farm. He drove to where she was waiting for him. He stopped the truck in front of her, then watched as she threw her bag into the bed of the truck. Emily got in without saying a word. Luke started driving toward the farm.

Luke glanced at Emily and then back at the road. "I take it all went well."

Emily smiled a nasty smile. "I had a lovely homecoming. I told them how wonderful I was feeling. They were so happy for me it left them speechless."

"I am glad it all worked out for you."

"So am I, so am I."

It seemed that everyone was at the farm when Emily, Luke, and

Jack arrived. They were working in the hay field. Jack found a shady spot to curl up in while Emily and Luke joined everyone else in the hay field. Luke's Mom was driving the truck Rhea was on the truck stacking the bails while Dan, his Dad, and Steve were throwing the bales on the truck. Emily took one look and then climbed up on the truck with Rhea while Luke took over for his Dad.

While everyone was home Luke's Mom saw the chance for a family meal so she let her husband drive the truck. She went to the house to start fixing supper. Emma finished bailing the hay and then went off to the barn to milk the cows.

There was very little talk between the guys but the two girls on the truck were talking. Dan and Luke didn't know what the girls were talking about but they were both worried. There were things that the girls knew that everyone else in the family didn't know. There were things each of them knew that they shouldn't be telling one another about.

Emily stood beside Rhea on the truck with a smile. "Rhea, it has been a while how are things going?"

"I have been spending some time with Dan, getting to know him again."

"How is that going?"

Rhea smiled. "It has been interesting so far. He has some rough edges."

Emily laughed. "Are you planning to smooth them out?"

"I thought I would give it a try. What about Luke and you?"

"I am afraid Luke needs to be molded and shaped before I have to worry about his rough edges."

Rhea looked back at the brothers. "Do you think they are worth the effort?"

Emily looked at the brothers too. "It could be fun finding out."

"You know they do have some good points."

"Yeah, they have nice parents and a nice sister."

"Rhea laughed. "You two have a rough trip?"

"The trip was okay but the homecoming was a little rough."

"Sorry.

"It is for the best I think."

Luke stood near a couple of bales of hay looking at his brother. "How long have you and Rhea been dating?"

"About a week give or take a day or two. What about you and Emily?"

"We aren't dating anymore we stopped after a couple of days."

"Does she know that?"

"We talked about it."

"Now I understand."

"Understand what?"

"Nothing at all."

"You got that right."

"Is there something wrong with her?"

Luke smiled. "No, there is nothing wrong with her. We are not dating but we are getting to know one another."

"Luke, I think that is what people do when they are dating."

"No, we just had to change. I needed to talk to someone besides Jack. Emily just needed a vacation from her job and things. You know, sometimes it just doesn't take long to figure things out. Sometimes you have to step back to get a good look at where you are."

"I know what you mean I didn't think I was going to like Rhea but she is not the person most people think she is."

Luke looked at his brother. "Those two are doing an awful lot of talking."

"I noticed, what do you think they are talking about?"

"I think they are talking about us."

"That is what I was thinking too."

"You think they shouldn't be talking to one another?"

Dan laughed. "I think we are in trouble that is what I think."

Luke looked at his brother. "You have no idea."

"What does that mean?"

"That means some nights are rougher than others."

"Luke, what did you do?"

"Nothing I am going to get arrested for."

Dan smiled there were a lot of things that his brother could have done that wouldn't have gotten him arrested. "Do you plan on telling me about what you did?"

"Not here in the hay field."

By the time all the hay was in the barn, the chores had been done. Supper was on the table so they all sat down at the dining room table to eat. You had to say the food smelled good, yet there was more than food going around the table.

As the food was being passed around Roger Richardson looked at his son. "Luke, were you planning on telling us just what happened to you?"

"Dad, I thought I would eat before talked about that."

Emily jammed her elbow into his ribs. "Why don't you tell them now?"

"Or I could just tell you now if that is okay with everyone."

"Your mother has been worried I think she would like you to ease her mind."

"Okay Dad, I will tell you all about it but it would be best if I start the story on Friday night."

"Start it anywhere you want just start it."

"Okay, just remember that I will take questions when I am done with the story not while I am telling the story."

Dan laughed. "You are stalling so just tell the story and get it over with."

"Emily and I went to the Circus Bar last Friday night Dad was there for a little while with us then he went home. Emily and I were sitting there minding our own business talking about different things until the pool table was free. She wanted to play a couple of games before we left so we started that. Everything was going along fine until her ex-boyfriend walked in with some redhead. Emily walked over and broke the pool stick over his head. He went after her. I wasn't going to let that happen so I got in between them. We hit one another a couple of times then Linda got the shotgun out. Emily and I went out the back door we got in my truck then went for coffee at the truck stop.

Emily didn't want to go home she wanted to go for a ride. I had a load on my trailer that had to go to a small town in Connecticut so Emily, Jack, and I drove over to the yard. We got in my rig and headed south.

After that one load led to another load which got us another load. It went on like that all week until we finally got a load coming back home. When we got here we stopped by the police station to get things straightened out with them then we came here."

Luke's father looked at him calmly. "Is that it?"

"That is the short version it tells you all the things we did without a minute-by-minute account."

Roger looked at his son. "Luke, I have heard a lot of stories in my life and you left a lot out of yours."

Dan smiled. "I thought so too."

Roger looked at his younger son. "Dan, what were you doing all week?"

"You know me I was here taking care of his place while he was off running the roads just the same as I always do."

"That is all you have to say about the week?"

"Dad, I don't understand what you are getting at you knew where I was all week."

"I would like to know why these two young ladies are here today and you boys don't want to tell me. If you don't want to tell me there must be a lot more going on here than there seems to be. We will all meet here again tomorrow we can have another nice meal. The four of you should be able to come up with something believable by then."

Emma was smiling at her brothers. "Don't be too hard on them they are just boys."

Roger looked at his daughter. "I have heard some things about you this week."

Emma looked at her Dad as she handed him the keys to the car. "I think I will stay here for a little while."

Roger looked at his daughter. "I take it Steve will be staying too?"

Emma shrugged her shoulders. "I guess."

The truth was what they had told him though they had left out a couple of little things. They say it is the little things that make the story. Roger wanted to know all the little things the boys already knew he knew most of what had happened. Their father always seemed to know more than he should. A lot can happen in a week.

PART THREE

Chapter 31

The Family Deals

Emily, Rhea, Emma, Luke, Dan, and Steve sat in the kitchen at the table looking at one another all of them feeling just a little uncomfortable. They had done well all week long but now they had to share what they had been doing. Luke got up opened the refrigerator and took out a beer.

"Anyone else want one?"

Dan looked at the three girls."I think we could all use one right about now."

Luke got three more out then went back to the table. "Dan, are you planning a party? I don't think there has ever been that much food in that old frig."

"The cupboards are full too. Rhea bought food and Mom bought food so we will not need anything for months."

"You cut more hay than usual."

"Yeah, I had a lot on my mind so I mowed."

"I have done that before it didn't solve anything but it seemed to help me relax."

"Yeah, I relaxed right into three days of hard work."

"Tomorrow's load has already been delivered and the truck needs to spend a day at the shop getting ready for the next round of hauls. I will be here to help."

Rhea nodded. "I work tonight so I will get some sleep then come back in the afternoon."

Emily took the last sip of her beer. "I quit my job so I will be here to help."

Emma nodded. "I will be here too."

Luke got out six more beers and then passed them around the table. "Dan, you have nothing to worry about you have a crew right here."

"Not me I have to work tomorrow. It looks like you are going to be the only one here in the morning."

Emily opened her beer and then looked around the table. "I need to wash my clothes."

Emma was on her feet. "The boys have a washer and dryer here."

Rhea got up from the table too. "Come on I can show you where everything is. I even know where there are some clothes you can wear so that you can wash the ones you have on."

Emily looked at Rhea. "Are they your clothes?"

"No, they used to belong to Linda she left them behind."

Emma smiled. "I didn't know she had left anything behind."

Emily looked at Rhea. "You seem to know a lot about what goes on around here."

Rhea smiled. "You learn a lot when your clothes are soaking wet from the rain. Dan and I talked about a lot of things while I was sitting here in Linda's clothes waiting for mine which were in the dryer."

"What was the most important thing you learned?"

Rhea laughed. "I don't know about the most important thing but it was the most uncomfortable thing. Linda didn't leave any underwear behind."

Emily had just past her clothes out the door to Rhea to put in the wash. "You couldn't have told me that before I gave you everything."

"I didn't want to be the only one that found out a little too late."

Emma was laughing. "You can't leave behind something you don't own."

Emily walked out of the bathroom. "You know this shirt is a little too tight."

"I had the same problem."

"Does it look as bad as it feels?"

Emma was still laughing. "Hell yeah!"

Rhea had a smile on her "Oh dear."

"What is wrong?"

"I think we are about the same size and I am now seeing what Dan saw."

"It is that bad?"

Emma shook her head. "Girl, those are a couple of things that will hold my brother's attention."

Rhea was calm. "We are going to have to burn all of Linda's clothes after this."

Emily wanted to cry or punch somebody. "Oh, this is just great!"

Emma started for the kitchen. "Go back in the bathroom I will have Luke get you one of his shirts."

When the girls got back to the table the guys were finishing their third beer. They all sat down at the table and Luke got them all another beer. "I think I should have bought more beer."

Dan went down into the basement and came back with another case of beer which he put in the frig. "I went to the store too."

Luke looked at Rhea, his sister, and his brother. "What have you three been doing while I was gone?"

Rhea smiled. "I bought groceries, did chores, took care of the milk, and learned how to rake hay."

Emma smiled. "I have been working here for two days."

"I bought a tractor and found a girlfriend."

"I saw the tractor it looks good how does it run?"

"Not quite like I expected but I am really happy with it."

"I felt the same way about mine even the little imperfections are good."

"I thought a tune-up might be in order myself but I was wrong."

Emily looked over at Rhea. "I get the feeling we are the tractors they are talking about."

"You know they are talking about us too. You never did say how the truck was running?"

"A little rough right now but I think I can fix it."

"I noticed that with my truck it is a little hard to steer at times but I think I have it under control."

Emma looked at her brothers. "You two are in trouble and you don't even know it. As for you gals you are not in control of anything at all."

Dan smiled. "Emma, we are all good. The thing is Steve hasn't said a word he just sits there drinking our beer."

Steve smiled. "It is all good to me. I love a good beer and I have a good beer. What more can I ask for."

Emma laughed. "Dream on boy, dream on."

They were all laughing maybe a little more than they should have been. It took a couple more beers before Emily started to talk. "Jim was sitting in the living room with my father they had the wedding all planned out. I told that child molesting rapist just where he could go. I told my father to take his job and shove it."

Rhea banged her fist on the table. "Good for you they ought to grab Jim Campbell by the privates and cut them off!"

"I think we better cut you off if you are going to get rowdy."

Dan was about to say something else when Emily jumped up out of her seat. "I took my bag and left the house I am homeless."

Emma set her beer down on the table. "I am so glad I didn't go home I would have missed all this."

Steve laughed. "So this is what family life is like."

Dan shook his head. "This is the fun part."

Emily looked around. "I need a place to stay."

Luke shook his head. "I don't think that is a problem tonight we are all too drunk to drive."

Rhea was shaking her head. "We can't be I have to go to work."

Luke put six more beers on the table. "Not tonight."

Rhea started to laugh as she grabbed another beer. "Oh good."

Emily looked around the table. "Where are we all going to sleep?"

Dan raised his hand. "I have a room."

Rhea stuck her hand in the air and gave Dan a high five. "I claim the guest room."

Emma laughed. "I get Luke's room."

Emily looked around the table. "What about me?"

Luke looked at her as calmly as could be. "Your room is open no one is sleeping in the bathroom. Hell, this time you can close the door if you want."

"What are you talking about you said the door was closed?"

"It was after I found you in there on the floor naked. I saw you then I closed the door."

"I am not going to stay in the house with a liar."

"Okay, give me back my shirt before you leave."

"You want your shirt!"

Emily was on her feet and about to take off the shirt when Rhea spoke up. "Your clothes are still in the dryer. You should have another beer while you wait."

Emily started to sit back down. "I guess I might as well."

Emma looked at Emily and Luke. "I want to hear the rest of that story."

Just before Emily sat down she punched Luke in the face almost knocking him out of his chair. Luke yelled while everyone else laughed it was clear they had all had way too much to drink. Six people and two cases of beer add up to not enough beer or too many people, in this case, it was not enough beer.

There are times in a person's life when things happen that everyone knows can't happen but somehow they seem to happen anyway. This was looking like one of those times. Luke and Dan had a rule which they never broke it said when the beer ran out it was time for bed. Tonight they didn't want to go to bed they wanted to have more fun and more beer. They were all drunk but not so drunk that they did not know they couldn't drive.

Rhea was thinking about how wonderful the phone was. It went everywhere she went and it didn't drink beer which was good because too many people were already drinking the beer. All she had to do was call the right person and they could get more beer. Rhea made the call she told her friend where she was as well as how to get there.

Sheri Carson was a very good friend of Rhea's they worked together at the truck stop. The most important thing about Sheri was that she owned a seven-passenger van. The second most important thing was that she didn't drink. Sheri had just gotten home from work; she was just about asleep when the phone rang. If anyone but Rhea had called her she might have told them where they could go.

Rhea was in trouble she never would have called if she wasn't. Sheri had to get out there to pick up her friend and then get her sobered up as best she could before taking her home. Dressing quickly she jumped in her van and headed for the farm.

She got to the farm just after nine and everyone was sitting in the kitchen drinking the last of an old bottle of whiskey they had found in the cupboard. Everyone was glad to see her at first. There was something wrong Rhea noticed it right away.

"Sheri, you don't have any beer with you."

"No, you asked me to come to get you there was never any mention of beer."

Rhea laughed. "I forgot."

"I can give you a ride home if you want."

"Sheri, that is what I need I need a ride."

Sheri and Rhea walked out of the house and got in the van. Before they could leave the yard everyone else got in the van too. Sheri wanted to kick them all out of the van but Rhea needed her help. She was going to have to take them out to eat someplace where she could get some coffee into them.

It was time to go out and have a little fun. Rhea and her five drinking buddies wanted more beer while Sheri was hoping to get them to drink coffee and maybe get something to eat. It was going to take some doing to get the six of them to drink coffee.

They didn't go out to eat though Sheri did her best to get them to do it. The six of them were not in an eating mood they had other plans. They had run out of beer at the farm all they wanted was to buy more. The package stores were closed but the bars were still open.

The Circus Bar was open and all they wanted was a couple of beers then they could go back home and get some sleep. That was the plan after all they were having fun. It was one of the few times when the brothers and their sister were out together. Most of the time when they went out they split up going in different directions and doing different things.

Emily had been out before she had even gotten drunk before but until tonight she had not realized she had never had any real fun before. The five people she was with were fun even if they were not your normal party crowd. Luke was never around, Emma had her own crowd, Steve was always on the move, Dan was usually very serious about everything and Rhea was the Pastor's daughter.

Rhea had been drunk before but that had been when she first went out and she had not thought about it until the following morning. She had suffered all the next day which lead her to promise herself that she would never do it again. That had been the plan but not every plan is carried out. As she took another beer in her hand she heard Linda Fields announce the last call so she ordered another round.

Luke was sitting with his back to the bar across the table from his brother. They were all laughing and having a good time something he hadn't done in a very long time. He was thinking about Emily she was a little crazy but she was okay in time they might even become a real couple. That was if she could find herself a place to live.

His head started to hurt on the right side as some girl started to scream. Something flew past him as he did his best to try and figure out just what was going on. Rhea and Sheri were on their feet, Dan was gone so was Steve. Emily and Emma were swearing at somebody. Luke stood up he was in the middle of a fight.

Dan was beating on anybody that came at him but there were at least a dozen of them while there was only one of him and maybe Steve it was hard to tell. He saw Jim Campbell coming after him but there was nothing he could do he already had his hands full. Dan knew he was going to have to take a few lumps but it would not be the first time.

Luke was on the move and Jim was the first one that he hit. He held nothing back he wanted Jim on the floor which was exactly where Jim ended up. Fists were flying people were falling like trees being cut down in the forest. The fight wasn't going to last long but anyone that came at Luke was going to go away hurting.

His head was pounding though as he stood beside his brother he didn't feel it. He was holding his own though his vision was a little blurry. He didn't need perfect vision to hit something as big and ugly as Jim. When Jim went down he just hit anybody that came his way.

Emily was standing to the left of Luke hitting people with a cue stick she had found on the floor. Emma was using her feet as well as her hands her brothers had taught her well. Rhea was to the right kicking guys in the lower regions causing them to fall to the floor in front of her. Sheri was looking toward the back door she didn't really care about anyone else but she just wanted to get Rhea out of there.

Linda Fields had her shotgun in hand but it was all over by then. Better than half a dozen guys were on the floor between the bar and the table where the Richardson group had been sitting. There was blood on the floor as well as on some of the tables, a few stools, chairs, the bar, and the pool table.

Linda put the shotgun back behind the bar as the police arrived on the scene. Jim was put in handcuffs as were most of the others. Linda gave the police the story just the way it had happened then sat beside George. It was like nothing that had ever happened in their bar before. It was going to take a few days to clean up the mess the fight had left behind.

Laurie looked around the bar. "Mom, I think it is time to kick some people out of here."

Linda nodded. "I am afraid you are right."

Laurie shook her head. "They sure tore us up."

Linda smiled at her daughter. "We have handled worse."

George looked at his wife. "I don't know about that."

Laurie got three beers and put them on her parent's table. "That was crazy."

"I saw the wildest woman I have ever seen tonight."

"Who was that?"

"She was, our daughter, she was as rough as they come. You should have seen her come over to the bar. She caught one of those boys in the chin with her foot."

Laurie shrugged her shoulders. "I saw my friends in trouble and I helped them."

Linda smiled. "You had the shotgun."

"I wanted to kill Jim so I didn't dare touch the shotgun."

"You should have seen our daughter standing there beating those boys with a pool ball in her hand."

"I did that once."

George laughed. "I remember that."

"A fight in a bar when we were young."

"Mom, you want to tell me what happened?"

"I think we should get some sleep we have a lot to do in the morning."

Chapter 32

Monday morning Luke woke up early to find himself sleeping on the kitchen floor. He had a pillow and a blanket as well as a headache. He got up off the floor and then put the pillow and blanket on the couch on his way to his room. He got himself some clean clothes and then went back down to the kitchen. He started a fresh pot of coffee going then went into the bathroom for aspirin and a shower.

There were a lot of things that he remembered about the night before like Jim Campbell hitting the floor as the fight was getting started. He remembered seeing Jim go down several times as he tried to get back up. Emma had been standing with him and Dan giving out as much pain as she could. He also remembered seeing Laurie standing by Emma giving Jim's friends some really hard hits. Steve had been there as well as Laurie, Emily, and Rhea.

Emily had a cue stick in her hands swinging it like a major league ball player. She may not have been knocking them out of the park but she had seemed to be knocking them out of her way. He couldn't remember if she had broken another cue stick even though it had passed close to his head more than once. If she had she was going to need to go to work for Linda for a while.

That had not been his first bar fight but it had been one of the wildest. He should have felt bad about the fight but he didn't. The truth was he had not even thought about it. He had been hit as he sat at the table. While he was wondering what had happened the girls, Dan and

Steve were tearing things up. If the fight had lasted ten minutes it had lasted longer than he thought.

Luke stood looking at the face in the mirror. It looked a lot older than it had a week earlier. Even though he knew he had been acting younger he didn't feel very young. Life sucked more often than not and the harder he looked at things the worse they got.

Things had to change but they were changing too fast he hated change. It might be best if he just got in his truck and didn't come back to town. His Dad wasn't going to get any better it was all downhill to the end of the road.

When he walked out of the bathroom he got the largest coffee cup he could find and filled it up. Cup in hand he went out to the barn where he found Rhea feeding the cows and horses. Luke sat down on a bale of hay and then sipped his coffee.

Rhea also had a big cup of coffee but hers was already half gone. "Did you make a fresh pot?"

Luke nodded then spoke softly. "Yes, I did."

"I would kill for a cup of fresh coffee."

"Rhea, how many times have you had a night like you had last night?"

"Counting last night just one."

"That is what I thought. I have to tell you I was very surprised at what you did last night."

Rhea sipped her coffee. "I know I let things get out of hand right from the start I never should have had so much to drink. I lost control of myself last night."

"The drinking was nothing I was talking about the fight at the bar. You were kicking guys between the legs. You hit that one guy in the knee with a beer bottle not to mention the chair you threw."

"I have never been in a bar fight before."

"I get the feeling most guys in this town would feel a whole lot better if you were never in another."

"Luke, I think we should get these cows milked before I drink all my coffee."

"I think you are right because one cup isn't going to be enough this morning."

"One cup is never enough but today I am thinking a pot of coffee might make me feel almost normal."

By the time they finished the morning chores Emily, Emma, Dan and Steve were sitting in the kitchen the third pot of coffee was ready on the stove. Dan took care of the milk while Emma took care of the eggs. Emily got up from her chair and started breakfast. There was not a lot of talking as they passed the aspirin around the room.

Rhea and Luke got their second cup of coffee and then sat down at the table. No one said a word they were all doing their best to live with pounding headaches. After a few minutes, Rhea got out the dishes while Luke refilled everyone's cups. He started a new pot of coffee. When he finished he was just in time to sit down to eat.

They were eating in silence doing their best to try and block out what had happened the night before. The truth was none of them had a clear memory of everything that had happened. There had been a blow to Luke's head followed by fists, feet, cue sticks, and a chair or two. It all happened fast then they were out the back door and in the van.

Sheri dropped them all at the farm and then got out of there just as fast as she could. It was clear from the things that she said to them that the six of them need never call her again. They had all stumbled into the house and then up the stairs to the bedrooms. There were four bedrooms so they had each managed to find one.

Emma was in Dan's room, Emily was in Luke's room Rhea and Dan each had a room Luke went to the kitchen for a coffee. He didn't get any coffee he went to sleep on the kitchen floor. Steve had fallen asleep on the couch in the living room.

Now they sat waiting for the pain to ease enough so they could get on with the day. They were just finishing breakfast when someone knocked on the door. When Luke opened it he was put in handcuffs as were the other five then they were taken to the station and locked up. Though they were all allowed one phone call they only made one call they called the boys Dad.

Roger Richardson didn't have to go to work anymore. On his first day off he had planned to sleep in. The day was like so many days before it was just not meant to be. Luke had called they were locked up in jail after being involved in a brawl that had caused a lot of damage to the Circus Bar. Luke didn't remember all that had happened but he did remember that he had not started the fight.

Roger drove over to the bar finding it was locked so he went up the back stairs to the second floor and knocked on the door. Laurie Fields opened the door and smiled at him. "Good morning Uncle Roger."

"Good morning Laurie, is your Dad up?"

"He is on his third cup of coffee. Would you like a cup?"

"I would love a cup."

George Fields looked up at Roger. "I take it your kids are in jail?"

"They are, I came by to find out what happened so that I know whether or not I should leave them there."

"Emma and the boys didn't start it but they finished it up in short order. The six didn't hold back once the fight started they took out everyone that came their way. Roger, I haven't seen anything like that since you and I took on that bar full of bikers."

"We tore that place up that night."

"Linda was doing a lot of damage that night as well."

"She broke my jaw."

George laughed. "She always was handy with a cue stick."

"As I recall we were supposed to be on the same side."

"Linda had her eyes closed when she swung that thing just like she always did."

"I am not so sure about that I still think she hit who she was aiming at."

Linda smiled. "I never worried about hitting your thick head. I didn't know you had a glass jaw."

"It wasn't glassed it was damaged from the fight and you hit the weakest spot."

Linda laughed. "Broken glass is still broken glass."

Roger smiled as he shook his head. "George, how bad is the bar?"

"There were at least twenty people involved in the fight. Jim Campbell started it he hit Luke in the side of the head with a cue stick then all hell broke loose. Your kids and their friends were holding their own but Emily Rice, Rhea Conner, and Laurie did more damage than your boys did. They even had Steve Benson with them I thought he was working out of town. I haven't seen anything like it since the good old days."

"You drop the charges against the six of them and I will have them over here cleaning this place up for you before they have a chance to think about it. Laurie, you helped give Jim and his friend hell?"

"Yeah Uncle Roger, I had to protect the bar and my friends."

"Well, you had to defend your home and your friends."

"Why do I get the feeling there is more coming?"

Roger smiled. "Don't look at me."

"Dad, is there something you want to say?"

"No, I am just sitting here enjoying my coffee."

"Then why do I feel like there is something more coming my way?"

Linda laughed. "Laurie, don't let them get to you they are just giving you a hard time."

"Why?"

George finished his coffee. "The question is why not?"

Linda smiled as her daughter breathed a sigh of relief and frustration. "You two need more coffee?"

"Linda, we are truckers we always need more coffee."

"George, you drink much more and I am going to have to open up the bathrooms in the bar for the kids."

George looked at his wife with a smile on his face. "It wouldn't be the first time."

Roger had three cups of coffee with his friends and then made a few phone calls before he walked up the street to the police station. He talked with the Chief before he went to see the kids. "Tim, how are things in the cop business?"

"Roger, you here to bust my chops because I locked your kids up?"

"Hell no, you were just doing your job."

"Bullshit."

"Maybe a little, is the coffee here any better than it used to be?"

"I am the boss everything is better."

Roger sipped the coffee. "This stuff still tastes like crap."

"You want to throw it out?"

"No, I think you should give it to the kids then throw out the pot."

Tim smiled. "What did you and George decide to do about the fight?"

Roger set the empty cup down on the desk. "We were thinking the kids could clean up the bar and do some other work for George because they were defending themselves."

"We should talk to the judge about this."

"Tim, you know George can't do anything and I am sure you know I have cancer."

Tim smiled as he shook his head. "You two are so full of it."

Roger coughed as he placed a hand on his chest. "Cancer cough and it hurts."

Tim smiled even though he didn't want to. "Go, get out of my office, out of my station, and take your kids with you."

"Do I get all six of them?"

"Yes, make it fast or I will arrest you and George just for laughs."

Roger smiled as he stood up. "You should do something about that coffee before it kills you. I think it already made me sick."

"Get the hell out of here."

Roger left the office and then got the six young people out of jail. "I got you out but there is a price."

"Dad, with you there is always some kind of a catch."

"Luke, I wasn't in a fight in a bar last night."

Luke knew better than to argue. "Right, what kind of deal did you make?"

"The six of you are going to help clean up the bar you helped break up last night."

The statement was easy to say but getting the job done was going to be a little harder after all everyone had a job but Emily. Luke was the one that told his father the way he thought it was over coffee at the Circus Bar. They were all surprised as they surveyed the damage. None of them could believe how bad things were after all the fight hadn't lasted that long.

"Dad, we all want to help we know we have to but four of us have jobs and there is the hay on the farm that we have to get in."

"I didn't bring you all over here to go to work cleaning I brought you here so you could see what you have to do. As soon as you finish your coffee you can all go to the farm. Get your hay in then take care of your animals then get back here and start cleaning this place up."

"Mr. Richardson, I need to go home to let my parents know what has happened."

"Rhea, they know and I am sure once you get done here today they are going to have a lot to say to you but for now they have left this matter in my hands. As for your job I had a long talk with your boss and you are on vacation."

Luke shook his head there was a smile on his face. "You know for a minute I forgot who you were. I knew you were my father but I forgot that you were more than that. You are Roger Richardson the quiet man that knows more than he ever lets anyone know. You sit and you seem to know nothing of things but in fact, you know a lot."

"Luke, I found out your truck will be out of action for at least a week."

"Dad, my trucks are just fine and I don't get vacation time."

Roger smiled. "Dan, you do now I will be driving your truck for at least a week. You see I retired last week. You and I bought a garage where we are going to park the trucks."

"Was it last week or this morning when you retired?"

"Luke, I retired on Friday so I could spend some time with your mother."

Luke shook his head. "I still don't believe it but it will do for now I guess."

Roger ignored Luke. "Emma, you are on vacation too. All of you are on vacation until this bar gets fixed up and back in business."

Emma nodded her head. "Okay Dad, I will do what you want."

"Now let's get moving I have things to deliver today and you have things you need to be doing."

The six of them didn't say anything else they just walked out to the cars and got in. Roger drove out to the farm and then took the box truck to make Dan's deliveries for the day. The six of them got more coffee as well as several aspirins. It might have been that they had a lot to talk about but right then they had nothing they wanted to say to one another.

By the time they had finished the haying as well as the afternoon chores, the guy's father had already come and gone without a word. He had dropped off the truck without saying a word to any of them. Emma, Emily, and Rhea worked in the kitchen together while the guys had been out in the barn.

As they sat down to eat they had things they wanted to say to one another. As they started eating none of them seemed to want to be the first one to say anything. They had all let things get out of control for different reasons. As much as it may have seemed like they were all intelligent young people it was clear they were not as smart as they thought. Though they may have been smart they were young and the beer canceled out the brains.

At last, Emily spoke up she simply couldn't wait any longer. "I don't know about the rest of you but I want to know why your Dad seems to have so much control in all of this?"

The guys had come into the house and sat down at the table. What they all needed was sleep but there was still work that they were supposed to do. They could refuse but things just didn't work like that you had a job to do and you had to get it done. Life was not easy it was just life and you did what you had to do.

Luke got up and poured himself another coffee he was already four cups over what he usually drank. "About fifteen years ago the world was not what it is today. We were all a lot younger for one thing. Our parents were all friends back then, more or less. Emily's parents were trying to get a business started and it was not going well. They were having trouble finding people who would work for them for next to nothing.

"What they got was three drivers Rhea's father, George Fields, and our father. Our mothers worked in the factory. When things started to pick up George bought the bar our mothers quit their jobs to stay home with us. Then George wrecked his truck and our Dad pulled him out of the truck.

"Rhea, that was when your father quit driving and moved out of town."

Rhea nodded. "I hated moving because this was my uncle's farm. I used to come out here all the time but once we moved I could only come back a week or two a year."

Dan was surprised. "You were in my first-grade class at school."

Rhea smiled at him. "I sat right beside you."

Emily shook her head. "We all rode on the same bus that year. I had forgotten all about that."

Emma laughed. "I wasn't with you old people."

Luke looked at his sister then shook his head. "What I didn't remember I got from Jim Campbell at the jail."

Emily shook her head. "That was what you were talking to him about."

Luke smiled. "In a way we were, he was trying to tell me that your parents and his were the best of friends which is why you would marry him eventually."

Emily shook her head. "I think I hate small towns."

Rhea finished her coffee and then looked at the empty pot on the stove. "I have never felt like this before, hung over and trapped in a soap opera."

Emily nodded. "We don't call it that we just call it living in a small town."

Emma laughed. "We are all here because of Dad. Some people like him some hate him and they all listen to him."

Dan looked over at the empty coffee pot. "We should get into town there is nothing left for us to do here."

Steve looked at everyone. "What about my parents?"

Dan shook his head

Luke waved his hand as he headed for the door. "Come on kids we best get moving before Dad comes after us."

Dan got up. "He is right about Dad. Come on girls they have coffee in town."

Rhea nodded. "Coffee and aspirin I need more aspirin."

Dan laughed. "Little kids can't have any more aspirin."

"I know what you mean Dan, I feel like a little kid being sent to time out."

"Emily, Dad doesn't put us in time out he just puts us to work."

Emma laughed. "Dan, you know with him it is the same thing."

Without another word they all went out to the yard Emma had her own car, Rhea and Dan got in his car while Emily, Jack, and Luke got in his pickup. There was going to be a lot to do, it was going to be a very long week. There were still a lot of things they had to settle that had nothing to do with clearing up the bar.

Roger Richardson got home at about four in the afternoon. He sat in the living room watching the TV. He had enjoyed the work though he was tired. He was thinking about how things had been when he had been younger. Everything changed there were always new challenges and he loved a challenge. After a few minutes, he drifted off to sleep.

Rachael stood in the doorway looking at her husband with tears in her eyes. They had planned to travel when Roger retired but there would be no traveling now. There would be trips to the doctor and the hospital, those would be their only road trips. In time even those trips would be too much for him. Then one day he would be gone.

She would grow old alone, something that she had never expected to do. If not for Roger she would never have become strong enough to do it. He may not have been the perfect husband but he had been the right one for her. As she watched him sleep tears rolled down her face. It wasn't right or fair it just was and she hated it.

The wind was blowing just a bit as the lights of the town came on. Stars hung in the sky as they always did. People watched television or playing computer games. It was as it was every night yet it was different. Every night was different for someone. Things were always changing as time moved on. Rachael stood by the window tears in her eyes why couldn't they have more time together?

Rachael went to the kitchen where she started to clean. She washed the walls and then the floor. Going into the dining room she dusted everything. When she was done she went into the bathroom and cried. The world simply wasn't fair.

Chapter 33

Fixing up the bar was not as easy as they thought it was going to be. There were some changes George had been wanting to make at the bar. Looking around he thought he might as well make them while the bar was already closed. Besides a little free help was the best kind of help to have. There was no reason why he shouldn't get the most he could out of them.

Emma, Emily, Rhea, Luke, Dan, and Steve worked alongside Linda, George, and their six kids. They had coffee in the morning soda with their lunch and a beer at the end of the day. It might have been a punishment yet it didn't feel like it at the end of the day.

Every night after work Dan gave Rhea a ride home and then went back to the farm where Emily and Luke were waiting for him. They would eat then Emily would do the dishes after which the three of them would watch TV before they went to bed. They seemed to settle into the routine almost too quickly.

Emma went home most nights to spend time with her parents. They turned in early most nights which was not the way it had been before. When their Dad went for his first treatment Emma went with him and her mother. That night Emma went to work and cried every time she was alone. She might have seen it with people she didn't know but this was her Dad.

Emma did spend a night or two with Laurie and Steve because she needed to get out of the house. She could have gone to the farm but she wanted to be with her friends because they made her laugh. Each member of the family handled the whole thing in their way.

Roger talked the boys into leaving the stake truck on the farm and moving the box and Luke's truck to the garage. He bought a car hauler for the garage. He was spending his time getting the place ready for the boys to use. There were so many things he wanted to do even though he knew he would not have time to finish them all.

Two weeks after the fight the bar was set to reopen on a Saturday night. The day before at seven in the morning Roger Richardson went into surgery. Sitting in the waiting room with his wife and three kids were the Fields family, Emily, and Rhea with their parents. The hours passed slowly but when it was done the Doctor said he was doing well. The truth was they had gotten what they could and bought him some time but they didn't get it all.

Roger was tough but he wasn't going to win the battle they all knew that. Even though they all knew how things were going to go they didn't talk about it. Roger wasn't going to talk about it so no one else would either. They all respected Roger's wishes as they talked about everything else they could think of. There were no tears Roger didn't want to see them. There would be time enough for that when his battle was over.

The next morning at eight in the morning the Circus Bar reopened. Most of the people in town stopped in though not everyone was in the mood. Six people were out at the farm working in the hay field. Though they had been spending a lot of time together they were not talking much except about things that didn't matter. They talked a lot about the farm the girls wanted more cows the boys were thinking they already had enough.

Luke got two sodas out of the refrigerator, he sat down at the table and then handed Emily one of the sodas. "I am going to have to get back out on the road Sunday night."

Dan refilled his coffee cup and Rhea's then sat back down at the table. "I figured you would. Don't worry I can take care of things around here."

"I know I wasn't worried about that we have a bigger problem."

Dan looked at his brother surprised. "What problem?"

Emily raised her hand. "That would be me."

Dan still didn't see a problem. "What is wrong with you?"

Emma shook her head. "This town is going to love talking about that."

Steve looked confused. "Talking about what?"

"The fact that I am here."

"So what Rhea and I are here too."

Rhea put her cup down on the table. "Dan, I don't live here it would just be the two of you here every night."

"So what, she needs a place to stay."

Emily smiled at Dan. "I need to go home is what they are saying. I walked out of the house with nowhere to go, I was in a bar fight, I got arrested and I have been here for two weeks."

Dan looked at Rhea but he was talking to Emily and Luke as well. "There is no reason for her to leave if she doesn't want to."

Rhea smiled but Emily spoke up. "Dan, I would love to stay here on the farm I like it but if I don't go home and make things right with my parents I really won't be happy anywhere."

"I suppose you are right but I was just getting used to having you all here I don't think I want to go back to living alone."

Rhea rubbed the top of his head. "Don't worry I am not going to stop coming around I am not done molding you yet."

Luke smiled at his brother. "Dan, this place feels like home for the first time and it is because you have made yourself at home here. It is also because there is more to life than just the two of us and Jack."

Rhea took his hand. "Dan, I never lived life until I came back here and spent time with you. You have to understand life to live it and I didn't understand it. Getting drunk was something I never thought I would do because my father told me not to. Now I know why he told me not to. I have done a lot over the last twenty-eight days that I never thought I would do but I don't regret any of it I have learned a lot."

Emily looked at the others she had never thought she would be sitting here. "So have I, most important of which was never sleep naked under the bathroom sink."

Emma shook her head. "You had to mention that again."

Steve smiled. "Emma has been naked in the bathroom too."

Luke shook his head. "Now that is a story I think we should keep to ourselves."

"Luke, I wish you had said that earlier it was in the church newsletter this week. I should have known Dad couldn't keep it to himself."

"Rhea, you are so lucky that I know you are full of it."

"I am sorry but at least I didn't make you wear that awful shirt of Linda's that was too tight everywhere that counts."

Dan smiled. "I liked that shirt on you."

Rhea looked at him. "Dan, shut up or Emily will be driving me home."

Luke smiled. "I thought Emily looked good in my shirt."

Emily laughed. "That isn't your shirt anymore."

Just before ten, Luke took Emily home and Dan took Rhea home. Steve took Emma home spending a little time talking to her parents. Dan dropped Rhea off while Luke sat and waited for Emily to come out to let him know everything was okay. He wanted to be sure she was okay before he headed home. Dan left Rhea's a good fifteen minutes later than Luke left Emily's. Rhea was in her house and bed while Emily was still sitting on the front porch with her father.

"Emily, I should have left you alone but I thought you were just nerves."

"Dad, I have a good idea why you did what you did. Why don't we just let it go."

"I didn't realize Jim was such a complete fool."

"That is a nice way to put it. I want you to know I will never be that nice to him again."

"I just didn't understand."

"Dad, it is not true you knew just what he was like but he is a guy and guys need to do guy stuff before they settle down."

"You think I want him doing that to you?"

"That was just the point he wasn't doing that to me he was doing that to every other skirt in this town."

"You want your job back?"

"No, but I need it."

"I fired Jim."

"Why?"

"I did it because he is a rapist, as well as a child molester."

"You didn't do it for me you did it for the company."

"I did it because what he did was wrong."

"I know that girl and she would just as soon rub up against you as him she doesn't care as long as she gets what she wants."

"Then maybe they should lock her up too."

"Maybe they should lock her up and let poor Jim out? Dad, if that is the way she is what did Jim do that was so wrong?"

"She will just do the same thing to someone else you know that."

Emily shook her head a sad smile on her face. "Here we go again. Poor Jim that girl made him do it."

"I didn't say that I just think that she should have dated boys her age."

"Dad, Jim knew who she was and he knew how old she is and he knew she was his damn cousin! He took her to his bed just the same! The only difference between them is their sex. You kept pushing me at him like he was something special but I want you to know there is nothing special about that pig."

"Emily, I am sorry."

"Maybe so Dad, but it isn't enough right now it just isn't enough."

"What are you going to do?"

"Tomorrow I am going to pack my things and see if I can get my room back out at the farm."

"Emily, please don't be mad at me."

"Dad, I am not mad at you I need time to think, I need time to figure out what I should do next."

"Out at the farm with Roger's boys?"

"For now, and before you ask again yes, I do still want my job at least until I get things straight in my mind."

"You can't do that at home?"

"I don't think so."

"Why?"

"Because you and Mom are here and you would try to fix it."

"That is what parents do."

"Yes, but that is not what I need right now. I need to figure out how to handle things myself."

"We should go in and tell your mother."

"Dad, I am not mad at you or Mom. I am twenty-four years old and I think it is time I figured out just what it is that I want out of life."

"I think you are right."

Emily went into the house to her room where she sat on her bed and cried. This was not the way things were supposed to be, her parents were supposed to care more for her than they did Jim. No matter what they did they couldn't make right what had happened to Jim's father. She needed to decide what to do next. She couldn't live on the farm she needed a place of her own. Emily would only stay at the farm until she could find a place.

Emily didn't sleep she had too much on her mind. Her parents didn't want to let her go. Luke didn't want to commit to her or anyone else. He liked her she could tell but he was scared it wouldn't work out. That was fine with her she was in no hurry Jim had made sure of that. Trust was not something she had a lot of at the moment. She just wanted to let things go and see what would happen in time.

Rhea was up early she had a cup of coffee and then drove to work. She had been up most of the night thinking about a lot of things most of which had to do with Dan Richardson. He was a really good guy but he wasn't the guy she had thought she would marry. Dan wasn't a Pastor and she had learned that she was not going to be a Pastor's wife. Dan had faith which was more than most of the young men that she knew had.

Emily might not know it yet but she was not going to stay home. She would try to move into the farm because she felt safe there but that couldn't happen there would be nothing but trouble if she did that. It was going to have to be different someone was going to have to help her before she did something crazy. By the end of her shift, Rhea knew what she was going to do to help Emily as well as Luke and Dan.

When Rhea got home she took a shower and then dressed in her jeans and a shirt she had gotten from Dan. It was comfortable and it was his so the fit didn't matter. The shirt fit her no matter what size it was. The outfit was just what she needed when working around the farm. She went to the window to look at the pickup she had bought. It may not have been something her father would have bought her but she liked it.

"Rhea, can we talk for a minute."

"Sure Mom, is something wrong?"

"Not that I know of but you are up to something and I would like to know what it is."

"What makes you say that?"

"First and most importantly you are my daughter. The second reason is the pickup you bought yourself."

"I like the pickup and I thought it was time I had something of my own."

"Are you going to tell me the rest?"

"Emily Rice is going to need a place to stay so she is going to ask the guys to let her stay at the farm. I think that is a really bad idea."

"You mean because Dan is there?"

"No, it is because we live in a small town. If she is left out there Emily and Dan will become our Linda and Roger."

"You know about that?"

"Mom, everyone knows about that. People have to talk about something even if it isn't true."

Her Mom smiled. "That is what Linda said fifteen years ago. We all did what we thought was right back then just as you are doing now. One thing changed all our lives. When George got to hurt your father knew he had to become a pastor and Roger knew he had to stand by George and his family. The thing that most people forget is that there were two people in that truck that day. Big Jim Campbell was riding with George. He jumped out of the truck and then was killed by the trailer."

"I didn't know that."

"Most people don't they have forgotten all about him."

"Was he a good man?"

"One of the best but he never should have been in that truck."

"Mom, I have to go they are waiting for me we have to get the hay in the barn."

"Rhea be careful and remember Jim Campbell is nothing like his father."

Rhea thought about what her mother had told her on the way out to the farm. There was so much they didn't know about what had happened when their parents were young. They had made choices that had made things the way they were now. Emily's parents felt guilty about the death of one man so they tried to make his son a part of their family. The problem was the son was not his father. He seemed to be just the opposite of his father. Where one seemed to have been a good man the other was a creep.

This was even more of a reason why Emily could not stay at the farm Jim would make sure everyone in town started talking. Her idea was better after all Emily would still have a place to live. She could still go out to the farm when she wanted and she would not have to live alone. It seemed to be the perfect plan as long as Emily agreed to it.

Luke was getting the baler ready to go when Emily parked her car by the house he had expected her to come back but not today. He had expected it would take more than a day to get things to put right with her parents.

"Emily, I didn't think you would be here today."

"You want me to leave?"

"No, I just thought you would need a little more time to work things out."

"I do but I can't do it there too much has happened, I need time to think and I need a place to stay."

"You want to stay here?"

"I would go back on the road with you but I have to go to work in the morning."

"I am not going to be here."

"I had that much figured out before I got here."

"I don't mind if you stay but I think you need to talk to Dan not me."

"I was going to but he is going to tell me it is your farm so I ask you now then I will ask him."

Luke laughed. "I see you have this all worked out so I will just let you handle it. Dan is out raking the field he will agree to your idea if you bring him a cup of coffee."

"Do you think I should talk to Rhea first?"

"Emily, I thought you had this all worked out?"

"So did I but I forgot about her."

"You move in here she won't forget about you."

"I was thinking the same thing maybe I should go somewhere else."

"Okay, where?"

"I don't know I was thinking I was going to stay here and help out when I wasn't at work."

"You talk with Rhea when she gets here then the two of you can let Dan and I know what is going on."

"You are going to leave it up to us?"

"Dan and I lost control around here weeks ago. As long as we are all in agreement it will be okay."

Luke got on the tractor and then went out to the field to start baling hay. As he went out to the field Rhea pulled into the driveway parking her truck behind Emily's car. Rhea waved to her as she walked toward her. Emily was nervous though she didn't think she should be.

"Emily, I thought you would be here this morning though Dan was sure you would be at home still getting things back in order there."

"You want a cup of coffee we can't start for a while?"

"I didn't think you were a coffee drinker."

Emily smiled. "I don't usually drink a lot of coffee. There is nothing wrong with a cup now and then. I think it is good for you."

"I take it things didn't go well with your parents?"

"You could say that they just don't seem to understand that I am tired of living their lives I want to live my own."

"You want to come back here don't you?"

"Luke said it was okay with him but I had to talk to Dan. Luke and I thought it might be best if I talked to you first."

"Emily, I don't think it would be a problem but we live in a small town and if you were here alone with Dan people would talk."

"People are always talking."

"I know but do you want them talking about you the way they talk about Cassie Edwards?"

"Not really though people don't bother me that much."

"That is just how Linda Fields felt sixteen years ago."

"What does that mean?"

"When people started talking about her and the guys' Dad she didn't care she thought it would all blow over after a while."

Emily poured them each a cup of coffee and then sat down at the table. "You think that they would do the same thing to Dan and me if I stay here?"

"You know Jim better than I do what do you think he will say?"

"Damn it! When does my life become about what I want?"

"Right now, it is all up to you. I am not telling you what to do just think about everything involved then do what you think is best."

"I see what you mean but I still feel like everyone is running my life but me."

Rhea nodded. "I know but the first thing you have to do is decide what you want to do."

Emily looked into the bottom of her empty cup. She wanted to throw it against the wall but it wasn't hers. "Oh hell, what is the point!"

Rhea placed her cup on the table. "Now that we have that settled, we should get out there and help the guys before Dan comes in here looking for us."

Dan had finished the raking; he was on his way back to get the truck. As he started toward the garage he saw Emily was already driving it out to the field. He jumped onto the back of the truck with Rhea to ride back out to the field.

Rhea stacked the bales on the truck as Dan passed them up to her. While they were doing that Luke baled up the hay and then went to the barn to do the chores. When he has finished the first load of hay was ready to be stacked in the barn. While the guys did that Rhea and Emily took care of the milk then the four of them went back out to the field.

When they finished the second and last load of the day the guys went to work stacking it in the barn. The two girls went into the house and then straight to the kitchen. Rhea got out the cups and then placed them on the table. Emily filled two of the cups with hot coffee and then put the pot back on the stove. The two of them then sat down at the table. At first, they didn't say a word each of them wondering what they were going to say to one another.

Rhea looked at Emily. "Emily, did you ask Dan if you could stay here?"

"I asked Luke and I talked to you but I didn't say anything to Dan."

Rhea nodded. "I thought you would come out here for a place to stay. I thought about it all night and I think I have a better idea. What would you say to share a place with me?"

"Are we going to throw the guys off the farm?"

"I thought about it. There is a small two-bedroom house not far from here and the owner just wants someone to keep an eye on the place the rent is really low for a two-bedroom house."

"Why are you doing this?"

"Because I think it will be good for all of us."

"What am I going to do tonight? I really can't go back home again I will end up right back where I was before."

"I thought you might like to spend some time at my parent's house. It shouldn't be more than a night or two."

"This should be interesting."

Luke grabbed a cup off the table. "What should be interesting?"

Dan took the last cup off the table and let his brother fill it. "What are you gals talking about now?"

"Emily and I are going to share a house not far from here."

"Rhea says I can stay with her and her parents until we can get into the house."

Luke sat down at the table. "No more week-long trips in the truck with you I guess."

Dan sat down at the table with the others. "Pastor Emily Rice. I am not sure I could get used to that."

Luke laughed. "I don't think she could."

Emily shook her head. "No way Pal."

Luke looked at Emily. "I thought you were going to stay here with Dan?"

Emily nodded. "That was the plan until I talked to Rhea. I like her plan better."

Dan laughed. "That means I still have to eat my own cooking."

Rhea shook her head. "Not all the time if you are lucky."

Chapter 34

Luke was back on the road with Jack but things were different somehow. He still loved to drive but there was more to life than just driving a truck. Jack had his seat back but he didn't sit in it much anymore. Jack was getting old he needed to be home where he could do things he wanted to do. Time has a way of changing everything whether we like it or not. He was not sure what he was going to do if he didn't have Jack with him anymore.

Luke had been back on the road two months but it seemed more like a year. There was just too much time to think about things he didn't want to think about, things he didn't want to even know about. He knew what was going on with his Dad at home. Even if he wasn't there he kept in touch getting daily updates. As much as he loved the driving he was sure it was time for a change of some kind. He had to decide where he was needed the most.

The dinner was empty except for the cook and the waitress. The waitress brought him a soda and then took his order. Luke watched her walk away and he shook his head. Even she didn't look at him the same way anymore. It was worse than starting over. He missed the farm but he didn't want to stop driving.

The waitress brought his food smiling as she set it on the table. "What happened to your girlfriend?"

"She went back to work so Jack and I are on our own again."

"That reminds me we have a bone in the kitchen for Jack."

"Thanks, he will really like that."

"What will it take to make you happy again?"

"I was just asking myself that question."

"Maybe you need to find yourself a partner that can talk."

Luke grinned at her. "Why are you looking to change your job?"

"Sometimes I wish I could but I don't spend enough time with my kids as it is."

"I didn't know you were married."

"You aren't supposed to; if most of these guys think I am available the tips are bigger. Are you going to stop driving?"

"I thought about it but I like my job. It isn't that I like being alone I like the road and I like being my boss most of the time."

"That is what my husband used to say right before he ran off with some redhead named Linda something or other."

"I had a wife named Linda once but she wasn't a redhead and I have known a redhead who wanted to get me into trouble but her name wasn't Linda."

"I will go get that bone for Jack."

When Luke left the diner he was feeling a little better about things. He still thought he should find a way to be home more but the job was the job you couldn't change it whenever the mood hit. He was a trucker he liked being a trucker but he missed a lot by not being at home.

By the end of the week, Luke was no closer to an answer than he had been at the start of the week. There didn't seem to be any answer to his question so he did the only thing he could do he quit his job. He drove the truck home. He parked the rig near the garage and then walked to the house for a cup of coffee. He sat at the kitchen table thinking about what he had just done.

He was supposed to park the rig at the garage his Dad had bought for Dan. Luke hadn't done that because he didn't want anyone to know he was back until he had talked with Emily. Long-distance relationships were hard to keep together at times. She needed to know she was first in his mind so he had to be sure she was the first one he told about this change.

Luke also needed a new job but that would have to wait until he figured out just what it was he wanted to do. He had a few ideas about places that might be good. He just had to be able to get a job at one of them. It was true that he needed high pay but he could work for less if he had to. He might have to sell the horses but he would do his best not to let it come to that.

Luke called Emily and told her he was home and that he had quit his job. He then asked her if she would give him a ride back to his former place of employment so he could get his pickup truck. She said she would be right there and she seemed upset.

As Luke sat there he thought she should be happy to have him around a little more. Why did she sound upset with him? Maybe it wasn't what he had told her that had bothered her maybe he had just caught her at a bad time. Luke knew her job wasn't easy they expected a lot from her. Why wouldn't they after all one day she was going to own the company?

As he sat thinking about things he was wondering if he should have called her. He could have waited for Dan to come home but he just wanted to talk to Emily. He wanted to let her know why he had quit his job. She had left her job before she would understand why he had done what he had done. She might even offer him a job after all it had been a good place for his Dad for a lot of years.

Jack was curled up in his usual spot which he didn't move from when Emily arrived. A good dog knows when to get up and go. A really good dog knows when to stay home. Jack was a really good dog; he also had a bone to work on. There was no need to follow Luke everywhere after all he was a grown man. There were some things he was just going to have to handle on his own.

Luke stood up and looked at Jack working on his bone. "No need for you to come with me I got this," Luke said then went out the door.

Luke got in the car and Emily pulled out of the driveway before his door was even closed. "You quit your job? Just like that with no notice, nothing at all you just quit? Jobs don't grow on trees these days you know? What the hell were you thinking?"

"Hi Emily, I want to thank you for giving me a ride over to get my pickup. Yes, I quit my job. I quit it just like that without notice. Yes,

I do realize that jobs don't grow on trees anymore. I was thinking I wanted to be home a little more than I am."

"Hi."

"Hi, I think we should talk."

"You are crazy, you know that right? You can't just quit your job. People see that and they don't trust you so they don't hire you. You might be the best driver there ever was. You have to know that won't matter to them. It won't matter because you quit without notice. You might do the same thing to them."

"I know that."

"Then why didn't you give a two-week or even a one-week notice?"

"I didn't want to wait that long I might change my mind."

"This isn't like you."

Luke laughed. "I know it is more like you. I guess you were in the truck too long."

"I was only there a week."

"I guess it was a long week."

"Don't try to be funny."

"I wasn't."

"You don't understand how serious this is."

"Emily, I do understand. I don't think that you are hearing me."

Emily just looked at him she had a lot of things going through her mind none of them was anything she wanted to say out loud. She stopped the car in the parking lot where Luke's pickup was parked. "Rhea and I are having dinner at the farm with Dan tonight I will see you then."

Luke didn't say a word he just got out of the car and then stood watching her drive away. That had gone over like a paper bag on an open flame. He wasn't sure what she was mad about after all he was the one without a job. Women were like a bottle of wine you had on the shelf for a while. You just couldn't be sure which way it had gone until you opened it. Emily was crazy she had to be to get so mad at him because he had quit his job. You would think he had taken money out of her pocket.

Luke waved a dismissing hand in the direction Emily had gone. There were other things he could be doing he didn't need to deal with the drama now. Getting in his pickup he drove over to his parent's house and then mowed their lawn. He went into the house when he was done to have coffee with his Mom.

"Luke, what is going on you rarely drink coffee this late in the day?"

"I quit my job this afternoon. Emily is mad at me though I couldn't tell you why. Mom, you would think we were married and had a house full of kids the way she reacted."

"I can tell you she is not going to have a baby."

"Mom, I knew that but what other reason could there be for her to get all mad at me? It was my job and I thought she might be happy to have me around a little more."

"Give her time to calm down I am sure she will tell you what is bothering her."

"Mom, I am not sure what I am going to do next I could have used a little support instead of a slap in the face."

"Give her a chance to think about it I am sure she will calm down and stand beside you."

"How is Dad doing?"

His Mom smiled. "He is doing fine. He seems to like being home more and more. He spends more time with me and he still has time to play cards with George."

"I have to get going Dan is going to have questions when he finds my tractor and trailer in the yard."

"Luke, everyone needs a change now and then there is nothing wrong with that."

Luke smiled at his mother. "Mom, you don't have to tell me that Emily is the one that needs to hear that."

Luke left the house with plans to get to the farm just so he could find out what was going on. The Circus Bar was not the farm but he found himself there just the same. Going inside he took a seat at the bar and then ordered a beer. It was early yet he had some time to kill before Dan got home. Even though it was Friday there were not that many people in the bar.

Linda set a beer on the bar in front of him. "Luke, you look like a man with a problem."

"I quit my job and Emily is mad at me though I don't know why."

"You know the day after George's accident when we all knew he was going to live everyone came in here even your Mom. We closed the place that night and we got a friend to watch all our kids then we started drinking. Big Jim was dead George was alive but he was never going to walk again. Emily's parents wanted to close the business after all it was their truck that George and Big Jim had been in.

I bet you have never really looked at the pictures in here, have you? If you had you would have noticed that George, Big Jim, your Dad, our Pastor, Emily's Dad, and I are in every one of them. Your Mom took most of those pictures Emily's Mom took a couple even Rhea's Mom took at least one.

Jim's wife Connie worked here for a little while because we were all good friends back then. That night we sat in here and we all got drunk. We got so drunk that night that we never left here we just passed out on the floor. When morning came we got up and drank gallons of coffee before everyone went home. I was never that drunk before nor did I ever get that drunk again.

Everyone drifted apart after that everyone but your parents stopped coming here. Your Mom and Dad helped get this place on its feet. They helped get everything ready for George when he got out of the hospital.

If it wasn't for them I don't think George and I would have been able to hold onto this place."

Luke looked at her wondering just what was going on. Why was she telling him all of this now? "I never heard any of that before."

"I am not surprised we don't talk about it anymore."

"Why tell me all that now?"

"I thought it was time that you knew what it was like back then, back when all the stories started about your Dad and me."

"Dad said you were friends so I accepted that."

Linda smiled. "That may be true but you always had questions I know because my kids had questions. Your Dad came in here every night and he went upstairs with George. They never said what they were doing they just got drunk then your Dad went home. I was getting mad and your Mom was mad. It was like we were not even a part of their lives anymore. Then one Sunday morning your Dad brought you all over here and he made us all breakfast. George came down here on his own that morning for the first time.

"I think your Mom cried as hard as I did that morning. George wasn't supposed to be able to get out of bed on his own but he had the will and your Dad was there to help him. George can't walk far but he can get in and out of bed on his own thanks to your father. It was never me he came here to see."

Luke saw the tears in Linda's eyes she was happy as well as proud. Luke reached across the bar and hugged her. There were even tears in his eyes by then. "I have to get home I hear we are having guests for dinner tonight."

As Luke went out to the truck he was thinking that there was so much he didn't know about his parents. Just because you live in a small town and you know all the stories that people tell it doesn't mean you know what happened in the town. Luke was beginning to understand that the past was so much more important than he had ever thought it was. His parents were so much more than he had thought. They were people who had more to their lives than just their children. The more he thought about it the more he was sure he had done the right thing when he quit his job.

He was going to get a short-haul job so he could be home more because he wanted to get to know his family before it was too late. It might cost him a little money but that didn't matter. There were a lot of things in the world that was so much more important than money. Besides he would find a way to make it work he always did.

For the first time in what seemed like a very long time, he was feeling good about things. Nothing was perfect but he would be home on nights he could spend time with his family and with Emily. He was going to be around to help more than he had been. He was going to stop running away from the past. This was his chance to learn how to deal with the way things were. It was going to make him a better person.

Chapter 35

Luke drove back to the farm parked the pickup by the garage then walked to the house. Emily's car was parked near the house beside Dan's car. This was one of those times when he really wished he had taken up smoking so he could stand outside a little while longer. He didn't want to face them just yet but he had put it off as long as he could.

Going into the house he heard them talking in the dining room so he went to the kitchen to get himself a beer before he went in to face them.

When he did walk into the dining room they all looked up at him smiles on their faces. Now he knew he was in trouble.

"Am I late?"

Dan passed him the potatoes. "No, we just sat down."

"I went by the house and mowed the lawn then I stopped by the Circus Bar and talked to Linda for a bit."

"I knew you went by the house Mom called."

"I guess she wanted to let you know I wasn't hiding anywhere."

Dan passed his brother the meat. "I hear you quit your job."

"It seemed like the thing to do at the time."

"Do you have any idea what you want to do for work next?"

"I have a couple of ideas."

"That is good."

Emily couldn't take the whole nice guy routine any longer. "You should have talked to us before you just quit your job."

"Emily, did we get married the night we all got drunk? I have to tell you if we did I don't remember any of it."

"Marry you? Pal, you are lucky I am even talking to you."

"That is funny I don't feel lucky."

Rhea slammed her hand down on the table. "Okay, kids I think that is enough. We need to talk not argue. Luke, you need to be told what has been going on around here."

Luke looked around the table he had a feeling he was losing control of his life. He smiled, hell he had lost control of things months ago. "Okay, which one of you is going to tell me just what it is that I need to know."

Emily looked at him while Rhea and Dan were looking at her. "We bought a couple more cows."

"Okay, you bought a couple more cows that are not that big a deal. Did you find someone to take the extra milk?"

"That wasn't a problem."

"We made a couple of changes or at least we are going to."

"What kind of changes?"

"Build a milk house as well as a free stall barn."

Luke was calm he sipped his beer and then smiled at them all. "I want to say that I have enjoyed spending time with all of you but I think I need to go now."

Emily looked at him a little nervous. "Where are you going?"

"I think I will go see if I can't get my job back. I don't think I am needed here anymore but the money is."

Emily shook her head. "That isn't what we said."

"Emily, you have been yelling at me since you found out I quit my job."

"We planned this diner so that we could tell you what we were doing. We all thought once you heard us out you would agree with us. You quit your job then I overreacted. I should have stayed calm but I lost my temper."

Rhea looked at Luke she could see the same look she had seen on Dan's face when she first talked to him about expanding the farm. "Just listen to the whole plan before you say anything else."

"The three of you have a plan. This should be good I can't wait to hear it."

Rhea got up and went to the Refrigerator she got out four beers and then brought them back to the table. She gave one to every one of her friends and then sat back down. "I came up with the idea then I convinced Emily it was a good idea. The two of us came over here and told Dan about it. He took it about as well as you are at first but he came around."

Luke picked up the bottle of beer she had put in front of him. "How many of these did he drink before he opened his eyes to this great plan of yours?"

"I gave him coffee."

"Okay, what is this big plan of yours?"

"We turn this place into a dairy farm we have a deal with the closest dairy they will take the milk."

"I know you want to do this but it costs money which is something that is in short supply these days. At least now I know why Emily was so mad at me all of you need that big check of mine to make this work."

Emily looked at him the anger was gone from her eyes she was scared now. "Luke, we want to help we want you to sell us shares in the farm."

"You want to buy shares in the farm? You are crazy all three of you this is no time to start something like this."

Emily looked at him with a business look. "There isn't going to be a better time."

Luke sat there looking at Emily doing his best to understand just what was going on. "I am on the road all week when I get home I find you three are moving on without me. This is the reason I quit my job I am missing everything I want to be a part of. Don't get me wrong I think you are all crazy but there are three of you and only one of me. So we are going to go into the dairy business."

"You need a job."

Luke looked at Emily. "Are you my wife?"

"Thankfully no, I have enough problems already."

"You want to run a dairy herd on this place you are going to need a lot more than a new barn and a milk house. You don't have enough pasture."

Dan looked at his brother. "If we don't have enough pasture we don't have enough fields for hay and we are going to have to start growing corn for the cows."

Rhea was looking at her empty bottle. "The place we are renting has a lot of land with it and it used to be a dairy farm it already has everything we were going to have to build here."

Luke looked at her. "If we could get it I would never be here I would have to be on the road almost all the time the three of you are going to be here doing the work. What you want to do is not going to work as a part-time job it is going to be full-time and then some."

Rhea nodded her head. "We already had that figured out I am going to quit my job it pays less than everyone else so I will be the one working with the cows."

Emily got up she got them each another beer then sat back down at the table. "Dan and I will be here every afternoon as well as all day on the weekends."

Rhea shook her head. "Saturday morning we all go to church."

Emily looked at her she wanted to say no but that wasn't what came out. "I don't go much."

"You might change your mind. Dan and I would love to have you come with us."

"We will see."

Luke looked at Jack then at his brother. "I go back on the road Jack is going to have to stay here and ride with you."

"Not a problem I like Jack."

"I will call Helen in the morning and see what I can do about getting my job back."

"You are going to have to be around to sign papers from time to time."

Luke smiled. "Rhea, don't you worry about that I am sure Emily has that all worked out."

The girls left then Dan got out two more beers. "We are in way over our heads aren't we?"

"Submarines don't go this deep."

"You have a plan though."

"I don't know as I have a plan but I have a couple of ideas."

"Luke, I am sorry I know why you wanted to change jobs. He is going to be okay for a while you can find a good job closer to home when he needs you."

Luke sat back in his chair. "You are all crazy, we owe money on this place and we owe money on the garage we can't afford another loan."

"Dad paid for the garage we have Cora and Kevin Farley running the place with Dad's help of course."

"What the hell is going on around here?"

Dan looked at his brother. "We want to do something together and Rhea sold us on the farm idea."

Luke shook his head. "If we are going to do this we have to start right. We go partners then we rent to own the farm you are talking about."

Dan was wondering just what Luke was thinking. "Why rent to own?"

Luke sat calmly. "I think we are getting in over our heads but I am willing to try this as long as we don't get in too far over our heads. If things don't work we can cut down the size of the herd and come back at it a little slower."

Dan looked at Luke surprised. "You would be willing to do that?"

"Everybody has a dream and I don't see why mine should be more important than anyone else."

Dan shook his head. "As long as we go at this a little slower you are going to give up control of this place?"

"Dan, a good idea is not always as good as it looks from a distance."

"What do we do now?"

"Let's just get drunk and forget the whole damn world."

"That sounds good to me."

"I know but I have to get my job back in the morning then I have to come back here to help with the haying."

They finished their beer and then went to bed though Luke didn't get much sleep there was just too much going through his mind. They had talked a lot and as he lay in bed he realized why Emily had been so mad at him. She had worked it all out on paper she knew what they could do before they talked to Dan. When he told her he had quit his job he thought she would understand. Now he understood that she had accepted him for who he was and planned accordingly she wasn't ready for him to change.

By morning Luke was tired, short-tempered, and glad he was going back on the road. He did the morning chores and then left Dan to clean the barn. He drove over to the trucking company where he found Helen Conroy in her office. He placed the coffee he had bought her on her desk then grabbed a chair and sat down. "Good morning Helen."

"Luke, what do you want?"

"I was hoping to get my old job back."

"Sorry that position is filled."

"That was fast, who did you get?"

"You."

"Me."

"I figured you would be back so I just didn't do anything about your statement on Friday."

"Thanks, I really need the job."

"Luke, you are a good driver, and now a day that is something rare. Drivers your age usually can't drive, we are glad to have you here."

"Helen, I didn't know you thought so highly of me."

"Don't let it go to your head."

"You don't need to worry about that I promise if I ever think about quitting again I will talk to you first."

"Luke, I know things happen which don't always let us do things in the right way. I know your Dad, he is an old friend of mine. Did you know I knew him before your Mom did?"

"No, I never knew anything about that."

"He was something when we were young I can tell you that. I would have married him if he had asked me."

"You liked him that much?

"He was hot back in those days."

"You liked him I take it."

"I spent a lot of time with him when we were in high school. Those were some very good times. We even stole a car once."

"You did?"

"Yes, it was my Dad's car and I left him a note but your father didn't know about that. We drove around for the better part of the night. It was the best night of my life. I used to wonder what it would be like if we had gotten married."

"Okay, that is enough of this I have to get moving I have hay fields calling my name."

"I thought your Dad was something. You are sure to tell him I am still thinking about him."

"Thanks for understanding Helen, as well as the history lesson. I promise I won't soon forget the last couple of days. I have to tell you things have been a little crazy the last month or so."

Helen smiled at him. "Now get out of here I don't have time to visit I have work to do."

"Thanks again," Luke said as he went out the door.

Luke drove over to the garage his Dad and brother had bought. Roger was sitting in the office reading a book while Kevin Farley was working on a car in the garage bay. There were two bays in the garage where Dan's trucks were parked at night. The spare truck as well as the tow truck were packed behind the garage during the day when not in use. The flatbed and box truck was always parked out behind the garage.

Roger put his book down when his oldest son walks in. "Luke, your Mom told me you were in town."

Jack found a spot on the floor near Roger while Luke stood by the desk. "I quit my job yesterday; I got it back this morning. Helen told me to say hi to you."

"She is a good friend."

"She told me some things that made it sound like you had been more than friends at one time."

Roger smiled. "Helen and I had some really good times when we were young."

"So she said. It sounds like you two were a bit on the wild side."

"I might have married her if I hadn't met your mother."

Luke shuffled his feet. "You are getting thin."

"I lost a couple of pounds and a little hair. The women like my new look."

"I wasn't going to say anything about the hair."

"It is no big thing they tell me it will grow back."

"Rhea, Emily, Dan, and I are going into the dairy business."

"Your brother was telling me about it I think you should ask your sister to help."

"Emma? Why do you want her to help?"

"She is spending too much time at home she needs something to do."

Luke was surprised. "I will talk to her about it if you think it will help her."

"It will. Why did you quit your job?"

"I wanted to spend more time at home."

Roger looked at his eldest son. "I know you think it would be best if you were here but it would only be harder on us all. There is nothing we can do it is up to the doctors and God."

"It is hard to do nothing."

"I know but it would be even harder if you were here day after day."

Luke shook his head. "I feel like I should be home."

Roger shook his head. "I would be on the road if it was you or your Mom because there is nothing to do here. Life is never easy it just is, we have to do the best we can. You kids are trying to build something for the future. I will be happy watching you all doing what you need to do."

"Then I guess I best go talk to Emma."

Luke went out the door and Jack watched him go. Jack had a new job now he was going to stay with Roger. Times changed he knew Roger needed him now even if no one else knew it. People thought they knew it all but they were not the only animals with brains.

Luke drove to his parent's house where he hoped to talk Emma into joining them at the farm for a meal. He was also going to have to tell Dan that Jack would not be riding with him. Jack as always had gone where he wanted to go. It was funny how things were working out everything was changing and all he could do was watch. He felt very alone as if he were no longer a part of life at all. Everyone had plans and dreams all he had was the truck and the highway.

Emma was in the kitchen having a coffee when Luke walked in. "You have enough left in that pot to give some coffee to me?"

Emma pointed at the cupboard. "You know where the cups are."

"It is nice to see you too."

"What do you want from me this morning?"

"I wanted to invite you out to the farm for a meal."

"Tonight?"

"That was the plan."

"I have a date tonight."

Luke smiled. "You can bring Stephen with you if you want. I will buy more beer on the way home."

"Food and beer, I think we might make it unless you are cooking."

"Rhea and Emily are doing the cooking."

Emma smiled. "Then I think we can make it."

"The girls are spending an awful lot of time together with you boys aren't they?"

"Dan is spending time with them. I am a truck driver I am never home so I am not spending a lot of time with anyone. Even Jack isn't riding with me anymore."

"Why not?"

"He is with Dad."

"You left him with Dad?"

"No, Jack decided one of us had to keep an eye on Dad."

Emma hugged her brother. "That was a real nice thing to do."

"Thanks I hope it helps in some way."

Luke went back to the house picking up some beer on the way. He was sure Emma would join them even if it was just to help from time to time. This would all work as long as they were all getting along. Families didn't always get along he had learned that. He wasn't a fortune teller so he would have to wait and see just like everyone else.

That evening the six of them sat at the dining room table for supper talking about farming as well as living arrangements. Emma surprised them all by agreeing to help as did Stephen. Their jobs would affect the time they could spend helping but they would help as much as they could. It all just seemed to come together as if they had all wanted to be farmers all along. They drank a little too much beer so they all spent the night at the farm.

Sunday morning the girls made coffee, and breakfast and handed out the aspirin. The guys took aspirin with their morning coffee and then went out to the barn. After the chores, they went into the house to eat their breakfast and get more coffee.

When it was time Dan went out to rake the hay. Every one of them was enjoying their time together. This would be the end of haying for the year. They had a cookout planned for later in the afternoon to celebrate the end of the season. They had gotten two cuttings of haying that year.

When the day was over Emma and Stephen left the farm. Emily and Rhea cleaned up the kitchen Dan did some work in the barn while Luke got his things ready to go. He packed his bag and then took it out to the truck. He stood looking out across the field. This had started as his dream and now he was sharing it with everyone it seemed.

Sunday night Emily and Luke sat in his rig at the farm looking at the star-filled sky. It had been a wild couple of days for them filled with lots of people with no real time for themselves. They had gotten off to a rough start and then just made believe it hadn't happened.

Emily looked at him wondering what she should say to him before he left. "I am sorry I acted the way I did when you got here Friday. You wanted to do something for your parents and I was mad because my plans to pay for the dairy farm were all messed up. I was wrong I shouldn't have been upset."

Luke smiled. "It is no big deal I understand my timing could have been better."

"You know I am not a farmer but you are and I was thinking that together we might find something to keep us happy."

"If you wanted to make me happy you could see if the next time I am home we could spend some time together without my family."

"We can do that as long as you call ahead and make an appointment I am very busy you know."

Luke smiled. "Do you think you could do that for me?"

"I think with some notice I might be able to find some time for you."

It was an hour later when Emily climbed out of the cab. She stood by her car until Luke was out of sight. No matter how good things were you could never have it all the way you wanted it.

From that night on Luke was on the road more and more not even coming home on some weekends. They talked most nights but it was not the same as having him home. Rhea had Dan and Emma had Steve even if she didn't know it yet. Emily had Luke but she didn't see him every day and he was more than a phone call away. As time went on they seemed to come to a point where they were more friends than anything else.

Luke glanced at the empty seat beside him. He had planned to be home every night but the best plans don't always come to pass. Now he was on his own even more than he had been before. The nights would be darker the roads would be longer. Still, it was his job there was no reason to be upset the job was the job.

Luke drove more and more finding it easier and easier to stay out on the road. The longer he was out the longer he could lie to himself about his father. Though it might seem like a good idea it was costing him more than he knew. He was getting his bills paid while avoiding his Dad's condition and Emily's.

That was August and by September Emma, Rhea, Emily, Dan, and Steve were in the dairy business which was nothing like they thought it would be. It was not as easy as they thought it was going to be. They had so much more work than they thought they were going to have. Rhea did her best as did Emma, Emily, Steve, and Dan but there was just so much that had to be done.

As fast as money came in the farm sucked it up like a dry sponge. There were never enough hours in a day even when they were working together. It felt like they were dogs chasing their tails all they were getting was dizziness. As they worked together they were getting closer together and Emily was feeling more and more alone.

Chapter 36

By November things everywhere else seemed to be slowing down everything but the work on the farm that is. Luke was never really home though he did stop for the night a few times he was always gone before sunrise. His Mom made him promise to be home for Thanksgiving so he worked his schedule out that way. Helen gave him four days off. He agreed though he didn't really want to be home that long.

It was hard for him to come home now that everything had changed so much. Dan had taken on more jobs because some of the places he had delivered for had gone out of business. He was now using the car hauler more as he picked up cars that had broken down. He hauled them to the garage where Kevin would fix them. The trouble was his hours were not as regular as they had been before. He had been called in on a couple of repossessions though he said he didn't like those.

Emily had gotten a promotion at work which meant she was working long hours. She was still helping out on the farm when she could but her time there seemed to be less and less each week. Luke talked to her a lot on the phone but it was harder and harder to catch her when she wasn't working or on her way to bed.

Emma was there every morning with Rhea but in the afternoon she was at work. The farm left little time for any social life she was too tired most of the time. She didn't have much time to spend with her parents either. It was getting to the point where she would do anything to sleep more than four hours a night.

Rhea was working on the farm seven days a week though on Saturday she did only that which had to be done which was mostly the milking. She only had the cows Dan still had the horses and the chickens. Rhea had found the job rewarding but a lot harder than she remembered it being.

Emma was with her almost every morning unless she was at her parent's house the night before. Rhea was up every morning at three-thirty; she had a cup of coffee and then went out to the barn with a cup of coffee in her hand. She started the milking at four-thirty; and finished at six-thirty. She cleaned everything up and was out of there by eight.

Jack was still with Roger they spent time at the garage though not as much as they had at first. Jack was nine years old now which meant he was a little slower though he still liked to run he just didn't run as much. This worked out just fine as Roger was a little slower too. Everything had changed as things seem to do as life moves on. There was nothing to be done no one could stop time.

The first week in November Donald Fields got his license and he needed a job. His sister Cindy was also looking for a job so Laurie sent them both to the farm. They had never worked a farm before but that was alright with Rhea she could train them. They worked together helping ease Rhea's workload in the afternoon.

There were other changes around town as well. Laurie was doing more at the bar giving her parents more time together. George took Linda on a cross-country train trip to visit relatives they hadn't seen in years. It had been a wonderful trip for both of them.

Laurie took care of the bar while making sure her sisters and brothers did everything they had to do. They all joked with her calling her "Little Mom". Laurie didn't mind she liked helping her family and her friends.

Luke was on the road finding that things were changing for him too. He had no reason to go home every week so he took longer runs as well as sending money home to his Mom and money to Emily who made sure the bills at the dairy farm were getting paid. Luke knew what was happening and he accepted it as the way things had to be.

By the week of Thanksgiving Luke had made up his mind about

what he had to do. He had thought it all out over a long time knowing that he had to do the right thing. Still knowing and doing were two different things.

Luke sat in his pickup thinking about it all wishing things were different. He had set out at the age of nineteen with a girl he didn't know expecting to find happily ever after. He hadn't found it with her. He didn't know if he would ever find it now. It seemed to him that when he was a little kid in a hurry to grow up he had been closer to it than he had ever been. At the age of twenty-five, he knew there were no better days ahead of him.

Thanksgiving was hours away but he was sure there was nothing to be grateful for after all life was a lot of hard work as well as hard times. When you had worn yourself down then you were gone. People were sad then life went on without you and in time they forgot all about you. He wanted a beer, no he wanted several beers but he wasn't going to the bar his father would be there. He wasn't sure he wanted to see him.

There were times when the good memories seemed better than reality. He had been on the road a long time his thoughts of his Dad were all of a man in good health. It might not have been true but it was what he wanted to remember when he thought of his Dad.

The best thing he could do was go out to the farm. He would be the only one there he could hide out without actually hiding. If he got very lucky no one would know he was there until morning. He knew he wasn't going to be that lucky but he could dream. It didn't cost anything to dream which was good because that would be all he could afford. There were a lot of things you could get but nothing was better than the free stuff.

Luke was no fool he knew he was depressed but in the modern world who wasn't? Life was a battle every day even if the days were good. You couldn't enjoy life someone or something was always there to spoil everything. He wanted to be a kid again but even then he had wanted something more. The people of the world were in a hurry to get everything they could out of life. What people didn't seem to realize was that when you had it all you still had nothing. Money wasn't everything it was just money and worth a lot less than they thought.

What was important could not be bought or even owned it was given freely and it was shared. The world was in a hurry to accomplish nothing while losing everything. The truth was lost and the world believed in lies. Luke shook his head he had been alone far too long.

Luke had left his rig to get serviced then walked over to the garage and got his pickup. He had gone out to the truck stop for coffee but never went inside. All he had done was sit there thinking about all the things he hadn't done right. When he had been there about an hour he headed back toward town.

Luke should have gone home but instead, he went to the park and sat on a bench drinking a coffee from a fast food place. The coffee wasn't that good but it was hot. A cool breeze was blowing which meant he had to be a bit off his rocker to be sitting there.

"You look uncomfortable."

"Laurie, what are you doing here?"

"I was on my way back to the bar."

"You always do that?"

"Leave the bar?"

"No, go out for lousy coffee when you have better coffee at the bar."

"Sometimes I just need a change."

"Why get a cup of lousy coffee just like the one that I have?"

Laurie smiled. "I was on my way back to the bar when I saw you and thought you might need a friend."

Luke moved over to make room for her on the bench. "Laurie, since when are we friends?"

"To be honest we are not friends anymore I am friends with your sister."

Luke shook his head. "You know life sucks most of the time."

"You are talking about most of the dates I have had as of late."

"You should try dating while you are on the road most of the time. My dates are phone calls from time to time."

"That sounds rough to me."

"It can be if you are crazy enough to expect anything to come from it."

Laurie looked at him thoughtfully. "What is it you were expecting?"

Luke laughed. "That is what I am sitting here thinking about, among other things."

"It sounds like that is way above anything I can help you with."

"It is out of my reach at the moment."

"Do you have any idea what you are going to do about your problems?"

Luke shook his head. "I don't have a clue so I think I will go home and have a beer this coffee sucks."

"You are right about the coffee. I think I should go back to work hanging with you is depressing the hell out of me."

"For a bartender, you are not very helpful."

"We are not helpful we are just good listeners."

Luke nodded his head. "Right, you don't talk you just sell drinks."

"That is right I nod, pour, and take the money."

"You are all heart."

"No, I am all about the money. I need all I can get people to start fights in my place."

"Are you ever going to let me forget that?"

"I doubt it."

"I have to get going."

"Yeah, you better before you start a fight here."

"I love you too."

"Don't tell anybody else that. I am looking for a real man."

"I have got to go. Talking to you is depressing the hell out of me."

"I already said that about talking to you."

"You have made me feel worse than I did before."

Laurie smiled at him. "Then I am done here."

When Luke drove by the garage he thought about stopping but decided against it. Dan's car hauler was gone the delivery trucks were in the yard. There was no need to call anyone by now they all knew he was home. That was the good and the bad thing about a small town.

Luke walked into the house, going right to the refrigerator he got out a beer and then sat down at the kitchen table. As he sat there he was trying to think of one good reason that he had for being there. The truth was he really couldn't think of one. It was true after all that times had changed. He was needed on the road more than he was needed at home. Emily had made that clear to him when he had tried to be home more.

He finished the bottle of beer and then went out to the barn to look at the horses. How long had it been since he had gone riding? He really didn't know but it had been a long time that was for sure. There was no reason he couldn't go now. No one needed him to be anywhere or do anything so he could go horseback riding if he wanted.

"What are you doing?"

Luke was startled though he did his best not to show it. Luke turned slowly. As he smiled he was sure she knew she had startled him. "What are you doing here?"

Emily was standing there a smile on her face a beer in each hand. "I brought you a beer but I think I will take it back to the house."

"I just thought you would still be working."

Emily handed him a bottle of beer. "I should be but Dan called to let me know that you were home so I came over to see you."

"Thanks for the beer I was about to go for a ride."

"You are going to ride on a horse?"

"Yes, I thought I would ride a horse."

"You remember how to do that?"

"I think so it has not been that long."

"Are you sure about that?"

"I am as sure as you were about remembering to close the bathroom door after a few drinks."

"I thought you were going to forget about that."

"So did I but it hasn't happened yet."

"You want some company?"

"Sure if you remember how to do it."

"I am as sure as you are."

"If we fall we fall together."

"I remember just how to do it; you saddle the horses while I get something out of the house. When I get back I will show you I know how to do it."

"The bathroom is on the right don't fall asleep."

"I have a gun in my car."

"There you go a couple of jokes and you go looking for a gun. It might be better if you just worked on developing a sense of humor."

"You could develop a lump on your head."

Emily went into the house and Luke saddled the horses. When she came back out of the house she had a backpack on. Luke looked at her thinking of a lot of things that he wasn't ready to talk about. "I think I know that pack."

"You should Dan told me it was yours. Where are we going?"

"I thought we would follow the logging road up the mountain it goes up about two miles."

"I don't think I have ever been up there."

"Not many people go up there but I keep it open just like it was when I bought the place."

They mounted up and then crossed the pasture to where the road began. It was a nice ride up through the pines. They didn't talk much it seemed to be enough for them to just ride up the road toward the top of the mountain. There was something about the road beside the fact that it was long it seemed comforting for some reason.

When they reached the property line Luke noticed that the state had not been keeping up their part of the road. "Are we going to keep going?"

"No, maybe another time it is going to start getting dark and that part of the road has trees and branches all over it."

"Where does the other road go?"

"That goes over to your dairy farm."

Emily laughed. "You are kidding!"

Luke smiled. "No, it goes right to that stand of trees behind the house."

"I haven't had time to really look the whole place over."

"There is a lot of land to that place."

Emily dismounted, took off the backpack then got out two bottles of beer. "I thought you might want something to drink when we got up here."

Luke dismounted and then tied the horses to a tree before he took the beer from Emily. "This was a good idea. I hope the horses remember the way back to the barn."

"We haven't had that much to drink."

"Speak for yourself I got started before you got to the house."

"I didn't know that or I would have brought you coffee instead of beer."

"That sounds like you."

"Don't start that."

"Start what?"

"You know what."

"If I did I wouldn't have to ask."

"You make it sound like I am treating you as if we were married."

"Is that what I was doing?"

"You know it was."

"Maybe we should get started back to the house you need some sleep you're getting cranky."

"Don't push your luck, Bub."

"Yes, Dear."

Emily was laughing. "One of these days you are going to get it."

"Promises, promises, or was that a threat?"

"You are never going to find that out up here."

Luke finished his beer. "Then I guess we best get started back to the house."

Emily smiled at him. "For someone who is never home you seem to expect a lot."

"I thought I heard an offer."

"You expect a lot from a couple of beers."

"I was thinking about what you might do for more beer."

"We should go back to the house and see what develops."

When they got back to the barn things went along as they should. Luke took care of the horses while Emily went into the house to make them something to eat. The ride back had been even quieter than the ride up the mountain if that was even possible. Emily was worried because everything had changed so much since they bought the other farm and went into the dairy business. They were friends but the six of them were so busy they never spent any time together. Luke was never home anymore which was not completed because of the farm she realized.

The truth was he had wanted to be home more and they had sent him back out on the road to help pay for the farm. Luke had wanted to quit the job because of his Dad now he wanted to stay on the road for the same reason. If he had seen his Dad more he would have been able to handle the changes better. Now he didn't want to know about the changes he simply wanted to stay on the road.

There were times when you have been dealing with something for so long that you seem to forget that it is as bad as it is. Emily, Rhea, Emma, and Dan saw his father every day so to them, he was doing okay. Luke hadn't seen him since he had shaved his head. He had waited until he started to lose it then he shaved it off. Seeing him like that for the first time was going to be hard.

Luke finished with the horses and then went into the house where he found Emily setting plates of food on the kitchen table. "It looks good what does it taste like?"

"I don't know I seldom eat my own cooking."

"So I get to try it first? What if I die after tasting it?"

"I won't eat it."

"Well things could be worse you could have lied to me."

"I hear your Dad has a surprise for us in the morning."

"I heard about that and I was thinking it might be best if I didn't go to the house for dinner."

"You know that is a really bad idea you are gone more than you should be as it is."

"That isn't what you told me when I wanted to start driving locally."

"I know I was thinking about the farm I had it all worked out. Well, I thought I did but I hadn't thought of everything I hadn't thought about your Dad."

"That is over and things are what they are but we need to talk about us."

"I am not so sure I want to. I mean we are okay aren't we?"

"That was what I wanted to talk to you about after all as everyone keeps telling me I am never home anymore."

Emily was nervous there wasn't anything good that was going to come from this conversation. "Can't this wait until after the holiday?"

"I think we have to do this now."

"Okay, I am not seeing anyone else and I don't want to see anyone else."

"I knew that already I was thinking that maybe we should talk about what comes next."

"I can't ride off into the sunset with you in the truck."

"I know that."

Emily looked across the table fear and surprise in her eyes. "Oh, crap."

"Well, I was hoping to talk to you about something else before we started talking crap."

"There are times for humor and there are times when you should let it go."

Luke looked at her then shook his head. "I never let the crap go in the kitchen."

"Luke, I am going to kill you in a minute if you keep fooling around."

"Okay, I was thinking we can't keep going the way we are going. I think it is time for a change."

"Oh, crap."

"Yeah, it might be but you never know if you don't try."

Emily could feel her stomach starting to churn. She had been here before with Jim and it hadn't ended well then. "What do you have in mind?"

"I was thinking you might want to come over to the farm for a time."

"I am here so how long do you want me to stay?"

"That is up to you."

"What does that mean?"

"That means you can spend a night or just move in."

Emily took a deep breath. "You want me to move in with you and Dan?"

Luke shook his head. "I was thinking if you move in it might be best if my brother moved out."

"Did you tell Dan about this plan you have?"

"I thought I would talk to you first."

"So in other words this is all on me?"

"That is not the way I said it."

"No, but it is the way it is."

"Not much point in asking Dan to move if you are not going to be here."

"Oh, crap."

"Is that what you think of my idea?"

There was a lot Emily wanted to say. All she could say was. "Oh, crap."

Chapter 37

Dan had gotten back to the house just before dark. He had seen the pickup as well as Emily's car but there was no one in the house. He got in his car and then drove over to help Rhea with the milking. When he got there he went out and cleaned the free stall barn with the bobcat. Once that was done he loaded everything into the manure spreader so it would be ready to spread in the morning.

Dan stood in the darkness looking up at the stars. He had been planning to talk to Rhea but there was never time for them to sit down and talk. If she wasn't busy he was or if they did have the time there was always something else they had to talk about. Tonight he was going to sit her down and talk about what he wanted to talk about.

Rhea was done milking by the time Dan walked into the milk house with two cups of coffee. "I thought you might need this right about now."

"Thanks, there are times when for two cents or a good cup of coffee I would think about selling this place."

Dan gave her a weak smile understanding how she felt. "I take it you have had a rough day?"

"Just a little, I lost a calf this morning it took some time to deal with that then the tanker broke down in the yard when it came to picking up the milk. That was just the start of my day so you can guess how the rest of it has gone."

Dan smiled. "I have a good idea how the rest of it went, all downhill.

Luke is home he is with Emily though I have no idea where they are. Their cars are at the house but they are not. As far as I can tell it seems to be all things as usual."

"How is your Dad doing?"

"He is bald but other than that he seems to be holding his own."

"I hear he has a surprise for us tomorrow."

"I might have one for him as well it all depends on how things go tonight."

"Are you working tonight?"

"No, I am going to be here then I am going home to talk to my brother if I can find him."

"Where do you think the two of them went off to this time?"

Dan shrugged his shoulders. "I think they went off on a horse ride or the horses said no so they took them for a walk."

Rhea smiled. "They are riding? I have been working with the horses."

"You have been working with the horses?"

"Yes, if you don't they can give you some problems when you try to ride them."

"I don't know anything about that. I have to be honest; tonight I don't care about any of that. I have other things that are more important to me."

Rhea looked at him wishing they were someplace else right then. "What are you up to now?"

Dan put his coffee cup down on the window cell. "I was thinking we should be spending more time together. I know with the farm and my job as well as everything else it just doesn't seem possible."

Rhea looked at him. "You have a plan?"

"Oh yeah, I have a real good plan."

"Shouldn't we talk about this in the house?"

"Should we?"

"There is coffee in the house."

"We don't need coffee for this."

"Oh crap!"

'"The crap can wait we need to talk."

"Oh, crap."

Dan smiled. "You have been spending too much time with Emily."

Rhea was holding her cup in both hands. "You want to spend more time with me."

"I was thinking that it might be a good idea at this time."

"You don't think we would be moving a little too fast?"

"Would you like to buy your own tractor first?'"

"I thought we were talking about something along those lines."

"I guess you could say that."

Rhea put her cup down. "Okay, what about the tractor?"

"You want to go in on a partnership?"

"I have always been looking for a really good deal. What have you got?"

Chapter 38

On Thanksgiving morning it was cold at three thirty in the am. Dan was up he had the coffee on though he didn't feel he was awake enough to know for sure just what he was doing. He filled the two pellet stoves and then added wood to the kitchen stove before he went off to take his shower. He had to get moving he had promised Rhea he would be there to help her with the milking.

When he walked back into the kitchen after his shower his brother was sitting at the table with a cup of coffee. "Luke, you don't look so good."

"Dan, I feel like crap this morning I guess I haven't been getting enough sleep."

"I know what you mean I had a rough night last night I guess I was thinking about a lot of things."

"That will get you into trouble every time."

"Luke, where did Emily and you get off to yesterday afternoon?"

"We took the horses out for a little bit."

"Where did you go?"

"We took a ride up the mountain."

"While I was working over at Rhea's place you two were off enjoying yourselves?"

"Yeah, I would have to say it was enjoyable. We went for a ride got up to the top had a beer then rode back down to the house. Emily made a supper for us which was quite good."

"I must have passed her on the road last night."

"You went over to the dairy barn?"

"Rhea needs all the help she can get."

"I was told Laurie had her sister and brother over there."

"They are one in the morning and the other in the afternoon. They help out a lot but Rhea still does most of the work she needs more help."

"I would think she would it can't be easy for her."

"It isn't, I expected her to call it quits before the end of the year. Now that she has helped in the morning and the afternoon she is in a better mood."

Luke got himself another cup of coffee. "You would never have let her quit."

"I didn't plan to I had a plan that I thought would help."

Luke smiled at his brother. "I thought you might. You were the one that got her help in the afternoon."

Dan filled his travel mug. "No, Laurie did that her sister and brother were looking for work. We should be going."

"Why rush Emily is there to help her."

"We just leave them there to milk over one hundred cows?"

"That sounds like a good idea."

"Only for you after all you get to leave in a couple of days while I am stuck here with both of them."

"I have to say that sounds good to me."

"We have to get going."

"Alright, we can go. I am only going because I want to eat turkey before it is time for supper."

Rhea was up early as always she started the coffee and then went out to the barn to get things started in the milk house. She hadn't slept well mostly because of some of the things she had talked to Dan about. They had all been working very hard which was why she had been feeling alone most of the time. Everyone else had a job to go to but she lived with her job.

Emily walked into the milk house with two cups of coffee and handed her one. "Morning, did you sleep at all last night?"

"Not like I wanted to I slept a little less than usual."

"Me too, Luke is home he had to talk about things."

"Dan and I did too. I guess those two are related."

They smiled at one another then Emily asked. "Where should I run the spreader?"

"You can spread it in the field across the road if the spreader is full."

It was then that they seemed to realize they had gone from talking about talking with the guys to spreading shit. They started laughing and went on laughing as they heard the tractor start up. Rhea tried to calm down. "I think the guys are here."

"Yeah, I think they want to spread a little more crap this morning."

Rhea calmed down a little more as she whipped a tear from her eye. "Oh, I have to tell you I needed a good laugh this morning."

"I think we both did, it may have something to do with not getting much sleep."

"I think I better get to work or we will never get out of here."

"Let's see if I remember how to do this it has been a long time."

Rhea went out to the free stall barn and turned the first twenty cows loose. She followed them into the barn and then hooked the stanchions up as the cows stuck their heads in them. Emily started washing each cow utter so that the area would be clean when Rhea started hooking on the milking machines. As they worked they heard the Bobcat running as Luke cleaned one side of the free stall barn.

Rhea was enjoying all the help everything was moving right along she couldn't remember the last time things had gone so well. Working together they finished everything up in record time. There was time for a really good breakfast before the guys went back to care for the horses and chickens.

Having breakfast together was something else the four of them had not done together in months. There had always been one or more of them missing when meal time came around. To be honest, in the morning most of them were lucky to eat at all. Coffee had replaced breakfast most days and a really good meal was seldom eaten by any of them. If it wasn't fast as well as small they simply didn't have time for it.

Rhea showered and then dressed in her good clothes which were something else she hadn't done in a while. The truth was she didn't leave the farm much anymore. When she did leave she wore jeans and a clean shirt she had no time to get dressed up. Besides she wasn't going to be gone long she couldn't be, there was just too much to do around the farm.

Emily stood in her room looking at herself in the mirror. The good news was she didn't look as old as she felt. Work was dragging her down as she was in the office six sometimes seven days a week. She was the first one in and the last one out most days. Her social life was a cup of coffee in the morning with Rhea then maybe a cup of coffee with her parents as they talked about the business.

When she was dating Jim she had thought she had a good life but she had found she was wrong. She had enjoyed the time she spent with Luke but it had been all too short then she was back at work. The only people she went out with were Rhea, Dan, and Luke on those rare times when he was home. In other words, she had no real social life anymore which didn't seem to matter much.

Going down to the kitchen she found Rhea sitting at the table with two cups of coffee. "Are you going to drink both of those?"

"That depends on you I guess."

"In that case, I will drink one."

"The guys should be back in a little bit they will want to leave right away."

"If I am not done with my coffee they will have to wait."

"Don't you think we have kept them waiting long enough?"

"Rhea Conner, are you suggesting that we should do something different?"

"No, I was just thinking we have to go so we can get back I have to milk the cows again this afternoon."

"That is not what you were talking about and we both know it."

"Things have to change we both know I am right."

"Of course, they have to change but that doesn't mean that we are going to run out and get married tomorrow."

"No not tomorrow."

Emily sat back in her chair. "Dan asked you to marry him."

Rhea nodded her head. "Yes, last night in the barn over coffee."

"It sounds so romantic. I always wondered just how farmers handled that sort of thing."

"We went out under the stars and he said we could have hot coffee if I said yes."

"So you said yes."

"Of course, I did it had been a long day and I needed a good cup of hot coffee."

"What about Dan do you need him?"

Rhea smiled. "I need him more than I need the coffee."

"Well, then I guess it is a marriage made in the kitchen."

"The marriage was agreed to in the barn the coffee was made in the kitchen."

Emily smiled. "Luke asked me to move in with him in the kitchen over dinner last night."

Rhea smiled. "He is finally sick of his own cooking is he."

"His and Dan's I guess."

"I like Dan's cooking."

Luke was sitting at the kitchen table looking at his brother while he was thinking about their father. He wanted to say something but he simply couldn't find the words. It had been too long since he had been home. He had been given a job which he had done very well. The problem was he felt it was costing him more than he could afford. If he wasn't on the road he would have to watch his father slowly die. Luke didn't think he could handle that.

"Dan, how is Dad doing?"

"You mean besides the fact that he saved his head and looks like Elmer Fudd?"

"Yeah, I mean besides that."

"He is a little thinner though not as much as you would expect. He wants to go back to work so he goes over to Rhea's and spreads manure for her from time to time. He hangs out in the garage with Kevin sometimes. He spends more time with Mom now. Most afternoons he goes over to play cards with George."

"I should be home more."

"Dad says you are doing what he would do if it was one of us that was right where he is now."

"Do you believe that?"

"No, he does though so I guess that is all that matters."

"I wasn't going to come home for the holiday but I got five calls asking me to come home and my boss got three."

"Mom said she called Helen as did Emma but Dad didn't tell me he called her too."

"He didn't Emily did."

Dan laughed. "That is something I didn't expect."

"You are not the only one."

"I am sure she thinks you two are married."

"No, she just wants me to know what I am going to get if we ever do get married."

Dan finished his coffee. "Two cars or do we all ride together?"

"Two cars I need to go over to Emily's parents after we eat."

"We will take two cars then, Rhea and I will need to leave early anyway."

They put their cups in the sink and then went out to the car and the pickup. Dan drove off in his car then Luke followed in the pickup. It would be a good day Thanksgiving always was. The fact that things had changed would be ignored today. This was a family day may be the last Thanksgiving they would all have together after all Jack was getting old.

Luke was worried about what his Dad was going to say to him when they finally had a chance to talk. He had given Emma the house and then sold his truck to buy the garage for Dan. As far as he knew there was nothing his Dad could give him. Luke didn't want anything from his parents but there was a part of him that envied his sister and brother.

Chapter 39

Emma Richardson got two more cups of coffee and then shut off the coffee maker. Walking into the dining room she set one cup on the table in front of her boyfriend before she sat down beside him. They had been dating for just about a year. He wanted her to move in with him she agreed it was time to step things up a little which was why she had invited him to Thanksgiving dinner with the family.

Though they had been dating for well over a year she had not told anyone in the family that they were dating. With things the way they were she felt that it was not that big a deal. She had never said they were not dating either. They were together but they were not together.

Her Dad came first everything else could wait. Now things were changing she wanted everyone to know that she had found a nice guy. As nice as he was she still was not ready to move in with him after all she was needed at home.

It was true that everyone knew about her and Steve even if they didn't talk about it. There was no doubt that her brothers were going to give her a hard time. This also meant that they were going to give Steve a hard time. It was true he knew them but he was about to hear from them.

Her parents had given her their house she was not going to move out on them. If he could not accept that he was not the man she thought he was. In truth, if he could not wait they were not going to last anyway. She wasn't testing him and if he thought she was they were not going to last. Emma had told him why she couldn't move in with him that should be enough.

Stephen looked at his watch. "It is getting late we were supposed to be there by ten."

"It takes time to milk all those cows but they will be here on time give or take a minute or two."

"While we are waiting why don't we talk about the nice place we could buy if we got a place together?"

"Because I already told you this is not the time."

"I get the feeling you don't want to live with me."

"Stephen, I do want to live with you but now is not the time and you know it as well as I do."

"I was hoping I could change your mind and you would let me move in with you."

Emma laughed. "You want to move in with my parents and me?"

"Emma, I want to be with you wherever that is."

"I think you have lost your mind. You know my Dad, do you want him sitting at the kitchen table staring at you?"

"He is not as scary now that he is bald."

"I know."

"Still he is still scary enough."

"You are smarter than I thought you were."

"I am one of the best."

"I thought you were until you said Dad was not as scary as he used to be but you saved yourself."

"I like your Dad and I think he likes me."

"That is a good thing for you and me. Still, do you think he likes you enough to let you share a room with me?"

Steve smiled. "I have to admit you may have a point but I never said I was going to share a room with you."

Now it was Emma's turn to smile. "You want a room of your own?"

"That was my plan when I started talking to you."

"I think you are crazy."

"Emma, I want to be with you and I will sleep wherever you and your parents say I can."

"Including your own apartment?"

"Yes if that is all I can get."

Dan walked in with Rhea. "Emma, where are Mom and Dad?"

Before she could say anything Emily and Luke walked into the room. "Emma, where are Mom and Dad?"

"Hi everyone, this is my boyfriend Stephen. Stephen, these are my brothers Luke and Dan."

Luke looked at him. "He is kind of thin and doesn't look like he could pick you up."

"Luke, we should have him come out to the farm more we can have him clean the barn every day until spring that should build him up a bit."

Luke shook his head. "Sorry Stephen, I am afraid you will have to go."

Stephen didn't move or say a word he just sat there looking at them. Rhea shook her head as she pushed Dan out of the way. "Stephen, don't listen to them they are just giving you a hard time I am grateful for the help you have been giving me with the cows."

Emily punched Luke in the side as she pushed past him. "Yeah, these three think they are funny. Rhea and I will tell you how things are around here. We will give you credit for all you have been doing"

Rhea nodded her head in agreement. "First things first do you have any money with you?"

"Yes, is that your way of telling me I have to pay for Thanksgiving dinner?"

Rhea smiled as she shook her head. "No, but tomorrow you are going to take Emily and me out to a nice place so we can tell you how this family operates."

Emily looked at Stephen as if she were sizing him up. "After that, we will stop over to see Rhea's father Pastor Conner he will explain what is expected of you."

Stephen finished his coffee and then calmly set the cup down on the table. "I don't think I have ever met a bunch of people so full of it. After the summer we all had together why are you doing this to me now? Why the new guy treatment?"

"We had him right up until you mentioned my father."

Emily nodded in agreement. "Yeah, I think you are right."

Dan looked at his brother. "I wonder what these three have been up to while our backs were turned."

"I was just thinking the same thing."

Emma smiled at her brothers. "I am willing to share a good thing with good friends."

Stephen squirmed in his seat. "All of a sudden I feel like a piece of meat at the market."

Luke laughed as he looked around the room. "Emma, where are Mom and Dad?"

"Dad said all I had to do was tell you we would not be eating here and you would know where to go."

"Mom agreed to have Thanksgiving dinner at a bar?"

Emma shrugged her shoulders. "I don't know you are the one that is supposed to know where we are going."

"It isn't the place to have our Thanksgiving."

Dan looked at his brother. "Luke, I think it is the perfect place today."

Stephen looked at Luke. "Now that you have all had fun picking on me shouldn't we go to dinner?"

Luke shook his head. "I don't agree we have just started having fun at your expense. However, if you are all in a hurry to eat then I think we should go."

Stephen looked at Emma. "I am in trouble aren't I?"

"Oh yeah, you are in big trouble."

They all left the house driving to the bar in three different cars. It was true that the bar was within walking distance from the house but the cows would have to be milked in the afternoon. Rhea wanted to stop by her parent's house before they went back to the farm. Emily wanted to go to her parent's house before they went to help Rhea and Dan with the milking. Emma had to go to work in the late afternoon so she had to have her car as well.

When they got to the bar Laurie opened the door for them and then followed them into the center of the room. All the tables had been put together to form what looked like one long table in the center of the room.

Covering the tables as well as the bar were red and white checked table clothes which gave the place a completely different look. The pool table had been covered with a sheet of plywood which had then been covered with two checkered table clothes to match the rest of the room.

Laurie's sisters and brothers were all sitting around the room drinking coffee or soda whichever they preferred. Linda walked out of the kitchen wearing a dress and an apron. "There is coffee in the pot on the bar and soda in the cooler at the far end of the bar."

"Linda, do you need any help in the kitchen?"

"No thank you, Rhea, the girls and I can handle it."

Emily was looking around the room all Linda's daughters were sitting there watching the parade on the big screen TV. She wondered whose girls were helping in the kitchen. "Luke, do you want coffee or soda?"

Luke looked at his watch. "Coffee I guess it is still early."

"Oh please, you are acting as if I asked you if you wanted a beer."

"I thought we were going to have coffee."

That was when the elevator door opened and George rolled off the elevator followed by Roger Richardson, Pastor Jason Conner, and Walter Rice. Needless to say, everyone was more than a little surprised to see the four men together. Laurie and her sisters brought out the fruit bowl, cheese platter, crackers, and a bowl of nuts.

Emily and Luke were getting a cup of coffee. "Luke, you have to take me home."

"Why are we leaving? Is it because your Dad is here?"

"No, it is because I need to get out of here."

"Are you feeling a little underdressed for this wingding?"

"I see dresses and skirts while I am the only one wearing slacks."

"All the guys are wearing pants."

"In case you have forgotten I am not one of the guys."

"I haven't forgotten."

"Then will you please take me home?"

"I don't know what you are talking about I think you look just fine."

"You do?"

"Sure you're slacks are the same color the turkey was before someone chopped off his head and pulled out all its feathers."

"Knowing that makes me feel so much better."

Luke smiled at her. "I knew you would. I have that effect on people."

"You mean other people want to kill you too?"

"Only the ones like you with no sense of humor."

"You are one sick person."

"Yeah, but you love it."

"You keep telling yourself that."

"Ain't love grand?"

"Moron."

"Witch."

Emily was smiling. "Hanging around you has changed me."

Dan filled two coffee cups and then handed one to Rhea. "I thought the surprise was the fact that we were eating here."

"I think there was a little more to it than that,"

Luke looked at his brother. "I thought for sure Dad was done with this kind of stuff."

Dan sipped his coffee. "He just slowed down a little he hasn't stopped."

Emily looked around the room again. "Did anyone else figure out that our mothers are in the kitchen with Linda?"

Rhea was looking at the people in the room as well. "I have a feeling that there is more going on here than a dinner."

Luke leaned up against the bar. "This is what I was talking about when I was telling you I had no idea what was going on anymore."

Dan laughed. "I was here all the time and I never saw this coming."

Rhea sipped her coffee and then looked at Luke. "I talk to my Dad every day and he never said a word about this. Mom and I go shopping together once a week and she didn't say anything about this."

Emily smiled. "I work for my parents I see them every day and they never said anything about this."

Steve looked at Emma. "I don't see my parents here."

Emma gave him a dirty look. "Your parents live in Florida."

Laurie Fields walked over to the coffee pot got a coffee then stood there with the others. "I take it you have figured out that our parents are good at keeping secrets?"

Luke nodded. "When did you find out?"

"This morning when Mom said we were having guests and then told me who I could let in here."

Steve smiled. "My parents aren't here."

Laurie looked at him. "I guess that says a lot about what we think of you."

Steve looked at Laurie. "That hurt."

"Good.", Laurie said with a smile.

Steve looked at Emma. "What did I do to everyone?"

Emma smiled. "They are just letting you know they like you."

"I think I was better off before they liked me."

That was when Jim Campbell and his mother walked into the bar. Connie went to the kitchen while Jim got himself a cup of coffee. Laurie walked to the bar to refill her cup. "Jim, you haven't been around for a while."

Jim looked around the room. "I am doing my best to make a few changes in my life."

"You think you can win Emily back?"

Jim looked at Emily but spoke to Laurie. "It is too early to think about anything like that."

"What are you doing?"

"I go to AA meetings, work, and sleep. That is about all I have been doing."

"I heard the charges against you were dropped."

"Your Dad told me to grow up or stay locked up. I told him I would do my best to grow up."

"You plan to do that on your own?"

"No, I have my Mom."

"I think it would be best if you sit with me."

Jim looked at Emily. "I think that might be the safest place for me today."

Laurie smiled. "Normally there would be no safe place for you but today you might get a pass until after we eat at least."

"That long?"

"If you are lucky."

Chapter 40

Not long after the group meeting by the coffee pot all the food was brought out and set up on the pool table. Everyone sat down at what looked like one long table. The Pastor said grace before they all got up and formed a line behind Linda. One by one they filled their plates got drinks then returned to the table. By this time the parade was over the football game was on and the guys started yelling at the TV. Even the Pastor seemed to agree that the quarterback wasn't worth much.

When the halftime show started the sound was turned off. Roger Richardson looked around the table knowing that this could be the last time he would be able to join all his friends and family for a Thanksgiving meal. He was proud of his children as well as his wife and their friends. Even though they had not always been together they had always kept in touch. Whatever happened to him he knew he had been lucky to live the life he had.

George looked at everyone. "I want to thank you all for coming. I have wanted to do this for a long time but never got around to it for one reason or another. So while I have you all here I want to invite you all back here next year and every year for as long as we own this bar."

Linda was standing beside her husband a hand on his shoulder. "I know things have been hard over the last year. So many things seem to be changing. I want you all to know that I am happy to have you all here today."

Roger Richardson looked around the room remembering good times as well as the bad. It was his life sitting there at the table with him. He was with his friends as well as his family for the first time in a very long time. It had been too long a time. It was his cancer that had brought them all together. Even though he was dying from it he was thankful. Because of it, he had once again found all that was important in his life.

Roger cleared his throat which got the room quiet as everyone turned to look at him. "Life isn't always what you expect it to be, that is something we learn as we go. You think you will always be young but you are not. You believe that you will live forever but no one does. You are surprised when your children grow up even though you knew they would.

"Today I am happy with where I am in my life. I see my family and friends here; I know I have had a good life. I may not have been the best husband, father, or friend but I have done my best. I want to thank you all for putting up with me because I know it could not have been easy. I know I have a hard time putting up with all of you."

Everyone sat there quietly not knowing what to say. Pastor Conner was the one to break the silence. "Amen."

Everyone started to laugh as they also started to breathe again. Somehow right there at that moment if only for that moment they were all just fine. They had come together faced the past and the future and survived the whole thing. It was just what it was they were going to deal with it all in time.

It was getting late the cows had to be milked and the barns had to be cleaned. Rhea, Emily, Emma, Dan, Luke, and Stephen stood up to go but Dan told them to wait. "I have something I want to tell everyone before we leave. I had planned to do this a bit differently but seeing as we are all here I might as well do it now. I asked Rhea to marry me and she said yes. We are going to get married in January because that is as long as we want to wait. We know it is short notice but that can't be helped."

Roger smiled. "It is about time you settled down."

Luke shook his brother's hand and then hugged Rhea before turning back to face everyone. "Emily and I are not going to get married in January because we have rushed into things before. She is going to move into the house to keep an eye on things while I am on the road. This means that Mom and Dad are going to get Dan back at least until he gets married."

Roger looked at his oldest son. "Not the smartest thing I have ever heard but it is okay. Emily will have you straightened out before summer. The only thing that surprises me is that it took you two so long to get this far."

"Thanks, Dad, you have more faith in Emily than me."

Roger smiled. "She is a planner which is the only reason you two have made it this far."

Emma looked at her brothers and then at everyone else in the room. "Sorry folks the only thing I am doing is going to work."

Roger laughed. "That's my girl."

Stephen looked over at Roger. "You wouldn't happen to have an empty room that I can rent until I can get my life set the way I would like it would you?"

Roger smiled. "No."

Steve nodded. "Emma and I are engaged."

Rachael stood up and hugged Steve. "We can talk about the room."

Roger smiled at him. "We can talk about the room."

Emma looked at her father more than a little surprised. "MOM, DAD!"

Jack was lying in his usual corner watching Luke and the others as they left the bar. He could have gone with them but they didn't live in a bar full of food. There was a lot to be said for being the only dog around after Thanksgiving dinner. Roger was in no hurry to go home which was a very good thing for an old dog with bones. Jack might even spend the night at the bar. There was no hurry the house would still be there in the morning. In the meantime, he was looking at a couple of really good meals.

Rhea, Emily, Dan, and Luke went back to the farm. Steve took Emma to work and then went back to his place. He was one step closer to Emma and with a little bit of luck, he would marry her in less than a year. It was hard to say she was awful stubborn.

Laurie got two cups of coffee and then set one on the table in front of Jim. Sitting down at the table with him she shook her head. "Looks like you are stuck with me."

"Something tells me that you are the one that is stuck with me."

"Whatever it is I will talk to you."

"Can I ask you why you are talking to me?"

"I could lie to you but the truth is you need someone to listen to you and that is something I am good at."

"You are a bartender and I am trying to quit drinking."

"That would make us the perfect odd couple."

Friday and Saturday they got a lot of work done around the farm. Saturday night they all went out to eat at the country club. As they ate they talked about a lot of things avoiding the one subject they all knew they had to talk about.

Rhea was the one who finally brought it up. "Boys I want Emily to stay with me until the wedding."

`"She is going to move in with me.", Luke told her.

"Luke if you were home every night it would be one thing but you are rarely home. I think it would be best for all of us if we leave things the way they are for now."

Dan sipped his beer. "I was looking forward to spending time with Mom and Dad."

Emily looked at Dan with a smile on her face. "I think Steve is going to talk his way into the house in no time at all."

Luke nodded. "You might have a point there."

Rhea was surprised. "You mean you all agree with me?"

Dan smiled. "We talked about it yesterday while you were shopping with your mother."

"Why didn't you tell me?"

"We thought we would see how long you could go without saying anything."

"Luke, I would kill you if we were not family."

Luke laughed. "We are not family yet."

"No, we are not but I have plans for your brother which do not include me being in prison."

Emily laughed. "They say the Pastor's kids are the first to snap."

Luke agreed with her. "I have heard they can be very unstable."

Rhea looked at Dan. "Aren't you going to help me?"

Dan nodded. "Just as soon as I am done eating this is really good food. It is also very expensive food. I am not going to waste any of it."

"There are more important things than the money you know."

"Rhea, you should never waste food."

"Dan, you are about to find yourself living alone for the rest of your short life."

Luke laughed. "Now she is planning to kill us all."

Emily laughed. "She wants to be a serial killer."

Rhea was laughing now. "With the three of you around I am amazed I could hold my temper this long."

By Sunday morning everything was settled between the four of them. They decided to keep the girls together until the wedding. Dan would care for the horses and the chickens while Luke was on the road. They were sure everything would work out just fine that way.

They all went to the Richardson house for dinner at noon. Steve was there with Emma which seemed to make Roger happy. The more he talked with all of them the better he looked. He was happy for his children as well as for his wife knowing she would have them all to help her after he was gone.

Sunday night Luke went back on the road feeling good about everything that had happened over the Thanksgiving holiday. He stayed on the road until Christmas. When he got home he found his chickens had been sent over to Rhea. He agreed with the idea after all it was the smart thing to do.

Emily was learning to run her parent's business though she didn't want to run it. She had plans of her own which didn't end with the partnership on the dairy farm. Emily had other ideas as she looked around the small town. There were so many things they could do that would make her money as well as help the town.

Rhea and Dan were busy with the farm and their wedding plans. They had a lot to do in a very short amount of time. The wedding would be at the church and the reception would be at the Circus Bar.

The whole thing would be catered by Linda and her girls with help from her friends. Rhea was happy while Dan was worried.

Emma and Stephen were getting closer though Emma did her best to slow things down. Her main problem was that she was starting to see things the same way Stephen did. They were spending more and more time together there was no reason why they shouldn't get closer. Emma could see this was true even if she didn't want to admit it. This was not the time there was just too much going on. Her father was dying and her brother was getting married.

Luke did his best to stay on the road but the holidays and family made it hard. He was running week-long runs until after the wedding. Once the wedding was over he was on the road a month at a time. This brought in a lot of money but that was all it did.

By the time spring came around the garage was making good money showing a good profit. They had bought more cows for the dairy which was now holding its own. Emily had found more work for her parent's company which was now running three shifts. Everything was looking up or almost everything was.

When Luke got home the first week in May the house was empty which he had expected after all it was too early for Emily to be home. He smiled, Emily had called him telling him she was planning on moving back to her parent's house. She had not told him when she would move just that she was going to move.

He put his clothes in the washer and then took a shower. When he was done he made a pot of coffee and then went out to care for the horses. He was surprised to find a new bag of horse feed in the bin. It surprised him that Emily had bought the feed before she moved out.

Once he was back in the house he poured himself a cup of coffee and then went to seat by the kitchen window. As he was sitting there he was thinking of all that had happened in one short year. Who could have seen it all coming? How could anyone have prepared for it all?

The front door slammed shut then Laurie Fields walked into the kitchen. She got herself a cup and then poured herself a cup of coffee. "Well, how are you doing?"

Luke looked over at her. "Laurie, it is good to see you please come in and make yourself at home. Would you like to join me for a cup of coffee?"

"You never knock when you come into my place."

"You own a bar."

"Yeah I do, and you drive a truck. I am sure glad we got that cleared up."

"This is my house, not a bar or a truck."

"That explains a lot."

Luke smiled even though he was trying hard not to. "You just come over here to give me a hard time?"

Laurie looked at him doing her best not to smile as she sat down at the table. "No, that is just a bonus I got."

"Let me guess you are here to tell me that Emily moved out?"

"No, I am here because you are my friend and I didn't want you to come home to an empty house."

"You were a little late for that."

"You didn't call me and tell me when you were going to get in so I think I did damn good, all things considered."

"You did and I want to thank you. There was no need I already knew she was gone before I got here."

"No, you didn't."

"No, but I knew she was planning to leave. It isn't easy being with me when I am never here."

Laurie refilled their cups and then sat back down at the table. "You are even harder to live with when you are home every night."

Luke smiled. "It has been said once or twice."

"Don't worry you will always have me to talk to."

"Everyone talks to the bartender."

"That doesn't mean you will always talk to me."

"Of course it does."

"That is what you say now."

"Yes, it is."

Laurie shook her head. "I may not always tend bar."

Luke laughed. "One day my sister is going to marry Stephen, will you go to the wedding with me?"

"Even if I am married, I will leave him home no matter who he is."

"Why would you do that?"

Laurie smiled at him. "Someone will have to stay home and watch the kids. When I party I want to party not sit with the kids watching other people have fun."

"You do something like that and people are going to talk."

"They talked about my Mom and your Dad they can talk about us."

"You like horses?"

"Yes, and I will even come over here and feed them while you are gone."

"What do you want?"

"I want to stay at the house while you are gone."

Luke laughed. "Just what reason could you have for that?"

Laurie sipped her coffee before she answered. "My parents, my sisters, and my brothers are all at the house I would like some time to myself."

"You want time to yourself at my place?"

"No one else is here during the week."

"I am here Friday through Sunday from time to time."

"I am the owner of a bar which is busy on the weekends as well as being open late on the weekend. I need to stay there on the weekends."

"That just might work."

"You know it will."

Luke shook his head. "When do you want to move in?"

"I already did. Emily moved out and I moved in. I even bought horse feed."

"Thank you."

"I saved the slip."

"I will pay you back."

"Oh yeah, you will."

Luke smiled and then finished his coffee. "What else do you want?"

Laurie finished her coffee and smiled. "We can talk about that another time. You are out of coffee and I have to get back to the bar."

"I will go with you. I might have more fun there than I will here."

"We always had fun didn't we?"

Laurie looked at him as they walked out of the house. "No, not always. I think there were more good times than bad."

Once they were in her car Luke looked at her. "I wish I had never met Linda."

"If it had not been her who would it have been?"

"I guess we will never know."

Laurie laughed. "You are such a shithead."

Luke smiled at her. "There you go talking shit again."

Chapter 41

The Story Ends

Someone is going to read this story and they are not going to be happy about where it ends or the way it ends. The truth is this is not the end for some it is a beginning. The world is not filled with happy ever after stories because those kinds of stories are not real stories.

Someone will want to know about Laurie and Luke did they get married did they split up? What happened to them? Did they settle down and raise a family or did they walk away from one another? Were they left as some would say living in sin for all their lives or did they do the right thing by one another?

What happened to Emily? Did she go back to Jim? Did she do good for herself and the town? What did she make of her life? You want to know just what she did.

What about his sister Emma did she marry the guy she brought to the Thanksgiving dinner or was he just a nice guy she spent some time with on her way to meet Mr. Right? Did she keep her job or give it up for a life as a stay-at-home Mom? What did she find when all was said and done?

What about their father Roger did he live or did he die from cancer he was fighting? Why aren't all these questions answered? Why did the story end leaving all these questions unanswered? What good is a story that ends with so many questions waiting to be answered?

The story ends the way it ends. It ends this way because that is the way that life is. No one has all the answers but everyone likes a good story. What happens to these people? We all know what happens life happens. The good, as well as the bad, will happen as it always does. So let's just leave them on a high note a good day a day to be remembered. Let's just leave them at a good place and give them that happily ever after type ending that we all want.

Our lives are filled with highs and lows there is nothing we can do about that some days are just better than others. If you want to have a different ending then you can tell me what happened in your story. As for me, I like this ending because it leaves open all the possible endings. It also leaves us with new beginnings; new roads that no one has traveled yet. It leaves us to dream of a future that might be which at times is more than enough.

Sit down with a friend and have a cup of coffee or something a little stronger if you like. Talk the ending of this story over just to see where it all takes you. If you chose something to drink that is a little stronger than coffee, remember the most important lesson you learned in this story.

"Don't sleep naked on the bathroom floor with your head under the sink."